To Val + Geoffrey.
Enjoy + Enjoy Myanmar (the rest!). Regards.

REGINA
A Novel of Some Extremes

Robin Anderson

MINERVA PRESS
LONDON
MONTREUX   LOS ANGELES   SYDNEY

REGINA
Copyright © Robin Anderson 1998

All Rights Reserved

No part of this book may be reproduced in any form,
by photocopying or by any electronic or mechanical means,
including information storage or retrieval systems,
without permission in writing from both the copyright owner
and the publisher of this book.

ISBN 1 85863 967 0

First Published 1998 by
MINERVA PRESS
195 Knightsbridge
London SW7 1RE

Printed and bound in Great Britain by
Antony Rowe Ltd, Chippenham, Wiltshire

REGINA

A Novel of Some Extremes

For Melford – the original Amanda

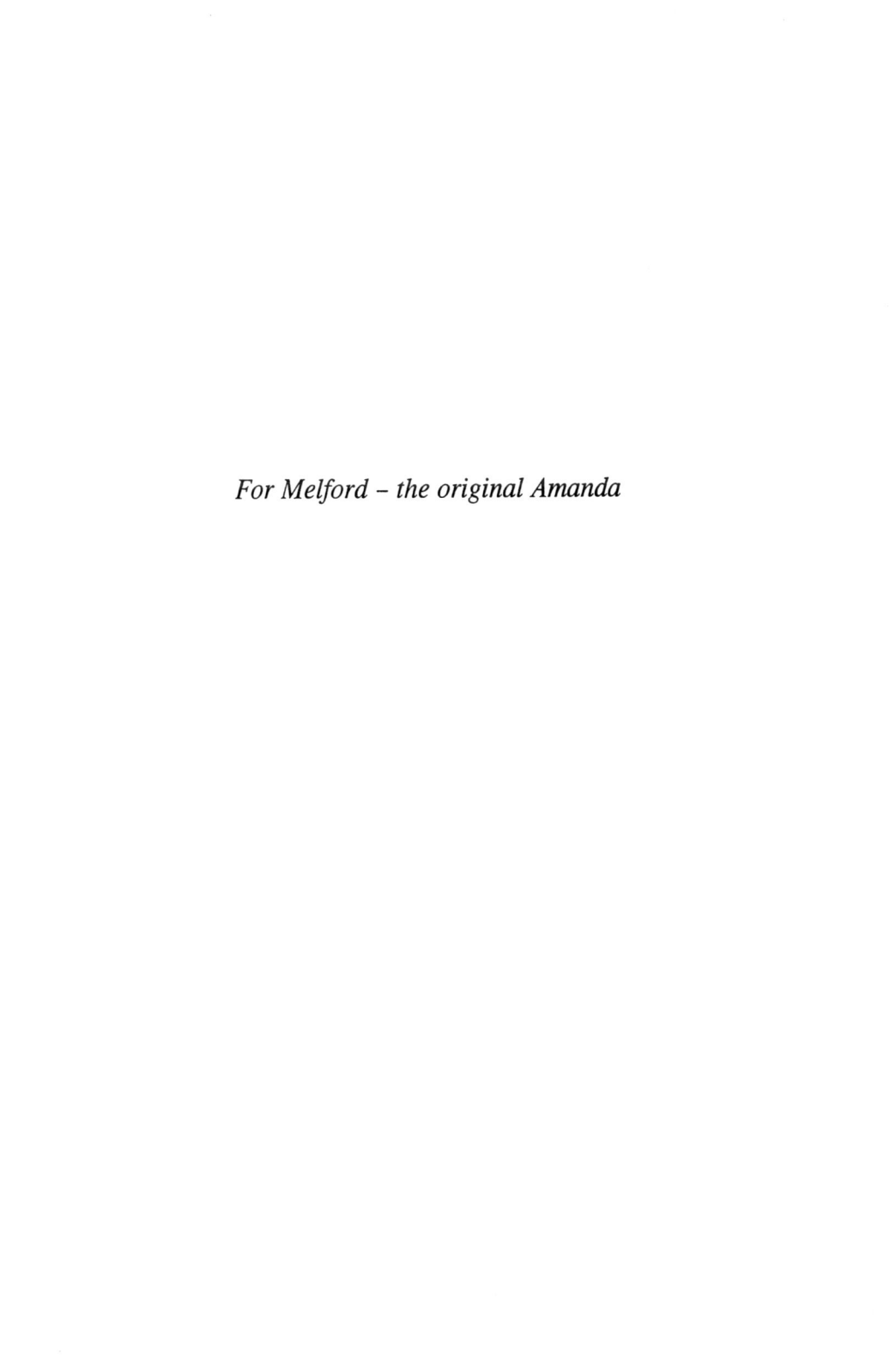

Contents

One	The Present	11
Two	The Sixties	24
Three		41
Four		64
Five		80
Six		99
Seven		120
Eight		134
Nine		142
Ten		166
Eleven		190
Twelve		201
Thirteen		211
Fourteen		233
Fifteen		252

"You ungrateful little cunt!"

Big Joe glares down at Regina sitting behind the large, mirrored desk. Regina glares back up at Big Joe. Regina calmly takes a Sobranie cigarette from the mirrored cigarette box. He places the cigarette in a silver holder, manipulates a silver lighter and calmly applies the flame to the tip. Regina inhales.

"Possibly. Yes, a definite possibility." Regina smiles and exhales. "But let's face it, my dear Joe, with that face of yours you'll never view a grateful one."

Chapter One

The Present

Regina is a legend in his own time. One of the favourite, self-inflicted reasons for his pseudonym goes, "Darling, as one who was born as Alicia in Wonderland – dreadful name, Alicia – I created a delicious cocktail made up of Dietrich, Swanson, Turner plus a soupçon of Bette... added a tremendous zest of talent and, lo and behold, I created ME!"

Designs Exclusive is one of those discreet doorways off Carlos Place in London's elegant Mayfair – Carlos Place being a small street achieving more in its mere few yards than Rodeo Drive desperately strives to achieve in millions of dollars, additional yardage and designer labels. "After all," claims Regina, "it does house – apart from Designs Exclusive – the three responsible Big Cs; the Connaught, Connaught Champagne and those divine Connaught crisps." The last pronouncement is accompanied with lightly clasped hands, lowered lids and a definitely hallowed voice. One enters Designs Exclusive through the highly lacquered door which today is gleaming in a bright burgundy colour, highlighted by silver and grey and deemed by Regina as the "top in power" colour of the moment. What Regina as top designer, rules, goes. Then again, what Regina as top designer, rejects, also goes. Clients arrive 'by appointment'.

"How sad that as yet we are not by appointment to 'Her'," Regina has been heard to murmur on more than one wistful occasion. At thirty-five ("I shall always be as old as the number of my premises so I have no intention of moving") he has conquered all realms of design. His Carlos Place address deals essentially with that desperate set of ladies who are chauffeured between Richou, Harry's Bar, Michaeljohn and who occasionally venture through "that ghastly souk in Knightsbridge." The ladies who remain loyal to Mayfair with its familiar Fortnum's, comforting Bond Street and – naturally – Designs Unlimited.

Clients are bullied, calmed, coaxed and sometimes asked to leave. However, they always return for more. He is the darling of London's bored society and – dare he say it – the vital nouveau riche. Regina is adored by the ladies and treated with scepticism and caution by their spouses. His style is daring, flamboyant, original and at times futuristic. Regina claims the power to make the most beige of ladies beautiful and the loudest of ladies toned and tranquil.

But now, knowing the initial recipe, surely there must be a further reason for the name. Regina has the answer for this too. "Well my dear, She had a book written about Her by that divine Mr Lacey. Should he one day choose to write about me we would expect a reusage of That Title now, wouldn't we?"

A gloved finger presses the neat, silver buzzer. The burgundy and silver door opens and the client enters through the revered portals. The hall, with reflective, recessed lamps, appears to reach through to eternity. The client, slightly intimidated and deliberately confused, pauses in this temple of images. A few moments pass and ahead of her the wall of mirror slowly O'Sesames ('opens' for lesser mortals) to reveal the heavenly Sharoo. The wondrous Sharoo is a great beauty. The therefore beautiful Sharoo is also Regina's bodyguard, personal assistant, mother figure, psychiatrist, karate expert, jester, soothsayer, astrologist, Girl Friday, chauffeuse and friend. Sharoo is, in fact, simply Sharoo!

Stories about Sharoo vary as much as those over Regina's pseudonym. Regina claims he met her in a male brothel in Tangier. Sharoo claims she is a Kenyan princess who was pursued, disposed of and suitably abused – basically everything that makes Kenyan princesses top liners in the Sunday newspapers. A more solid theory is the one of original roots in Jamaica leading to the glories of Mayfair via Brixton; but nobody, particularly Sharoo, is commenting. Sharoo is tall, she is thin – paper thin – and with a wonderful punk Afro hairstyle which at present is furnished in stripes of silver, burgundy and natural black to follow the decor. Her outfits are designed by Regina with Sharoo's heritage always in mind. The drapings to her dress are very Masai at present and an elongated silver cane, similar to a crook but doubtless the sublimation for a spear, hints of a tropical Bo Peep.

Occasionally, a client in the throes of being 'processed' and on a return visit to the showroom is visibly taken aback with the emotion of seeing the elegant fabric of her drawing room curtains walking towards her or perhaps the damask on a treasured fauteuil taking on a new life form in that of a blouson jacket on the elegant frame of Sharoo.

This latest client, greeted with a warm, dazzling smile and whispered "please, this way" follows the swaying, reed-like Sharoo through into the start of Phase Two. Even the simple gesture of taking her coat is completed in a spiritual, ballet-like movement.

The salon is the original drawing room to the large, converted late eighteenth-century house. A main conversation area comprising of a sofa, low table and a pair of chairs, gently beckons the client and she is asked by the solicitous Sharoo to "please, be seated". She sits down dutifully and waits, her eyes darting around curiously at the lavish decor about her. Though unaware of the fact, she is being prepared for the happening of Regina.

The salon theme contains the silver tones subtly hinted at by the main entry hall - and Sharoo's hair! - plus a blending of the additional colour tones as carried by Sharoo's total look.

A silver carpet washes the floor and soft festoon shades of the palest grey veil the tall windows. Walls are lacquered in a translucent silvery grey with cloud and smoke effects in wisps of deeper grey and the deified burgundy. Mirror bands form the architraves and skirtings with additional mirror bands placed below the traditional cornices, thus enhancing the original mouldings which, in their turn, are lightly silvered. The ceilings are in mirrored panels creating a further spacial effect enhanced by the inset of large, modern canvasses imbuing one with a further dimension of colour.

"My dear, it's madly Sistine and will never tire," Regina explains against comments over this particular feature. "It is simply the most amazing coincidence but one of my specialist painters is named Miklos Angelos! He's Greek of course, but it is in the same area - Mediterranean - isn't it?" A confused, tiny smile usually accompanies this bon mot. More salon works of art are attributed to mysterious artists. "They are simply dedicated and I have been asked never to divulge." Regina totally overlooks the source of one such art work which spent the best part of a weekend on the Bayswater Road railings before being 'discovered'.

Sharoo's musical whim of the moment, whether Barry Manilow, Boy George, Delmingo or the Brandenburgs, filters softly through the heady atmosphere. The conditioning client is offered coffee – decaffeinated perhaps? – tea or perhaps a glass of champagne. One well-known actress, without any of the preliminaries, was handed a personalised Redmile mirror, a silver straw and a line.

The music fades to a hushed whisper. Sharoo smiles mysteriously, moves back a few paces from the mesmerised client and announces simply, "Mr Forbes."

Reginald Forbes arrives. No simple doorway for him. He materialises from behind a mirrored screen behind the mirrored desk. He is a striking sight. Of medium height and of slight build, he still spells presence and style. He is immaculately dressed á la decoration. The suit, from Tom Gilbey, is double breasted, and tailored in silver grey silk. He wears a pale silver toned shirt with burgundy stripes and with plain burgundy collar. The tie is burgundy silk and the shoes a burgundy patent leather with silvered buckles. His hair is silver blonde and kept to its impeccable trim by "that divine, butch Paul at The Berkeley". Regina stands admiring his new client, his head is held slightly to one side. "Mrs Clarke." A statement, not a question. "Good morning."

He glides over to her, takes her hand and shakes it warmly. "How very kind of you to telephone and make an appointment to see me." He smiles brilliantly down at her. "I was delighted to hear that you, too, were so enchanted with the project I carried out for Mrs Grahame. She was a delight to work with. Those marvellous sculptures originally so wickedly obscured and what about that divine Chinese screen which was positively lurking in the garden room?"

Mrs Clarke and the likes are overwhelmed by this brilliant technicoloured technique – "staking one's claim" as the office says – and enhanced by Regina's incredible charm. There is a hint of naughtiness intertwined with a steely professionalism which from the moment of meeting, oversees all. He continues, "Thank you for your husband's letter acknowledging my terms of business. Mr Clarke has suggested a budget but doubtless you and perhaps I can talk to him about this?" A larger smile accompanies the remark.

He turns his elegant head. "Sharoo, please."

Sharoo acknowledges the quiet command with a slight nod of her head. She picks up a burgundy folder with its few pages of grey paper from the mirror-topped desk and moves to one of the chairs facing the client. Mrs Clarke realises her disadvantage – surely not intentional? – from having been placed on the sofa and making herself so extremely comfortable amidst the soft grey silk cushions. The chair upon which Sharoo arranges herself is a triumphant bergere with the seat at a higher level than the sofa. The client is therefore at the lower, focal point of a neatly contrived triangle. Regina is looking down at her from her right and Sharoo, with silver Cartier pen poised above her pad, looking down at her from her left. Regina relaxes, asks "may I?" and helps himself to a Sobranie cigarette from the box on the low table.

"I know your block of flats, having recently completed a project there," he enthuses. "I am delighted with your choice of Number Five. You certainly do have the advantage of that magnificent view over the park." Sharoo is responsible for this spontaneous knowledge having checked out all relevant details earlier and leaving the necessary brief notes for Regina to glance over prior to the meeting.

Regina continues. "Mr Clarke has also sent a set of the existing plans as requested, or at least he asked your architect's office to send us a set. I have had a chance to look at these with my architect and assistant and I am sure we will be creating a highly desirous home for you." The conversation carries along with Regina taking Mrs Clarke by the beringed hand and leading her through a suggestion of schemes and treatments. Sharoo's offer of a further cup of coffee is shushed by Regina. "It must be time for the first sip of champagne," he announces. "After all," he smiles at Mrs Clarke once more, "we do have our first of, I trust, many successful meetings to celebrate."

The inimitable Sharoo produces a tray with mirrored bucket, a bottle of Cristal and three silver and grey glass goblets. Mrs Clarke murmurs rather weakly, "How divine." – Regina's expressions are catching.

"Aren't they?" he cries. "I get them from that wonderful little kiosk in that designers' heaven – the V. & A.!" The exposed goblets are filled to the brim.

Arrangements will be made for Regina, along with Ray, one of his able assistants, plus architect Bob, to visit the newly acquired flat. The proposed layouts are to be presented to Mr and Mrs Clarke and then final details worked upon. A future meeting, presided over by Regina, will exhibit the prepared schemes, colour perspectives, relevant texture boards and scale models to the essential rooms. Parallel with the process are the costings "for Mr Clarke's eyes only," hisses Regina and receives a conspiratorial, champagne giggle from the cushion enveloped Mrs Clarke.

The meeting is ending. Mrs Clarke is now completely malleable to whatever Regina deigns to suggest. She is, in other words, completely overwhelmed. Sharoo offers a final glass of champagne as Regina stands. As far as he is concerned, the meeting is over. He directs his gaze from Sharoo's pad back to Mrs Clarke. "Please excuse me. I have to go over a briefing with my architect before I meet my next client." The name of a prominent City company, much in today's news, is mentioned. "Sharoo will arrange our next meeting and any meetings I require on site prior to seeing you."

Mrs Clarke's extended hand is lightly blessed with a soft touch and Regina disappears – as silently as he arrives – behind the mirrored screen. "What talent, what charm, what genius," breathes Mrs Clarke, taking her last sip.

Sharoo murmurs some matching platitudes and a few words like "confidential", "exclusive", "ultimate", plus phrases of "will not be discussed" and "as he see you". She helps Mrs Clarke to her feet and they move through towards the main entrance. There, in a fleeting moment to assist her with her fur jacket, Sharoo murmurs a few more words and they part on the front steps. The burgundy door closes.

Inspired and with a hint of mystery and intrigue now added to her step, the excited Mrs Clarke trips along Mount Street onwards to Harry's Bar. Her thoughts in a cloud of Cristal and herself in a cloud of newly sprayed 'Dorelle' – "Reginald Forbes did their salon too, you know" – she cannot wait to compare notes with Mrs Grahame of the shamed, Chinese screen fame.

*

"My dears. What an extraordinary woman! What on earth did she think she looked like? I suppose one could give her credit and say that perhaps it was her deliberate mistake!" Regina and Sharoo are now in the offices at the back. Here is a different scene. An atmosphere of activity and purpose replaces the hushed, theatrical ambience of the front salon. Regina is leaning up against the edge of his work desk. Sharoo is draped in his chair. Across from this secluded alcove which offers privacy and yet gives immediate access to the remainder office space, is the architect's area. Bob is concentrating on a plan, hunched over his drawing board. He occasionally scratches his balding head with his pencil and sniffs loudly. Regina rolls his eyes heavenwards for Sharoo's benefit. "At times..."

Charles, another assistant, is busy working on a decorating schedule at his particular desk whilst Beverley, the visual artist, is contemplatively daubing paint tones onto a selection of fabrics she is interpreting into a perspective.

Sam, the long-suffering general secretary, is busy clattering away at her typewriter. Having once been told that she was a Minelli lookalike she wears nothing else except a black jump-suit, white shirt and a scarlet bow tie. A black bowler has made its appearance on more than one occasion for the benefit of would-be sightseers at Morton's during Happy Hour. Three other design assistants complete the small, highly skilled group of staff. David, Ray and Vanessa are out at the moment. The first two are on sites with Vanessa "doing the rounds" which means viewing latest papers and fabrics at selected wholesalers and drinking a lot of Sainsbury's Soave.

The commercial side to Designs Exclusive is housed at the large studios in Pimlico Road near to Sloane Square. The commercial sector is headed by Ray's boyfriend, Steve, and a further team of seven designers. The contracts office, managed by Big Joe and Big Chris, is also based here.

Regina checks his watch. "I must not be late," he announces for the benefit of the office. "I am meeting the managing director of the Peter Brown agency for a drink which I am sure will lead to lunch." Sharoo gives Regina a look and laughs. She is aware that he is meeting Peter Brown himself. Peter and Regina are long-standing friends.

"I have not made a reservation for you anywhere. Shall I...?"

Regina laughs with her. "Yes, dear. I clarify that. I mean yes to it's Peter, but not yes to a reservation. He will no doubt have arranged for somewhere. It's not a business meeting, but as we all know, all work and no play simply will not keep your dear Regina gay."

Bob, the only male member of the office who is not gay, pulls a wry face, whilst Sam gives a short bark, her idea of how Minelli laughs. "Perhaps she is confused with what Garbo promised the world to do in *Ninotchka* and did, sounding exactly like a seal," was a favourite Regina criticism.

"Two matters afore I go... God, I'm getting worse by the moment – it must be the influence of Mrs Clarke. Bob, can you and Sharoo sort out a time later this week for you and Vanessa to view the flat with me. We'd better not appear too keen but let's get the ground work done." He pauses. "Poor Mrs C. Actually, she's very rich Mrs C – she is so pallid and strained I suggest we cheer her up a bit. A touch of the phallic! A column or two with an embodiment of the dawn – sunrise tones! And of course, the touch of burgundy. That should see her with a new grip on life. Perhaps old man Clarke... where have I met him before? He's a frightful old bore but, as I say, lethally loaded – he too may take a new grip on himself. From drab Mrs C to lucky Mrs C. With me it could be a revitalisation for her as his sun also rises!"

A disgusted snort – or laugh from Sam – and a few groans from the remainder. Regina stands. "Sharoo darling. If you get that columnist again, you know nothing about the wedding. Also, do check that appointment with Regal Oil – you know how vague old Simpson can be. You had also apply a verbal soothing balm on Big Joe. I put his dainty nose out of joint earlier. Suggest a drink before lunch tomorrow or else later today." He sees Sharoo's questioning expression. "I asked him to explain why his idea of overtime is the same as my idea of office time. He is not amused, having devoted the whole weekend to Carlton Terrace and so sacrificing his precious fishing. I was told in no uncertain terms as to what an ungrateful noun I was."

"Will do. The two of you should try and grow up one day." Sharoo makes an additional note and looks back at Regina. "That it?" He nods. She lifts the telephone and begins dialling.

Regina speaks briefly to Bob. He has a few quick words with Beverley as he glances over her shoulder at the perspective. "Sallow up that yellow, Bev darling," he instructs. He signs a letter Sam holds out and looks over once more to Sharoo who is talking to Mr Simpson's secretary. The secretary is apparently as vague as Mr Simpson. "I will be back at four, no later. If possible see if you can get hold of Sir James' office and suggest Sir James and I meet at Fisher Fine A. as opposed to The Ritz. It means I can definitely see

Big Joe and also, I would like to go over that list of Jackson extras with him."

He concludes by blowing a kiss at Sharoo and waving graciously to the office. "Be good," he carols and sweeps out with nobody having paid the slightest attention to his exit with its regular display of official love.

Regina pauses on the top of the outside steps. He adjusts his silver fox coat and grimaces at the cold wind. A dumpy passer-by with an equally dumpy child looks up at him curiously. He gives her a dazzling smile and she scuttles on. Regina looks up and along the street, descends the steps, crosses and walks briskly over to the Connaught entrance. The top-hatted doorman greets him with a cheery "Morning, Mr Forbes," and holds the revolving doors for him.

Regina flashes another dazzling smile and sweeps through. He traverses the lobby and glides smoothly past reception to the Oak Bar.

*

The Connaught. That reassuring sanctuary as to how everything can be. I arrive and make my way through to the Oak Bar. I seat myself comfortably in a deep, tapestried chair, order a very dry vodka martini – they make the best in London – eye the bowl of fresh potato crisps with a certain amount of malice and give the room a cursory glance.

Nothing and nobody has changed. Even the clientele look the same as from my last visit – merely freshly dusted.

I am looking forward to seeing Peter. He has managed to contact me at The Berkeley where I am presently staying – so much for me attempting to remain incognito! He has suggested we meet for a lunchtime drink – perhaps even lunch? – but most important of all he tells me he has the most illuminating and outrageous news. He goes as far as to say that it could be deemed sensational news. I may be wrong, but I suspect that the news must involve Peter himself. However, I may be incorrect and curiosity is certainly getting the better of me. It will be torture having to sit and wait to hear him out.

I calculate rapidly. It must be at least seven months since I last saw him and that was in New York. My drink arrives and I take a tentative sip. Perfection. I unfurl the early edition of *The Standard*, glance at the headlines and still studiously avoid the crisps which now appear to have taken on an inner glow and resemble a bowl of glowing Kruger Rands.

"Mr Brown, sir," announces Michael.

I stand up. "Peter," I say.

He stands, beaming. He is as immaculate and as suave as ever and – as always – looks extremely pleased with himself.

"RA. How well you look!" Peter holds out his hand in response to mine. "My, it is good to see you. I was delighted to hear on the drums that you were dashing in and out on one of your 'don't let anybody know I'm here' visits. But especially delighted to actually catch you at your hotel."

"Well," I say, sitting once more and gesturing to him to do the same. "I can't wait. I mean, nobody could have their appetite whetted to such a degree as you have mine. The lure of such riveting gossip is such bait that you knew I would not refuse. Forget the 'incognito' bit. Even the flow of art treasures to the New World is staunched when Peter Brown and intrigue are hand in hand. Everybody comes out of hiding!"

I glance at the hovering Michael who appears uninspired by my verbose opening with Peter and add "Peter?"

"Oh. A large gin martini, please Michael. Straight up and with a twist." He grins affectionately at me. "How is America et all?"

"America is still America. And more American. Et all is fine and sends love." Peter is stalling, I can tell. He and I continually go through this small social ritual. The conversation starts with the searching question as to how the latest port of call was. Peter, with his London-based international public relations company, is always arriving 'in' from somewhere. Likewise, myself, who with an antique export business concentrating on America, spends most of my time flying 'out' back to my bases in Texas and New York.

Peter pulls at his cuffs – he has always done this – and scoops up a handful of crisps.

"I envy you few things," I continue, "but that ability to devour those lethal crisps is too unfair. The mere factor that you can gulp down any junk food you desire – not for a moment that I'm suggesting that what you have just stuffed into your mouth is junk – when I seem to spend my time calorie counting, jogging and using a gym so as to retain this highly desirable, if somewhat worn, physique! It's simply not on, Brown!"

"Put the other way," Peter replies with a twinkle, "and I am being decidedly subtle and putting my PR experience to the fore; perhaps the quantity and quality of the martinis you consume compensate for my junk food substitution? Given the choice between a Big Mac or a Whisky Mac, I'd go for Big."

"My dear Peter, you always do."

We both laugh. He is still playing 'The Game'.

"My God, RA. Isn't that Geoffrey Lay over there, in the corner?" Another PR ruse. Distract or detract.

I turn my head. "So it is. He certainly is not looking in the best of frames, is he?"

Geoffrey Lay is a business competitor to Peter. A tension exists between the two following Peter's successful coup over a contract covering the promotion of a new Sotheby Parke Bernet-type operation on America's West Coast. Due to my personal contacts in America I was able to see Peter ahead of all competition. There was also my help with regard to setting up some of the initial financing Peter required for his new American base.

Geoffrey Lay continues to pointedly ignore us. His female companion, a terrifying marron-glacéd ogress, determinedly avoided by designers and dealers in London alike, is again taboo to the majority members of the gossip press and public relations world.

"God help the two of them," Peter says with glee. "With Lay as her Custer her stand socially will simply have to fall. If it has any self-respect, that is!"

I join him in more laughter. We continue playing 'The Game'. He fills me in with more information on his latest projects, spicing his sentences with pieces of irrelevant but highly colourful gossip. I ask about Paul!

"Paul." He turns this new topic over in his mind for a brief moment. "We're going through a roughish patch," he acknowledges.

Paul is the latest person in Peter's never ceasing quest for the perfect relationship. I have seen Peter through so many, but this particular one appears to blossom the more rough the patches become. A contradiction perhaps to seed on stony ground? However, taking into account Peter's barometer-like temperament, I know he will always weather the storm – which he does, with an admirable alacrity.

I gesture to Michael for a repeat of the martini flow. "I realise we are having drinks, but you will join me for lunch, I trust? I was not able to get through to Sandi again after I had snatched your call."

"Of course I'm joining you for lunch," answers Peter. "Drinks are on me, though."

Michael sets down a second round. "Ah, delicious," Peter smacks his lips, "and now, RA, enough build up." He takes a long sip. "My news." He pauses dramatically.

"Go on," I hold up my drink, "I'm bracing myself for it."

"Am I being fair, I ask myself?" Peter looks solemnly at his glass. "Perhaps I should leave such a bombshell until after lunch."

"If you decide to do that, then you can take it that those crisps you have gutsed down is lunch!"

Peter looks at me with mock dismay. "But you never know. This news could make or break your calorie count. You may either revert to a violent liquid lunch of more martinis followed by many, many more martinis, or in addition to the martini marathon you may add to this several bowls of these tantalising crisps. Even worse, all this and a five course meal in The Grill."

I shake my head and start to laugh.

"That's right, you may laugh now, but wait – let it not be said that Brown is completely heartless or cruel." He takes another sip. "It does cross my mind that the described reaction could apply to both good news or bad, so, knowing that whatever I say I will remain guilty for your overweight, heart attack or God knows what..."

"I'm still braced."

Peter smiles. He is looking his wicked, dashing best. He knows he has wound his solo audience to a feverish pitch of intrigue. Eyeing him I can well see why hearts, male and female, go on a merry flutter when his rakish, gypsy charm is in full flight.

"Right." He raises his nearly empty glass and gestures again to the solicitous Michael. "I say this now – and I do mean it – to us!"

I reciprocate.

Peter puts down the glass and tugs again at his cuffs – an infuriating habit.

"Regina's getting married."

I choke.

"Furthermore, Regina's meeting us here. Yes. Now." I gulp another mouthful of martini. "I took the great liberty of suggesting he joins me for a drink. He has no idea you are even in town... yet."

He regards my stunned expression with some concern.

I snarl at him. "You cunt!"

"My dear!" I spin round in my chair. "Everyone in vogue appears to being called that this morning."

There stands Regina.

Chapter Two

The Sixties

Being the Friday prior to the Christmas break, the office was in its usual pre-Christmas panic. I was seated at my desk, working my way through the proof for a forthcoming sales catalogue and trying to retain a modicum of calm – and dignity – amidst the last minute rushings and cheery carolled greetings. Outside, a freezing rain was steadily falling and an occasional extra strong gust of blustering wind would blow the drops against the black window panes in loud, staccato fashion. My office, a large room on the first floor of a newly constructed building off St James, was finished in a pale pine panelling, smoothly waxed and with a deep charcoal-coloured carpet and matching charcoal-coloured ceiling. A tall brass desk lamp and further strategically placed table lamps added a warm, cosy glow to the area.

Curtains and upholstery in varying tones of copper and cinnamon added extra touches of warmth. A log fire, hissing in the Adam fireplace, gleamed from the highly polished grate. Stretched out in front of the fire was Petrina, a geriatric old lady of a pug who had been a loyal friend and companion for the past twelve years. Several seascapes, luminous in heavy gold frames and cleverly lit by pin spots concealed in the ceiling, further enhanced the warmth of the pine. Above the mantel, in another heavy elaborate gilt frame, was a charming eighteenth-century painting of two silver pugs, both of whom Petrina and I claimed were ancestors of my totally spoiled and pampered friend. Petrina for one, never looked as if she would gather the energy nor the will to contradict this minor claim to a family tree.

I checked the leather-bound desk diary on my right. There, marked down for the evening, was another of Peter's unlimited pre-Christmas parties. This particular engagement had the added distinction of two exclamation marks, plus a question mark, inked in alongside it. I gave a small sigh and smiled. As always, it was Peter in one of his many romantic guises. We had Peter the matchmaker; Peter the twentieth-century cupid; Peter as the baritone Dolly Levi of the gay world. Of course, he was going to be there, he being Peter's latest find, unlike any of the others and this time, "definitely for keeps, RA."

"Anything else, Mr Anderson?"

A statement, not a question.

Clare, my secretary, doubtless in a clairvoyant mood so already wrapped and booted against the cold December night, stood by the door.

"No thank you Clare. Have a very good Christmas, my regards to your mother and thank you for all the arrangements and bits of Christmas details you have so kindly – as always – taken care of."

She stood smiling at me. I looked down at the catalogue and then back up at her.

"Everything all right?" I always asked this question and no doubt would have been totally taken aback if Clare had said something was not all right.

She laughed. "Oh yes. Absolutely. You have a good Christmas as well and thank you for the presents. I can't wait to open mine and I know Mother will be thrilled with hers."

I smiled and she smiled again, and as if on cue, said in her singsong voice, "Now, you won't forget the cake?"

"Never," I said, my hand on my chest.

More giggles and a glance at Petrina. "And Petrina will have some too?"

"Petrina has been dreaming about it for weeks," I smiled.

"Goodnight then. Goodnight Petrina. Merry Christmas, again," and she was gone.

Dear loyal Clare! Though the affectionate butt for a multitude of office jokes, she was brilliantly efficient, wholly reliable and a guardian angel with her many little kindnesses and thoughts. She had presented a tiny Petrina to me within the first month of joining my staff, all those years ago. "One always needs someone to talk to," she had said, coyly. "Now this little lady here. Her mother went out for a walk when she knew she should not have and met this gentleman dog. Fortunately he was one of her kind," she had blushingly explained. However, while Petrina revelled in the talent of being pampered and petted, it was Clare who happily offered the pampering. I too became part of her little game. Firstly, there was the birthday cake for Petrina – "lovely chicken livers and bits of beef," then a cake for my birthday and naturally the annual Christmas cake had to follow. Clare produced the most alcoholic fruit cake I have ever had the pleasure to devour!

She typically lived with her mother, a widow and a smaller, older version of the sparrow-like Clare, in a pretty thatched cottage outside Lingfield near to East Grinstead. Her great passions in life – apart from managing her mother and myself – were baking, making jams and jellies, and keeping bees. The honey from the five hives in the garden was delicious and Clare always giggled when I said she had been caught displaying her wares in Fortnum's. She was one of those extraordinary little women whom you knew would cope with any crisis, albeit political, emotional or even physical. One could picture her battling against hordes at the likes of a Rorke's Drift; dealing with the Japanese in Java; coping with an earthquake or typhoon and simply getting on with the job. I got up from my chair and walked across to the discreet bar concealed behind the panelling to the right-hand side of the fireplace. Petrina raised her head lazily, eyed my movements, then promptly collapsed again and was soon snoring.

I poured myself a comfortable shot of Bells, added a cube of ice and a jet of soda. The ice-bucket, siphon, decanter and glass had already been set out by Clare. Clare was remarkable with her invisible movements. One had never witnessed her attending to any of these minor little luxuries, but whatever one required Clare always had anticipated. I returned to my desk and picked up the telephone. Glancing at my watch I noted it as being twenty minutes to seven. I called my answering service, gave my code number and made a rapid note of my messages to the flat. I thanked the voice, wished her a Happy Christmas too, checked a number in my desk address book and dialled the stage door to the St George's Theatre off the Strand.

After a few rings the telephone was answered by Arthur, the elderly doorkeeper.

"Good evening Arthur, it's Mr Anderson. Has Miss Adamson arrived yet?"

"Evening, Mr Anderson. No, but she should be here any minute. Is there a message?"

"No, thank you Arthur, I'll call her back. She left a message with my answering service. In case I don't get through, would you confirm with her that I will be collecting her after the show, as previously arranged. I will try again, though, before the curtain goes up."

"Very good, Mr A. Nasty night, isn't it?" Arthur put the telephone down before I could agree with him. I dialled a second number.

"P.B. Promotions."

"Peter Brown, please."

"May I ask who is calling?"

"Robin Anderson."

"Good evening, Mr Anderson. Sandi here. Merry Christmas."

"Good evening, Sandi. Sorry I didn't recognise your voice. Merry Christmas to you, too. Is He about?"

"Oh yes, indeed. We have just come in actually and we are very cold and rather short tempered. But, one moment, I'll get him for you between snarls!" I laughed with her.

A few clickings and I was through.

"Robin?"

"Peter, good evening."

"Good evening, dear. How are you? How was New York?"

"Cold. Listen... about this evening..."

"Hold – hold on one sec." I could hear a few muttered expletives in the background, probably into another telephone. He came on the line again. "Sorry about that. You were saying... yes, about this evening, you are coming, aren't you?"

"Yes. Of course. But not for too long as I... I mean..." I faltered.

"Typical, RA. Typical. Anyway, arrive, because this amazing boy is going to be there."

"I know. He's the whole reason for the party, isn't he?"

"What? Oh, good God no. No, no, no, no, not Tim. Well, yes. Tim is part of the reason for the party. But, my dear, for you! My Christmas present!"

"What do you mean? My Christmas present? I'm too old for Christmas presents."

"Ha! I detect first night nerves! One is never too old for Christmas presents. It's the birthday presents one has to avoid. This is vital if Old Man Time is to be kept in abeyance... hold on again," a few more mumblings from Peter in the background. "Still there, my ancient one? Good. No, the one – the boy – I mentioned to you... I must have... this student, or at least, ex-student from the Royal College of Art. Last weekend, in Brighton, he was at Ken's."

"Yes, you may have mentioned him. Yes, come to think of it, you did!"

"Oh, piss off!" said Peter with his usual charm when discussing grand amours with me. "You know damn well I mentioned him but you were in one of your states as you were rushing to the airport to catch one of your inevitable flights to New York... makes one wonder who it is in New York..."

"Very amusing."

"I know. I'm devastating. Imagine how I feel waking up with me each morning."

"And the rest!"

"Jealousy. Do I detect that little green monster fairy? Listen. Dress casually unless you are doing one of your boring, formal stints later. I look forward to seeing you around nineish. Who knows, tonight may be... the night! Byeee!" He jammed down the telephone.

I leaned back in my chair and contemplated the remains of my Scotch. Petrina making one of her supreme efforts again, raised her head and looked at me sleepily.

"Yes, Petrina," I said, looking at her, "your Uncle Peter is at it again." She did not react. Petrina, like myself, had been through a number of Peter's passions selected for our mutual bliss. No doubt she was secure in her knowledge that whomever Peter came up with, she, Petrina, would have the final say.

I pulled open a lower desk drawer and took out the case housing Peter's 'party' present. Inside was a small box containing a pair of leather armlets, a pair of rhinestone-encrusted handcuffs and a rhinestone-encrusted cock ring. I had spotted these on my last trip to New York when browsing through The Pleasure Chest. These were the fun items for Peter's Christmas stocking. "The stocking will doubtless be a pair of stapled together leather chaps," I had drily remarked, knowing Peter's preferences.

The main gift, albeit again leather bound, was an eighteenth-century book with a fine fore edge painting. Peter had been introduced to this particular art form by me several years before and had now formed the foundation of what would eventually be a very fine collection. I had originally met Peter six years ago at a party given by a highly flamboyant barrister who lived in the City near to St Bride Street. I had recently amicably divorced my wife and beginning to take a keener interest in the gay scene, something that I had not particularly pursued previously. Before, my interests had taken me to a few downmarket pubs in the Soho and Earl's Court areas where clandestine meetings followed by sleazy hotel rooms appeared to be the call of the day. Whereas trade in New York or the major cities of Europe had seemed easier to obtain, London, because we lived here, had created its own social problems. Experiences had been essentially one-night stands when the opportunity did arise. Although I was aware of numerous people in my business and social circle being active participants in the London gay scene, I strictly did not mix business with pleasure.

One evening, in a pub off Marble Arch, I had bumped into a business colleague who expressed as much surprise in seeing me as I had at seeing him. We had bought each other a few drinks and in a more relaxed mood I agreed to go on with him to a party off Farringdon Road. The party was given in the top floor flat of a large converted house. We walked up several flights of stairs past darkened offices, to be greeted at the top landing by our host who was dressed in a leather biker's jacket, leather trousers, boots and a leather hat, complete with visor flap. Several chains were draped around his neck, and armlets, again in leather with metal studs, adorned his biceps. Bunches of keys jangled from his belt. He was pure New York and not exactly what I expected to see one's friendly barrister wearing. The party turned out to be enormous fun.

There must have been forty people, if not more, of varying ages and types. There were young men in their late teens and early twenties; those in their thirties or early forties and a smattering of slightly older gentlemen who nonetheless were being amazingly spry. I was definitely part of the business suit brigade and a marked contrast to the leather or casual look. George, the leather-adorned host, greeted me warmly when introduced. He collected a glass from a young man who was passing with a full tray of drinks and pushed the tumbler into my hand.

"This is a special home brew," he laughed and added, with a broad wink, "it's also guaranteed to get you whatever you wish!" With that he moved back with an extra loud jangling sound and was swallowed up by the growing crowd. I was left standing, rather sheepishly, holding my drink.

A young man with long dark hair, wearing a pair of jeans and a heavy orange-coloured sweater, came over to me. "Hi," he said, "I'm Mark."

"Hello, Mark," I replied. "My name is Robin."

"Robin," he repeated. "I don't seem to remember seeing you at one of George's gatherings before." He sipped at his drink, eyeing me over the top of his glass.

"No. This is the first of... er... George's gatherings I've been to."

"Aha," said Mark, "that explains it. I was about to give old George a dressing down for hiding you. You are quite glorious."

I went crimson.

"Don't be embarrassed," said Mark, smiling broadly, "that is meant as a compliment."

"Well, thank you. Thank you."

Mark continued smiling, turned, glanced back over his shoulder and moved on across the room.

Feeling decidedly foolish, I took another large mouthful of my rather strange tasting drink. I was about to move on and claim a refill when my attention was taken up by a tall, dark-haired man in leather, who looked to be in his early thirties. He was dashing in almost a Latin way and was being adored by a quartet of young men who were hanging on to his every word. He must have felt my gaze for he turned and glanced over to where I was standing. He smiled and beckoned me over with his glass. At the same time he lifted a jug of the home special with his other hand and made a gesture of pouring.

"Hi," he said, "do come over and join me." He gave a look of dismissal to the group around him but they, unlike me, did not notice his wicked fleeting expression.

I pushed my way through a dramatically gossiping couple. "Hi," he said again, "I'm Peter Brown. I know you're Robin Anderson. Antique dealer and exporter extraordinaire!"

"I am Robin Anderson," I replied. "As for the rest..."

"Modesty, I like it!" continued Peter Brown. "You are very well known, if I may say so and I do say so!"

I bowed slightly.

"I have a PR business and have been asked to handle the account of one of your rivals."

Before he could continue, one of the group whom he had been talking to, interrupted, saying, "Aren't you going to introduce us to your friend, Peter?" Peter Brown frowned. He quickly introduced the four to me and then turned his back to them and moved over more closely to me.

"I haven't seen you at any of George's parties before. Is this the first one?"

I was beginning to feel like the unhappy sore thumb and wondered as to how many more people were to comment over this being my "first time" before the evening was through.

"Am I that obvious?" I quipped, trying to match him with his vibrancy.

"Well, no. Not really."

"Oh."

"I didn't mean it quite like that," continued Peter, laughing. "One is apt to play on one's words though. Put it down to the world of promotions and PR. Only obvious, I assure you, by being a total new face and for George, that is a major achievement! He'll relax over you for at least a year!"

We both laughed. Peter refilled our glasses once more. We chatted for a few more minutes but by this time I was getting edgy about a dinner appointment and kept glancing at my watch.

"Look," said Peter, noticing my anxiety, "let's meet again. I would like to see you and discuss business as well – particularly the new account I began to tell you about earlier before les girls were overcome by their curiosity! Why not meet for lunch next week? I'll get Sandi, my secretary, to give your secretary a call. St James', isn't it? Then we can arrange something."

"Delightful idea," I agreed, "and I do look forward to that."

Peter smiled, patted me on the shoulder and turned away, moving over to a young man who had just arrived.

He was wearing a tighter version – if possible – to what our host was wearing.

Sandi, Peter's secretary, telephoned Clare the following day. We met for lunch which was a success from the first martini and it was well after four when we finally left the restaurant. This was the beginning of our very close friendship. As Peter had said afterwards, "Thank goodness you weren't wearing leather and I didn't have to fancy you. Those sort of relationships with me never last!"

I collected my coat and Petrina's coat; buckled her into the latter; checked the lights and the door and walked down the dimly lit hall to the lift. The offices, in one of those newly built but heavily disguised blocks to appease the local planning committees, had the added boon of a basement garage. I took the lift directly down to this. The building, in a discreet side street, was ideally situated for travel purposes to and from my flat in Knightsbridge, Heathrow and also for the main route out of the West End for my country escape in Oxfordshire.

I opened the car's passenger door for Petrina who inelegantly clambered in and collapsed again on her Anderson tartan patterned rug (Harrods best cashmere) on the front seat. She gave me a baleful glance as I moved her over slightly. The glance frequently accused me for the indignities she had to suffer in her attempts at agility at so vast a canine age of seventy-two. I appreciated Petrina's penchant for a Rolls Royce but the model I chose to drive helped me – I thought – in preserving a discreet youngish image. Baleful glance duly delivered and responded to by a cheerful tickle to her stomach, she promptly fell back into a doze. I eased myself into the driver's seat, inserted the key into the ignition, turned on the motor and adjusted the tone of the stereo cassette player whilst allowing the engine a few moments to warm up. I reversed carefully out alongside a rather hazardous concrete column which had, on more than one whiskied occasion, been responsible for several markings to the otherwise immaculate blue paintwork. All such 'incidentals' I blamed on Clare and her efficiency with the decanter, particularly after a more frustrating day than usual. I eased the car, a pale blue Aston Martin, into the main traffic flow and across to Arlington Street where I slowly passed the Ritz before turning left into Piccadilly.

The traffic was crawling along and the Hyde Park Underpass was choked up with fumes from endless revving exhausts. Out of this it was again into more solid jams in Knightsbridge. I sat for many wasted minutes as the lights appeared to continuously change but with no apparent response from the frozen traffic. An MG Midget, in bright canary yellow, drew up alongside me. The young man in the passenger seat gave me a long look through the side window, then turned to his companion obviously commenting on the driver in the car alongside. Both then – in unison – looked again and slowly edged forward as their lane began to shift. I smiled to myself and put my hand over to give Petrina another rub. Hopefully their comments were favourable! My mental comments, in return, most certainly were. We travelled side by side through the remainder of Knightsbridge – the frustrations of the traffic momentarily overlooked – and it was with a cheerful waving and hooting that they zoomed off through a clearing in the traffic. I reversed the tape to the cassette and continued the rest of my journey.

This was so typical of those occasions where you fantasise as to what would have happened had you either noted their registration number and followed that lead through, or, much easier and obvious, rolled down the window, introduced yourself and invited them back for a drink. Who knows, the evening may have developed into a cosy, amusing dinner somewhere camp or, better still, into a satisfying threesome! I shook my head and smiled to myself again. These were certainly lecherous thoughts for one who had always led such a quiet life barely intruding in more than the outer fringes of the gay scene. Peter was always regaling me with the wildest of stories and continually suggesting visits or cruisings to the more outrageous clubs or discos. I usually refused on the pretext of there being something else planned for that particular evening or, quite simply, that it was "not my scene". "How do you know that?" Peter used to question me hotly. "Had you not been trolling around that Elephant's Graveyard (the nickname for the gay pub in Quebec Street off Marble Arch) you would never have come on to George's party and think of a major tragedy in your life – you would never have met me!"

I always fobbed this one off by saying that he would have met me through business anyway as it had been part of his personal Five Year Plan!

This created a further uproar. "You'll never know your type or your scene if you don't give everything a chance," he would argue. "You go around with your head in the clouds – and not even pot clouds – with this B Grade movie attitude that somewhere sometime there will be someone who will walk into your life – doubtless with preference at Claridges or at some lush tart-arty party – and all will be totally correct even down to a Cartier toothpaste squeezer on the KY tube and Porthault cum towels and, duly anointed, you will both mince or waltz off into a subtly technicoloured sunset together. Well bullshit! That simply does not happen. Relationships are relationships. Gay or straight. Look at you and your ex-wife! It's the same in the gay world. People, no matter what their scene have to find each other and work at it."

Once I had interrupted him, angrily, and retorted, "You are a fine one to talk about relationships. You say I am full of bullshit. You and your birth sign certainly show you as pure Taurus the Bullshit! I suggest you practise what you pontificate!"

This was one of several times that he had attacked me on the subject and certainly the only occasion I could remember that he had brought my ex-wife, Leslie, into our conversation. Basically, I knew that what Peter was saying was correct but, in my turn, being Virgo and a romantic Virgoan at that, I was convinced that somewhere there would be this someone – to coin a song – and this person would be there and the technicolour sunset would exist. Judy Garland eat your heart out! I further excused Peter by the fact that his background housed all the obvious traits for his supposed aggression as well as an egotistical and sometimes almost violent attitude to life. He was a human bulldozer, mentally and physically. Born to an alcoholic mother with a layabout as a father, his childhood was spent in a neverending scene of violence and despair in the seamier side of Eastern London. He, too, as I once said making light of some of the appalling incidents he confided to me, was good, B Grade movie fodder, but then his scenario had been real.

"Aah, yes RA. And unlike yours, which you are still waiting to have written."

*

The interior of the car was warm and snug. With the music filtering gently through the speakers and the reassuring click, click of the windshield wipers, interspersed with Petrina's soft snoring, I sat perfectly relaxed, looking forward to the evening, dinner with Amanda and the thought of a quiet weekend in the country. Should my dinner with Amanda not be too late (she did have two shows on a Saturday and probably would not want to go drop into Annabel's for our usual nightcap and a sobering spin around the floor) I would collect the few parcels of food and the laundry waiting at the flat, collect Petrina and travel down to the cottage in the early hours of the morning.

The cottage was a small pebble-dash horror I had spotted several years prior, down near Henley. I had returned to view it several times and as the price was so reasonable and the setting so perfect, I was convinced that with the aid of an architect friend of mine, plus my own abilities as a decorator, I would be able to create something worthwhile. The cottage had stood derelict for several years with all potential buyers reacting as I had done initially, simply throwing up the proverbial hands in horror at the general appearance and state of the building. This was also the time that I was going through the painful process of divorcing Leslie. She had gone and fallen in love with a schoolteacher, several years younger than herself, who resided in Hong Kong and had been over in London doing some advanced studies. Though his curriculum had not originally included Leslie, his interests in her – they met at a talk on John Ruskin at the V. & A. – had started over a cup of instant coffee in the museum's cafeteria and had grown in strength from this sloppy moment. Leslie had been with a companion who had known Tony from Cambridge days and had taken great delight in aiding and abetting the nurturing of the blossoming friendship. I had no idea as to what was going on. At this stage I was extremely busy with my antique commitments abroad and Leslie, who freelanced in journalism and fashion writing, continued to lead her own life in much the same way she had prior to our getting married.

Our marriage was still a surprise to me. I had met Leslie, invited her out a few times and the two of us had eventually ended up in bed. I am still not sure as to who seduced whom, but it all seemed very cosy and jokey at the time and as we both had no immediate family ties to think of, we decided to create our own. The wedding was a registrar office affair with a small reception held at The Dorchester. We gave a very good luncheon in the Oliver Messel suite and in an extreme champagne haze, made our way to Heathrow and off to Barbados for a few days at the Sandy Lane Hotel. I left Leslie in Barbados and went on to New York. She remained in Barbados for an extra day or two and then joined up with the great chum who, in the not too distant future, would have Leslie staying with her in a repeat performance for the second honeymoon, only this time the groom stayed.

New York had proved very heavy and hectic. I had been there two days when, after a particularly long session with some associates who had travelled from the West Coast to meet up with me, I had taken myself along to the Four Seasons where I had gone and gotten totally drunk on an endless fountain of vodkatinis.

From the Four Seasons I had made my way down to the heady precincts of Christopher Street and had wakened next morning in some studio apartment off Gramercy Square, my head like a piston machine and my companion, a petite blonde young man now clad in a brightly coloured shortie robe, leaning over me with a cup of steaming black coffee and a phial of amyl nitrate should I have thought that this would be a preferable alternative to the coffee. As it was, I savoured both and then, without actually planning to do so, savoured the young man as well.

After a shower, I was found sitting on a large, brightly coloured cushion on the floor having a totally celibate coffee and talking to Karl who, by this stage, was dressed in a khaki jumpsuit and assorted scarves and rummaging through a large khaki shoulder bag.

"I must say it was such a relief to see you walk into The Knockout last night," he said, unfurling some cigarette papers and rummaging again in the bag for some loose tobacco and a small plastic sac. "I never thought I'd require Durex," he continued holding up the plastic sheath, "but they are ideal for holding one's grass!"

I watched as he expertly rolled the joint, pinched the ends and lit up. He took a long draw and then held the thin length over to me. I shook my head to show 'no'.

"You sure?" Karl questioned. "Is there anything else perhaps...?" The concerned almost maternal look took on a slightly bawdy smile.

"No. No thanks. I'm fine. Simply a little heady that's all."

"Yea, I give good head too, remember?"

"I do and I don't feel like that sort of head at this very minute. No hard feelings (God, was every word going to have a sexual connotation) but I would prefer to say yes to another cup of coffee."

"I could die for the way you say cawfee," he chortled, "it's so English."

"There is a rumour," I answered. I nearly added "And don't die," but I was getting the message that although Karl might have been blessed with the basics of bed he was not too blessed on the cerebral front. I simply was in no state to have to explain what I thought was a fairly hilarious remark – and this feeling without a joint.

He was studying fashion design and had great plans for his future. "You name 'it' and I mean 'it' when discussing this particular field, Mona and I'll be leaving them so far behind that even that telescope at Mount Palomar won't spot them!"

He regaled me with his scholarly doings whilst busying himself at the gas ring behind the large fabric screen. I had to confess that I had never seen such activity over a cup of instant coffee before. He sashayed over with the cup and caught my gaze wandering around the small room. He kicked back at the screen with his foot, nearly spilling the coffee over me. "Don't for one minute think that I was responsible for that piece of deadly nightshade. This studio is temporary, just t-e-m-p-o-r-a-r-y." He was standing above me, still holding the steaming cup. "But let's forget me and return to you!"

"I thought you had," I said, pulling at my jacket which he was partly standing on.

"Uh? Oh, pardon me but I have such big feet." He looked at me again, "And you know what they say and you know." Karl was obviously relishing himself in the dual role of Gramercy's Park's answer to Mae West and 'The Stud!'

"But as I was saying, the relief of seeing you walk in. You looked like one of those mean, macho, moody executive marvels from *GQ* - though a slightly smashed one. Mona, was I flattered when you came over and stood alongside my bar stool and offered me a drink!"

"Well, and why not," I said, trying to look mean, macho, moody and not hung-over from my low level position on the floor. I was frantically striving to recall Karl and The Knockout but it was all extremely vague.

"Yes, you offered me one drink, then another and then a final one before you said - I think you said - you had 'to sail'! I suggested we bought some vodka and came back here and you said that was what you had in mind anyway. You in my bed and never mind! If those looks I was getting from some of the other girls could have slain, I would have been the deadest of corpses. Oh Mona," he looked down at his khaki running shoes, "you were terrif. You are some catch and some guy is sure lucky!"

"Well," I was flattered and embarrassed, "I thank you. But this terrif catch has to go." I pulled myself to my feet. "Tell me, do you call everyone you meet Mona?"

"Sure. It's to do with the sweet smile - not odour - of success. Get it, the smile of the Mona Lisa."

I didn't get it, but I answered "sure" anyway. I checked my wristwatch. "Good God, it's almost ten and I'm due for a meeting at noon. Give me your number and I'll try and call you later but now I must dash and find myself a cab."

Karl hastily printed a number on a pad symbolically headed "NO SHIT" and handed it to me. The name Karl was heavily underlined. I looked at him again.

"In case you forget, Mona," he said with a grin. "Last night I felt that you could have been my true destiny. You kept calling me 'Lisa' and then I realised you were saying 'Leslie'. It's that damn fascinating accent!"

'No Bullshit' didn't even make it to the yellow cab.

The memory of the night was crumpled and thrown into a litter bin as I raced along the sidewalk towards Fifth. I hailed a cab and sat feeling totally terrible as we headed across town before taking a parallel run up towards The Pierre. A groom of merely two weeks and I was already off the rails (I didn't want to play on the words straight and narrow even though it was with a young man, to boot!). With firm resolve I told myself that this was the final of all flings and with added determination I further purged my guilty soul by tipping the driver an extra five dollars. "Come again," he shouted, jovially. I simply shuddered at the thought. When I told Peter the story, he whooped with mirth. "Karl marks the start!" he had chortled.

I shook myself out of my reverie, changed down and flicked the indicator on turning left to Ennismore Gardens. My flat, in a large, grey-faced house, was made up of the basement and ground floor. There was the benefit of direct access to the private gardens.

The ground floor comprised of a large, elegant drawing room, finished in my favourite old golds and autumnal tints. A small dining room, with canopied ceiling and marbleised walls, was set off from this. There was an adequate kitchen and small staff quarters for two. The other main room on this floor was the large library and, like the drawing room, was enhanced with graceful vistas onto the gardens. A steep staircase led from the panelled entrance hall to the lower floor. Here there was the main bedroom, decorated in a deep spinach green and tan with its own adjoining bathroom and dressing area. A small guest bedroom with private shower and walk-in wardrobe completed the sleeping quarters. An additional feature to the main bedroom was the small patio with a spiral staircase leading up to the garden. The staircase was known as 'Petrina's Penance' as it was the only way she could get into the garden unaided. Otherwise she had to be taken out via the front door and to the main gates.

I removed my gloves and checked the post on the console table in the main hall. I removed Petrina's coat and unlocked the front door. Trini, the Spanish housekeeper, had left the lamps burning in the drawing room and library. A gas fire was burning cheerfully in each of the two rooms. I put down my briefcase, hung up my coat and then moved downstairs to my dressing room where I put my jacket on the back of the clothes press and took out a cardigan from the eighteenth-century tallboy. I kicked off my shoes, put the trees into them and slipped on a pair of comfortable Gucci loafers. All this accomplished, I returned back upstairs to the drawing room. I poured myself a large Scotch from the silver drinks tray on a commode and went over to the main sofa of the three grouped round the fireplace. Petrina, needless to say, had scrambled on to another of the sofas and was snoring quietly. I picked up the antique styled telephone from the side table and dialled the theatre again.

"Arthur, Robin Anderson for the second time!"

"Ah, yes sir. I gave Miss Adamson your message. Hold on and I'll see if I can put you through. There's plenty of time... curtain doesn't go up for three quarters of an hour yet."

"Hello?" Amanda's husky voice came on to the line.

"'Manda, darling. Robin."

"Darling!"

"As Arthur told you, I called earlier. It's simply to confirm that I am looking forward to seeing you for supper, that is if you are still free?" Amanda and myself were always very open about our dates. As I travelled down to the country fairly early on most Fridays, it was only on rare moments that we ever planned a late supper on this particular day of the week.

"Of course I'm free darling, and gasping to see you. As I've said before, it's all part of the glamour of a West End hit. Everyone thinks you are unapproachable or more so, uninvitable, due to those throngings of stage door johnnies. Not true and boring, very boring!"

The second 'boring' was announced in a higher octave.

I smiled. Amanda was always at her most outrageous when not on the stage. As Peter often said, "my dear, she makes camp straight!"

I made a few more calls and added a few pencilled notes to my diary.

"Well, good evening madam." Petrina had finally deigned to take herself off the sofa and was stretching at my feet. She yawned, shook herself and busily wagged her ridiculous tail whilst sneezing with great enthusiasm.

"Ah, of course, dinner time."

I got up and walked through to the kitchen. Petrina, deciding it was high time to sing for her supper, was jumping up and down with short, puffy barks. "Don't overdo it," I admonished her.

I collected her bowl and biscuits. Trini had left out a delicious concoction of chicken livers, chopped vegetables and meal. At times I was under the distinct impression that Trini's gourmet capabilities were solely for the benefit of Petrina and the occasional dinner parties I deigned to give came as an intrusion.

Leaving Petrina to snuffle her way through a quantity of food that appeared almost as large as she was, I poured an additional Scotch and retreated back downstairs to bath and to change.

In my Dougie Hayward blazer, burgundy velvet trousers and blue and white striped shirt from Michael Fish with matching tie, I checked myself in the mirror on the back of the dressing room door. "Not bad," I murmured and returned to the basin cabinet where I added an extra splash of 'Equipage'. My mother had once described me as a taller Tyrone Power and had never been able to get over what she had produced. I, unfortunately, had never been able to justify or match the comparison and so had disagreed with her all along the way. However, that evening, with a slight narrowing of the eyes and blurring of the vision, I was almost able to tease the reflection into a reasonable lookalike.

I came upstairs. Petrina had finished her feast and was back on the sofa.

"Approve?" I questioned.

She gave me a negative stare and closed her eyes. This reaction was followed by the heaviest of sighs. No doubt she expected me to be shrouded in the heaviest of guilt as it was obvious to her that there was a delay in leaving for the country and, judging by my attire, there was an evening planned out and she was not expected to join in.

Chapter Three

Peter's house, in elegant Clabon Mews, backing onto Cadogan Square, was only a few minutes from Ennismore Gardens. I had deliberated calling a car hire service I frequently used or else taking a taxi – but, as I would be collecting Amanda and possibly going on to a club after supper, I felt it more convenient to take the car.

The bright orange painted house was ablaze with light and I could hear the Beatles shouting for 'Help' into the cold night air. I duly parked and walked quickly towards the welcoming open front door, my breath forming a vapour trail in the chill behind me. Several figures were grouped by the entrance, none of whom I recognised. Peter's parties were always fairly bizarre. Tonight was 'mixed' which admitted to any interpretation. David Wainwright, a fairly close friend, was standing inside the doorway holding an intense conversation with a young man, who was as intense looking as the topic being discussed. David raised his hand in greeting without looking away from the young man who appeared to be becoming more intense and was now pulling his cape – which looked like an old carpet from Portobello Road – more anxiously around his narrow shoulders. I eased my way past them into the main hall and then the main ground floor room. Peter's house had recently been decorated by a young man who was responsible for some of the more avant garde sets being pursued by one of the television channels. He had been called back to create a further set for the evening's frolics. There were revolving lights, strobe lights and banks of candelabra, all creating a stumbling arena what with mirror-adorned walls, patent reflective screens and acrylic louvred window shades. The inevitable Barcelona chairs and other knee-jarring embellishments, accepted only because of their affiliation with Maestro van de Roe, had been cleared as much as possible to the room's perimeter. The centre of the large room was thronging with a tightly packed group in all types of garb, puzzling sex and of all shapes and sizes. The noise was deafening.

"Darling, Robin!"

With a great shriek, a tall, extremely glamorous figurine dressed as some wild gypsy from a rock version of *Carmen*, swept over – quite a feat – to me. I was swamped in a heady embrace and kissed expertly on the cheek. April Ashley held me back at arm's length.

"So distingué!" she throatily chortled, emphasising the last syllable.

"April, dear. You look stunning."

April flicked open her black fan. "Olé!" she cried.

"If only," she sighed. We both laughed, embraced again and she was swept off by another group of admirers.

Peter had to be complimented. Everybody of note in London's eccentric gay and theatrical set was there with a notable sprinkle of society figures. Kenneth Williams was hysterically regaling a convulsed group with some latest, outrageous tale. A genial Norman Hartnell, resplendent in a strawberry brocade waistcoat, was busily engaged in animated discussion with a young lady sombrely and elegantly clad in a distinctive Jean Muir. Adding her own inimitable touch of tone was Elvira, a splendid Duchess of unknown years and a great beauty in her time, who was earnestly talking to Boris, a large young man clad in a pair of jeans with a diamanté-encrusted denim jacket. Elvira moved a hand in recognition at me and returned to her deep conversation with the husky bit of beefcake.

"RA! You've arrived." Beaming warmly and clinging to an equally beaming young man was Peter. "Meet Tim. Tim, this is RA whom I've mentioned to you endlessly. He looks very grand and boring but he's not, actually!"

"Thank you, Peter," I retorted. Tim beamed all the more and made a vague attempt at a half salute.

"Nice to meet ya, RA," he said, hiccoughing gently. He turned and gave Peter a playful nip on the earlobe. The nip should have caused a roar of pain – or would have with a lesser being, but Peter seemed unaware of the vampire attack and they two lurched off happily into the crowd. Peter appeared to have forgotten the promise of my Christmas present in the heady excitement of his own pursuits.

I edged my way through the crush towards the conservatory at the rear of the house. I was hoping to find some breathing space, get another drink and perhaps spot a familiar face. The crowd seemed to be growing at an enormous rate. Peter had always had the great failing of inviting anyone he fancied or thought would be amusing. Most of the time he had forgotten his invitation and arrivals were always being greeted with a complete blank and puzzled stare. A rider and pillion passenger at a set of traffic lights or a group in a pub were always being made welcome. Peter would supply the address and the drink and then simply allow the whole party to create itself.

I paused and spoke to a few faces I recognised and finally pushed my way through to a garden seat and some chairs which had been pushed into a semblance of a conversation area by the French windows to the small back garden.

He was dazzling.

Regina was draped – boa-like – across the garden seat. His long blonde hair fell elegantly across one eye ("Madly Betsy Drake, darling, and madly peek-a-boo!" he was later to say), partly covering one of a pair of amazing Susy Parker-type cheekbones. One hand, resting languidly on the back of the ironwork to the seat, held an elegant antique ivory holder with its smouldering, yellow Sobranie. Large blue-grey eyes with the slightest smudge of blue glitter to the half-closed lids were analysing the room with lethal dedication and no doubt, accuracy. A black velvet jacket, white ruffled lace shirt and a pair of yellow velvet pants – the colour of the Sobranie – tucked into long lizard-skin boots completed the impact.

Peter, now puce but minus Tim and still beaming, pushed by.

"Peter, who on earth is that?"

I half expected Peter to yell. "Happy Christmas! It's him, your present!" but received in reply, "Taboo, dear! Anyway, not your type – much too flash!" and he was gone.

"Taboo dear needs another drink," said a modulated voice.

I turned quickly back to the young man on the seat. He was not looking at me but holding out his glass to one of the people sitting with him. His companion took the glass and stood up to make a move. I glared at this extraordinary young man and felt myself flushing angrily. His companion had by now moved out of earshot. Not only was I annoyed at his mocking Peter but I was doubly annoyed that he must also have heard my remark. He slowly directed his gaze more accurately at me.

"Actually, I apologise." He paused and took a draw from his holder. "That comment was trite, if not a bit too flash."

I could not believe it. I was about to make some futile reply such as "only to be expected" or "wouldn't know any better", but realised how even more pathetic it would have appeared and turned away, very angry.

"Angel cake!" A large, burnished Brunhilde in swathes of coppery Sekers silk, copper bracelets, armlets, earrings, anklets and mostly concealed belt, burst through the group nearest to me. Pru Pru Wendelfoot, one of London's most determined and adventurous partygoers, flung her large marshmallow-like arms about me and planted a large lipstick smudged kiss – copper coloured – on my cheek.

"Second kissies!" she screamed, pressing her lips to my other side.

She increased her wide-eyed smile – if possible – as she stood back either to admire me, or her handiwork, or both. She suddenly looked about her wildly. "Where... where," she began, "oh, there he is!" She leaned back and dragged forward a tiny man who had been bravely attempting to follow in her large wake ('Miss Red Sea' she was usually known as due to her colouring and cleaving her way through seas of people).

"Darling," she paused and looked at me dramatically. "This is TOM!"

I looked at TOM!

Pru Pru had the skill of being able to speak in capitals. With the production being staged in front of me and my anger and confusion following the confrontation with the young man on the seat behind me, I was not too sure as to whether Peter had summoned Pru Pru to present TOM! as a joke present for the evening, or if TOM! was Pru Pru's genuine escort. Peter and myself had often discussed Pru Pru's paramours. The larger she became, the smaller they seemed to be. Peter put it quite succinctly: Pru Pru in bed with a lover was reminiscent of the midget atop the fat lady in the circus who says to him, with nanny-like smile, "Oops, I think you've found a wrinkle!" Peter is always threatening to invite Pru Pru to join us on one of our annual breaks abroad. "Imagine Pru Pru topless or starkers on Super Paradise! Merde. Poor Mykonos," he used to chortle. "Paradise with no chance of being regained," I would reply, with exaggerated shudder.

"Hello TOM!" I said. "Pru Pru, how marvellously different you look," I lied.

"Liar!" she retorted in full voice. "I can tell what you think. Marvellously different indeed! That could mean I look like a truck driver in DRAG en route to The Dorchester. But you, darling, genuinely look DIVINE! TOM!" she shouted into his ear next to her, "isn't RA heavenly? He's NEVER in town on a Friday so you see how important this party must be!" She put her hand in front of her mouth and twisted her lips ferociously into an enormous stage whisper. "He hasn't been to a basically GAY DO before and therefore will not leave me for ONE SECOND as he feels his REAR," she shrieked at this pun, "REAR – get it? – virtue has to be protected... TOM!" She bounced round, but TOM! had gone and I was left by a gesticulating Pru Pru ballooning off in hot pursuit of her threatened midget man.

I slowly wandered into the kitchen and began talking to a few people surrounding a large bowl of crudities and dips. Pru Pru reappeared with a chastised-looking TOM! Pru Pru continued to lecture him in her loud voice, her one hand holding him and her glass and the other working energetically to and from the food bowl. She paused in mid sentence to blow me a large kiss. TOM! was showered in bits of celery stalk. Peter's Tim, looking dishevelled and much the worse for drink, reeled over to Pru Pru and leaned against her gratefully. I thought for one moment he had gone to sleep but he nodded now and again as if agreeing with her continued berating of TOM!

I looked up at the clock on the wall. Time enough for a last Scotch before going to collect Amanda from the theatre and go on to supper.

Peter loomed up alongside me. His smile was definitely of the slack version.

"Peter I'm about to leave. The party is great. But then they always are."

"If Amanda feels up to it, come in after dinner?" slurred Peter. "This is going on for a time."

"I'll see how Amanda feels," I promised.

"Sorry about the present... he hasn't arrived... couldn't come or something. Some message from someone."

"Not to worry," I smiled, "probably just as well. I do have to go on." I gave him a gentle push. "Off you go and see your guests. I'll call you in the morning, but not too early. And I look forward to seeing you and Tim on Tuesday," I added.

But Peter had already swayed off back to the main party. I set my glass on the counter top and stretched out my hand to the whisky bottle.

A hand moved across mine. "Allow me," said the modulated voice, "and this time I do apologise."

I looked down at the young man standing next to me. He placed his holder in his mouth, took the bottle and my glass and poured a healthy measure into it.

"Ice?" I nodded, waiting for the next dash of vitriol and debated as to whether I would even attempt to control a reaction this time. He dropped a cube in and raised an eyebrow. I nodded again and he dropped in a second lump.

He took the cigarette holder from his mouth momentarily. "Soda?"

"Please." I could feel the tension. "A splash only."

He placed the whisky bottle back on the countertop, picked up the siphon and squirted the soda with professional accuracy into the tumbler. He put down the siphon, brushed back the hair from his face, removed the cigarette holder once more, raised his own glass and said "cheers".

"Cheers."

It was a bit of an anti-climax. I had expected the whisky to be thrown at me or accidentally spilled but there was none of this.

"I am Reginald Forbes."

"Reginald," I nodded. "I am Robin Anderson."

"Hello, Robin,"

I refrained from replying "Hello Reginald" as the whole situation was becoming ludicrous.

"Fun party, isn't it?" I said.

"Yes, if you like these sort of parties," he replied. "I don't."

I looked at him. Who on earth was this poisonous young person?

"I'm sorry you do not approve," I said, "but Peter is a great friend of mine and I always think he entertains brilliantly."

"I wouldn't go as far as to use the word 'brilliant'," said Reginald Forbes, "but I would use the word 'irrational'."

I looked at him in astonishment and shook my head. I put down the half-finished drink and turned abruptly away.

"Mr Anderson," said the voice, "I wasn't invited, anyway. A friend of mine was asked here, to meet you I believe, but sadly he couldn't make it and so he suggested I came instead. We were both at college together and I gather he met your friend, Peter, in some strange club!"

I continued to look dumbfounded.

"Oh yes, Phillip, my chum, has mentioned you several times. He says Peter never stops talking about you in the nicest possible way and so I decided to have a look see myself." He half closed his eyes, smiled and took a further draw on his cigarette.

My mind raced as to what I would be saying to Peter next morning, but I simply could not get over the gall of Reginald Forbes.

"Reginald," I said, "do you seriously expect me to believe what you are saying? I mean, do you really go around behaving or acting like this and expect people to take you seriously? I mean, this is Clabon Mews, London, not Sunset Boulevard, LA."

"And you would be William Holden and doubtless I am already cast as Gloria Swanson," laughed Reginald. "No, seriously, it's all totally true. I admit I was reasonably foul back there but when you are an uninvited guest at a party where you know nobody, it can be fairly alarming and one immediately puts up one's defences."

"I don't accept that you don't know anybody here," I argued. "Why, you seemed to have gathered a perfectly adequate circle of admirers – even to having one fetch and carry for you."

"Charisma, Robin," said Reginald Forbes, "charisma."

"Well, Mr Charisma or Mr no Charisma, I must be going. I appreciate you coming over to talk to me and I am sorry you have not enjoyed yourself. Say hello to your friend, Phillip, for me and say I look forward to meeting him another time. With Peter." I made to leave but he lightly touched my sleeve.

I turned round and looked down at where he stood looking up at me. "Goodnight and I do hope we meet again," he said.

"Of course," I replied, feeling fairly bewildered and also irritated at the young man's extraordinary attitudes and behaviour. I said a few more goodnights and made my way towards the front door. I was not too surprised to see Reginald Forbes standing there. I had already got his number and knew that this was one very tough number – strychnine sweet as Leslie would have said.

"We meet again," I murmured.

"Indeed," he replied. "Would you by any chance be heading past an underground? I have to get back to the West End."

"Anywhere near Piccadilly?" I gave him a bemused look.

"No, not what you think. I'd rather like to talk and I can easily get the tube from there and change at Earl's Court."

I had to admire the tenacity of the man and said, "Piccadilly it shall be."

The traffic was still bad and so the journey into the West End took longer than I expected. I was not too anxious as I knew that Amanda would be happily dealing with backstage admirers and also having a glass or two, and besides I could not help being fascinated by the strange individual sitting alongside me.

"Heavenly car," he said, "are you rich?"

"I could just hear Amanda 'another boring hustler darling. You really should know better... he wore what?'"

"Comfortable," I replied.

"How reassuring but how dull," said Reginald. He eyed me over the lambswool coat he had somehow conjured up from the night air. "One should be hideously, extravagantly, horrendously rich," he announced.

I looked at him again. "Do you always wear eye make-up?" I asked.

"Only on special occasions."

"And this sadly wasn't." I said this as a fact, not a question.

"Well, it's improving," he said.

"Look," I checked the rear-view mirror and pulled out to overtake a bus, "I really think you ought to stop playing your games. You do appear to be fairly absurd. You have been both exceptionally impolite but also fairly civilised. I appreciate," I continued, stopping his would-be comment, "that you were a stranger there, etc. etc. but people know how to behave and there is a time and a place." God, I thought to myself, I sound like the local Presbyterian minister in the small village in Ayrshire where I was brought up.

"So I have been offensive. I'm sorry."

There was silence. I shook my head. This young man was impossible. He was an amalgamation of every screen siren Hollywood had produced and carried off the roles with no self-consciousness whatsoever.

"I tell you what," he said, "we're almost at the Dilly. Why don't you come to lunch with me and Phillip tomorrow? I know you usually go down to the country and Ealing is on the way to Henley."

The homework had been very thorough. I again looked at him. "That is very kind of you – and Phillip – but it so happens I will be going down later tonight and will not be back in London until Wednesday as I do have a great deal of paperwork to catch up on." Why on earth was I making excuses to this rather annoying young stranger. "But, as I said back at the party, I will make sure that Peter is in touch and no doubt we will meet again." I pulled over to the pavement. "I suggest you nip out here," I added, "and don't talk to any strangers."

"I can still catch a final few at The White Bear – drinks that is," he grinned. "Goodnight and thank you." He got out of the car, leaving the door semi-open. He looked up at the Wriggly sign and struck a pose, arms outstretched towards the car, his feet placed in ballet position, his coat draped over his shoulders. A few passers-by paused and looked at him curiously. He started to croon, "We'll meet again, I know where, I know when…"

I leaned across and pulled the door shut. With a crash of gears I pulled away amidst hooting from several irate drivers behind me. I glanced into the rear-view mirror. He was still standing there, still singing I imagined, a small gathering around him and his arms held imploringly at the departing tail lights of my car.

"Outrageous, silly queen," I muttered to myself and I inched my way up Shaftesbury Avenue. I checked the cassette, pulled on the knot of my tie and settled back in the plush seat, my fingers drumming in time against the alpine horn steering wheel to the latest sounds of The Springfields. "Bloody outrageous, silly young queen," I repeated, adding emphasis to my earlier reaction. However, I would be deceiving myself if I had claimed not to be fascinated. Although Peter had claimed Reginald was "too flash" – and I had to agree – I nevertheless had been fascinated by the young man during the few minutes I had seen him at the party and more so on the drive up to the West End. The old saying 'every cloud has a silver lining' no doubt could be changed in his case to a 'silver lurex lining', and in fairness to the young man he had attempted to redeem himself to a certain extent and could not have been more polite with his thanking me or in the invitation to lunch the next day. "Banish the thoughts," I continued, muttering to myself. "You're too old for this sort of game and anyway he would not fit into your scene at all."

Unlike Peter, I was far to circumspect to introduce to my 'straight' circle several of the young men I had become lightly involved with. Peter endlessly referred to me as "two faced" or else an uptight "old closet queen", but the terms were said on occasions more out of frustration and friendship rather than as a hurtful criticism. I had explained – or tried to exempt my actions – to Peter by showing that most of my circle were either friends from my days with Leslie or else those in my business circle.

"Most of the dealers and designers you deal with are gay, anyway," Peter would leer, "or else, like you, do the married and social bit and then dash back from the country seat on a Sunday evening after a pissy weekend leaving the wife to follow up on the Monday or Tuesday with the baskets of vegetables and her diary full of the luncheons and her good deeds for the week. Whilst wifey spends Sunday evening with the papers, a snack, and a latish film on the box, his nibs is into the casuals and off to the A & B for a few stiff gins and something else as stiff later!"

My preference to date had always been for the fey and rather frail flowers one would see around the rather more sordid West End havens. As Peter said, "Bliss for you RA would be death amidst a welter of never-ending nellie waiters."

"That being so," I had replied, "you will appreciate my dilemma and the reason why I cannot mix A with Z."

"Of course you'd say that," Peter would continue. "It all goes back to that quotation that it doesn't matter what you do as long as you don't frighten the horses." Peter was always inclined to muddle his pointers when angered and the whole incident ended in a burst of laughter.

But Reginald. I had found him physically attractive once the initial reaction to his attitudes and behaviour had been appeased and, with his presence and obvious style – an acquired taste in all senses of the expression – he would obviously be in control of any gathering.

"No," I said, drawing up at the stage door of the St George, "no."
"Anyway," I said, as I locked the car, "can you imagine the reaction of Amanda to him?" – knowing Amanda, they would doubtless hit it off immediately – or else the Robinsons, or Tony and Bobbie... but I cleared these thoughts from my mind as they were irrelevant and as far as I was concerned that was the one and only meeting with Mr Forbes. As I nodded to Arthur and went down the concrete stairs to

the dressing rooms behind the stage, I gave Reginald one last thought – I wondered what he planned to do with his future or whether a career was planned or else would he simply be swallowed up into that nebulous waste of a Pollyanna and never never land.

*

Amanda was poised in front of the dressing table, a glass of champagne in her hand. I handed her a bottle of similar vintage I had brought with me as I knew Amanda's love affair with the bubbly – her favourite after the show pick-me-up.

"How lovely, RA," she smiled, holding a deliciously sculptured cheek towards me for a kiss. She waved an elegant hand at whom I took to be two of the backstage crew sitting alongside her. I did recognise them from the last of a show I had seen at the Criterion.

"Of course, you've met Stella and Simon, haven't you?"

"Er, yes," I said, nodding at the two. "On the opening night at the party at San Lorenzo." Stella and Simon beamed. I had no idea of meeting them before but had taken the plunge as I felt sure that this claim was as safe as any. Amanda was always adored by the rest of the cast and backstage crew alike. She had this immense charm of making the most menial of the team feel totally important and was never too fussed or too busy to listen to, or advise on, the smallest problem or detail. "Remember, it's all teamwork, darling," she would say to me. "Okay, at times one can barely hold back some devastating retort, but my love affair with the lighting manager and the director never falters and I am passionate about the rest of the cast!"

Stella and Simon, exactly like a pair of denim-clad Tweedle Dum and Dee, continued beaming.

"Stella is helping Mavis with the dressing and Simon has just been appointed Junior electrician," explained Amanda, sensing my slight awkwardness.

"Congratulations," I said, "may I?" I gestured to the bottle I had brought.

"What a lovely idea and why not," cried Amanda. She checked herself in the brightly lit mirror. "Isn't it wonderful?" she said, eyeing the flawless reflection – "not that" she added, gesturing back to the mirror – "but the fact of only two shows tomorrow and then four days out of purdah." She turned back to her mini audience. "Imagine, after eight months I can now look forward to four civilised lunches, all in a row and maybe even a movie."

The show was closing for the Christmas break and after seven performances a week to capacity houses, I could quite understand the exhaustion members must have been feeling. Amanda Adamson was the star of the show and apart from the frenetic costume changes, she was barely off centre stage. *The Bliss of All* was one of those spectacular American imports that was obviously around for some time. The music was being hummed and whistled along with the Beatles' hits and the whole production had been praised as a worthy sequel to the likes of acrobatic and high kicking *West Side Story*. As Amanda had been frequently quoted as saying, "When you have to kick, you kick!"

I had known Amanda for several years. She was one of those fascinating women, who though still in her twenties, gave out that aura and sense of sophistication which seems to have been imbued in certain types of womanhood, since the days of Circe. She had been compared to a reborn Rita Hayworth, a young Betty Bacall, but quite simply, to me and her vast following she was the one and only Amanda Adamson.

We had met at a dinner party given by two acquaintances of mine, Angus and Sarah Carr. Sarah I had met through some buying and selling, and had been a guest at their tasteful house in Montpelier Square on several occasions. Angus was one of those fierce-looking sorts whom you see travelling to the City each morning, secure in the back of his chauffeur-driven limousine and protected from the outside world by the pink bastion of the *Financial Times*. I had seen Amanda Adamson – as had all of London – in several hit shows and I was fascinated to meet her in person. She had a tremendous gay following and had outraged several members of Equity when it had been reported that Amanda had shown up with a young group at a pub one Sunday evening in the East End and spontaneously joined in a drag cabaret with the pub's 'Amanda Adamson' – a young man who was known as Clive off stage, and worked in a bakery in Bermondsey. The Bermondsey Amanda and the real Amanda had been a sensation and the cabaret had continued long after hours with part of the greatest applause coming from 'the old bill' who had dropped by for their late night pint.

As required of a star, Amanda Adamson never let her public down. She was smaller than I had expected her to be, but the elegant face, the incredible figure, seemingly endless legs and a tumble of auburn hair, plus the elfin face with its much copied beauty spot to the left cheek, created a total mesmerising person. Her voice was low and husky and I was to learn to admire the caustic and barbed wit which she never abused, but more than this her delightful camp attitude to the majority of situations. Sarah had placed me on Amanda's left at dinner. She had Angus who was at the head of the table next to her, but I was happy to say that he was more or less left to the wiles of a bridge-playing title seated on his other side, for most of the dinner. By the time we had reached the main course, Amanda and I were firm partners in 'mini crime'. Her discreet asides regarding a few of the guests and her general style of gurgling conversation had me laughing through the whole meal. She was totally enchanting and one could feel the great warmth she felt for both Sarah and Angus, though the latter was always being kindly mocked by her.

"Darling Sarah," she had said afterwards, "she is so sweet, but God, some of those dinners can be quite horrendous. Particularly when they are to 'welcome' some of those highly dubious associates of Angus's from the lesser Americas or elsewhere as remote. Even Tommy Tucker would find his singsong put to the test at one of these suppers."

Amanda had known Sarah before she had met and married Angus. Sarah had been an established actress and Amanda had been in the heady euphoria of landing her first bit part in a West End show with the famous Sarah Hope. Amanda was fresh from drama school and in between dancing lessons, singing lessons, and tramping from agent to agent, she had been working in Harrods where she seemed to be having more success in convincing matrons that they looked stunning in more than the little black dress, than convincing an agent she was the next happening in the realms of show business. Sarah Hope had been into the department on several occasions and Amanda always remembered her great charm and friendliness. "She made you feel two million dollars," Amanda used to say, "and I never forgot that lesson." All this was now history. Amanda had charmed the critics, found a great ally and friend in Sarah and had gone on from show to show, before landing the role of Ruby in a revamp of Robin Miller's *Dames at Sea*. From there it was instant stardom.

Amanda's only criticism against Sarah had been her giving up the theatre when she married Angus. "She was Queen of Comedy – in the biblical sense, darling – before becoming Queen of the Comedy of Errors. I realise she is blissfully happy with Angus, but from the selfish point of view, as a colleague, what a waste. Yet she sincerely does not miss it and has happily sublimated that adoration and applause in Angus, Arden and 'appiness as she says!"

When I realised that Amanda was to call a taxi, I had offered her a lift back to her house in Chester Square. The house had recently been successfully featured in *Vogue* and I had in fact seen the property in its early stages of redecoration as Sarah had taken me around for my advice on some of the mirrors which had been purchased through the sale of the property by the previous owners to Amanda.

Amanda had firstly declined my offer as she was going on elsewhere, "unless, of course, you feel up to a party for a minute or two," she had added.

"I would be delighted," I had replied. Sarah was fluttering about like the proverbial mother hen. I was fairly amused as I would have thought that with me, of all their friends, Sarah would have been the most intuitive, but this did not appear to be so that particular evening.

Amanda had collected a wrap of silver and green and we left. The new party, in a vast basement flat off Lots Road in Chelsea's World's End, was given by Amanda's hairdresser, Jon Jon, who lived in a blissful melange of art nouveau with his friend, Boris the beautiful – Amanda hissed, "But sadly, also Boris with the BO," she added mischievously. Boris was an artist and determined to start a new trend with his sculptures created out of old iron bedsteads of which the Thames offered a never-ending supply.

My admiration for Amanda had increased more and more that evening. Her total acceptance that I would not be put out by this particular party scene, plus her obvious fondness for Jon Jon and Boris, could not have endeared her more to me. The house had been ablaze with light, and music with a distinctive ethnic beat was echoing down the cul-de-sac. The party had been going for some time and was now in full swing. Jon Jon, a plump, hysterical glitterboots in spangles, his hair adorned with strings of rhinestones and glitter dust, shrieked with delight on spotting Amanda. "Manda," he cried, "heaven, heaven." He twirled in front of her. "How divine of you to come. You look ravishing and I loooove the hair." He grinned evilly and sucked in his cheeks. "Darling," he said, seeing me for the first time hovering behind. "Who is she?"

Any ice after this greeting, was broken. Beautiful Boris, very sweaty and marvellously muscled, came over with two glasses of punch and was introduced to me. He was staggering to view. Boris must have been all of six feet four, with wild black hair, a huge barrel chest and covered with hair. He had one of the most compelling and handsome faces I had seen, and the bluest of eyes. He obviously adored Jon Jon and kept glancing in his friend's direction through the entire time we were there.

"The gentle giant," Amanda had said afterwards. "He dotes on Jon Jon – in fact, left a wife and daughter amidst ghastly scenes to be with him. He had been one of the part-time workmen on the building site when Jon Jon was doing up his premises in King's Road. Jon Jon had got frightfully smashed on Saturday at Alvaro's – you know how lethal those long, wonderful Alvaro lunches are to all that endless hedonistic lot, and returned to the salon early evening to check how work was progressing. Boris was still there doing some final touching up – paintwise – and Jon Jon, who had eyed this Adonis – his description on more than one occasion, asked him out for a drink. They had gone to a local pub where they had happily consumed far too much with Jon Jon well in the lead. Some bright oik had made some cutting comment about Jon Jon and the "filthy queer" bit and next thing found himself on the pavement outside with a broken jaw. Boris and Jon Jon had toasted this incident with further drinks – this time uninterrupted – and then gone on to a club Jon Jon knew – gay of course – where Boris was the star of the evening but stayed close to Jon Jon, arm around his shoulder, mumbling that this was what it was all about and how much he admired Jon Jon for being what he was. Well, the inevitable happened. They went back to Jon Jon's flat in Lot's Road and there Boris remained."

Amanda had paused for a sip of coffee whilst regaling me with the story. She went on. "Jon Jon was horrified when he woke up next morning. Knowing how drunk they had both been he was terrified that Boris the Beautiful would awaken and become Boris the Bloody.

"Jon Jon had crept out of bed – or the sacrificial couch as he always calls it – and sneaked out to the sitting room where he had proceeded to call me. He and I are great soulmates and I can so clearly remember him saying, 'Manda darling – this could be the prelude to my last will and testament. I have Boris here – you know, the Adonis I have never stopped doing a Pavlov over-salivating and masturbating – well, he's in bed, asleep and I don't know what to do.'" For Jon Jon to be at a loss of what to do in this particular situation was certainly something very new. However, Boris the Beautiful remained Boris the Beautiful. He had come into the sitting room whilst Jon Jon was hissing into the telephone to me, gently taken Jon Jon's arm – I had heard the shriek – smiled and said good morning and that was the last I heard from Jon Jon for at least two weeks before he came back down to earth and called me to say that I should not have worried, and that, as he had anticipated, everything was wonderful."

From this first meeting with Amanda and my introduction into her viewpoints and her obvious knowledge and acceptance of the scene, there were no secrets and our friendship grew. Sarah was delighted with our getting together and my ego went through a great shot in the arm due to endless press speculations about our relationship. The gossip press had a heyday and even Peter had to admit that his PR Organisation could not have created such publicity even if there had been the slightest case of authenticity. Trust Peter always to have the last say. Amanda had gone through several of my emotional traumas and I had seen her through two, both with attractive young actors who, when they found she was more prepared to be sincere in a relationship as opposed to being an open door to success, left her feeling drained and totally disillusioned. She had been married once before, but the husband had left her and she did not seem prepared to go into any further details.

We finished the second bottle of champagne just as Albert knocked against the open door and poked his head round to check how much longer we were going to be. After a few more minutes of conversation we emptied our glasses and set off.

I had selected Burkes Club for dinner as I knew it was a favourite haunt of Amanda's and a place where she could relax even though being in public. The impeccable Luigi greeted us warmly on our arrival and led us through to our table. Several people waved to Amanda or the two of us and we sat down gratefully in a corner, partly sheltered from the main room by an arrangement of palm trees.

I ordered us each a dry martini, and took a menu from the ever attentive Luigi.

"I'll have something very light," said Amanda, "perhaps the sole and a green salad." I settled for some cutlets and tomato salad, and organised a bottle of Pouilly-Fuissé.

Amanda took my hand across the table. "Darling, this is nice." She smiled. "I have so looked forward to our dinner and it's lovely to have you solo."

Our drinks arrived and I raised my glass to her.

She took a sip and gave a long sigh. "Pure, heavenly sin," she breathed. "Quite, quite delicious. Now, tell me about New York."

We chatted about New York, mutual friends there and stopped only when our food arrived. Dinner was delicious and I happily ordered a second bottle of wine whilst Amanda broke all her rules and asked for a large helping of the gateau.

"Well, after all, it is almost Christmas," she said. "Anyway," she added, "with two performances tomorrow those calories won't have a chance and will be gone in a flash."

"The 'in' word for this evening, obviously," I commented dryly.

"I'm sorry, I've lost you on that," said Amanda.

"I'll explain." I proceeded to tell her about Peter's party and Reginald Forbes and the journey to Piccadilly.

"Another boring little hustler," said Amanda, right on cue, "you really should know better. His get-up alone, even though these are the swinging Sixties, should have flashed the warning light. Where does Peter find them?"

"Actually, in retrospect he really was not that bad." I was astounded to find myself defending Reginald. Amanda looked at me.

"Oh dear, darling Robin, I believe you are being serious. You're not planning to see him again are you?"

"No, but I was fascinated. It seems extraordinary how different the young are today – present company excepted – from my day. I mean, when I was twenty nobody would appear like that in public, never mind behave like that."

"Darling, you are not a fuddy duddy, at all," said Amanda. "There have always been people like your Reginald – I'll rephrase that – like that Reginald, but slightly more discreet perhaps. My only comment is that he sounded very unpleasant to start with even though he does appear to have become Miss Charm as the evening progressed. Anyway," she concluded, "let's forget Mr Forbes and discuss Christmas."

We carried on with our mutual plans for the coming Christmas week. Christmas was on a Monday and Amanda was coming to stay with me in the country as from the Sunday morning. She would be returning to London on the Wednesday although we had been invited over to lunch with some friends nearby but had decided to opt for a quiet Christmas dinner by ourselves, and apart from a few neighbours in on Christmas Day for a glass of champagne, it was going to be very quiet and selfish. Amanda had several scripts she planned to read as she was hoping to feature in a film when she left *The Bliss of it All* at the end of the following summer season.

Having finished our coffee, we left the restaurant, stopping for a final nightcap at Annabel's. I dropped off Amanda, promising to call her around mid-morning from the country and set off back to Ennismore Gardens to collect my briefcase and Petrina. I had already collected several cases of wine from Bury Brothers that afternoon and these, along with Clare's cake, were securely locked in the boot of the car.

As I opened the front door, the telephone was ringing. I glanced at my watch. It was a quarter to one and I was about to leave the call to be dealt with by the answering service, but thinking that it may possibly be Amanda or America, I quickly moved across to the hall table and picked up the receiver.

"5849," I said.

"Mr Anderson?"

"Who's calling him?"

"Is that Mr Anderson?" I recognised the voice immediately and my irritation was instant.

"Yes, it is Mr Anderson. And what can I do for you at this late hour? It is after quarter to one in the morning!"

"Oh I am sorry, but I was convinced you were out as your answering service has taken my previous calls till now." I had visions of my service switchboard agog with endless calls from a dulcet Reginald Forbes and no doubt the messages had not been simple and straightforward.

"I've just got in," I answered, wondering why I was sounding so on the defensive, "and I am now on my way out as I'm leaving for the country."

"Oh, I had hoped when you answered this time that you had changed your mind and I would be seeing you for lunch after all."

"Well, that is not possible. I would have thought that one of your concert audience in Piccadilly may have obliged," I added, totally unnecessarily.

"One has," said Reginald, "in fact he's getting me a drink."

"Aren't you home yet?" I asked.

"No, I'm here with Edward. He thought my carolling fairly amazing and asked me back for a drink. I'm in his flat which is fairly close to you." I gathered that as he had my telephone number, which he had clearly looked up in the directory, he had also got my address. "Look," he added, lowering his voice, "it is a bit awkward here – as you are driving to the country would you mind awfully if I asked you to hold on a few minutes and I'll nip round and perhaps you could drop me off in Ealing on the way – please!" The 'please' sounded quite panic-stricken.

"Of course," I said, and the line went dead.

I was furious with myself for being so weak, but again I was also curious as to what Mr Forbes had now gone and got himself into. I was also more than excited at seeing him again.

I went through to the library, checked my briefcase, told a not too curious Petrina who had followed me into the room, that she could relax for a few more minutes, and settled myself into my favourite chair with an unexpected Scotch.

Reginald Forbes had sounded agitated, but then as Mr Forbes gave the continued impression of always appearing to be in various stages of trauma I sat sipping my drink and generally sliding into a semi-doze as tiredness, resulting from my recent trip, the lateness of the evening and no doubt the fair quantity of alcohol I had consumed, took effect.

The sharp buzzing of the front door ansafone and Petrina's startled bark, woke me. I rubbed my eyes, yawned, automatically smoothed my hair and made my way into the hall. I checked the ansafone.

"Hello?"

"Robin. Reginald." He sounded totally brisk and together and not at all like the fraught voice of a quarter of an hour earlier. I again felt an annoyance starting within myself for being so gullible and allowing myself to be tricked into what would no doubt prove to be another of the young man's games.

"Ground floor, to the right," I said. However as I pressed the release button, I resolved to let him in, offer one drink and then set forth for the country without further delay.

"You are so kind," he breathed as he arrived at the front door. "It really was too awful." He swept past me into the main hall and through into the sitting room. "Do come in," I muttered, following him. He moved to the centre of the room where he stood looking around, his left hand on his hip, his coat draped around his shoulders, chin up and his right foot pointing outwards.

"Very pleasant," he said, "a bit contraceptive, but very pleasant. Oh!"

The "Oh" was directed at Petrina who had sat up on the sofa having made her great gesture of a few barks. "What a divine pooch!" He crossed quickly to Petrina and knelt down to speak to her, tickling her under the chin. Petrina, being a total tart, sagged sloppily and turned on to her back to present a large black stomach which was immediately tickled.

Appalled at her double-crossing I said, "I seem to remember Campari, correct?"

"Please," said Reginald, looking up and giving me a dazzling smile. "Isn't she marvellous?" he cooed and returned to scratching a now totally won over animal.

I came back and handed him the drink. "I was actually sitting in the library but would you prefer to stay out here?"

"The library sounds wonderful. I do like this room," he added again, looking round. "That's a Piper, isn't it?"

I was most impressed. Piper was still fairly rare to be appreciated at this time, but I reminded myself that he was an art student and more likely assessing the value of the various paintings and objects in the room.

"And a Bacon, Robin! How marvellous." He moved over to the violent oil above the fireplace. "And look, what an enchanting pair of watercolours!"

I caught myself looking at his excited face with renewed interest. "He genuinely knows and cares," I said to myself. His gaze moved towards the coffee table, positioned between the three sofas. "Pre-Colombian," I said, pointing to the clay heads that had been specially set out on acrylic cubes, "and the piece of marble next to them is part of a Roman foot from an excavation outside Carthage."

My art collection was of great pride and joy to me and I found myself warming to the subject and certainly fired by Reginald's exuberance. While he moved on to study a further group of enamel boxes on a Biedemier table near the window I quickly refilled our glasses and returned to continue with our art appreciation. This was not as to how I had imagined the arrival of this rather terrifying young man to turn out.

"Really sensational," concluded Reginald. "And for the second time this evening, I apologise. The room is not contraceptive. It simply is the ideal backdrop for these marvellous paintings and pieces."

"Come through," I said, and led the way into the library. I pointed to an armchair facing mine. "Perch yourself over there." He hesitated, stopping for a moment in front of one of the bookcases filled with heavily tooled first editions. "Later," I added, "or if you are very good, you may even be asked back."

He gave me a sidelong look and I groaned inwardly. God, how arch that must have sounded. I really was so inadequate at being relaxed in such a situation and my awareness of this made me feel even more awkward.

Reginald unfurled himself from his coat - we had been so engrossed in our conversation that I had forgotten to take this from him - and arranged himself in the armchair.

"You were so understanding to let me come around, out of the blue like this," he said.

I held out my hand for his glass. "Don't mention it. But out of curiosity, what happened?"

"Oh, the usual," he said, running his hand through his hair and patting it back. "After you drove off and I continued with my amazing bit of busking, and after a ripple of desultory applause, doubtless swept away at my obvious success I decided to take this star into The White Bear as I had threatened, and wallow in the waves of audience adulation." He paused to sip at his drink - the third while I simply looked on in astonishment at this incredible verbal flow. "However, the English are so good at allowing celebrities their privacy that everybody pretended not to notice me, with the exception of one fan who eventually plucked up courage and moved over towards me at the bar. Not wanting to be too aware, I stood staring at his reflection in the mirror behind the bar and it was either due to the sandblasting or else the soft focus of cigarette smoke, but he appeared to be fairly presentable so I turned and beamed in with my full charm."

"Poor bastard," I murmured.

"I would have agreed, but later the boot – literally – was on the other foot!" He could certainly embroider a tale and I was already smiling as the saga was further unfurled.

"He asked me if I was a stranger to London and of course, I said yes. As this was the first utterance I made I came over heavily Gabor-like and veeery foreign. I was ziz poor student and alone in the big city wiz ze digs in Bayswater. He, in turn, was a barrister with an apartment which turned out to be at the top end of Draycott Avenue. Ted – his trade name, no doubt – drove one of those sinister minis with everything blacked out and his apartment was the same! I realise G Plan looks sinister at the best of times, but put all that black leather upholstery with black walls and drapes, plus carpet et all, and it makes Hammer Films nursery quality. Added to this, Ted poured me a drink – in a black-edged tumbler which added a definite funereal touch to the proceedings, and disappeared to reappear looking like Ghengis Khan on a wild night out. He was holding this strange harness and a pair of boots and asked me if I would put these (I quote) 'upon myself', and this before I had even finished the first drink! Totally taken aback, I lisped, as opposed to lapsing back into my former accent, whether he would mind if I telephoned my friend first of all. He looked a bit confused at the lonely student suddenly having a friend with whom to clear the coast, but gestured to the telephone – black GPO and E-V-I-L, and returned to the bedroom, no doubt to gather more toys for the anticipated playpen. That is when I telephoned you."

By this stage I was roaring with laughter. "And then...?"

"Then he returned and I out Zsa Zsa'd Zsa Zsa. I clutched my coat and said that my friend was furious and would kill me if I did not return immediately. The thought of a violent friend seemed to add zest to Ted's plans, but he was having difficulty in saying anything as he had added a leather mask to his attire and so I sprang like a demented gazelle to the door – thank God this was in polished pine and not painted black as I would no doubt still be there beating the walls for the exit. And here I am!"

By now I was doubled up with laughter. Petrina, thinking she was missing something, had come through from the sitting room and, giving me a strange look, immediately jumped onto Reginald's lap.

"I don't know how much of what you say is fact or fiction but it makes a good tale."

"I assure you, Robin," said Reginald, "whatever I say is always somewhere based on fact!"

It was now well after three in the morning and the wild thought of asking Reginald to stay over and then driving down to the country before lunch was a wickedly delightful thought spinning around in my mind. I could not help it but I was fascinated by the young man.

Reginald looked at me. "I think it's perhaps Ealing time?" he said. "As I have already said, you have been very kind and I have enjoyed myself and seeing your flat."

I started to protest and say that I would do the same for anyone in need – I was more tight than I had imagined – but he continued, "If you do not feel like driving down I'll get myself a taxi!" I looked at him. "Oh yes, I could easily have done this earlier but I did want to see you again and you were so determined not to see me for lunch!"

"No, I'll take you back," I said, "I really should get down to the cottage as there is so much to organise."

He smiled. I got up, not too unsteadily, and crossed over to him. I leaned forward and gave him a tentative kiss on the cheek. He smiled again. "Come on," he said, "let's get into that car before we both do something you – not me – may regret."

I straightened up, the caution signals flashing. 'He doesn't like me,' my mind said.

"Now don't think that," he admonished. "It is late and I would much rather we met again. If you are going to do that drive I would appreciate the lift – otherwise, as I said, I'll get a cab and perhaps you'll ring me over the weekend. Here," he took out a piece of paper from the coat on the chair, "let me give you a telephone number – for the second time, perhaps?" He laughed, rummaged for a pen and wrote down the figures. "There," he smiled, "if you don't call me, I'll call you!"

Chapter Four

I wakened feeling ghastly. I gave a slight groan and turned over on to my side, scrunching up the pillow and burying my head into it. A cold grey light was coming through the gothic-styled window leading out to the small balcony and the light patter of falling rain did not help to bring about a general feeling of morning well-being. I pushed the slight body alongside me, which lay silently in a total state of comatose. I raised my arm and looked at the wristwatch – half past nine! I sat bolt upright, throwing the slumbering Petrina across the bed. She gave a yelp of indignation and then sat up languidly, gave me a glare, stretched and yawned. A second ferocious look and she hopped off the bed and padded out to the corridor. I yawned, gave a second testing groan, cleared my throat and pushing aside the side curtains to the large four-poster bed tottered rather unsteadily into my bathroom. I looked at my reflection, added a third groan to the morning's series, and took down a terry robe from behind the door. A splash of cold water, a few expert whisks with a comb and a quick swirl of pure Listerine, saw me slightly more prepared to face the day.

I shuffled downstairs through the small TV room and into the kitchen-dining room behind. Petrina was sitting expectantly at the doors from the kitchen to the outside dining patio. I opened the door, gave a further shiver, and quickly retreated back into the warmth of the kitchen. With the kettle firmly placed on the Aga and the instant coffee impatiently spooned into a mug, I sat with a glass of orange juice and the *Telegraph* which had been pushed through the letterbox with the usual company of buff envelopes and those last minute maddening Christmas cards from people whom you hoped had forgotten about you, as you had not sent them a card and had no intention of doing so, even at the eleventh hour.

I glanced at the headlines, filled my mug from the whistling kettle and proceeded to go through the mail in a half-hearted manner.

Christ! Reginald! It all came rushing back to me! I had driven him to Ealing as planned and had asked him about his Christmas arrangements. Phillip, I was told, was going back to see his family in Norwich, but he, Reginald, was more than likely at a loose end and apart from seeing some past cronies from the art school he had attended he would be working on a portfolio he was preparing and taking in one or two films he wanted to see. Then and there I had suggested he spend Christmas down at the cottage with me. I had added, hastily, that there would be a house guest – female – but he was more than welcome, and why not bring his various bits and pieces and work down here on his portfolio in company and also join in some of the Christmas merriment! He had thanked me and said it was a marvellous idea and he would call me at around ten o'clock to discuss times of arrival and exactly how he would be coming down. I was appalled. "You arsehole," I said to myself, spooning in another lot of coffee granules to my mug. Petrina, who had been let in again and was energetically snuffling her way through a saucer of warm milk, looked up at this self-assessment. "Yes," I said to her, leaning forward to wipe the milky whiskers off her chins, "your old man is a prime arsehole." Amanda would obviously be furious at the intrusion into her much looked forward to break. I wildly hoped that Master Forbes would live up to his expectations and cancel, but somehow I knew – and hoped – he would not.

As if by telepathy the telephone jangled, breaking into the Saturday morning concert on the kitchen clock radio.

"Nettlebed 47?"

"Robin, good morning. It's Reginald."

My heart sank. "Good morning," I replied. "Sleep well?" God, how stilted I sounded.

"Like a vestal," answered Reginald, with a chuckle. "You obviously got down there in one piece!"

"In no time at all," I lied. On reflection I had very little recall as to the journey down. A few cases of wine were neatly stacked in the kitchen and my briefcase had been in its usual place on the desk in the television room, so I assumed I had been fairly together.

"Have you had time to reconsider that very kind invitation?" continued his voice.

"Why reconsider?" I asked.

"Well, it was late and there is such a thing as a mellowing due to the booze and the hour, so if you do wish to cancel out I quite understand?" So it was for me to cancel out. Clever little blighter. How very typical of Reginald to swing any blame right into my camp. "Besides," he continued, "you do have a house guest and she may be put out at the inclusion of a third party."

"You wouldn't bother Amanda."

"Amanda?"

"Amanda Adamson, my house guest."

"Not the Amanda Adamson?"

That is eleven out of ten for diplomacy, I groaned to myself.

"Yes."

"Of course, you and she are great friends, aren't you. You are always being billed if not cooed in the papers!"

"Look," I decided to be positive and, as they say, in for a penny in for a pounding. "Do come down and I am sure you will enjoy yourself." I could just hear the playback from Peter after Phillip had told him that I had asked Reginald down to stay and then had cancelled out. Peter would accuse me of being two-faced and unfair, and more concerned with my reputation with the locals rather than the feelings of the young man. "Typical, uptight, selfish old closet queen," I could hear him saying, "as if Manda would mind, she probably would have found the weekend actually livened up for a change. I can just picture her relief at having someone human and amusing around as opposed to those dreary locals you entertain!" This conversation would be shouted over the telephone whilst Peter was no doubt ensconced with some young wild friend or friends and having a totally uninhibited and lively time.

"I would really love that," confirmed Reginald. We discussed train times and I suggested he arrived as soon as possible. "I've got to go over to Wallingford to collect the turkey and such, from there, so why not catch the 12.20 from Paddington to Didcot, rather than go to Henley, and I will meet you. We can have a bite to eat with Lulu, a mad woman I know who owns a pub called The Angry Bull and then finish our shopping in Wallingford before coming back here. I suggest a sensible supper of steaks and a salad as a break before all that gorging!"

"I'm heading for the front door, now."

"Don't forget your portfolio, your purpose for coming!" I said, laughing. I felt marvellously elated and almost forgave myself for my pompous-sounding last sentence. 'You're becoming paranoid, RA,' I said to myself, and burst into a merry carolling of *Come all ye faithful*. The implication caused further merriment. "And why not," I said, as I sank into a bath.

Amanda was charming about Reginald's unprecedented arrival. "I told you last night that I thought he sounded great fun," she pussy-catted over the telephone. "One thing, darling," she added, "we cannot go on calling him Reginald and he certainly doesn't sound a Reg, so let's settle on Reggie, if he has no objection!"

I winced at the thought of Reginald's reaction to 'Reggie' but I had to agree that it was more acceptable than the stuffy 'Reginald'. "Agreed."

I checked out what was 'Amanda's room' with adjoining bathroom. She always had the small bedroom overlooking the back rose garden and the several bits of topiary which were Edward, the gardener's, pride and joy. The room, done in a delightful toile of pink roses and ribbons, had a delicate four-poster bed in painted pine, a dressing table and chair to match, a small chaise and its own separate bathroom. The floor was in painted pine strips, with stencilled patterns, and a small hand-woven rug picking up the pink roses theme.

The third bedroom, billed the bachelor room, was all butch, ochre and beige with a vast Empire bed in polished mahogany, and a tallboy to match. "Wouldn't have minded being a general and entertaining the army in that," Peter had said. "Imagine all those boots and privates!" This bedroom had its own shower area, as well as a small balcony overlooking the driveway.

I was very pleased with the final result of my much-criticised purchase of the years before. From the small two up and down it had been, I had created a gothic style dwelling of considerable charm. The main sitting room extension, part of the upper area which also housed my bedroom, was warm and comfortable with its large stone fireplace and small minstrels gallery, serving as a miniature library. Basically furnished in a warmly patterned Percheron linen with dragged walls in a heavy sand, the ivory carpet added the ideal background to the large sofas and scattered wing-back chairs. Pieces of Victorian papier mâché furniture and some gothic pieces of pine, added to the general cosy clutter. Large vases of dried Queen Anne's lace, thistle, protea and wild grasses, were the substitutes for the usual summer and spring colours from cut flowers, and a large jade plant in a mock Ming bowl, added a final touch of the exotic to the room.

Arched gothic styled doors led on to a terrace from which one could walk out to the lawn, and a yew hedge and ha-ha separated the house from the neighbouring fields. I loved the place and was always very happy whether down there solo or with one or two specially selected friends. The latest extravagance had been a swimming pool. "One way to get those local lads to strip off," Peter had said. There was also a barbecue area nearby to the swimming pool.

Warmly dressed in a comfortable pair of old cords, boots, sweater, and an old suede jacket, I spent the next hour doing various household chores. Fetching additional logs from the shed behind the garage I stocked up the log bins, both in the television room and sitting room. I collected also the remainder of the wine and obligatory cake from the car and double checked the bar cupboard. The basic Christmas stocking up had already been done – several crates of champagne to bring unlimited Christmas cheer to Amanda, some whisky for myself, plus the usual sherries and sticky liqueurs so favoured by the local ladies. There was only one bottle of Campari so I added several extra to my shopping list.

A present! I rummaged through the small storeroom at the top of the stairs where several suitcases had been placed. The ideal answer – a small watercolour of a lone female figure on a beach, reminiscent of Russell Flint. I had purchased the painting mainly for the frame, a delicate tracery of gilded gesso and wood, but typically had placed it on a shelf planning to do something with it at a later date and then forgotten all about it.

Amanda's present had already been extravagantly wrapped by Clare. Her passion in life was collecting porcelain cats and I had found a small Egyptian cat in the brightest of blues, in the sale of a private art collection from a house on Long Island, outside New York. The statue was a collector's item and should have been bought as an investment, but my fondness for Amanda I deemed more than this.

Wrapping paper was scrawled on to my jot pad and I returned downstairs with the painting which I hid carefully in one of the cupboards in the library. I had done nothing about Christmas decorations as I was adamant that the house in itself was decorative enough and did not merit any additional dressing up. I also loathed

Christmas trees. "He's afraid the fairy on top may give him away," Peter had quipped, the last time he had spent a Christmas with me. At that stage his companion had been a heavy young man named Sy. Sy- "and he does, because of me" – this again, from Peter, had again been destined to be around forever but as with the others had gone off on to pastures new.

It obviously was going to be an interesting few days. I was not concerned about Reggie and Amanda, but fascinated to see Peter's reaction when he and Tim arrived for lunch on Boxing Day. Although I would have been criticised had I cancelled Reggie, there was also the turnabout that I would be getting myself involved with someone who was not my scene, and when matters did go wrong there would be a great deal of 'I told you so, much too flash'.

The train rumbled into Didcot station. A few passengers dismounted and for a few moments my heart sank. He wasn't there. I could not quite believe my feeling but I was totally thrown! Within a few hours I was reacting to this young man as if he was perhaps one of the most vital matters in my usually planned and totally controlled existence.

"Robin."

I turned round. It was Reginald, but one with a difference! I do not know whether I had expected him to arrive in velvet, ruffles and tight yellow cords as of the night before, but here he was in car coat, long scarf, jeans, albeit snakeskin boots and carrying a light duffel bag. My face lit up.

"There you are," I said, the relief obviously showing in my voice.

"Did you think I wouldn't show up then?"

I smiled. "There was a moment... I didn't see you at first."

"Next time I'll wear a scarlet cloak."

I put his bag on the back seat. Petrina was very pleased to see her new friend from the evening before. She jumped up and down with a series of welcoming barks and was waggling furiously. Reginald was subjected to a slurping of passionate lickings and then she settled herself determinedly upon his lap.

"Push her away and she can sit on the back seat, if she's a bother," I said, sliding into my side.

"No, no. She's adorable." Petrina received a large kiss on the head which led to further snufflings, snorts and wrigglings. She was determined to claim Reginald as her own.

"Any difficulties with the journey down?" I asked, as we sped past Didcot's tallest piece of architecture, a hideously stained gas cylinder on the outskirts of the town.

"No, Paddington was surprisingly quiet. The only complaint, though, was there was no buffet on the train. Typical BR, but fortunately I had a bottle with me and so I was able to have a nip... brandy," he added grinning. He leant back across the seat and rummaged in the duffel bag. "This is for you." He held up a bottle of Glenlivet whisky.

"How very generous. You really need not have. Bringing yourself was enough." Again the foreboding. Did I sound too arch? Christ, I was becoming a case!

"Not at all. Besides, I adore giving presents."

"And receiving them?"

"Of course!" We both laughed.

"Let me fill you in about Lulu, where we're off for lunch. She's a fairly jolly lady who appears to have been married several times; claims to have been a prime dancer from Martha Graham's encampment, but sacrificed all for the love of her life. One is not told as to what happened to this man who altered her destiny, but there have been a number of replacements and at present she is deeply involved with a man who cultivates locally exotic fruits by hydroponics. The fruit market is certainly not being threatened by a glut as he seems to be spending most of his time at The Angry Bull looking soulfully at Lulu."

I changed down and manoeuvred a particularly icy corner. "Lulu appeared on the scene about three years ago. The Angry Bull had been empty for some time and one day, driving past I saw that the 'for sale' sign had disappeared, and a few cars were parked on the verge outside so obviously The Angry Bull was back in business. I did not call in on this particular occasion, but I did hear that it had been bought by an ex-American dancer and so I decided I simply had to have a look. I called in a few weekends later and lo and behold! – there was this amazing Amazon – how you would imagine, if possible, an overgrown Isadora Duncan to be, happily pulling pints behind the bar. I hope you'll like her," I added, slowing down by a heavily beamed building, warm lights glowing from the small leaded windows. There were several cars outside and I drove on a bit further down the lane. "I'll have to lend you a pair of Wellingtons, those snakeskins won't take kindly to the mud and slush."

"Presents," grinned Reginald.

"Robin, desperate darling," Lulu boomed out from beyond the bar. She turned to a few faces I didn't immediately recognise – "Desperate because he hasn't seen me for at least three months," she trilled by way of a totally unmerited explanation. She swept out from behind the bar, arms outstretched, paused and rushed towards me rather like Giselle towards her prince. Considering the largeness of Lulu and the smallness of the bar, she managed the whole gesture with extraordinary lightness and grace.

"Angel," she murmured, embracing me and kissing me delicately on the cheek. "Lulu's missed her favourite big city man." The 'man' came out 'may yan' with a hint of the Blanche du Bois. I glanced at Reginald. He was smiling at Lulu. It was obviously love at first sight. It did occur to me that at this rate all my women friends were about to have a new ardent admirer in their midst.

"And who is this?" demanded Lulu. "He's gorjus!" She pushed me aside and placed her arms on Reginald's shoulders. He turned on that dazzling smile. Lulu spun round admonishingly. "Where have you been hiding him?"

I flushed. Lulu was never one for tact. She was always having Amanda in fits of mirth at her attempts to launch me with a local yokel. 'He bottles it all up inside and it isn't healthy' she would say to Manda. 'At his age it is necessary to express his deepest emotions. If he likes boys he must find one to love.'

Lulu was always first at giving advice on life and loving, although her own private life was always in the utmost strife.

"Hello, I'm Reginald. I am a designer and a friend of Robin's." He held out his hand and added an extra few dazzling watts to the smile.

"I'm Lulu," said Lulu. She beamed down at him. "You're delicious! Hector!" The tone changed from tone to command. A mournful figure by the bar looked up. "Two glasses of that extra special hot punch for Robin and Reggie. My special Christmas recipe," she twinkled at us.

Reggie! It had been accepted without comment. Indeed, the smile was even broader.

Hector held out two steaming tankards which Lulu grabbed. "Merry Christmas, darlings."

"Merry Christmas, Lulu, and thank you," we chorused in unison, and burst out laughing. I turned to him.

"To us," I said.

"To Robin and Reggie," he replied, eyeing me wickedly over the brim of his tankard. He took a sip. "Good slogan that, R and R."

We lunched in the low-beamed dining room behind the bar. The fading light outside and the heavy snow clouds allowed Lulu to show her Christmas decorations to their best advantage. A cheerful tree glowed in the corner of the main bar. In the dining room, streamers and swags of glittering fairy lights added to the festive scene. Sprigs of holly and mistletoe, strategically placed, festooned the ceiling. Silvered acorns and bunches of conifer were clustered around the bright red candles glowing on the scarlet tablecloths.

Lulu, after several arch comments about the dish of the day, served up a delicious steak and kidney and oyster pie, with lashings of sprouts and chestnuts. This was followed by a mouth-watering treacle tart and cream. Petrina, always thoroughly spoilt by Lulu, had also had her fair share of the latter. Several glasses of an iced Côtes du Provence helped us down the meal, and by the time we had decided on a glass of port, the atmosphere was mellow and very relaxed.

Lulu, having made sure that Hector – the 'hypochondriac hydroponic' as Reggie was later to dub him – was in control at the bar, sailed over to join us. Clad in a loud mauve angora sweater and apricot-tone long skirt, she made a vibrant and distinctive clash against the scarlet tablecloth. Her hair, pulled up in a knot, reminiscent of Widow Twanky (perhaps that was the role she almost made famous before whatever it was happened, Reggie had evilly hissed) was decorated for the festive occasion with a sprig of holly and a few purple and gold glass balls.

"Darlings," she said, "it's been hectic and we open again in a few hours. I don't know how I'll manage, but as I have in the past I shall no doubt continue."

I looked at Reggie who winked. Lulu saw the wink.

"Ah," she cried. "So he's been mocking me behind my back." She clasped Reggie's hand. "He thinks we are all like him," she said, "that we have had it so easy. No problems... but I do love him so." She clasped my hand with her free one. "Now," she continued, "you boys look so happy. And, as I say, that is all that matters. Hector!" Hector appeared around the door. "Another port for my guests," she demanded, "and a glass of punch for me. Hector is being very heavy," she added and then went on to discuss the Christmas plans she had made, insisting that I brought Reggie and Amanda around the next evening.

"It depends on Amanda, Lulu," I said, "but we will definitely be over on Boxing Day with Peter and Tim."

"Oh, that wicked Peter!" cried Lulu.

"Anyway, we must go," I said, throwing back the recently arrived glass of port. "We've still got to collect a few things in Wallingford. That was delicious, Lulu, and thank you for the drinks. Shall I do this now, or would it be easier to put it on the account?"

"Oh, the account, darling," said Lulu, "should you not settle I will demand Reggie in return!"

After fond farewells we put on our coats and moved out into the cold late afternoon. A light snow was falling. Petrina, despite the several helpings of treacle tart and cream, showed a sudden bout of enthusiasm by leaping up at one or two falling snowflakes. Needless to say the unexpected exercise exhausted her and in the car again she promptly went to sleep on Reggie's lap.

"What a fun person Lulu is," said Reggie, "though one is never too sure whether she is Blanche or Garbo – the accent and attitudes!"

"Yes, I am sure that at times she gets rather angry with herself for being so adamant about the Martha Graham bit and the American heritage. Today there were definite hints at a tragic Russian ancestry."

We both laughed. Reggie felt in his jacket pocket. "Do you mind if I smoke in the car?"

"Not at all."

He lit his cigarette and took a long draw. I had put an orchestral tape of festive songs on the cassette and was feeling delightfully warm, mellow and romantic. I knew that perhaps I was being totally wrong, but nothing could have spoiled the minute.

Until Petrina threw up.

*

We returned to the cottage without further mishap, a very sheepish Petrina sitting in silent embarrassment in the back of the car. Reggie had managed to basically mop up his jeans with a cloth kept for wiping the windshield. He had been hugely amused by the incident, much to my relief. I still did not understand his way of thinking and I was still very aware of his mental frolics from the party the night before.

As it was snowing quite heavily, I turned the car and reversed up to the stone patio by the front door.

Reggie was right behind, with a box containing part of the groceries we had collected. "Kitchen's through there to the left," I called. "The switch for the light is on your right inside the door."

I returned to the car and took up the remaining box. "Come on," I said to a moribund Petrina who was still sitting on the back seat. "Nobody is going to tell anybody." She gave me a pained stare and cautiously stepped out of the car. I closed the door, made sure Petrina had got to the front door, and scrambled into the driving seat again. Having put the car in the garage I made my way back to the house.

Reggie was in the kitchen and had already unpacked most of the contents of the boxes onto the central work table. "This cottage is magic," he said. "May I look round?"

"Sure thing," I said, eyeing the turkey and wondering if it was going to be large enough after all for the Christmas dinner, plus cold on Boxing Day. I had witnessed Reggie's appetite at lunch and it was obviously in the best of health. "Here," I added. "Bring your bag and I'll show you your room." I did not dare look at him when I made this announcement. I left him to get himself organised. He was back downstairs in a few moments, his anorak having been substituted for a bright tartan cardigan, more in keeping with the Reginald I had first met. His enthusiasm for the cottage was contagious. I found myself doing a repeat of the night before and explaining my various possessions, supplying anecdotes as to where or why they had been purchased. He was full of admiration for the minstrels' gallery and the miniature library it contained.

"We could enact a pantomime for Amanda," he said. "I could be Rapunzel and let down my hair to the Prince."

"Who would play the Prince?"

"Oh, Amanda. In pantomime the handsome Prince is always played by a girl."

I felt strangely jealous of Amanda.

By this stage we had returned to the kitchen where I made two mugs of coffee. I added a shot of brandy to each. "We may as well continue with the festive spirit," I said.

"RA," said Reggie, using my initials as the majority of people did. "If this goes on I'll believe you're trying to get me drunk and therefore defenceless?"

"Could be," I said, feeling slightly rakish. "Here!" I flipped across a packet of Sobranie cigarettes at him. "I got these for you so as to add a bit of colour to the weekend. Just in case you found the Benson and Hedges scattered around the place too contraceptive!"

"Touché," said Reggie, grinning and putting the packet in his cardigan pocket.

The evening moved into a convivial, comfortable mood. Having got his approval for the proposed menu we decided to eat late and I busied myself with the salad and general preparations for the stuffing for the turkey and was about to suggest a drink when Reggie appeared in the doorway. I looked up. "Telepathy," I said. "I was about to come in and offer a drink. However, please feel totally at home and help yourself to anything when you so wish. If you do feel like one there is Campari on the tray in the television room and perhaps you'd get me a Scotch?"

"Of course," he smiled. "By the way, would you mind if I used the telephone?"

"As I said, please be totally at home. As long as it isn't Australia?" I added.

"Not quite," said Reggie, and was gone.

I felt a slight twinge again, jealousy perhaps and twice within the hour. I really was getting it badly.

Having completed my chores in the kitchen I went back through into the sitting room where Reggie was sitting on the floor in front of the fire. He had a half-full glass of Campari and soda alongside him and a totally revived Petrina was snuggled in the bend of his knees. He had put on a Van Cliburn tape and the setting could not have been more harmonious. Perhaps this time there would be no sudden mishaps. I settled in the chair.

"This is marvellous," said Reggie, "and I really must thank you."

"It's early days," I replied, sipping my drink.

"No, really. I mean it. This time yesterday I was getting ready to do my great stand in for Phillip and thinking to myself, well it's at least something to do over this dreary holiday period, little realising that this evening I would be sitting here and enjoying myself so much. And meeting such a lovely girl." This latter sentence was added to a very cosy Petrina.

We sat in silence for a moment, the only sounds apart from the music, being Petrina's contented snoring and the occasional flurry of snow against the windows behind the tightly closed curtains. A crackling from the fire broke my reverie.

"Tell me," I questioned, "when we met Lulu you introduced yourself as a designer! I understood that you had recently finished a course as art student. Hence the portfolio and such?"

"Correct, but an art student with the ambitions of being a designer. However, my first impressions of Lulu told me that the description 'student' would cause her more fascination than a definite career and so I plumped for the latter. Now she is debating as to whether I may be associated with you business wise as opposed to only socially wise, though..." he looked at me "...after her Papal-like blessing following lunch I somehow feel she's already issuing the banns!"

We both laughed.

"Tell me more about this designing though."

"Well, since leaving college I have been doing some part-time work with a small design firm in Ealing. Basically, though, even in so short a period I seem to have become their bookkeeper, estimator, and perspective artist – all at once, and part-time has become almost full-time. Well," Reggie continued, "several years back I did have aspirations of becoming an architect. I went so far as to arrange an interview with Siefferts, but quite honestly, I came to view architecture as I do the work of the early cubists. I am all for art form and technique, but basically, my total enthusiasm is in colour and design with colour. The more I visited the galleries and the more I visited the V. & A. – almost my second home – I became convinced that I would be happier in creating environments or interiors as opposed to the basic shells. Don't get me wrong," he added, feeling for a further Sobranie (I realised I should have invested in several packets), "I am not dismissing architecture but I do feel that architects' ideas and interior designers' ideas do not always go hand in hand, and it is up to the one side of the profession to compliment and involve itself with the specialist abilities of the other."

I looked at him with renewed interest. "But what about the likes of Robert Adam or, take more recently, Frank Lloyd Wright? They were responsible for both the interior works of design as well as the exterior shell or frame as you put it."

"Ah, yes. I cannot disagree or argue with that fact. But you are giving me exceptions. It's like comparing Coward with the likes of Tennessee Williams. Noel Coward was both brilliant at his writing and at his acting, whereas Williams gives us the most sensational scripts but allows the likes of a Brando to create the ultimate of a role – therefore showing the author and actor as a perfect vehicle for each other."

Our conversation went on in this vein. Reggie had opted for a course in the finer pointers of art with the plan of studying with one of the leading design houses in London before making the venturesome step of launching his own design career. I had heard a similar story many times before, but here there was a determination and also that quality of a sharp and witty mind, plus an inherent style, which one is born with and that no amount of education or training can produce. I avoided the obvious in asking Reggie what he would have done with the cottage! This would be too unfair and anyway I was convinced that I would have ended up defending my English country house look against the intrusion of something that would no doubt be spectacularly original and possibly more 'way out' than I was used to.

We talked for a bit longer and after a friendly bantering over one or two design ideas and general topics, I pulled myself from the chair and went through into the kitchen to prepare supper. We had agreed finally on salad, potatoes in their jackets and a Spanish omelette, followed by some particularly delicious runaway Brie we had spotted in Wallingford.

Reggie followed me as far as the television room where he expertly added a few logs and some coal to the fire. He poured himself a further Campari, checked my Scotch which was standing on the kitchen table, and returned to seat himself in front of the television set to watch the end of some programme. The devoted Petrina had followed him and had taken up her claim, once again, upon his lap.

Supper was a relaxed and jokey affair. We were well into our second bottle of Barola when the telephone went. It was Amanda.

"Darling, I'm just checking to see that my lovely host has not been devoured by the sheep in snakeskin!"

"Far from it. He's having a lovely time."

"I'm delighted," said Amanda. "We've had a frightful second audience and the cast and myself are all going along to Popote for supper. Christopher has arranged some frolic so no doubt it will be the greatest of fun. Darling, I'll be with you mid-afternoon tomorrow. Love to you both." And she was gone.

"Manda sends love," I said to Reggie. "I had no idea she believed in proxy," I added.

It was almost midnight by the time we had finished supper. Reggie announced he was going up to take a shower. "Put on your electric blanket," I instructed. "I should have done both some time ago, but I was so interested in our conversation that I forgot." I stacked the dishes in the dishwasher, added the soap powder and turned the machine on. Mrs Law, the local daily, would not be in until Tuesday morning to do a tidy before Peter and Tim arrived for lunch, and so I was under strict orders from her as to how to maintain the cottage whilst Amanda and myself were there for the two days. Dear Elsie, she had arrived on the doorstep offering to 'do' when I had moved into the cottage and I had been totally indebted to her ever since. She was a great admirer of Amanda's and I had to be very firm about her not coming in over the Christmas break to fuss over us. "You've got enough on your hands with your own family," I had admonished her, "and Miss Adamson and I will be fine." I had given in and agreed to her doing a few hours on the Tuesday morning. As I said to Amanda, the likes of Elsie were amazing in that they did not appreciate how valuable and rare they were. Nine times out of ten, most of my colleagues or friends with weekend cottages or flats, did not have the good fortune or the luxury of an Elsie. I felt very spoiled by her constant mothering.

Reggie was singing in the shower. Though I had been happily cajoled into a romantic and mellow state by the cosiness and success of the evening, I did not expect it to lead to more. Remembering back to my younger days and those anguished evenings when one was invited to stay and it was obviously expected that you were meant to share your host's bed, even though one had no desire to, I was always adamant that the air was sufficiently cleared and that whoever stayed with me was given the final decision himself. As with Reggie, the spare bedroom was offered and no mention to a night's connubial bliss was made.

I checked both fires, put the screens in front of each, put out the lights and made my way upstairs. Reggie's door was ajar and the light was on. I knocked. "Need I say who's there," came the voice.

I put my head round the door. Reggie was already in bed, his still damp hair pressed against the pillows which he had stacked up behind him. Petrina, the traitor, was snuggled against his hip. He was holding a magazine.

"Have you got everything you need?" I asked, my throat contracting slightly and feeling strangely dry. He was so beautiful, sitting there with his bare chest gleaming in the lamplight, a faint down of blonde hair shining between his slim pectorals.

"Thank you, yes." He smiled. "See you in the morning."

I nodded. "I'll leave the door slightly open in case Petrina wants to move about." I then said goodnight.

Walking through to my room I slipped out of my clothes and put on a dressing gown. I busied myself in the bathroom, automatically washing my hands and face and brushing my teeth. I looked at my reflection in the mirror above the basin. "Silly mutt," I said to myself. "What did you expect?" I towelled my face and put the towel on the rail. I was relieved at Amanda's expected arrival. This would make the situation much easier, "and stop any thoughts of a romp with young Reginald," I added to myself.

I put out the bathroom light and crossed the dressing room back into the bedroom. Reggie was sitting in the bed.

"Goodness," I said, making light of my surprise.

"Goodness has nothing to do with it," grinned Reggie. "Lust, pure lust."

I walked over to the bed and looked down at him. He smiled and to my amazement, appeared to be rather nervous.

"Reggie, you don't have to," I said.

"But I want to," he whispered.

I took off my dressing gown, never taking my eyes off him. I slowly pulled back the bedclothes and got in alongside him. He snuggled back into the bed and looked at me. I took him tentatively into my arms, still staring at him. I moved closer, pulling him more firmly towards me. He closed his eyes. I kissed him lightly on the left eyelid, and then on the right. "Dear Reggie," I whispered, "dear, dear Reggie."

Chapter Five

"J'arrive!"

Amanda's cheery cry came from the front door.

I put down my pen, got up from my desk and walked through to the hall. She had let herself in and was standing in the doorway, pulling a long scarf from around her neck, and stamping the snow off her boots.

"Darling!" she cried, seeing me appear. "How lovely. Merry Christmas Eve and all that nonsense."

I held out my arms and clasped her in a warm, if cold, embrace. "You're frozen," I said. "Here, let me take your coat. You get yourself into the sitting room and thaw out. I was about to get some tea," I added. "Would that suit, or would you prefer something a bit more in keeping with the Yule feeling?"

"I'm on holiday, remember?" said Amanda, shaking out her long auburn hair from under her fur hat. "I'd adore something sticky and lethal, like a whisky mac."

"You're on. What a splendid idea and far more nourishing on such an evening as opposed to old man Grey." I followed her into the sitting room.

"Isn't this marvellous!" said Amanda, moving over to the fireplace. "I have so been looking forward to our break down here." She turned to me. "The guest?" she whispered.

"Oh, Reggie's still about," I laughed. "In fact I'm surprised he's not back. He and Petra went out into this appalling snow about half an hour ago. For Petrina to even put her nose out of the door in weather like this is unheard of, but she's obviously madly impassioned over Reggie and so she's bounded out with him in her new coat, and God knows what they are up to!"

"Is everything all right?"

"Couldn't be better." I smiled at her and handed her the glass of amber liquid. "I'm sure it's going to be a very merry Christmas for us all."

It could not have been better. Our night of tenderness and, at moments, of heightened passion, had gently brought us into the start of a wonderfully intimate and almost shy day. I had got up fairly late as opposed to my usual routine of being up and about, albeit a weekday or the weekend, by half past seven, without fail, and gone downstairs to organise breakfast. Reggie was still asleep and curled up on the side of the four-poster. Petrina, who had decided that she had been tactful for long enough, had eventually joined us as the first morning light began to break, and was fast asleep next to Reggie's neck. I smiled down at the two of them, pulled the blankets a bit closer to the sleeping young man, put on my dressing gown and opened the door, closing it quietly again as I stepped onto the landing. I was ecstatically happy, proud, excited, nervous and in a slight dilemma about the events of the night. Being a Virgo and a total romantic at heart, my mind was racing ahead with the most preposterous imaginings and wild schemes. I shook my head with disbelief and smiled as I organised the croissants and brioche in the oven and set out the breakfast plates, cups and saucers and cutlery, on the kitchen table. 'Caution, old son,' I said to myself, not for the first time. 'You've been through this scene too often to imagine that this time it will be different.' But Reggie was different. I had enjoyed his company, our conversations and I had certainly enjoyed him in bed. His fevered responses, occasional inhibitions and a certain *naïveté* had both thrilled and touched me. Overall, his great tenderness and total loving, mixed with this gentleness and quietness led me to a spilling of emotions and endearments that I had forgotten were capable of being aroused and which I imagined I had lost to myself so many years ago.

I checked the oven, the coffee, and moved over to the fridge to get out the marmalades and a jar of Clare's home-bred honey. Sandi Shaw, shrilling away on the kitchen radio, was confirming that there was always something there to remind her. Reggie's bottle of Glenlivet was still sitting on the counter top as if there to remind me. I smiled, I chuckled, I laughed with happiness.

The morning had passed contentedly. We had consumed an enormous breakfast, sitting opposite each other, touching hands and playing with each other's feet under the table. Reggie had wrapped himself in one of my endless dressing gowns.

Petrina, needless to say, had taken up a definite position by his feet and grunted with irritation every time he moved his foot towards mine, which meant a lot of grunting.

The Sunday papers had arrived and these were avidly devoured with Reggie causing us much amusement by lapsing into various accents as he read out cases of startled ladies who found themselves continually interfered with, or news of outraged members of the public complaining about rates, television licences – all as religiously portrayed by the *News of the World* or the *Sunday Mirror*. I bought every Sunday paper printed as this was one of my great weekend indulgences. I was delighted to find Reggie as engulfed as I was in the various elements of reporting and as to how stories or articles could change.

The only interruption to the quiet scene was the unprecedented arrival of Lulu's Hector who turned up with four large, brightly wrapped parcels. A large box and a smaller one were marked for Reggie, and of the other two, one was for Amanda and the other for myself.

"You've obviously made a firm fan there," I said.

"Hopefully I've made two this weekend," Reggie replied.

Hector stopped only to have a glass of orange juice, having checked the cardboard container to make sure that it contained 'nothing artificial'. Reggie and I were already well into the Buck's Fizzes and entering freely into the festive spirit. We had been discussing the possibility of a light snack instead. We spent a blissful couple of hours in bed, exploring, adoring and cuddling each other and finishing several more Buck's Fizzes. Amanda's impending arrival saw us reluctantly getting up and it was then Reggie had suggested taking Petrina for a short walk. "Perhaps it would be a bit more tactful if I was out when she arrived," he said, "and then you can have the great excitement of announcing me when I return!"

"That must be Reggie now," I said to Amanda who had curled herself up on the sofa.

"RA?"

"In here," I answered.

Petrina came bounding in, scattering snow all over the carpet. She barked with delight at seeing Amanda and jumped up onto her lap.

"Petra," I shouted. "Your manners! Get off." Petrina jumped as if shot, and beetled back to the door where she grabbed hold of Reggie's trouser leg and started worrying at it, growling with mock ferocity. "She's gone quite mad," I added, looking at Reggie and smiling. "Amanda, Reggie! Reggie, Amanda!"

"Hello," said Reggie, "this is indeed a treat. I have so been looking forward to meeting you for myself. Robin," he added with a mischievous sidelong glance, "had not stopped talking about you and I can see that so far there has been no exaggeration."

"I like it," laughed Amanda. "Flattery is always the best way to an actress's heart."

They had got on brilliantly and I visibly relaxed. There had been a split second when I thought Reggie had come on a bit strong during the introductions, but Amanda had not seemed to notice this, though I was sure she had, but was too much of a friend and too astute to take it up without giving Reggie a chance.

Knowing that he was so aware of our very close and long-standing friendship, she was prepared to make allowances for any nervousness. "First night nerves, darling," she later said, and as usual, her intuitive action had paid off.

The evening was fun, full of laughter and we all became very merry and mellow. I consumed a great amount of port and was feeling definitely in love with the world. Knowing how delicate the situation could still be – I felt Reggie would pray for the floorboards to open up if I suggested we all went up to bed – I excused myself, saying that I should see the two of them in the morning. We had arranged a late breakfast prior to facing the onslaught of several locals I had asked round for drinks before lunch. We planned a lazy afternoon, viewing the Queen's Speech and either reading or playing Monopoly or Scrabble and then doing the whole turkey, trimmings and cracker bit that evening.

I had got into bed and turned off the light. I had expected to lie in a sleepless forlorn and frustrated state, knowing that Reggie would be only a few yards away from me. I knew Amanda would not mind had we gone up to bed together, but I understood his hesitation and possible embarrassment, particularly as this was the first time he had met her. I could smell Reggie's faint shampoo and soap smells, as well as his own particular scent. I smiled and burrowed my face into his pillow and promptly went to sleep. I awakened later to find him asleep next to me. My joy was insurmountable. With a muffled sob I held him close to me and remained holding him until the first light of morning. I was falling uncontrollably in love.

*

Christmas Day. I turned the handle to the double doors leading into the sitting room and stood amazed. A tree, bedecked in glass balls, tinsel and ribbons, stood behind the sofa in place of the usual sofa table. Bright packages in a myriad of colours were heaped around the base. Sprigs of mistletoe and holly wreathed the picture frames. A large bowl of crystallised fruit and nuts, interspersed with more baubles, formed a decorative centre piece to the sofa table now moved over to across the one set of French doors to the patio.

"Merry Christmas."

Amanda, in a marvellous housecoat of ivory quilted satin with a vast extravaganza of a collar in apricot marabou, stood framed, Gilda-like, in the doorway behind me.

"Darling! Merry Christmas! But I'm amazed. When did all this happen?"

"The good fairy," said Reggie wickedly from behind Amanda. We all burst into peals of laughter.

"This calls for a celebration," I said. "Would anyone think it too early for a glass of Christmas champagne and peach juice?"

"It is after ten o'clock," said Amanda, "and if we were in Hong Kong we would be celebrating so...?"

With our bubbling glasses we stood around the room smiling at each other.

"But how, when?" I asked for the umpteenth time.

"It's all thanks to Reggie," said Amanda firmly.

We both looked at him.

"Well," said Reggie, "I'm not criticising the cottage." He looked at Amanda. "After what I said about the flat in London I wouldn't dare criticise the cottage." We all laughed again. "But, when I arrived yesterday I said to myself – very pretty, but it is Christmas and we could do with a tree. The point in question, how and from where? The tree and holly and stuff was easy. All those fir trees at the top of the lane and that is where Petra and I were when you arrived, Amanda. The baubles and such were much more difficult. However, being a top student and knowing that something amazing would be anticipated by the illustrious company I have the privilege to be amongst," he bowed towards Amanda and me and Amanda gave a theatrical curtsey in return, "I made a telephone call last night which caused some feeling of mystery and intrigue with mine host," I nodded in agreement, "and called the lovely Lulu."

"Aha!" I cried. "I knew passion of a mutual vein was brewing there."

"Indeed," continued Reggie. "Lulu was brilliant and instantly became the greatest of Russian spies with a touch of the Mata Hari. She casually threw away the information that she was sending Hector over anyway as we had left in such a rush that she had not had time to hand us our presents, and therefore there would be an added parcel - that ton crate of a box - in which she would slip a few redundant balls and bits, and hey presto, the tree! With thanks," he raised his glass, "to my beautiful second in command, Comrade Amanda Adamson."

"Well, you both deserve the highest of honours," I replied. "More champagne! And now, the presents."

Amanda was thrilled with her cat. "Darling," she cried, "you're too extravagant with me." She gave me a large kiss and started to unwrap a small parcel Reggie had set down for her alongside mine. "Reggie," she cried, "this is divine." She held up a small drawing in a simple frame. It was a black and white sketch of the St George theatre where she was currently appearing. "Did you do it?"

"From my architectural phase," replied Reggie, with a conspiratorial grin. "It is a listed building as you know, and those cupolas have been the demise of many an art student."

"I love it," stated Amanda, "simply love it." She hugged Reggie and kissed him warmly. "There!" She moved back and leaned the drawing against a lamp, placing the blue ceramic cat in front. "Isn't that perfect? My two most favourite presents ever!"

Reggie shyly handed me a similar parcel. "I'm afraid it looks as if sketches are in," he smiled, "but I was taken somewhat unawares."

"Don't worry, we've got the embryo of a miniature Tate here," I added, handing him his painting.

Reggie was delighted with the lookalike Russell Flint. The sketch he had selected from his works for me was a perspective of the Royal Opera House. I immediately placed it in a prime position on a small acrylic easel standing on the mantelpiece. The painting from the easel, a small Lowry, could go up to London. Amanda had given Reggie a snakeskin wallet – "I have been looking at it in the boutique window for days," she claimed, "and after MI5's description of you, I was able to overcome my frustration and actually buy it. I owe you my sanity, Reggie, in giving me the excuse!"

Her present to me was a beautiful casual sweater in a multitude of purples, blues, burgundies and tans. "What else apart from Missoni for the maestro?" she said. Reggie heartily agreed.

The later invasion by the locals for mid-morning drinks, had only added to our feeling of camaraderie, and Christmas dinner progressed as had the rest of the day. The noise of laughter made by the three of us, occasioned by a few barks by Petrina, was never ending. I had not known such fun, warmth and friendship for many years.

We had all changed for dinner. After the last lunchtime drink and guests had left, we sat around the kitchen with cups of tea or coffee, holding a general post-mortem on our earlier visitors.

"I think you've made a firm impression with the General," I teased Reggie. "Perhaps all those latent tendencies, bottled up from his military days, will suddenly burst to the fore!"

"God forbid," he said, in mock horror. "Talk about the charge of the Heavy Brigade!"

"I've got a medal that could jingle, jangle, jingle..." croaked Amanda. More laughter.

We had eventually gathered ourselves together and gone upstairs armed with various cocktails, to change for dinner. I had given the turkey a further basting, checked the pudding steaming away in its cloth and set aside the vegetables in final readiness before putting them on the Aga.

Reggie and Amanda had created a splendid Christmas fantasy with the table setting. Bright red candles, the centrepiece of fruit and nuts from the sitting room, gold crackers, and marvellous simulated rich green malachite and gold porcelain which I had found years ago in Portmerion, green and red wine glasses from Marano, near Venice, red paper napkins with a holly motif from Harrods, old steel cutlery with green dyed bone handles, a purchase I had made when casually shopping in Burford after a particularly good lunch at the Lygon Arms.

Amanda was a vision in an emerald green Hardy Amies, with a sequinned stole to match, trimmed in dyed fur. I felt decidedly dashing in my Turnbull and Asser smoking jacket of deep burgundy velvet, with matching bow tie and a Michael Fish shirt of fairly discreet ruffles. Reggie had stolen the show, however, even from Amanda, in a pair of outrageous silver trousers, silver waistcoat and a deep blue open-necked shirt with large puff sleeves. A Liberty scarf of blues and silver completed the outfit. The erstwhile snakeskin boots had been replaced by a pair of boots in blue suede.

"Darling, you're pure Bermans," shrieked Amanda, from the sofa, as he appeared.

"Don't you adore these pouf sleeves," lisped Reggie, pirouetting at the door. He and Amanda fell into further shrieks. I raised an eyebrow. To think I had been worried about Amanda and Reggie together! I was almost beginning to feel left out.

It was well after midnight when the three of us tottered upstairs to bed. This time there were no inhibitions. At the top of the landing Amanda had kissed the two of us warmly. "Darlings, bless the two of you for a divine evening and the most wonderful Christmas Day. See you both in the morning." Amanda's total acceptance of our togetherness added the final touch to this Christmas to remember. As if it was the most natural thing in the world the two of us walked slowly towards my bedroom, me with my arm around Reggie and Petrina hesitantly following at a discreet ten paces behind.

The second visit by the good fairy was in the guise of Elsie on Boxing morning. We had left downstairs in a fairly rough state and it had been my intention to get up early and do a semi tidy up before she arrived. However, she was well into the routine of things when I appeared downstairs.

"Elsie, good morning," I said as I entered the kitchen. "And Merry Boxing Day."

"Good morning, Mr Anderson," chirruped Elsie. She was organising the various plates and cutlery from out of the dishwasher. At least I had managed to stack this and turn it on before going up to bed.

"Coffee? It's just percolating nicely."

"Elsie, you're a saint and a genius," I said. I settled down on the edge of the table. "How was your Christmas?"

"Oh lovely, Mr A. And thank you for that wonderful hamper. Mr Law is really suffering from all that Madeira this morning!" Elsie's great Christmas treat was a regular hamper from Fortnum's. I had bribed her over the years with an assortment of gifts, but when I had on one Christmas occasion while speaking to Clare from New York, asked Clare to call Elsie and check on what she would really like as a present, she had shyly said to Clare that of all the wonderful things she had received in the past, nothing had quite competed with the hamper. And so the tradition had started, and Sid, Elsie's husband, could always be guaranteed his Boxing Day hangover.

Elsie chatted on as she continued her chores. "Miss Adamson was so kind as well. She gave me some really lovely soap and Sid is ever so pleased with his record." Sid was a great Mantovani fan and Amanda had added considerably to his collection of records. In their youth, Sid and Elsie had been enthusiastic ballroom dancers and Elsie blushingly admitted that over Christmas, aided by the Madeira and Mantovani, Sid became "ever so romantic" and would insist on spinning her round the sitting room.

I was about to explain that there was a third house guest, hence all the extra dishes and glasses, when a voice came from the door.

"Good morning." It was Reggie, already dressed and looking very bright and together.

"Reggie, good morning," I said, "sleep well?"

"Like an innocent," he replied.

"Elsie, this is Mr Forbes. Reggie, this is the amazing Elsie whom I have told you about, and who," I added, "is the only reason I slog it out of London for these long weekends."

Elsie chirruped again with laughter. "Oh Mr A. You are a one," she cried. I avoided Reggie's expression at this remark.

"Elsie, Happy Christmas." It was Amanda's turn to make an entrance. She stood at the door in the incredible housecoat.

"Oh Miss Adamson. How lovely you look." Elsie was Amanda's greatest fan and one of her greatest moments had been when Amanda had asked her and Sid to a charity performance of *The Bliss of All* attended by one of the royals. Elsie and Sid had been in the row right behind the house seats where the royal party had sat. Amanda had arranged for them to come backstage after the show and they had been in the wings to witness the princess congratulating the various members of the cast. After this excitement, they had then come on to a buffet dinner at the Savoy. Amanda was at one of the few formal tables and had placed Sid on her left, next to one of the vivacious blonde second leads in the show who had entranced him with her smile. Elsie had been placed between me and Piero Matthieu, who played the role of the acrobatic dancing lover in one of the big dance spectaculars, and she could not have been more feted. Piero got very drunk and very nostalgic, and claimed that Elsie reminded him of his mother whom he considered "ze most wunnerful woman" and Elsie could not have been more flattered. I left Elsie, Reggie and Amanda gossiping away in the kitchen while I went back upstairs to change. Peter had telephoned to say that Lulu had been on the telephone and they would drive down via The Raging Bull and meet us there, and then follow us back for a late lunch. "I hear you've got someone in tow, a pretty someone," he added. I felt a surge of annoyance with Lulu. I had wanted to present Reggie as a surprise as I did not want Peter to ferret around in his mind on the journey down and come up with any opinions which could be biased based on anything Phillip may have said about his room-mate, or else the impression Peter may have made at his own party. Even more worrying was my conveyed first impressions to Peter about Reggie after our first initial skirmish at Peter's party.

Reggie had straightened the bed and tidied the bedroom. I went through to the bathroom. A large note was lying on top of the closed toilet seat. "I love you," it said.

My happiness was incomprehensible. I turned on the bath with a laugh. "Sod Peter," I said to myself, "with you, Reggie, we can face them all." I looked again at the note. "The best graffiti I have ever seen in a toilet," I added.

*

The Raging Bull was crowded. Amanda was immediately recognised as she walked into the bar. Having been there on many occasions she knew most of the locals by name, and there were many shouted happy greetings and wavings. Peter and Tim were already there propped up against the bar and talking to an animated Lulu, heavily swagged in turquoise angora this time.

"Here they are," she shouted above the general noise. Peter turned with a large grin. He hugged Amanda and introduced her to Tim and then turned to where the two of us were, Reggie standing close next to me.

"RA," he said in his deep voice. "A belated Merry Christmas!" He looked at Reggie and did a double take which would have shamed any amateur dramatic society. "Good God!"

"I believe you've met," I said, keeping the whole matter as light as possible.

"Your party," said Reggie, holding out his hand.

Peter looked at him and at me. "I must say I was surprised to hear there was a third party at the cottage. I should have realised it would have been a gatecrasher."

Reggie paled. I looked at Peter in astonishment. I knew from old that he could be bitchy and directly to the point, but this was unexpected and certainly uncalled for.

"I invited Reggie," I said rather lamely, "and was delighted he could come."

"I am sure," said Peter, still looking at the two of us. "Reggie," he emphasised the 'gie' bit, "no doubt was also delighted to come."

Amanda, sensing the instant tension, came quickly to the rescue. "I understand you've all met," she said gaily, putting her arm through Reggie's. "I could be jealous," she continued. "If it hadn't been for RA here I would never have met my gorgeous Reggie. Reggie, come over and meet David and Sue." She steered him away from us and left me glowering at Peter.

"What the fuck was all that about?" I hissed.

"What the fuck are you doing with that obvious little fuck?" he retorted.

I was stunned. "That 'little fuck' as you have just called him happens to be a very nice kid, my house guest, and I think you had better change your tune if you still plan to come back to lunch. What the hell's got into you?" I added.

"I know his type," said Peter, unrepentant, "and I saw the play he made for you at my party. Phillip has told me all about him. He's made it obvious on more than one occasion, that all he is, is on the make and nothing will stop him. I must admit that I have heard that he has talent – artistic that is –" he put in snidely, "but your house guest, Reggie Forbes, caused a great deal of upset a few years ago and I assure you, had it not been that he knows Phillip and it would have caused an upset then and there, I would have thrown him out the other night."

"That's a choice one from you," I tore into Peter, "claiming concern for someone else's feelings. Since when does Phillip rise to such an elevated position? I imagined he was simply another of your toyboys."

"He's proved to be a good friend as well as a good fuck," Peter bulldozed on, relentless, "and the fact that he landed himself with your 'fun for the festivities' as his room-mate, is pure coincidence. End of subject!" Peter smiled. "You'll see."

I was furious. Tim came over and began chatting to the two of us and Amanda returned with Reggie. He was still looking pale but was obviously determined to ignore the incident. Peter turned on the full charm and had Amanda and Lulu, who had left Hector despairing behind the bar counter again, laughing at one of his many anecdotes.

The group was divided into two sets for the journey back to the cottage. Amanda travelled with Peter and Tim, and Reggie joined me in the Martin, with Petrina who had been left in the car on this occasion. I was feeling dreadfully unhappy for Reggie and I thought for a moment he was close to tears. What had happened to the mood of a few hours previous!

"I'm so very sorry," I began, "it's not like Peter..." I trailed off lamely.

"Yes, it is! I know he's a great friend of yours," said Reggie, staring ahead and clutching Petrina, "but he's a total shit. And so rude!" The word 'rude' came out with a break in his voice.

"Cheer up," I said. "Lunch will be okay. He's promised not to say any more."

"Say any more? Who's side are you on, anyway?" exploded Reggie. "A few sentences from that oaf and you appear content that he is not 'saying any more'! I'm quite aware at what he may think of me, and I'm pretty sure of what he was saying." He clenched and unclenched his fist. "Who the hell does he think he is to tear into a person like that? I appreciate he is the Midas-like Peter Brown whose agency can make a silk purse out of a sow's ear. Pity he seems to have overlooked the treatment on himself!"

"Now, come on," I said. "Let's drop it. What is important is that we are here together. It's just one of those unfortunate situations. If it's any help," I added, "he's obviously a bit jealous."

"Big deal, RA, I am not a child. That was not a display of jealousy. That was pure dislike and I really don't know for why."

"He probably fancies you rotten and is livid I got in before him." The comment could have been funny, with the added innuendo, but Reggie was not to be amused. We continued the rest of the journey in silence.

Lunch began on a more pleasant note. Peter seemed almost contrite, and was being very tactful and pleasant. Tim had immediately rolled a joint on arrival and was happily slumped out at the table, a large glass of wine alongside him.

Amanda was being enchanting. She and Peter did get on extremely well and he was a great audience and catalyst for her many witty and breezy stories. Elsie had prepared several dishes of cold turkey and salads and we sat in the dining room long after we had finished eating and Reggie had helped me clear the plates away. Peter had made one barbed comment about how expensive 'casual help' particularly over the festive period, could be, but this had been ignored. More wine flowed and I opened the first bottle of port which Peter had brought down as his contribution to the lunch. Tim was totally gone by this stage, and was sitting in a befuddled state with a further joint and a bemused expression on his face.

Peter had made one or two irritated comments to him, about pulling himself together, but had only received a slow grin in return. Although the picture presented by the group about the table in the late afternoon light – I had already put on the table lamp on the server and lit the Christmas candles – was Impressionist-like in its quality, there was a definite hypertension. I was desperately hoping that Peter would soon make his excuses and go, taking with him the spaced-out Tim, but my hopes were soon to be quashed. Peter opened another bottle of port!

Peter leaned back in the chair and held up the glass of port to the light.

"Not bad, for a Taylor's," he mused.

Amanda, holding a glass of green Chartreuse, looked at him. "I've never been able to cope with port, more's the pity, as I do love it so."

"I prefer brandy myself, preferably a marvellous Remy," I contributed. I looked at Reggie.

"I agree with RA. But I also never say no to a 'Stinger'. Better still, a 'Harlow Stinger'."

"I bet you never say 'no'," said Peter.

Amanda glared at him. "I know a Stinger, but what is a 'Harlow Stinger'?"

"Basically a 'Stinger' but with pernod floated on the top – reminiscent of Harlow's platinum hair," explained Reggie.

I had to give him top marks for control.

"Harlow's hair was much more blonde than yours, wasn't it?" continued Peter, with a rather childish drunken sneer. His 'Harlow' came out more as 'Arlow'. Amanda looked at me rather desperately.

"Naturally – or should I say unnaturally," continued Reggie, still determined to be good-humoured. "I suppose you could say she was a silver blonde." He smiled with an expression of mock self-pity. "I suppose I'm just plain old gold."

"Never as gold as perhaps in digger?"

Reggie slowly turned towards Peter, eyes blazing. The atmosphere was electric. The Harlow reference had been an open mistake.

"It may surprise you, Peter Brown, but not everybody drops their pants as often as you drop your 'aitches'."

The Achilles heel had been directly hit.

Peter gave a roar of fury at the accuracy of this barb to his childhood upbringing. Drawing himself to his full height, he threw his glass of port directly at Reggie. The ruby liquid hit Reggie directly in the face.

"Not bad – for a Taylor's," said Reggie, and calmly and slowly helped himself to a cigarette from the box on the table.

Befuddled by the amount of drink he had consumed and obviously at a loss to Reggie's brilliant thrust and parry, Peter turned his anger on the still smiling Tim. Amidst another bellow of fury and a burst of expletives quite creditworthy in their rich variety, Tim was punched and abused and dragged out to the car. Still shouting about "'ores" and "tarts" and with a final "you'll see!" he threw himself into the driving seat, slammed the door and skidded off down the lane, his Bentley narrowly missing Amanda's snow-bedecked Alfa.

Reggie had remained seated whilst the dramatic parting had taken place. Amanda and I looked at each other, shrugged and went back into the dining room.

"Sorry about that," said Reggie, the untouched cigarette smouldering between his fingers. "But Mr Brown is going to answer for a lot."

I looked at the young man seated in front of me. His expression was as serene as ever and he looked totally devastating and totally vulnerable sitting there. However, he had shown a side that I had not seen before. Reginald Forbes was utterly ruthless when crossed and he was as tough as fine-tempered steel.

The rest of the holiday break could have been strained and a dismal affair. Amanda, however, came to the rescue. She had helped herself to a further glass of sickly green liquor and sat down at the table once more.

"That was quite brilliant Reggie," she said. "I don't think I have ever seen our brilliant PR friend at a loss for words."

"He's obviously been lulled into a false security since Tim took his vow of stoned silence," said Reggie.

We all laughed.

Amanda had planned to return to London on the Wednesday morning. She had no performance until the Thursday, but needed the extra day to busy herself with the various bits and pieces that always seemed to be on a waiting list whilst the show held priority. We had made fond farewells, Amanda coming back from the car to give Reggie a further hug. I had closed the office for the week and suggested to Reggie he stayed on if he had no other plans. I needed a few days with him to sort out the hurt that Peter had so deliberately seemed to nurture. I had not heard from Peter and restrained myself from calling him. I would get Clare to ring Sandi once I was back in the office and organise a lunch. It was always so much easier to take up again at a rather formal occasion when matters like this occurred. Peter was, after all, my closest friend and ally and I was sure that the situation would sort itself out, despite Reggie's resolve not to even mention him.

I mulled over a comment a great friend had made to me on a similar occasion. This was the actress, Coral Browne, who claimed, quite rightly, "It's always virtually impossible, darling, to like a friend's 'friend'." I could see this may very well be the case with Reggie and Peter.

The remaining days were happy and uncomplicated. We spent a great deal of time walking and talking – poor Petrina had never had so much exercise – as well as a great deal of ecstatic times in bed. I learned from Reggie about his home life. He had been part of a family of four children, one brother and two sisters. He was devoted to them all and the other three had subsequently married. The two sisters had moved abroad with their respective husbands, and his brother ran the successful construction company his father had started up in Yorkshire several decades before. "So I do know my architrave from my elbow," Reggie had smiled.

His parents had retired on Jersey and had been quite happy at his ambition to move on in the world still evolving from his roots, namely building and decorating. "You'll be like an English Billy Baldwin," his mother had often said. She had flooded him with magazines on design and decoration and obviously the American Mr Baldwin had caught her eye. I was relieved to meet someone who had not come from a broken home, did not hate his family and seemed quite capable of accepting the fact that he was gay; the latter factor openly discussed by his contemporaries and without any visible emotional trauma thrown in. I ruefully reflected on my own background, where the subject of homosexuality had been taboo and only sniggered about over after dinner jokes, or cruelly exploited at school where the more obvious effeminate boy had been subjected to much bullying and the whipping dog for many a vicious exploit. Peter, in his way, epitomised the typical school bully, aggressive and hard-hitting, and probably the most frustrated gay of them all.

To return to Reggie. Our different upbringings were a major difference, plus the fact I was heading for forty-two and Reggie had just celebrated his twentieth birthday. Reggie, though a day scholar, had enjoyed his schooling considerably. "I was very good at tennis, though basically loathed the so-called blood sports - rugger and soccer - though it might have been a turn on to be a bum in a scrum." He had several close relationships with boys in his very early teens at school, "but nothing serious," he had added. "However there was one boy in my final year who totally overwhelmed me and the feeling was mutual. He was my first real teenage crush, and the first boy I actually did anything more intricate with as opposed to a mutual wank." Noting my fascinated expression, he went on – "Or in your layman's language, we fucked."

"Did you enjoy it?" I laughed.

"Put it this way, I've never regretted it and I never have claimed a headache!"

We discussed Reggie's future. I had always been adamant that I would not become involved in being a father figure, nor the Svengali to some young person. I had tried this once before and had been devastated to find myself alone and left to pick up the pieces after having pulled out every possible stop in helping a young man I had become involved with to start in a firm of solicitors headed by a gay friend. He had been the whizz-kid of the group from the day he began. I went so far as to help him in the purchase of his first small, but pleasant studio flat in Ladbroke Square, and also buy him a share in the friend's business. Peter had viewed the developments with his usual ferocity of expression. When Michael, the young man, had announced it was all over and that he was planning to live with a colleague he had met in the law firm, I was shattered. We were in Venice for an autumnal break and he had told me his news as we were sitting in Harry's Bar after a particularly pleasant dinner at the Gritti Palace where we were staying. I had gone and got myself totally drunk and had ended up in some sordid backstreet bar. I had awakened in some filthy doss-house off the Piazza San Marco – "who claims Venice is completely beautiful" – my wallet gone, as well as my watch and cufflinks. In a sorry dishevelled state I had found my way back to the hotel. There was a note left for me with the reception. Michael had returned to London. I later learned that he had hired a car and motored on down to Florence where he had already planned to meet his new companion.

I returned to London, called Peter and we had spent a soul-searching lunch at L'Escargot in Soho. We had tottered down to the A & B where I had met a young man on leave from his ship docked in Portsmouth. He came back to the flat and stayed for a few days. I gave him a farewell gift of some cash and he went off back to Portsmouth without any complications and seemingly quite happy. I threw myself into my work and never stopped thanking the powers that be that I had my office and a business that was doing so well. Dealing mainly in the export of antiques, I was also finding myself acting more and more as a consultant for firms and individuals wishing to invest in refurbished properties of quality. My company had been responsible for the total furnishings of a town house for a powerful American oil company in New York, and so a section of the office had been set up to handle the total refurbishments of such projects which were becoming more and more frequent. My flat in Ennismore Gardens was a perfect example of the ambience we would create for a collection of furniture or paintings and the company relied heavily on the services of an ex-member of the famous London design house of Colefax and Fowler whom we had bribed away.

In a way, Reggie's arrival on the scene could appear to have been brilliantly timed.

We quickly settled into a routine. From the small design firm in Ealing Reggie had managed to get himself involved with a large design and furnishing store in Tottenham Court Road and seemed quite happy, though at times frustrated, by the limitations of his role. Although his friendship with Phillip had cooled considerably he still lived in Ealing, but had seen a small flat in Fernshaw Road close to the Fulham Road that he planned to buy. The area was up and coming and he speculated that the purchase would be a wise move. His parents helped him organise the initial payment to the mortgage and the rest he was destined to cater for himself out of his meagre but regular salary. I offered him the choice of some kitchen equipment as a moving-in present. He wickedly said he would prefer to invest the same amount in an extra large and comfortable bed. He ended up with the bed and the kitchen.

The flat was a delight. Reggie had chosen ochre and white as a theme. The floors had been stripped and waxed, the walls painted ochre gloss with white woodwork and waxed louvre shutters to the windows. A modern sofa in an ochre and white geometric, and two marvellous gilt reproduction bergeres, upholstered in a leopard print linen from a fabric house sale, met at either end of the sofa. The central coffee table was made up of two piles of large old dilapidated leather-bound books, cleaned up and used as the base with a piece of smoked plate glass on the top. Large gold, white and yellow cushions added extra informal touches. Lighting was a series of large clay pots found in World's End and lit up the interior with intricate shadow play from the light thrown directly up on to the mouldings on the ceiling which added to the theatrical effect. Several of Reggie's paintings dominated the walls, and the hall itself was a complete *trompe-l'oeil* effect in black, ochre and white of jungle scene.

The bedroom was walled in the leopard skin fabric with a matching throw-over spread and a scattering of brightly coloured silk cushions in orange, ochre, green and gold.

We saw a great deal of Amanda. Her show was still a great success and Reggie had taken to giving her occasional suppers at the flat. She was always delighted by his invitations and he and she became firm friends. I was travelling to the States more and more and on several occasions I would telephone Reggie and Amanda would be there. We would have a merry three-way conversation and I would continue my business trip in a contented and happy way.

The slight with Peter had been glossed over.

He had gone so far as to send Reggie a note of apology. However, I kept their meetings to a minimum as the warning signs were still there, and one did not want to start up a second conflagration. Peter was the first to admit that he may have been wrong about Reggie and his initial purposes, and he was secretly impressed at the way Reggie had knuckled down to his job and also that he had managed to organise his own flat. Tim was still about, but more stoned than before and Peter was getting to desperation point with him. I had never bothered to ask Peter, nor Reggie, as to what the upset was. It had occurred five years before. Doubtless Reggie would tell me about it in his own time.

It was suddenly summer.

Chapter Six

London was sweltering in the most spectacular weather. It was 1970 and still considered the 'swinging capital of the world', and life could not have been more perfect. Reggie and myself had planned a few weeks in the South of France where I had rented a villa nearby Gassin, outside St Tropez.

It was a warm summer evening and we were sitting by the open windows to the drawing room in Ennismore Gardens. The sound of children's laughter echoed happily through the square. Petrina was lying panting on the sofa, not seeming to realise that she would be cooler on the carpet. Reggie had given up moving her off the cushions to a front window.

So much seemed to have happened and it seemed amazing that our relationship had reached this firming stage in only a matter of a mere seven months. Reggie was sitting holding a long glass of iced gin and tonic. He was in a pair of white trousers and an open-necked shirt. His feet were bare and he looked like one of those sun-kissed advertisements for some international summer drink. We had spent every weekend at the cottage and he had put the pool to good use and his tan was proof of this. We were due out later to an informal supper party given by Sarah and Angus. Reggie spent more and more time at the flat and had taken to keeping a fairly substantial wardrobe in the spare room cupboards. He refused to give up his flat and move in with me, although I had gone against all my former principles and suggested this on numerous occasions.

He checked his watch.

"I had better go and have a bath and change," he said. "I feel whacked. It's been a pig of a day." He stood up.

"Another drink, darling, before I disappear?"

He held out his hand and smiled. I took his hand, turned it palm upwards and kissed his palm gently and then slyly licked it.

"That would be nice."

"Lecher," he smiled, and walked over to the commode.

I looked at his trim, slim figure as he stood there in silhouette. Our relationship continued to thrill and amaze me. I knew that there had been nobody else as far as the two of us were concerned. Since our first night at the cottage there had been a love and mutual respect that seemed to grow and grow.

Our only disagreement to date had been over my suggesting he rented his flat and moved in with me. He had been adamant that this was something he would not do.

"I am not saying that it would never be possible," he had said, "but our relationship is still at such an early stage and it is only fair that on occasions we have the safety valve of me being able to leave you on your own, should you require to be so, or vice versa. I can be on my own if I feel like it."

Of course he was right, but I continued with my argument saying that if one was planning a future together, one may as well begin it now as opposed to waiting. "It's like those ridiculous trial marriages. I really do not see any point in those at all. You either marry somebody, or you don't. The marriage vows demand 'for better or for worse'. A 'trial' marriage leaves it totally open for one of the parties to walk away from the scene if it isn't working to their liking, resulting in the attitudes of either party remaining totally selfish. If you have committed yourself to another, you will make greater attempts to understand and adapt which would not have even been considered otherwise."

"Is this a proposal?" Reggie had cried, striking a camp pose with his hand placed limply to his brow. "Lordy, lordy Mr A, this is so sudden and so unexpected I do declare I've been suddenly taken over all queer!"

I had to laugh, but I did feel very strongly over my views. I had gone so far as to mention the conversation to Amanda when we had met for lunch a few days later.

Amanda had been to a meeting at the Savoy with her agent and the representative of an American backer who was hoping to have *The Bliss of All* open in New York at the end of the year, preferably starring Amanda. Details with Equity were having to be discussed and vital matters, such as salaries and benefits, had also been on the high-powered agenda.

My morning had been most successful, here again with an American client. I was in the final process of organising a large export order of a selection of early lesser-known Victorian painters and had been calmly and quietly buying over the past few years. These were going out to Houston for a decorative and furnishing fair being sponsored by a group of blue-haired American ladies, determined to bring a touch of European culture to their state. One of my New York contacts had suggested my organisation as a vital element capable of handling what this particular fair required, and I saw this as a brilliant opportunity to start promoting this particular period of art which was becoming more sought after as collectors were continually searching for new fields. Several Victorian artists were already in demand and the vogue was spreading.

When I had questioned a restaurant, Amanda had said with her utter throwaway charm, "Darling, the meeting will probably be horrendous and I shall be in the depths of a stunning, suicidal scene. I'll simply have to be convinced, by something sinfully calorific and totally against all my principles, that life is worth living."

We settled on the Mirabelle. I convinced Amanda that the croûte de foie gras gratinée, followed by the sole Mirabelle, would certainly take care of the required calories but added that no doubt the additional weight gained would take her right back to the suicidal syndrome. True to form Amanda had perused the menu and then sat back with a sigh, a glass of champagne in front of her. "Regime rules," she said sadly. "I had visions all the way in the taxi of all those compatible geese happily dedicating their livers to me, but I have to say no, I'm afraid." She leaned forward, smiled wickedly, and added in a stage tone, "You saw all those looks of recognition when I walked in. Now you wouldn't want them saying 'who is that large woman with Robin Anderson... wasn't he the dealer who used to date the actress, Amanda Adamson? I wonder what happened to her?'."

We both laughed and the maître d'hôtel shook his head admonishingly. "Never, Miss Adamson."

"I'll have the oeufs Florentine and possibly a sorbet afterwards." Amanda smiled up at him.

I ordered for myself. "Wine?" I questioned.

"No darling. I'll finish this delicious champagne and then go on to Perrier, please. Those legendary limbs daren't wobble tonight."

She was looking stunning and the American representative had thought the same. Amanda had her hair up in a chignon with a marvellous black top hat and veil. A sleek black Dior suit, black silk stockings with black patent shoes, a silk shirt in turquoise and white plus white gloves completed the fashion picture. She embraced the word 'star'! She was wildly excited about appearing in New York for six months. "I shall finish there and then take a break before beginning work on the film of the show. We're shooting in London and LA and I am so looking forward to it." She took another sip of her drink. "But RA, enough about me. When do you begin to rival 'Giant'?"

"Any minute. They have agreed to all the terms of commission and the handling of assorted costs. I should be out there after we return from the South of France as it may take a few weeks to set up."

"What does Reggie think about it all?"

"Typical Reggie. He says that no doubt he and I will end up making Mr Bell and the GPO even more rich! No, he says he'll miss me but there is Petrina who snores just as adequately and with you there to constantly hold his hand he feels sure he will survive."

"That young man is so divine." Amanda looked directly at me. "He is the best thing that has happened to you and don't you go and screw it up."

"Me?" I protested, wondering what she was getting at. "You know how I feel about him. Why, I've even asked him to move in with me..."

"Exactly," continued Amanda, setting down her fork and obviously gearing herself for a 'nanny' lecture. "He mentioned this to me. Don't give me that expression. Who else would he discuss it with? After all, he considers me – as I do – one of your closest friends, and I have been around literally from day one! Darling, don't push him. Reggie adores you and to him you are immensely important. However, he is much younger than you are. He's still a baby, especially compared to you." The latter was followed by a blown kiss.

"Very astute and amusing," I said.

"Don't lose your sense of humour." That was Amanda being amusing! "Seriously, he is determined to succeed in his design field. It is so obvious from the success he has already made in that dreadful concentration camp of a store. You may not be aware of it but several clients have approached him privately, offering to back him. Look at his flat as further proof. It is really so different and of it's time. Call it up-dated trad, as Reggie does, or whatever, but the flair and talent is there. He needs his independence from you and it is only with this independence that he knows he will retain your respect and that the relationship will succeed."

My mouth had dropped at this point.

"Don't sit there looking so surprised. He is a highly intelligent and talented young man. He is not like Peter's Tim, a lost soul who will only go on being kept by Peter until Peter finds another play pal who is at least sober and not stoned out of his brain the whole time. And that is only a matter of time. Tim will end up either with some raddled old queen in some downmarket place like Tangier – that is if he can find one particularly desperate enough to cope with a Tim – and only for as long as what are left of his looks last. It is a cruel, but typical story. Where will Tim be in ten years' time? In the depths, without a doubt, whilst Reggie, your Reggie, my Reggie – and, I really like to feel this – our Reggie, will be at the top."

"Your eggs are getting cold."

"That is a typical male chauvinist remark!" stormed Amanda. "As soon as you find yourselves being criticised by a woman – and both succinctly and correctly – you fob off their comments as if they are totally feather-brained. Well, you know what I say is correct. At least you won't be boring me with Reggie as you did over that pointless Michael."

I started to grow hot.

"Yes, you can sit there getting all steamed up," she went on, "but may I add the whole matter is totally one sided. All we have heard is what Reggie must do, or must not do, or listen to you going on as to whether Reggie really feels the same way about you as you do about him. What about you? What if you suddenly find the ultimate in a heavenly hunk in Houston? Not that you go in for hunks! You're not exactly the original immaculate conception. I have been through this scene on several occasions with you and Reggie is the only one I can honestly say I feel this strongly about.

"He wants you as an equal, not as a sugar-daddy."

I was totally transfixed, but there was no holding her.

"Has he ever asked you for anything? He could have quite easily charmed his way from your bed right into that design side of your business and sent that geriatric goddess ex-Colefax and Fowler, packing. That would have been the obvious thing to do. But he didn't, and you mark my words, he'll never ask you to help him in business. He's too independent and too proud, and more important, because your love and your respect for him have made him that." She paused, still glaring at me, and picked up her fork again. "The eggs are delicious cold," she grimaced and then winked. "What about another glass of champagne?" she added. "Lecturing to the unenlightened is thirsty work."

*

Reggie came back into the sitting room. The shirt and trousers had been replaced by a white suit with a navy shirt and with the trouser legs tucked into white boots.

"Don't tell me," he said, "they'll think it's Doris Day in *Calamity Jane*."

I laughed, "But without the need for the gauze!"

"Lucky for you you included the word 'without'! Aren't you changing?"

"No, I'll simply have a quick wash and have a shower when we get back."

"When you get back, RA. Don't forget I'm going to meet Steven and his friend from the display department at the store at Mandy's."

"Oh yes. Will that be fun?" I got to my feet and started walking to the stairs to go down to my bathroom.

"Hope so. Steven and Ray are sweet but very domestic. This is their great night out and they have asked me to join them before. They feel I'm a 'catch' as I seem to know everybody. This, due to Amanda coming into the store one day and insisting on meeting the window dresser responsible for the Fragonard-like setting for the spring bed linens. This was Steven, and Manda had been heavily primed by me prior to the visit. Steven has been a devotee of hers for ages. They've seen the present show seven times!"

"'Manda to Mandy's,'" I murmured.

"Not very original, Robin," said Reggie. "I said that to them this morning and they shrieked."

Sarah had asked us for nine o'clock and we arrived in Montpelier Square at twenty past. Most of the guests had arrived and were milling about on the patio off from the drawing room. We were ushered into the house by the Filipino manservant. A well-tended bar was immediately on our left in the library which had been specially rearranged for the evening. Sarah, with her usual precision and style, always made sure that on these more informal and crowded occasions one was well fortified with a large drink of one's choice before joining the ranks upstairs. We made our way upstairs to the first floor. Sarah was standing talking to an intense young couple and gave a warm smile when she saw us.

"Reggie," she cried, kissing him warmly on the cheek. She held him back at arm's length. "How marvellous you look. Robin!" I, too, received a kiss, but no similar compliment. Perhaps I should have changed after all. But into what? Another dark suit?

"Terence, Pamela, I want you to meet Reggie Forbes, the most elegant young man in London." Terence and Pamela, with Terence in particular, did not seem too impressed with meeting the most elegant young man in London, and smiled rather wanly at Reggie. Next to him they did look so very ordinary. Reggie radiated an aura of glamour and electrical excitement. His blonde hair, his dazzling smile, the tan and his general style of dress, made him a solo figure in the crowded room. Sarah, taking him firmly by the arm, moved through the throng towards a group by the fireplace. There were many familiar faces and I was soon busy talking to other friends or business associates.

"Darling, I've just met your Mr Forbes." I reeled round. Elvira. She stood there, exquisite and immaculately groomed, a smile playing on her carmined lips.

"Elvira! How lovely you look!" I leaned forward to kiss her lightly on the porcelain-like cheek, my mind racing at the 'your Mr Forbes' remark. Elvira, Duchess of Lewes. Considered one of the greatest beauties in her youth and still a reigning beauty in the upper echelons of London society, she was a brilliant raconteur, hostess, and when crossed – which was regularly – totally venomous. Stories about her abounded and she kept the gossip columns agog with her latest furies and feuds. Sarah always claimed it was safer to have Elvira in view as opposed to out of sight, and the two kept a very even keel with never-ending series of girls' luncheons and bridge.

Elvira put a delicate hand on my arm. Her carmined nails, in keeping with the ruby and diamond bracelet she was wearing, tapped my sleeve playfully.

"What a charming young man he is. And so pretty! You must bring him round to the house for dinner one evening. I'll call you." She blinked her large blue eyes at me – they were the only part of her outfit not carmined – and floated away, her chiffon dress of deep red, wafting in swirls of colour behind her.

"She looks exactly like Disney's wicked stepmother in *Snow White*," said Reggie, materialising next to me. "She is quite, quite extraordinary."

"Ah, the charming and pretty Mr Forbes," I cried. Reggie raised an eyebrow. "I feel we may have some trouble there," I added darkly. I reminded Reggie that Elvira had been at Peter's Christmas party.

"I was too interested in you, RA, to have noticed." He smiled evilly.

Supper was fun, light-hearted and amusing. Elvira waved graciously to the two of us on more than one occasion. We had collected our plates and glasses of wine and moved back on to the patio. I introduced Reggie to another couple whom I knew we would be seeing in the South of France and left him talking to them. Having finished with my plate I put it down, and moved over to talk to George Cooper who was standing next to a sullen young man who was obviously not at ease with the gathering. George was host at the party where I had met Peter all those years previously.

"Good evening, George." I nodded at the young man.

"RA, how good to see you. This is Don. Don, meet Robin Anderson, a long-standing friend." Don nodded with a surly expression.

"Is that him?" questioned George.

"Him?"

"Your new friend. The one you met at Peter's at Christmas?"

I should have known that Peter would have told George about Reggie. However, I was amused to glean from pieces of conversation I had with George during the rest of the evening, that Peter was taking full credit for the success of our relationship as it was he who introduced Reggie to me or vice versa.

"Some more wine, sir?" The manservant was standing next to me.

"Please," I said, holding out my glass. He turned to George's proffered glass and filled his. He looked at the surly Don. "Wine for you, sir?"

"No, I'd prefer a lager."

"Of course, sir."

"Don's from Australia," said George. "He's a master carpenter," as if this explained his friend's request for a lager. Where did George, like Peter, find them? I had to congratulate Sarah's manservant for not being the slightest bit ruffled. Sarah was always prepared for everything and he returned in a few seconds with a long glass of lager. Don took it and gave a second curt nod. He continued staring over my shoulder and ignoring George and myself.

"Which part of Australia, Don?" I asked, attempting to bring him into the conversation.

"Sydney," he said. "Is that gay sheila over there your friend?"

I was a bit taken aback and looked to where he had pointed with the nearly empty glass of lager. Reggie was standing talking again to a regally poised Elvira.

"If you are referring to the fair young man talking to the woman in red, yes."

"He's a doll." Don looked at me and smiled for the first time. "I congrat' you on your taste." He smiled again and gave a slight sway.

"Thank you." I felt it time to make a move from the two of them. "I'll be in touch," I added, and moved back towards Elvira and Reggie.

"Reginald's a designer," blinked Elvira, as if she had just been told that he was a direct descendant of the Pope.

"An emergent designer," corrected Reggie, smiling brilliantly at her.

"We must talk," said Elvira, tapping his arm this time. "I have been meaning to do something about my study for some time and I adore the description of your own sitting room."

I was beginning to see Reggie's wisdom in having an independent flat, particularly when the likes of Elvira decided to play at being the inquisition.

"Well, if you don't mind journeying to far off Fulham, you are very welcome to come for a drink and see the room yourself."

Elvira blinked again at Reggie. "Oh no, darling," she said, "if I journey to far-off Fulham, a drink would never suffice! I would have to insist on dinner." With that she floated off again.

"Is she serious?" queried Reggie.

"You had better believe it," I said. "She also likes pretty young men as dessert!"

"Hi!" I groaned inwardly. It was the drunken Don, swaying alongside me. "Who's the sheila in the red?"

"The one who was talking to Reggie earlier – this is Reggie, by the way. Reggie, Don."

"Hi, Reggie. Yea, the upmarket sheila?"

"That's Elvira. She's a Duchess."

"Oh."

"Why?"

"Oh, well she looked at me as I came over to you and said 'Honestly, Sarah' and I said, 'I'm not Sarah'." He looked down at his blue tight-fitting cotton jacket and bulging cotton trousers. He grinned at his well-filled crotch. "She must be blind if she thinks I'm Sarah."

Reggie and I had to laugh. Don joined in with us, though not quite sure as to what we were all laughing about. He looked at Reggie again. "Say, you really are a doll."

Reggie, instead of looking the slightest bit embarrassed, smiled more broadly. "You're not too bad yourself. Though a bit large for a doll."

Don held his thumb to under his nose and peered at Reggie.

"Would you like to find out?" He lurched slightly, and gave a leer.

"There you are." Saved, as always, by Amanda who had come in after the show. She swept over to us, clasping Reggie and myself by the arms and kissing us warmly. "Hello." She smiled at Don.

"Hi," said Don, lapsing into silence and focusing back on Reggie and then back on Amanda. He was beginning to look confused.

"Let me see if I can find you some supper," I said and led Amanda off. I had no doubt that Reggie could cope with the further passions of Don.

The party continued. Reggie came over to say goodbye. I saw Don and George lurking near the doorway. George waved with his free arm, the other was supporting a slumped Don.

"George has very kindly offered to give me a lift," explained Reggie. "He suggested that he shows Don a typical late night spot and so I suggested they join Steven, Ray and myself for a drink at Mandy's."

I stared at him.

"I don't think there is any danger anywhere," grinned Reggie. "Judging from Don's state I am sure he would be more of a Sarah than a stud."

I laughed and turned to a puzzled Amanda. "I'll explain. Take care Reggie, and I'll speak to you in the morning."

"Hmm, better, much better," said Amanda. "We're being allowed out to play."

"All work and no play – you know what they say!" I laughed in a slightly forced way.

"Darling, how cleverly you twist things," chortled Amanda. "With me it's all play or no work. Sort that one out."

*

The telephone rang whilst I was shaving. I snatched it up.

"You must have been late. How was Sarah?"

"What?"

I cursed myself as I recognised the imperious tone. "Elvira! Sorry! I was expecting somebody else."

Obviously," she sniffed. There was a curious pause. "What's this about Sarah?"

Trust Elvira's beady mind to pick up this remark. "Not our Sarah," I said desperately, "my secretary's mother, another Sarah. She's been ill," I ended lamely.

"Well, she's making it very confusing," snapped Elvira, "even if she is ill."

My curiosity gave over to me trying to sort this out further. "You are on the telephone very early, Elvira. You are usually an untouchable until ten."

"It's Reginald. I need to speak to him."

You old boot, I said to myself, and again blessed the Fulham flat. "Have you tried him in Fulham? Because that's where you'll get him."

Elvira was too wily to give herself away. "I didn't expect to find him with you, darling. I was calling to get his telephone number. Unless, of course, you're expecting him for breakfast or something?"

I ignored the latter part of the sentence. "Hold on, I'll get his number." I was not going to give her the benefit of rattling it off to her as if it were like Calais to another queen, and emblazoned across my heart.

I gave her the number and she thanked me and hung up. I quickly rinsed my face then dialled the number I had given out and got the engaged signal. Elvira was certainly quick off the mark, though I was surprised Reggie had not called. I dialled again before setting off for St James', but still obtained the busy tone.

The morning passed quickly. Clare and myself were busy working on the catalogue for the planned Houston fair. I was sifting through the photographs to be used in the catalogue when Clare buzzed me. "It's Mr Forbes," she announced.

"Put him through," I said absently.

"No, he's in reception," said Clare.

I was taken aback. Reggie had a policy of never telephoning the office unless it was something important as he did not want Clare nor anybody else becoming aware of the closeness in our relationship. He had met Clare on several occasions, but only with the strictest of formalities. For Reggie to appear at the office in person was totally unexpected.

"Show him in, please," I said, regaining some of my composure. A series of vivid thoughts rushed into my mind. He had been arrested; or beaten up. I did not know what to expect. There was a discreet knock on the door. "Come in."

"Mr Forbes," announced Clare, hovering. "Some coffee?"

I looked at Reggie who did not look in the least bit as if he had spent the night in a cell, nor as if he had been gang-banged nor beaten up. I sighed audibly. He was impeccable and wearing a suit.

"Reggie, good morning. Some coffee?"

"Please."

I nodded at Clare who bobbed her head and retreated back behind the door, gently pulling it closed.

"Well, this is a surprise," I said, gesturing to a chair. Reggie stood smiling. "Go on," I said, "sit down."

"In a minute," he said. He was carrying a briefcase and moved forward towards the desk. "May I?"

I nodded. He put the case on the desk and opened it. "Congratulate me," he said.

"Oh? And what is the occasion?"

He handed me a piece of paper. It was a company registration certificate. I looked at him. "What's this?"

He was brimming with excitement and smiling broadly. "Read it."

"Designs Exclusive. What's this all about?"

"It's mine!"

"What do you mean, it's yours?"

"Exactly that. I'm giving a month's notice as from Monday and starting my own company."

"You're what?"

"Yes, it's already registered. I'm initially going to work from the flat until the premises are ready and then take it from there."

"But... premises... office..." I was totally confused. "Reggie, this is madness. You've only been out of college for about eighteen months. You cannot walk before you can run. What about backing, administration... all right, I appreciate the firm in Ealing and your working only in the West End bit..." I trailed off and sat there staring at him in bewilderment.

Clare entered with the coffee and set it down on the table in front of the sofa by the window. I thanked her and then turned my attention back to Reggie. "Let's move over to the sofa," I said. He nodded and crossed the room. "I realise it's only gone eleven," I continued, "and I also realise that no matter what I say the deed is done, so instead of coffee and behaving as if this were a wake, why not a glass of something sparkling to celebrate the new venture?"

I went over to the bar cupboard next to the fireplace, checked inside the small Electrolux and took out a bottle of Veuve Cliquot. I took up two glasses and moved back to the coffee table. I manipulated the cork and there was a distinct pop.

"Well, that's a good omen." I poured a portion into the glass nearest to me, filled the other glass and handed it to Reggie. I then filled my glass, put down the bottle on the table, and raised the glass to him.

"To Designs Unlimited – and to my dear Reggie, of surprises unlimited." We solemnly sipped the champagne and then laughed.

"You so and so," I said, sitting down next to him. "Now tell me more."

Reggie had been planning the whole matter for several months. He had discussed the matter with his brother who had agreed to assist

Reggie with the initial backing in return for Reggie offering a professional design service to several housing developments in Yorkshire. Reggie's company would be responsible for the interior design to several show houses as well as the furnishings throughout. Richard, his brother, would see that Reggie received as much local publicity as possible and from this there would be no doubt a follow-up of private contracts from which Richard's firm would gain on the contractual side. Reggie would carry out the design work and the two companies would be of great benefit to each other.

The company had been registered with Reggie as majority shareholder and managing director. Richard was a fellow director, as was Amanda. I should have known she would appear in the setting up of it all. Reggie held seventy percent of the shares, Richard twenty percent, and Amanda ten percent. A shop front was already being worked on in Pimlico Road, along from Casa Pupo and an area which was already becoming noted for its antique and specialist shops.

"I was moving in when you were in Houston," concluded Reggie. "And the official opening was to be on the evening of your birthday with a small reception party. But I couldn't wait to tell you."

I simply sat there, smiling at him with total love and complete admiration.

"I did not make you a director as Manda and self thought you may have reacted to this. But you know it really is all yours – and due to you."

I still sat there. Reggie filled my glass and his.

"The publicity side is also well planned," he went on.

"Don't tell me."

"Yes, Peter. He's been sensational. The machine starts rolling as from tomorrow. That is why I have to give in my notice today."

I was now starting to feel very left out of it all. This had obviously been going on for several weeks. Peter was too slick a professional not to have already had the jungle drums giving a distinct beat and now the message was about to be sent out, load and clear.

"Last night was a blessing in disguise."

I looked at him quickly, immediately thinking of Don. Surely he wasn't going to add the Australian carpenter to his pre-planned team! "That blessing was hardly in disguise," I added sourly.

Reggie looked. "Not Don, RA." He laughed. "You're quick though. Obviously an early glass of bubbly helps your addled brain! No, Elvira!"

"What about Elvira?"

"She rang – as you must have gathered – since she called you earlier and asked for my number."

"And?"

"Well, she wants some design work done. I told her she could not have called at a more auspicious occasion and had she realised that, if she were serious, she would be my first client! She was a bit taken aback, but I tore in there and went on to explain that Peter was doing my PR – that impressed her, and I feel she has a hidden passion for our gypsy-like Mr Brown. I added that Amanda Adamson was also a client..."

"Amanda?"

"Of course, she wants her total flat redecorated whilst she's over there wowing them on Broadway later this year, and who but Reginald Forbes of Designs Unlimited would ever be considered for the task! Not only is she a director of his company but believes he IS the Seventies. To quote, 'I could be happy with Hicks, perhaps satisfied with Siddeley, but it will be fabulous with Forbes.' Peter is printing that in tomorrow's *News* in the story on Amanda's coup with the film contract. The first English star to be paid one million sterling for a musical."

I continued sitting.

"Elvira could not wait. She insisted, no demanded, to be my first client. It suddenly came to her that a simple study could not expect all this glory so it has to be the whole house. Mr Forbes, of Designs Unlimited, sees Her Grace at noon on Monday and, if Mr Reginald Forbes is not too busy, would he care to join Her Grace and a close friend, Mrs Dorella Devene, who simply happens to be the Devene behind the Dorelle cosmetic corporation, for a 'devene lunch intime' après." He did a neat pirouette.

I stayed sitting.

Reggie moved over to the Electrolux. "May I?"

I nodded dumbly.

He opened a second bottle of Veuve Cliquot. The buzzer went. I jack-knifed out from the sofa and went to the desk. "No calls for the next half hour, Clare," I snapped. I went back and seated myself again. Reggie gave me back the refilled glass.

"I am amazed and I am delighted at all this work. But who is going to carry it all out for you? Is Richard the Lionheart swooping down from the Yorkshire Dales with a literal army of men armed with paint pots and such?"

"It must be the champagne," said Reggie. "No, Richard Coeur de Leon stays in his own camp. We have our own militia here. The boys from the store. I have been working closely with Joe and his boys for six months now. We have completed two major contracts together. I mentioned this firstly to Joe about six weeks ago. They are not beholden to the store at all and are free agents who sub-contract themselves out. They are all for it and were delighted when they met Manda at the flat for an initial meeting for basic estimating purposes.

I was beginning to feel a total alien. All this planning had been going on between the three people I held most dearest to me and I had been totally unaware of it all. "But our plans, the South of France! The villa?" I said rather petulantly.

"Oh, nothing has changed. I will have to come back now and then the few weeks we are away. Joe and his right-hand man, Chris, are also away part of the time with their families – camping outside San Trop. would you believe. Joe's firm is doing Pimlico Road, but he has a top workforce and site foreman so there won't be any problems."

"I'm surprised you haven't told them they needn't use the camp site, but set up camp at the villa," I added sourly.

"What a charmingly unselfish idea, RA," smiled Reggie.

I glared at him.

"Come on, a leg pull," he said. "But it is good news, don't you think?"

"Brilliant. Little did I realise when I woke up this morning that the handsome prince had turned into a tycoon; the Duchess to a Tinker Bell and Amanda Adamson, actress, into Amanda Adamson, Associates. Where does this leave me?"

"As RA. Still best in the hay!"

"Let us sincerely drink to that." The buzzer went again. I went over to the desk. "Yes, Clare?"

"I know you said no calls, Mr Anderson, but it's the airport about that bill of lading on those items from Bangkok. They have been on twice and I do know how important it is to get the goods cleared."

"Right, put them through. Oh, Clare, before you do that, one moment." I covered the mouthpiece. "How sober do you have to be to hand in that notice? In the circumstances I feel I must compete with all this glory. If you and perhaps Miss Adamson are free to join me for lunch I would be delighted to meet you at the Connaught in shall we say an hour. Perhaps you would care to call Miss Adamson using the green telephone whilst I speak to the airport? Do finish the champagne, we can always open a third." I blew Reggie a kiss. "Right Clare, before you put them on would you set up a table at the Connaught for three, at 1.15 p.m. please? Thank you."

It so happened that Amanda was free for lunch and had seemingly been walking through the front door, having returned from her hairdresser, when Reggie telephoned. I knew the two had planned the whole morning brilliantly – after all, they were both professionals. I finished my conversation with the Customs and Excise and turned my attention again to Reggie.

"Things always happen in threes," I said. "Elvira, Amanda and certainly you will end up doing something for Dorella Devene. Elvira is already anticipating future years of free cosmetics and subtle visits to beauty farms preferably abroad and via some exotic watering hole. So I had better strike while the iron is hot. I wonder if Designs Unlimited would consider a slightly contraceptive approach – only slightly, I repeat – for the new offices planned for this humble company on Madison in New York. I mean, I should handle it all from here but my design department will be busy with Houston and as long as I may advise on the paintings and some of the more traditional furniture..."

Reggie, contrary to all his claims of office protocol, rushed across the room and flung his arms around me. I smiled down at him. "Do you think you can handle it?"

"And the offices?"

"Filthy sod. I mean, on this occasion only, the offices?"

"Of course," said Reggie, stepping back and straightening his jacket, still beaming. "I look forward to the challenge of Designs Unlimited working with your concern, sir. Antique and modern can form a perfect fusion. I mean, sir, look at us!"

Peter had certainly pulled out all stops for his new client. With Elvira, Amanda and the name of my own firm adding a slight touch of sobriety, Reginald Forbes was being animatedly discussed by the following midday. Amanda's interview featured him and their design partnership as he had said Peter would be doing. Hickey had Elvira's proposed refurbishment as his lead. "Duchess plans a total facelift", the headlines bitched, and went on to say that Reginald Forbes would be responsible for a facelift to the house in Wilton Crescent.

Peter had also had the proposed new Pimlico premises mentioned and stated that Mr Forbes would be abroad until September when he would be then returning for the official opening. He was travelling abroad to concentrate on a contract in the South of France for an international figure who was prepared to remain anonymous. Mr Forbes would not be seeing any potential clients until his return. Shrewdly, Peter had already organised the new business number with the Post Office and an individual twenty-four hour answering service had been put under contract to answer the newly listed number given to Enquiries.

Reggie had broken his news to me on the Thursday. By Friday evening his answering service had received over a dozen calls. The message to all enquiries was the same. The person or individual was thanked and asked to confirm the call in writing to the new Pimlico Road address. Mr Forbes would deal with each enquiry personally on his return in five weeks' time.

London's top fashion magazines were already vying for colour spreads on Amanda and the Duchess, both of whom they booked to photograph in their new settings. I was interviewed for a magazine, deemed the bible to the antique world and the connoisseur for all collectors. There was a rather dashing photograph of myself taken in the drawing room at Ennismore Gardens. Reggie had borrowed a Wassilly chair in white hide and chrome, and I was featured sitting in this alongside the William Kent commode.

"The old meets the new with Reginald Forbes", it was captioned. The caption caused great amusement with Reggie.

The same article appeared in the American edition of the magazine and here again Peter had suggested any enquiries be referred to a new listing. A registered office and the new number were given in the glossary at the back of the magazine.

As the publicity wheels spun into action, I kept looking at Reggie to see if I could discern any misgivings or the slightest betrayal of a loss of confidence. This was never apparent and I calmed down, knowing that he was already a winner. His photograph appeared in several papers. There was even a photograph published in one of the papers showing him leaving Elvira's house with Dorella Devene. Dorella had been so enchanted by her meeting with Reggie that she had been carried away and gushed to the press that Reggie was sure to be to modern design, what her cosmetics were to the modern woman. Yes, of course Reggie would be doing her refurbishment of the Bond Street Salon. Who else?

The last two weeks before leaving for France were frantic. Reggie was wholly involved in the initial designs for Elvira and scheduling out the works programme. Steven and Ray had handed in their resignations a few days after Reggie. "The management must love you," I murmured. A gay girlfriend of Peter's, Samantha – "don't call me mam, I'm Sam" – was being brilliant as the utmost in efficient secretaries. The boys adored her and she became a close friend and confidante within a few days of working with them. The base was Reggie's flat. As work progressed in Pimlico Road, more time was being spent there where possible. Martin, a freelance architect friend of Steven's, had joined the company and this saw the initial team formed. Whilst the answering service dealt with the new line, an ex-directory line to the office was in constant use among the staff and Reggie's telephone number at the flat was virtually unobtainable.

I had arranged with Reggie a time to meet me and look at the offices in New York. This was scheduled for late October.

"At this rate it looks as if the only time I will get to you is if I go on buying premises for you to furnish," I grumbled.

"Consider yourself privileged that you get me as well as discount," retorted Reggie with a grin.

I had not seen anybody so busy and so happy. Our relationship strengthened with all the pressures. Reggie and myself would not discuss the new business *ad infinitum*. If Reggie did want to talk about his company he would set aside a quarter of an hour of our time together. After that, it was us and he would not break into this pact if it were at all avoidable.

Peter and he had become firm friends and I was relieved. Tim had disappeared to Morocco and Peter avoided the subject about him so we did not question as to whether any news had been received from or about Tim.

Elvira sparkled with Reggie and she would coyly "borrow him" for an endless succession of galas and first nights.

Petrina seemed to have taken on a new lease of life as well. She was devoted to Reggie, and had appointed herself the new company's mascot. She was always at Fernshaw Road or in Pimlico and became a firm favourite of Sam's.

In what appeared to be minutes it was time to leave for the South of France. As Reggie had to be back in London every few days, we cancelled driving out to St Tropez and flew direct instead, hiring a car in Nice. Time was the ace factor and I was determined that he should have as much sea and sun as possible. The planned, leisurely drive through France would have to wait.

I collected Reggie from Pimlico en route to the airport. He had done his packing the night before and had set off for the site before I had even got up.

"See you later, slut!" he had called as he raced through the front door. Petrina had already gone to stay with Clare, though for a moment I had thought that Sam would win the day in her claim to look after the pug.

The shop front was gleaming with polished chrome and fresh paint, unusual for the Road. A well-placed bomb during the War had seen the reconstruction of a rather dull square concrete substitute. Reggie, with his modernistic chrome and glass front, had received no rebuffs when the necessary planning permission was applied for. He had created an effect similar to Tiffany's windows in New York. The main face to the window was in brushed chrome, with small picture-type frames looking into a series of room settings. As certain client's schemes were completed, an exact replica in miniature form of a stage would be put on display. It became a type of pilgrimage to go and view what Reginald Forbes had done for this or that celebrity or titled person.

The front of the shop housed a conversation area and reception desk with the switchboard. Behind this was the doorway to the inner sanctuary. "The slave quarters, darling," Reggie would say to a bemused visitor. "If you listen you hear the occasional scream – of delight, note – as another scheme of utmost originality is finalised!"

At Heathrow, Reggie completely relaxed. There was one moment when a photographer, arranged by the ever vigilant Peter, approached him and asked him to stand for a photograph prior to his leaving to meet his client in the South of France. "Don't they realise that I don't stand, I pose?" said Reggie, to an amused me, seconds later. "Are you prepared to tell us the client's name yet, Mr Forbes?" questioned the photographer. Reggie smiled his dazzling smile and shook his head.

"When I can," he promised. A few holidaymakers looked at him with curiosity while all the fuss was going on. Reggie preened. I made myself anonymous behind the *Herald Tribune*.

Chapter Seven

The South of France was idyllic. The villa, high in the hills west of Gassin behind St Tropez, proved to be the totally private getaway we had been looking for. We had three bedrooms, an enormous tiled sitting room and dining area, a vast kitchen and the most splendid terrace with a pool. The views were breathtaking. Rolling hills with pine and olive trees, huge bushes of oleander and the vivid greens of the vines, added to the enchantment. The weather was baking. Although I had vowed to avoid August in the South this was the only time that we could have actually managed. As it was, Reggie and I were determined to spend the majority of time up at the villa, travelling only to Gassin or nearby Ramatuel for provisions.

Jeannine, the wizened caretaker, appeared every second day. She seemed to have a passion for airing the beds, used or unused, and on the three days she was about, the flowering bushes around the building were festooned with Cardin drip dries. We lived on a diet of salads, fruit and barbecued local lamb and fish. Flagons of iced dry white local wines were consumed in vast quantities. Reggie spent a great deal of his time sunbathing or reading. He was most meticulous about working on his new projects for an hour or two each morning. As we were always up at sunrise, the 'homework' did not cut into his dedicated tanning programme. There were constant telephone calls to London and America, but basically it was a selfish togetherness and a much-needed break. We had arrived in Nice on the Thursday. Reggie's first scheduled return to check out Pimlico Road was for the following Wednesday. He would be in London until the Friday. I had several friends with villas in the area and so used this opportunity to arrange the obligatory dinner or beach luncheon.

We went down into St Tropez only once before Reggie returned to England. This was to dine with the friends of Sarah and Angus we had met in London. We had planned to meet on the quayside at one of the local bars, and then go on to a quayside restaurant for a late dinner.

We set off from the villa, loath to leave, soon after seven. Reggie had not yet seen the Byblos Hotel and so we were going there for a drink at first. It was also an ideal opportunity to park the car as the centre of the port had been sealed off, due to the usual congestion of summer pedestrians.

Reggie looked ravishing. Four days of blazing sun had turned his already spectacular tan into a deep rich gold. His blond hair was sun streaked and almost white in places. He was wearing a loose white coarse cotton shirt, intricately embroidered in white, matching trousers and white Gucci shoes. A simple gold chain with a medallion was hanging around his slender neck (this being a present from myself to celebrate our first three months together) and a white wristwatch with gold bracelet completed the summer picture. In contrast, I was in a deep blue silk shirt with white cotton trousers. The effect of the two of us together was fairly obvious. "No need to ask which one does the washing up," joked Reggie.

The Byblos was crowded. I ordered two large Negronis and joined Reggie on the terrace. He was deep in conversation with a young American couple. He looked up as I came over. "RA, meet Sy and Chuck. This is RA."

Sy was a typical American-type deb, very intense but also very pretty. Chuck looked like a typical Ivy-League jock 'on vacation'. Both were expensively dressed and determined to enjoy their stay in Europe. Reggie, with his typical lack of any inhibitions, had started talking to them whilst waiting for me to collect the drinks from the bar, as the terrace service looked as if it would take some time. He had captivated Sy but Chuck was studying him rather warily, 'probably ascertaining as to whether he is quite correct for the image,' I thought to myself.

We spent a pleasant half hour talking about the scenery, the weather, the food and how Bardot had ruined St Tropez due to her influencing hordes of tourists to visit the port, none of whom would have ever heard of it otherwise.

"It's like Liz Taylor and Porto Vallarta," surmised Sy. As neither she nor Chuck, nor Reggie for that matter, would have had any idea as to how badly the two places under discussion had changed with these unsuspecting sponsors, I left them gently arguing over the matter. I ambled back to the bar, ordered myself a refill, and then strolled again to the terrace to join the three.

Reggie looked around as I reappeared. "Oh, there you are," he exclaimed. "Good, I thought we had lost you for a moment." He went on to say what I knew was coming. "I've asked Sy and Chuck to walk down to the quayside with us and have another drink."

I looked at him for a moment, but then relaxed. Why not? Our host and hostess were destined to be fairly sobering for the evening and far better he ask the two of them now as opposed to ask them up to the villa. I was becoming crotchety and possessive.

I pulled myself together. "What a good idea. I am sure they will enjoy meeting the Smythe-Cunninghams."

Reggie looked at me and made a slight face, then laughed. He had been against the proposed dinner but as I had pointed out, they were great friends of Sarah's and Meg Smythe-Cunningham had a great many rich, bored friends who were definite client fodder!

The port was crowded with suntanned, excitable and happy holiday makers. The outfits and the posers were working at full tilt to outdo the other. Reggie was fascinated by the tableaux created by the stiff figures sitting on their yachts, obviously enjoying being peered at by the masses on the harbourside.

"They don't look as if they would begin to know how to enjoy themselves," he observed. "That must be an Australian yacht. Look at those gladioli in that hideous cut crystal!"

"Reggie!" A voice bellowed. I turned round. A giant of a man, with an enormous physique, squeezed into a pair of bright red trousers and literally bursting out of a bright pink shirt, was waving excitedly from a group of two very colourful young women and another man, almost his twin. Reggie followed my gaze.

"Joe," he shouted, "and Chris. How are you? The backbone to Designs Unlimited," he quickly explained to me. "The team, the builders."

Joe, Chris and the two women, whom I was introduced to as their wives, Viv and Pearl, came over towards us. I looked at Reggie. He was beaming broadly and genuinely pleased to see the four of them. He possibly fancies a big number like Joe, I thought to myself. Or Chris. I had to admit that they were spectacular examples of maleness in its prime. Joe was enormous with a boxer's beaten up face and towered above the pert and diminutive Viv. Chris was obviously the glamour boy of the twosome. "Don't you think he looks like a Ruin O'Neal?" Reggie commented afterwards back at the villa. Pearl obviously thought so as well. She clung to Chris's arm rather like a terrier holding on to a stick and kept gazing at him with total adoration.

Chuck and Sy were a bit taken aback at the jubilant group. Joe had given me a hearty handshake, saying he was pleased to meet Reggie's uncle. I gave Reggie a very old-fashioned look and made a mental note to mark that one down for the books. Chris shook hands warmly, his grip only slightly less vice-like. Viv and Pearl were "pleased to meet me", adding they were sure.

"A drink?" beamed Reggie, completely in command. Viv and Pearl had fallen for his charm and squeaking at how pleased they were to meet him after all they had heard about him. Not quite all, I said to myself, of that I was sure. Uncle indeed!

A silent Sy and Chuck suddenly decided that they should move on. They said how cute it had been talking to the two of us and with many wavings and smiles they set off along the harbour front.

Reggie's charm even succeeded in our getting a table for six at one of the crowded bars. I sat myself down between Joe and Pearl. Reggie was ensconced between the two young women who were now fingering his shirt and wanting to know who the designer was and where it had come from. Reggie remarked, "Palm Beach", much to their delight. It was, in fact, from an ethnic shop in the King's Road but Reggie had this unique style of giving his audience what they wanted, and they loved him for it. As Amanda had predicted, he was Mr Showmanship.

"Pearl, Viv, what would you like?" I questioned, aware of the jumpy waiter standing anxiously next to us. This question was received with a lot of "I dunnos" and looks to one another.

"Try a Negroni," I added, "you can have them either sweet or dry... they will certainly get you girls going," I concluded, with my best rakish grin.

"Oooh, sounds lovely," said Pearl, giggling. She fingered her hooped earrings. "You wouldn't be planning to lead us on, would you now? You do look like one of those bachelors gay."

Reggie snorted and turned his attention quickly to Joe. I looked up at the starry sky. "You, Joe?"

"I'll try one of them Brixton jobs," said Joe with a bellow. "Sweet." Chris and Viv and Pearl shrieked at this flash of wit.

"Yea, I'll give one a bash," followed on Chris. More shrieks. Reggie was sobbing with laughter himself and nodded his agreement with the order, "Though dry for me, please," he managed to gasp.

"Four sweet Negronis, large," I said, "and two dry, again large."

The drinks arrived and were tested with appreciative lip smackings. Joe insisted on ordering another round immediately. "Don't want to be kept waiting by these Froggies," he shouted. "Oi! Monsieur," he grinned at me. "Good bit 'a French that, eh?"

Pearl was telling me about the camp. She was very impressed with it all, but thought the swimming a bit unfair for the children as the beaches were so crowded. "And Tommy is such a devil with them topless women," she chortled. "His little eyes out on stalks, just like his dad."

"Wot's this about his dad's little stalk then?" demanded Chris grinning. "I 'aven't 'eard you complaining before, Pearl."

"Oooh, Chris! You are dreadful," shrieked Pearl, both she and Viv collapsing into their newly arrived Negronis.

Conversation went from decibel to decibel. More drinks arrived and Reggie and myself were continually doubling up with merriment. Joe and Chris were like Burns and Allen with their wisecracks and they never seemed to falter with their script.

Joe was becoming slightly melancholy with the fourth Negroni. He pointed at Reggie and said to me in a low, confiding voice. "That young guy is great. You mark my words RA, everybody will be talking about him within a year. He will be up there (jabbing at the sky) and me and my boys feel it a privilege to be in there with a winner."

Joe's comments were like music to me. The one thing that had been worrying me had been Reggie's rapport with his workmen. The English workmen, still the best in the world, irrespective of what anybody may say, would only give his best when he knew the person instructing him was as efficient in his knowledge of instruction as was the recipient. To have this praise, admiration and obvious loyalty from the salt of the earth like a Joe, was an accolade not easily earned.

Pearl looked at her wristwatch. "Oh Viv, we had better get back and see to the children." She turned to Joe and Chris. "Now don't you two have too many of those drinks, mind. You have to play rounders with the boys in the morning and I don't want you falling about like a couple of bears with sore heads." I looked at her. "Oh, we always do this," she explained. "Viv and I take the car back to the camp and leave them to get on with it. They can get a taxi later. Now don't you go chasing after one of those go-go dancers – topless I dare say – or you'll know all about it, Joe Knight," screeched Pearl.

"Yea, no kippers for breakfast," said Joe, with a mock sulk.

"Oh, you dirty bugger," breathed an indignant Viv, "and in front of strangers."

I collapsed. "I won't breathe a word to anyone," I smiled at a now giggling Viv. "In case the boys are not worthy of beach sports in the morning, why not bring the children up to the villa for a swim?" I could see Reggie's delight at my suggestion and I knew it would be both diplomatic and certainly fun.

With further shrieks and ribald comments, Viv and Pearl got themselves together and prepared to leave. I had gone so far as to suggest lunch and Joe and Chris had agreed to add to our already inflated stock of wine. A couple of crates of beer were also to be thrown in. "Bloody Frog beer tastes like camel piss!" grumbled Joe.

"I knew he was into odd things," screamed Pearl.

"Do you mind?" shrieked Viv.

"You obviously don't," shrilled Pearl. They all collapsed at this.

"Thank you again, RA," wheezed Viv. She looked at me and then at Reggie. "Oh, you do make such a lovely couple," she said with all sincerity. "Ooops," she pushed her hand into her mouth and looked decidedly sheepish.

"We'll have you as bridesmaids," quipped Reggie, unruffled. Further shrieks.

"They'd never manage the 'honour' job," bellowed Joe, to the still shaking two as they tottered across the cobbles.

We had one more drink with Joe and Chris before moving off to meet the Smythe-Cunninghams. On the walk to the bar at which we had planned to meet, Reggie asked. "What do you think?"

"They're marvellous, and they and yourself are very lucky having formed this new work team."

"They are marvellous, aren't they?" Reggie squeezed my arm. "Thank you, thank you, for being you, and thank you for inviting them up tomorrow. Can you imagine a set of miniature Joes, Chrises, Vivs and Pearls leaping about in the pool?"

"Sadly," I replied, "yes."

Dinner was a very sober affair in comparison to the festivities we had recently left. Our host and hostess were suffering from sunburn and were obviously put out that we were late in getting to the bar rendezvous. They also had been having an argument before we showed up. We were through much earlier than anticipated and, with relief, made our farewells. I attempted to compensate for the failure of the evening, by asking them to the villa for lunch on the Thursday that Reggie was in London. They accepted with alacrity and so I felt penance was being carried out and that the dinner disaster would be forgotten.

We were deep in conversation and moving across the front when we heard a now familiar bellow. I looked across at the bar we had vacated a few hours earlier. Joe and Chris were still sitting there, now visibly very drunk and causing some amusement to the surrounding observers. Joe had spotted us and was beckoning enthusiastically. I looked at Reggie.

"All right – one. Remember we will have to cope with their hangovers in the morning, as well as the long-suffering Viv and Pearl!"

They were delighted to see us. Joe was very drunk and becoming very amorous. He kept stroking Reggie's arm and saying how marvellous he was, meanwhile his eyes focusing every few minutes on the odd woman walking past.

"God, suppose he's basically a repressed queen," I said to myself with a laugh, "and Reggie is going to be responsible for bringing him out." I did not think I would be able to cope with this scene, nor Viv's reaction to Joe suddenly going overboard and chasing the boys. Joe's next move assured me that this concern was not for the immediate future. "Cor, get a look at that!" That, was a sinuous young blonde, with waist-long hair, in skin-tight pink stretch pants, high heel boots and a white silk shirt hanging open to her navel. Reams of chains adorned her neck and wrists, and she was sporting the most enormous pair of bronzed bosoms. Her sashaying slide along the harbour front was causing a great response. Cheers and whistles were coming from the drinkers and spectators on the front.

"It's that Brigitte Bardot," yelled Joe, his face red with excitement and glistening in the lantern light. He positively glowed with pure male animal magnetism. I could see Reggie had noticed this as well.

It was not Bardot, but a very good lookalike. The young woman's progress was audible from the whistles and calls as she continued on her self-assured way, calmly looking ahead, and disappearing from view.

"What a pair of tits!" breathed Joe. "Fancy getting your face between them. Reggie? Brrrrrrrrrr!" The latter noise was made by blowing through his large fleshy lips. I realised that the problem Viv would have later would not be Joe's turnabout, but Joe's overheating.

More drinks arrived. Chris was swaying in his chair and attempting to focus on Reggie, Joe and myself. His conversation had slurred to a halt. Joe had definitely got his second wind, obviously inspired by the Bardot lookalike, and was chatting animatedly with a highly intrigued Reggie. Joe glanced over at me and then over my shoulder. His smile broadened. "Reggie," he said, "get a load of that."

"That," was a frail young man making his equally swaying way in the wake of the earlier show-stopper.

I glanced quickly at Joe. The smile was still there, but it was not at all malicious. The man was really the total, genial, loving giant. He squeezed Reggie's arm. "Oi, monsieur."

The young man paused and looked over at Joe. He had already obviously noted our table out of the corner of his eye. His glance flickered over a slumped Chris who was grinning slackly; myself – a pause here – Reggie – he raised a well-formed eyebrow at Reggie – and settled again on Big Joe.

"Oui?"

There is nothing more queeny than a St Tropez queen and this young man was no exception. He was, perhaps, even the ultimate. He would have stood out in any of the established moneyed gay 'waterholes' whether on Key West, Ibiza or Mykonos.

He was in his early twenties, pencil slim and blonde. His tan was flawless, his hair long and silky and his mouth full and petulant. He was wearing full eye make-up which exaggerated a pair of enormous sapphire-coloured eyes (rather like you, on our first evening, I reminded Reggie later). He was drenched in gold diamonds and sapphires. His arms were adorned with bracelets and rings. A tie of gold chains with a diamond and sapphire clasp, was around his slim, bronzed waist. He was wearing a pair of white hipsters and his shirt, in white silk, was knotted across his chest. He had a pair of white thong sandals on his feet, and was carrying what could only be described as a white and gold evening bag.

He undulated slowly over to the table. Joe remained unfussed and smiling good-naturedly. Reggie had frozen and I was beginning to feel slightly uncomfortable. I simply hoped my illusions of Joe and Chris were not to be broken as I simply would not allow myself to sit there without defending the young man should they become unpleasant or verbally vicious. He was fascinating.

"Bonsoir," continued Joe. "Un drink?"

The young man knew a non-starter when he saw one. "Non, merci," he lisped, moving his head and turned to move on. Several people were looking at him totally fascinated.

"Monsieur," said Joe, not to be brushed aside, "I am sure you know where we can find some girls, birds, some oh la la." Chris practically fell out of his seat at this. The young man's eyes flashed and widened for a second. The people at the next door table tittered. He smiled sweetly at Joe, his expression in his eyes having hardened into one of lethal, cold and calculating fury.

"Oui Monsieur," he said. "La." The 'there' was accompanied by an elegant sweep of a beringed hand to a lighted doorway up the alley which was alongside the bar where we were sitting. He blew a kiss at Joe, gave a shake of his head and added in a heavy accented lisp, "You will enjoy eeet."

Joe looked a bit taken aback and was not quite sure as to who had won the round. The young man gave him another snake-like stare, smiled, spun round and continued on his sparkling way.

"Who was that?" said Reggie, to nobody in particular.

"Pity about the tits," barked Joe. More laughter from Chris who looked as if he was perhaps beginning to sober slightly. Joe was definitely heading for the winning stakes as to who would have the biggest hangover.

"It's how I imagine Elvira must have been," added Reggie, wickedly. It was my turn to laugh.

"No, even his bosoms were bigger than Elvira's," I continued, rather disloyally to Elvira.

This induced a shriek from Reggie.

"Okay. Let's go." This was from Chris, who had stood up. We all looked at him in surprise. "The club the skinny bird said." I jerked my head up in amazement and glanced at Reggie. He smiled a 'yes'. I was about to protest, but Joe was already on his feet with the light of battle in his eyes. He beckoned for the bill and handed over a mountain of notes. I only hoped that their business with Reggie was planned to cope with more evenings like this in the South of France.

Reggie knocked on the black painted door. A small shutter was opened and a mascaraed eye peered through. Reggie spoke to the eye and the door opened.

"Christ," breathed Joe.

Dolly Parton stood framed in the small doorway, or at least part of her anatomy did. A statuesque blonde Dolly Parton lookalike in a red sequinned dress with the most amazing cleavage and an enormous tumble of blonde hair, stood in front of us. "Welcome," she breathed, the front of her dress expanding with her intake of breath at Joe. "Oh, how big and spectacular you are, monsieur."

"You're not too bad yourself, miss," answered Joe. I could see him eyeing her cleavage. At any minute he would be sure to break into the famous "Bbbbrrrrrrrrrr!"

Reggie looked at me and gave me a wink. We were shown into a small, darkened bar area with a minuscule illuminated dance floor. A few other spectacular ladies eyed us from the shadows with momentary interest and then returned to their companions and their drinks.

Dolly Parton stood beaming down at us as we made ourselves comfortable on a purple velvet banquette. Chris had done a Petrina and promptly dozed off. Joe, now playing the suave ladykiller abroad, expansively ordered a bottle of champagne. I blinked. Joe had obviously not been abroad enough to realise what a rip-off joint these places could be. Background music had been filtering through a speaker when a popular disco beat suddenly bellowed through another, drowning the former. A few couples headed on to the floor in the dim light. Joe was tapping his foot with enthusiasm in time to the rhythm. A frail young man in black jacket and tight black trousers came over to us with an ice bucket and the champagne. He was heavily rouged and gave me a demure look as he struggled with the cork. There was a loud popping sound and a spray of champagne went over Chris, who remained dozing.

"Oh la la," said Joe, raising his glass.

Dolly waved from where she was standing. Joe waved back. "'Ave a glass darling," he bellowed above the throbbing music. He was obviously in for the kill. Dolly came over. Joe handed her the glass brought for Chris. She smiled and toasted the three of us and took a deep swallow. This was done in profile, for the benefit of Joe, and she was certainly spectacular.

"Dance, miss?" Joe asked, courteously, staggering to his feet. Dolly eyed the empty champagne bottle, clicked at the young man who was still looking at me, and pointed at the ice bucket. Dolly was no dodo when it came to business. She smiled at Joe and moved to the floor with him. I winced as I saw Joe's enormous hands go round her buttocks and pull her firmly to him. They swayed off into the dim recesses of the dance floor. Reggie was looking after them with a strange, fixed expression.

A few seconds later a heavily breathing, scarlet-faced Joe, staggered back and collapsed onto the banquette beside me. Reggie was stifling his laughter. "Everything all right, Joe?" I asked, mischievously.

"Christ, RA. No. That bird – she's fuckin' got an 'ard on."

Chris rolled on to the floor.

*

We returned to London a few days before the end of August. I had to be in Houston for the first week in September, but would be back for the official opening of Designs Unlimited on September the thirteenth, also my birthday. Reggie was determined about this for the opening date.

"All lucky dates for me have a three involved," he explained. "Furthermore, it's your birthday and it shows my business mind in having the opening and a party for you at the same time and so saving a fortune!"

The premises in Pimlico Road were splendid, very of today and very original. Reggie's team had managed admirably whilst he had been away with me, but I did point out that he had returned every four days so they were really not without total administration or guidance. I was determined that at no time was Reggie to feel he was dispensable. It was to be his business, he was the key figure and it was he the clients wanted. I gave Amanda as a parallel. She was the star and she had a brilliant cast. They were only as good as she was, but as I had said before, she also needed them to succeed. However, there always had to be a leader, no matter what other capabilities were about.

Reggie and I met at Wilton's for lunch on the first day of September, a few days after our return. This was another of my personal rituals I was introducing him to. September 1st, being the start of the oyster season, saw me religiously having my first dozen at Wilton's or at Scotts. Amanda disliked oysters intensely and so it was usually a solo affair as the 'ceremony' was brief and as light as possible. Amanda was the ideal luncheon companion as she was always going on to something, whether a fitting, rehearsal or a performance. Elvira and Sarah were the total contrasts. Elvira loved to sit and reminisce as did Sarah, and the whole afternoon would be lost. Reggie took only a short break as the letters of enquiry were now demanding action and I was on my way to the airport to get my transatlantic flight.

We lunched happily on our oysters, accompanied by an iced Chablis and followed by a creamy stilton. Elvira was sitting at a nearby table with a well-known political figure and gave a gracious wave to us when she saw us. She beckoned to Reggie who went over to their table. Reggie kissed Elvira fondly and I saw him shaking hands with her luncheon companion. They spoke for a few minutes and then he returned.

"Don't tell me, you're about to redo the Lords," I said.

"Maybe," said Reggie, and gave another look at Elvira's table.

"How is Elvira?" It occurred to me that since we had been back Reggie had been in daily contact with her, naturally discussing the proposals to the house; but I did know that she had asked him to escort her to a large Royal charity premiere whilst I was away and to the official dinner afterwards. I took it for granted that I would have been originally invited had I not been going to America. Now I was beginning to doubt it. Reggie was getting everywhere.

"Oh, fine, since her visit to St Tropez." We both laughed. "I wonder who that young man was?" went on Reggie, squeezing lemon juice onto an oyster. "He really was quite amazing."

"He obviously wasn't worrying about the rent," I said.

"No," sighed Reggie. "Some young men are so lucky at not having to slave for a living. I mean, when I contemplate what I have to cope with over the next few weeks, months... years! Mon dieu!"

"You mean me?"

"Yes, working to keep you, my darling," said Reggie. "I mean, if anybody is going to be giving diamonds in this relationship, it will be me!"

"Sad, but true," I agreed.

"Well, if that is the situation I had better get into practice." He felt in his hip pocket and pulled out a small case and placed this in front of me. "Here."

I looked at him. "What's this?"

"A bribe, to keep you on the straight and narrow." He smiled, "Go on, open it."

I looked down at the case and then back at him. There were tears in his eyes.

"Reggie?" I opened the case. A pair of gold and diamond links lay glistening on the velvet pad. "Reggie!"

"Do you like them?"

"Like them, they're beautiful... but!"

"No buts. They are a going-away present to make sure you come back. There are lots more in the offing..." he was crying. "Diamonds are, after all, meant to be forever as 'Sean the Brawn' would say..."

"Reggie, darling, don't. What on earth is the matter?" I was aware of Elvira looking across at us with her imperious stare. She was not blinking which was a sure sign that we were being given her utmost concentration.

"Oh, it's simply that I'm already missing you even though you are still here. Stupid, isn't it? I mean, here I am, perhaps one of the luckiest people alive and I'm snivelling away instead of appreciating it all."

I took his hand across the table. Elvira looked as if she had been stung. "Don't, dear, dear Reggie," I whispered, "please don't. I'll always be here and I will call you tonight or tomorrow, or whatever, as soon as I get to New York. You have so much to do and even though I will not be here in person I will be here, you must know that!"

He nodded.

"Thank you for the links, my darling." I looked at him. "They are almost as beautiful as you are."

"You mean, there is even an almost?" Reggie was looking at me in mock indignation. I sat back in relief and smiled. But I had been shaken by the scene.

For all his show and veneer, Reggie was still one very vulnerable young man.

Elvira had gone back to blinking at her distinguished-looking companion. We ordered coffee and Reggie lit a cigarette. We reminisced again over the recent days in the South of France and in particular the evening with Big Joe and Chris.

"I still cannot believe Joe didn't appreciate the fact that we were being set up by that bedecked queen, and sent to a transvestite or drag club," mused Reggie, going off again into peals of laughter. "His final two expressions that evening, one with Dolly's aroused passion, and two, the bill for the two bottles of champagne, were hysterical. No wonder they are prepared to do overtime for Elvira. She's to be photographed in the revamped drawing room in two weeks' time, by the way, so it's all stops out."

I called for the bill as I had to leave. We were passing Elvira's table when she called out. "Darlings." We went over to where the two were sitting. Elvira was sipping a glass of champagne and her companion was nursing a large cognac. "RA, how well you look. You know James, don't you?" I shook my head. "Oh, James Young, Robin Anderson. Do join us for a drink, darlings?" she smiled.

"Elvira, that is very kind of you but I cannot stay, I'm afraid. I literally am on my way to Houston."

"Dear RA." Elvira blinked at James Young. "He's so high powered and never out of a plane." James Young did not seem at all impressed at this comment and was looking at Reggie. I remembered who he was. Sir James Young, eccentric multi-millionaire, landowner and part-time politician. There were rumours of his Humbert Humbert pursuits, or penchant for nubile pubescents in their Lolita stage, but none of this had ever come to light.

"You'll join us, dear Reggie," tinkled Elvira, "I won't tell, I promise, that you are playing truant on my project."

"Cow," I said to myself. I had warned Reggie. Once these people employed you they really did demand one's balls for breakfast. Reggie gave one of his most dazzling smiles and sat down on a chair a waiter had hurriedly brought forward. I murmured a few pleasantries, said goodbye again, gave Reggie a last, long look, and left.

Chapter Eight

New York, the world's most exciting city. I never failed to feel that incredible surge of adrenaline pulsating through me as I crossed over the East River in some scabrous yellow cab and viewed that skyline. Today it is referred to as 'The Big Apple'. I still call it – and always will – 'The Big Amyl'. It is the ultimate of drugs and once you are hooked you can never break the habit.

My flight brought me into Kennedy early evening local time. As I simply had carry-on baggage I was through Customs and Immigration and in a cab within a matter of about half an hour. In spite of the lateness of the afternoon I was told by the large black lady at Immigration "to have a nice day and stay" and set forth determined to do just this.

Clare had made my usual reservation at The Pierre on Fifth Avenue. I checked in, went up to my room on the sixteenth floor, tipped the freckled, cheeky young bellhop with a five dollar bill, received a broad grin and a wink with the "thank you, sir", removed my jacket and tie, unpacked, and settled down with a drink brought promptly by another cheeky young man from room service. At this rate I would be going through a fortune in dollar bills! I dialled London. My watch said eight o'clock which meant it would be one a.m. the following morning, London time. There was no reply.

Although disappointed, I was not too concerned. Reggie was more than likely to be out to a late dinner, or somewhere having a nightcap, and so having let the telephone ring for a few seconds longer, I hung up. I tried also the Fulham number but again there was no reply.

There were several messages waiting for me. I was meeting a long-standing friend for a late dinner at Lutece and one of the messages was the confirmation to this engagement. Kurt and his wife, Carla, were at some gallery opening and were expecting me to meet them at nine thirty. Kurt had left a message with the address and details of the showing they were off to beforehand, in case I had the time to join them there, as opposed to the restaurant later. Kurt Rushmore – originally Rubilanski – PR, was the impressive coordinator with the various sales promotions and a major factor in the Houston deal. He was typical of the Bronx Jewish boy who had made good. Large, hawk-nosed, aggressive and ruthless, he was a great charmer and had in the past fancied himself as a bit of a ladykiller. He had met Carla on a trip to Europe several years before and the diminutive blonde Hungarian had totally won him over. He had been in Paris on business, and after a particularly depressing day – he found the French attitude to his American aggressiveness, plus the language factor, dispiriting – he was sitting in the Cambon Bar at the Ritz feeling slightly at a loss and alone. Carla had swept into the bar to meet a girlfriend for cocktails. She had set herself upon one of the banquettes and checked her face briefly from a bejewelled compact. She was obviously well known, as a champagne cocktail was served immediately. There was a brief exchange between the barman and herself which was carried out with a great deal of smiling and crystals of merry laughter from Carla. Kurt was riveted. He said afterwards that he only thought such goddesses existed in racy novels or Ross Hunter type films. Unlike the stylish Fifth Avenue American equivalent, she was petite, beautifully groomed in a couturier suit, a small beaded cocktail hat and a selection of jewels that would have been the envy of any jeweller's boutique in the immediate Place Vendome. Her elfin face was framed by a soft sweep of blonde hair and she sat poised, a cigarette holder in her gloved hand, smoking– to Kurt's added fascination – a cheroot.

She had sat there in silence, quietly reflected in the dim smoky mirrors, occasionally glancing at the bejewelled watch on her diminutive, gloved wrist. Kurt was to say later that she looked like a Dresden doll "one was terrified that if one spoke above a courtly whisper, she would break." Being Kurt and used to bulldozing his way into any deal and through life in general, he noticed her glass was empty and summoned the waiter over. He had asked the waiter to offer the elegant woman a drink. The waiter had looked at him askance, shrugged and went over to Carla. He leaned forward and spoke to her, gesturing discreetly at the corner where Kurt was seated. Carla turned and looked slowly towards him. Her large amber eyes had appeared slightly amused. She blew out a long cloud of smoke and murmured something to the waiter. The waiter looked at her, surprised, and returned to where Kurt was shifting uncomfortably on the plush upholstery.

"Madame is delighted with your offer and suggests that perhaps you would care to join her."

Kurt was flattered and delighted, but there had been second thoughts when he saw her amused glance whilst the waiter was repeating his request to her. That she had accepted his invitation led Kurt to hastily assume that she was some high class pick-up and he was not prepared for this. Although relaxed on his own home ground and knowing how to deal with the 'average New York hooker' as he so delicately put it, he was intimidated by the style and poise of a Carla. He buttoned the front of his Saks suit and moved in a lumbering fashion over to her. To add insult to injury, he knocked over a small brass table and a plate of hors-d'oeuvres spilled onto the deep pile carpet. He was now beet red, particularly as the minor mishap saw her give way to more merry laughter.

"Monsieur," she said, in slightly accented English, "that is always happening but they will not change the tables, perhaps it keeps the barman amused, no?"

Kurt mumbled something about the barman and her both being amused, and held out his large hand. She took it lightly in her gloved one. "Pleased to meet you mam, my name is Kurt Rushmore, and I am from New York."

"Enchanted, Monsieur Rushmore. And how kind of you to offer me a drink. My name is Carla Des Moines." She sat smiling at Kurt who was standing, feeling more foolish and embarrassed.

"I think I may have made a mistake. No hard feelings, mam, but I thought you were somebody else," he ended lamely.

"Oh, how sad I am not the lucky woman," continued Carla, playfully. "I would have enjoyed a drink with you."

Kurt was now totally perplexed. He had offered her a drink, got cold feet and now could appear even more foolish and reoffer a cocktail or else politely leave. He decided to leave, apologising once again, turning purple with his increasing embarrassment. As he was making for the exit a striking Carla lookalike appeared in the doorway. She ignored Kurt's stare and peered into the bar. Spotting Carla she gave a wave and a smile and moved over to her. Carla stood up smiling. The two women kissed each other on the cheek and sat down and became immediately immersed in a lively and spirited conversation. The barman swept down upon them with Carla's refreshed drink and a similar glass for her companion. Kurt cursed himself and spun round quickly to leave. He knocked heavily into a couple who were arriving. The woman gave a yelp and dropped her handbag as Kurt stood heavily on her foot. He began to apologise profusely once more, glancing back into the bar to see if Carla had noticed the incident. She had, and was saying something to her friend and again there was that laugh. She caught Kurt's glance and waved. He hastily left.

The story went on to take a turn as only Kurt could arrange. He had gone onto a solo dinner and as the evening progressed he became more and more obsessed by the woman he had seen in the bar. Even a visit to The Crazy Horse Saloon could not get his mind off her. He returned to his hotel and spent a sleepless night thinking of her, her poise, her looks and continually hearing her laugh. He was scheduled to leave Paris the next day, but cancelled his flight back to New York. He spent the whole of the following evening sitting in the Cambon Bar hoping to see her again, and the next. He realised that his chances were one in a million of meeting her again. He had looked for the familiar barman the first night after the incident, but he had not been on duty. He was also off the second night of Kurt's waiting. He had hoped to ask the man who she was, and if he knew where she could be found, but he realised that this would be the height of indiscretion and doubtless the barman would not be willing to divulge the information should he know, no matter how many francs were surreptitiously offered. They were, after all, part of the Paris Ritz and would Monsieur really expect them to give away any information on one of their regular guests?

Kurt had made his depressed way to the airport and checked in on the Air France flight. He had a few drinks in the departure lounge and made his way through to the aircraft when the flight was called.

He was greeted by a starlet-styled Air France hostess and shown through to the first class section. The seat alongside him was still empty but the cabin was filling rapidly. He ordered a Scotch on the rocks from the uniformed steward and settled down to read a lurid paperback he had been trying to concentrate on over the past twenty-four hours. A figure appeared with the hostess and was ushered into the seat next to him. He paid no attention to the woman as she busied herself settling into her seat. He merely muttered a gruff "good evening" and went on staring at his novel. The last thing he needed was to have a chatting woman next to him for the next seven hours.

A glass of champagne arrived and was placed on the pull-down table in front of her. A voice said, "What a good thing, monsieur, that the champagne is by courtesy of Air France or I may have missed out on my drink once again."

Kurt choked on his Scotch. "Mr Rushmore," the accented voice continued. "How nice to be seated next to someone one has met before. It makes the flight so much more entertaining don't you think?"

Of course it was Carla, and it was one of those extraordinary coincidences that do occur. She was on her way to New York as a representative of the jewellery organisation she was involved with. By the time they reached New York Kurt was completely besotted. He saw her every possible moment in the city and proposed to her within four days. To his surprise – and also to Carla's – she accepted. They had been wholly involved with each other ever since. I had been in the city and, with Kurt's secretary, was witness to their wedding at City Hall. Carla had brought a touch of glamour even to this most dismal of buildings, and received a rousing cheer from an old derelict as we left the main steps to climb into our waiting limousine. Carla had stepped back on to the pavement and blown a kiss at the old drunk. He had given her a courteous, old-fashioned bow. Her spontaneous gesture was pure Amanda and when I finally did introduce them to each other, they had become firm friends.

*

I was looking forward to my evening with Carla and Kurt. I poured myself a second drink – this time from the duty-free bottle I had brought – and made several more calls. I organised the valet service to collect my suit for pressing, had a shower and put on my dinner jacket, checked the image of the typical Englishman abroad, approved of what I saw reflected back to me and set off with a jaunty whistle. I was forty-two, successful, groomed, good-looking and in love. What more did I require to face an evening in New York?

Dinner was an elegant and amusing affair. Carla and Kurt were full of enthusiasm about the Houston deal. Carla was now acting as a liaison officer for Kurt and I had to admit that they were a prime example of a husband and wife being able to work totally together.

I went back to their apartment on Fifth Avenue, a few blocks up from The Pierre, and sat mulling over a glass of brandy. I longed for them to know about Reggie, but I did not know how well Kurt would have taken such a confession, even though so long a friend and of such good standing. I was sure that there would be no problem with Carla. Her sophisticated European upbringing allowed her to accept the majority of happenings without undue concern or dismay. I had never brought my private life to the fore with the two of them. They knew of my disastrous marriage and had heard of my close association with Amanda, and I had left it at that. I looked at Carla seated on the elegant sofa in front of the burning fire. Kurt was sprawled next to her, his beefy hand over hers. Carla caught my gaze and smiled. I decided that when Amanda was here for her show I would ask her to talk to Carla and explain Reggie and me. I would do so myself if there was a chance that I could get Carla on her own. I wanted him so much at that very moment to be there sharing such contentment and happiness as I was feeling. I finished my brandy and got up to leave.

"I'll be at the office at ten o'clock," I said to Kurt at the door. I kissed Carla who was standing next to him. "Thank you for a lovely evening and it was marvellous seeing the two of you again."

I walked slowly back to the hotel. The skyline above the Plaza end of the park was still ablaze with those endless lights which makes one sure that the city never sleeps. A cruising cab slowed down alongside me but I waved it on. I was totally at peace with the world. I took a decision then and there to call Carla before I met Kurt at the office and see if she could manage a quick lunchtime drink. I would then tell her about us. I was flying on to Houston in the afternoon, but felt I owed it to Reggie to do this. He was part of my life and would continue to be. Friends would have to accept him or else their status as friends would be questionable. I was humming to myself as I arrived at the hotel.

The telephone was ringing as I got into the room. It was slightly after two o'clock. I picked up the receiver.

"Robin."

"Reggie! I was thinking about you."

"Filthy thoughts, I trust!"

"Of course, everything all right?"

"Absolutely. Did you call last night – or at least, when you arrived there?"

"Yes, but you weren't in at either numbers. Where are you now, by the way?"

"Ennismore, as you know how neurotic Petra becomes if she feels she's being ignored."

"Rather like her owner."

"Nonsense, I tried you earlier but you were still out. No doubt you've just staggered in from The Trucks or some sordid dive."

Reggie's knowledge of the sleaze side of places he had not even visited never failed to intrigue me.

"Well, unless The Trucks has had a total refurbishment, no. How was Elvira after I left?"

"Charming. She is very excited about the plans for Wilton Crescent. She's going around telling everybody I see her in a Vermeer-inspired environment – soft yellows and blue. James Young is quite a dish, isn't he?"

"If you say so. You're a bit too old for him and the wrong sex, I'm afraid. He's into giggling young girls."

"So?" This with a giggle.

"You obviously didn't hear the word 'old'."

We chatted on for several minutes. He had been out with Steven and Ray and had been fairly late getting in. I lightly described the evening at Lutece. "Oh, and tell Amanda she's splashed all over Broadway – there's an illumination of her that almost rivals the Chrysler building in height!" After a few more minutes of conversation I rang off, ending by saying I would call him from Houston the next evening. I slipped out of my clothes and collapsed into the vast Empire styled bed. In a few minutes I was asleep.

Carla was most apologetic when I called her, but there was no chance of her seeing me before I left that afternoon. "Is there anything wrong?" she had questioned.

"No, nothing wrong. It is simply that there is something I would like to discuss with you."

"Look, RA, I'll see if I can switch my noon appointment..."

"No, darling," I cut in, "I'll be back in town next week and we can go through it all then. Besides, I would like to show you off and give you a glamorous, long lunch somewhere."

She laughed. "You are such a flatterer! If only Kurt had some of that subtle English charm."

"I'll call you from Houston," I promised.

"I do look forward to that, dear RA. And you promise that whatever you wish to discuss with me can wait?"

"MmMm."

"Good. Safe flight then and give my love to Monica. Also, to Bindi. You should get on like a couple of those proverbial houses!"

Chapter Nine

Houston was hot and windy. I was thankful for the almost over enthusiastic air-conditioning one was subjected to everywhere. I had visited the city on several occasions and much preferred it to its sister city, Dallas. At least the people of Houston did not seem to house the deep guilt of a popular president's assassination as did those inhabitants of their rival.

My hotel, The Warwick, was comfortable and I was settled in without any delay. My schedule was busy with only the Saturday and Sunday clear. I telephoned Monica Du Barry, the chairman of the Antiques Fair and a legendary figure in Houston's matriarch society. I had already spoken to her from New York. Monica and I had met ostensibly through Kurt and Carla. It had been Carla who had been the instigator of the Houston deal and she and Kurt had been adamant when Monica and her team had first broached the topic that I should be responsible for the handling of the European side.

I had introduced the idea to business associated in France, Italy and Spain, and their enthusiasm and response to the Fair had been greater than any of us had anticipated. From its original concept as simply a fair for the sale of antiques, the idea blossomed into a collection of loaned treasures from private and public collections going on display; as well as items for sale by auction and a series of lectures by top authorities in various fields of furniture and fine art. I had found wonderful cooperation from my West End sources and lecturers from several museums had offered their services. The Fair was scheduled to open the following Tuesday, with an address by the First Lady. I had the Monday, and, if necessary, the weekend, to check my side to the deal and in particular to finalise the auction of paintings I had sent over.

Monica had planned a grand soirée at her ante-bellum styled mansion in fashionable River Oaks for the Monday evening. She was flying in two orchestras for the occasion, one from New York and one from the West Coast. The vast gardens were to be sprinkled with marquees – air-conditioned – and a vast seated dinner for two hundred guests had been arranged. There were two dance floors, one a floating floor on the private lake, plus a special theatre with tiered seating for the spectacular midnight cabaret. We had been told that Streisland could be appearing, but in any case there were Ike and Tina Turner, Dinah Shore and a host of other stars. The Olympic-sized swimming pool was to be strewn with sprays of orchids and there were to be two crystal fountains gushing with champagne. A firework display was planned for the early hours on the Tuesday, the day of the Fair, followed by a spectacular champagne breakfast comprising of baked oysters, eggs and truffles, baked hams and hot corn biscuits.

I had driven out to Monica's for dinner the night I arrived. I expressed my admiration at her brilliant organising. "Let's say it has quite a lot to do with my late husband's organisation of oil wells," she drawled.

Monica was of Sarah's ilk. She had been a Goldwyn girl when she had been noticed by the small, dapper Hank Du Barry when he was on a business trip to Los Angeles. "What he lacked in size he was determined to make up for in dollars," Monica would continue when the hour was late and she had consumed a fair deal of Amaretto. "And honey, he had to make a lot of dollars!"

For all her comments, she had been steadfastly devoted to Hank. He had gradually created the empire of his dreams and she had given him the glamour, plus the eventual social accolades he had so desired. She had become one of the *grande dames* of Houston, and with her theatrical flair and her statuesque looks, plus her amazing warmth and humour, she was much loved and admired. When Hank had died she had shut herself in the vast mansion for a month, and had then emerged like a brilliant butterfly from its dull cocoon. "Hank and I promised each other a month of mourning either way, on the condition that after a month to the day, it would be party time for me – his Mighty Monica – or for my little Hank!" They had no children but their love and devotion for each other was a lesson to us all. Nobody quite realised the effort it must have cost Monica to carry out Hank's last wish. She missed him with an intensity that would be quite frightening at times, but she never allowed her emotions to come to the fore. Carla always said that had Monica died, Hank would never have been able to keep his side of the promise. He would have simply pined away for the woman he had so loved.

Monica's other guests had included a brilliant young lawyer and his wife. They were true Texans – tall, healthy and very glamorous. They were also highly amusing and I was enchanted by the two. Monica's closest friend, a bird-like woman named Angela, (a Clare lookalike but a Clare in Designer labels, champagne-coloured hair and a Fort Knox approach to any bauble she chose to wear) was also present. Her relationship with Monica was very close and they were very entertaining together. Angela and Monica disagreed on anything the other said.

Finally there was Bindi, the mysterious figure Carla had asked me to give her love to. One could quite see why. Bindi must have been about my age and was considered by Monica and Angela as 'the most handsome man in Texas, vastly rich and a bachelor to boot.'

This description had led me to the understanding that Bindi would possibly be gay. Perhaps Carla was giving me the welcome message I needed, that she had always understood about myself, and Bindi would be the key to this! Bindi was tall, at least six feet four, broad, tanned and a double for Clark Cable. He was so male and so American Mr Big that I was convinced that nobody could be this macho and mean it seriously. The baritone voice, charm, manners and style, were obviously devastating to the ladies. Even the massive Monica became coy and skittish and the diminutive Angela was reduced to a vaporous squeak.

"Probably as passive as a chiffon pie in the sack," I said to myself, quoting an expression I had heard in a San Francisco gay dive. "Just as well young Reggie isn't here." That was a sobering thought!

Dinner was light-hearted and relaxed. The Fair was enthusiastically discussed. Bindi had already been given a preview of the paintings I was hoping to sell. "I would appreciate it," he said, "if you wouldn't mind coming out to the ranch (of course he would have a ranch and no doubt a custom limo with gold steer's horns on the front) and advising me as to whether you think some would go."

Monica thought this a splendid idea. "Bindi has the most marvellous house," she exclaimed, "but his decorator just does not seem to finish it off properly. What it needs is a woman's touch."

"I'll see what I can do," I said drily.

Angela shrieked. Monica bellowed. "Oh, that English wit," she said.

Bindi just sat and smiled being Big Mr Butch. "Aren't my two favourite girls the best?" he drawled at me. More noise from the two. The young Texans joined in the laughter.

"Perhaps we should share them, RA?" continued Bindi, obviously enjoying himself. He produced a coin. "Heads for me. Tails for you?"

I gave him a hard look at his emphasis on the 'tails'. I was convinced I was right. Perhaps he fancied me. The picture of myself humping away on the vast passive form of Bindi caused a snort.

"You wouldn't laugh if you won me," Monica guffawed.

"Hank managed!" screamed Angela, now very pink and well away on her crème de menthe. "We heard that every time you made a century he bought another oil well... and you have hundreds."

The leader of Houston society collapsed. "Angela," she gasped, tears rolling down her cheeks, "and you ain't even got a wishing well!"

More shrieks and screams. I was laughing loudly too, one simply could not help but adore Monica and her sidekick. Even Big Bindi laughed, a rumble of thunder seemingly to burst out of him.

The evening continued in this vein. After a slight calm had been re-established Monica turned to me on her right and clutched my arm. "What are you up to over the weekend? We haven't planned anything for you as you may have wanted a bit of time to yourself."

"Well, there is the hope that he can view the ranch," interrupted Bindi. "Why not all of ya come over for a barbecue luncheon on Sunday?"

Monica thought this a marvellous idea. Angela squeaked in agreement. The two young Texans, who seemed to have contributed a fair share of fun to the evening, plus their looks and laughter, also agreed to come along.

"Good," said Bindi, "and I'll ask a few other folk as well to meet RA."

"That is very kind," I said, "and I would like to see if I can help with advising you on some paintings."

"Will you be able to look after yourself tomorrow?" queried Bindi. I was fascinated.

"Well, I had thought of a quick trip to the Keys, but that is not on now you are planning the barbecue. Property!" I added. "I have been fascinated by the thought of buying one of those conch houses on Key West, but have never had a chance to consider it seriously." I looked at Monica. "With all the business I seem to be doing in the States I feel the money should be invested in something here. Naturally I'll eventually get something in New York, but the Keys are a definite possibility and also a sound investment. I believe I wouldn't consider anything close to New York and the Florida sunshine is only a few hours away from the city."

We discussed Key West and the Keys. Monica had been there on several fishing expeditions with Hank.

"It's a divine island," she surmised, "and now is a very good time to buy. They are planning regular scheduled flights early next year, but at the moment there is an adequate air strip and a daily hopper from Miami. You can also drive along that nerve-racking causeway," she added, "as long as not too many roadies are in evidence." She laughed and was joined by Bindi. I mistook the term 'roadies' for a type of motorcycling police force patrolling the causeway, but Bindi put me right. Roadies were drinks one had in the car travelling down. They were usually served in plastic mugs and there were even special mugs made with a spout so that, should the ride become rough, none of the roadie was risked being spilled.

"Right," I said. The idea of Bindi and a rough ride seemed ideally suited. "What a pity you can't get to the Keys," mused Monica. "Maybe if you did get a house there we could all then come and stay."

"But why not get there?" interrupted Bindi. "Key West is only a few hours away. If we went early in the morning we could be back tomorrow evening. We could even stay overnight and safely be back in time for the barbecue on Sunday."

"I couldn't possibly go," said Monica. "It sounds divine but I have too many last minute things here with Monday's party. The decorators and caterers are arriving as from tomorrow, and even leaving them on the Sunday will be a luxury. And that goes for you too!" she turned to Angela. "You are needed here." She looked at Bindi and myself, the laughing Texans forgotten. "You two go along," she instructed. "It'll do you good."

I argued that I would be required to finalise the pictures for viewing prior to the auction.

"Nonsense," Monica continued. "That woman you sent out here has done wonders and all you will have to do on Monday is congratulate her on how clever she's been and then collect all the credit – and the cash!" Shrieks again.

"Bindi knows one or two of the agents in Miami and he can call them first thing and see if there are any leads. Bindi?" Monica turned back to him from me. "Keith whatsisname! The writer's friend who house-sits down there? He should be there. Give him a call? Yes, now he is probably the best answer as he would know private individuals wanting to sell." She poured another large Amaretto for herself and gestured to us to help ourselves. "Anyway, he's always fancied you, Bindi, so you may even get RA a discount."

This was a revelation. I looked at Monica. Having only met her once before, I had never thought of her being involved or aware of the gay scene. But now, it was all so obvious. An ex-showgirl, the midget, adoring millionaire and no children. Of course, Hank had doubtless been gay and had married this understanding woman in Tinsel Town. He had returned with the gilded Amazon and a Goldwyn Girl no less, set her up in the grandest mansion in town and they had lived happily ever after, each going their own way. It also explained Angela – I was dining with the local gay girls *en masse*!

Bindi laughed. "And why not!" He smiled at me, even the teeth were whiter than white and larger than life. "Are you on?"

More conversation about the prospects of a property on Key West followed. Bindi went off to telephone Keith Whatsisname – "How can I look him up in your address book if I don't know his name?" reasoned Bindi, standing up.

"Don't be ridiculous," Monica had retorted, "I don't know his name either, so he is listed under the Ws, under Whatsisname."

"Will we get a flight there and back?" I questioned, being too attuned to the hazards of trying to travel about Europe on a whim.

"Oh, Bindi will fly you. He has his own jet." I should have known. Conversation then followed about the Keys, with Monica's enthusiasm growing.

Bindi came back into the room. It was all arranged. Keith had been ecstatic to hear from him and even more ecstatic when Bindi announced that he would be flying down in the morning with a friend from London. Yes, Keith did know of several locals who had houses they may consider selling and he would be delighted to show us round. He, Keith, had insisted that Bindi and I stopover for the evening and he would organise a dinner. He would also make reservations for us at the Pier House Hotel.

I did not know what I was getting myself into.

All was happening so quickly but, I added as a sobering thought, I was in America and I was deep in the heart of Texas.

I was prepared to finalise further plans and arrange to meet Bindi in the morning, but he would not hear of this. "I'll follow you back to the hotel," he said, "and you pick up what you'll need for the night there. It will be warmer than here and Key West is very informal. You can stay over at the ranch tonight and we can leave at first light. The landing strip is only a mile from the house and we will be at the Key West in time for lunch."

He went back to the next room to telephone instructions for the early morning start to his pilot. There was obviously no argument against all this and so I agreed to all the arrangements. Following Bindi's Corniche - with horns - back into Houston proper, I was amused by the swing of the whole evening. Apart from the one comment about Keith, nothing more had been said that could be interpreted as being specifically gay, but I was much more relaxed about my Houston stay. I could not wait to speak to Reggie and after parking my car, I dashed up to my suite. Bindi had settled himself down in the bar and was nursing a large bourbon on the rocks.

"Reggie! Good evening, darling."

"Hi, how is the hit of Houston?"

"The Hit!" I went on to explain about the evening, about Monica and Angela and to describe Bindi and our planned spree to Key West. Reggie and myself had talked about the island on several occasions and it was Reggie who had first sowed the seed of the idea of a house there.

"It really does sound as if it is all Bigger and Better in Texas."

"It may be bigger but it isn't better," I assured him. "I don't think I'd trust you to set eyes on Bindi, though," I added. "I'd hate to be proved wrong."

We carried on talking. I gave Reggie some more news but was more interested in his London news. Reggie was highly excited about the business. Elvira was delighted with the way the decorations were progressing, Amanda too was happy and the business enquiries were rolling in. Several people had been on the telephone to see if they could come to the opening, and Reggie had even been approached by one of the television channels for coverage of the opening for late night news programme. This was Peter again, claimed Reggie, but I was beginning to realise that the name Reginald Forbes was already pulling them in. People were sitting up and taking notice independently. Reggie added to my assumption. "Three press mentions since you left. You've married a star!"

Reggie was also very taken up by the prospect of a house on Key West. "I can see Texas is doing great things for you," he teased. "In normal circumstances it possibly would have been a Tiffany hamlet, but now a Casa on the Keys – much better." Laughing, I rang off.

I rejoined Bindi who was happily talking to the waitress and on to his second bourbon.

"Sorry I was so long," I apologised, "but I had to call London."

*

I did not know what to expect by Bindi's ranch, but I was pleasantly surprised, and quietly impressed with the style of the establishment. After a half hour journey, driven in silence except for a flamenco tape playing a bit too loudly for my taste, he swung the Corniche off the empty freeway, through a pair of stone columns and proceeded along a gravelled drive broodingly guarded by sets of massive, dark trees. The house, a few minutes down the arrow-straight drive, appeared as a fairly low, heavily balconied two storey stone building, with an additional floor in the centre. The main front of the house was floodlit and geometrically placed flower beds with neatly clipped box hedges, gave one the impression of suddenly stumbling across a miniature Versailles in the middle of nowhere. The beds were partly illuminated and I could make out an enormous stone fountain in the centre of the forecourt. A pair of lanterns with burning gas jets added a further theatrical effect to the whole scene.

As we stopped at the base of the steps leading up to a pair of gigantic doors, one of these slowly opened to reveal a uniformed black manservant who stood smiling a welcome at us, despite the lateness of the hour. Bindi pulled my case from off the back seat and pointed gallantly towards the broad steps and the open door. "After you, RA."

"Good evening, sah." This was from the elderly manservant to me.

"Good evening."

"Mr Anderson can have the Blue Room, Max," said Bindi, close on my heels. He handed the case to Max. "A nightcap, RA? There is a bar in your room, though, if you want to go up immediately. Max will call you at five."

I was looking around at the hall in which we were standing. "Any preference for breakfast?" asked Bindi. "I usually have coffee, eggs and a steak, plus fruit."

"I'll join you. Why not, when in Rome..."

Max confirmed breakfast would be served in the Red Room at five thirty. He informed Bindi that we were being collected by the pilot at ten to six and would be flying at six o'clock. Bindi thanked him and walked over to me. "Now you see why I need your paintings," he said.

The hall was massive, and went up to the full height of the second floor I had noticed from the drive.

Two staircases, in white marble with elaborate balustradings in gilded iron and polished wood handrails, curved graciously to the first floor balcony. This ran the total perimeter of the circular hall. A second balcony matched the first and the whole hall was topped by an enormous glass dome. A gigantic crystal chandelier which could have weighed at least half a ton, hung in sparkling splendour to the level of the first floor balcony. Endless polished wooden doors, set in marble architraves, led off from the balconies to the various suites including, no doubt, the Blue Room. The walls were adorned with plaster mouldings and the whole finished in a fine ivory and gold drag effect. Even the skirtings had been fashioned out of marble and curved to the form of the wall. The basic finishes alone must have cost a fortune. The stairs were carpeted in a beautifully designed V'soske, in pale ivories, blues and golds. The silk drapes to the long windows were in gold, edged with ivory and blue fringings, with the swags finished in the same colours. Long mirrored shutters were closed across the windows for the night. Groups of gilt chairs and mirrored art deco style tables with blue, ivory and gold Tiffany lamps, added to the amazing effect of it all. A further fountain, as large as the one outside but this one in white marble, played in the centre of the hall, directly below the enormous chandelier. Instead of water around the base, there were myriads of ivory, gold and turquoise orchids.

He was quite serious and I had to agree, for all its perfection the walls boasted not one painting. "The decorator claimed the plaster mouldings and the competition from the windows and especially the chandelier, were enough," continued Bindi, "but I feel it needs cosying up. Some of those Victorian ladies in blue silk dresses and your very effective frames would be the answer I feel." I agreed, my mind working rapidly. Bindi could purchase the whole collection if the rest of the house was to be judged on this area alone, and even then he would still be wanting.

He ushered me through to a small library which would have happily swallowed up the drawing room at Ennismore Gardens, twice. The room, walled in a thick flame stitch linen of blues, tans, ivories, golds and greens, took up the basic theme from the entrance. The floor again was finished in a heavy V'soske in a large exaggeration of the integral fabric motif. Bindi was every decorator's dream. He obviously liked colour and a touch of the grandiose and theatrical. Although some of the pieces of furniture were of priceless quality, the rest, like the carpets, were made to order and very expensive. He poured me a large brandy with a twin for himself. I sat down in a leather chair to the side of the burning fire and he stretched his massive frame into a similar chair opposite me.

"Welcome," he said.

We spoke for a bit about Key West, Texas, his various businesses and Monica. At no time was a reference made to Monica and Angela or even the gay Keith waiting to see us later that day. Carla and Kurt were discussed with great fondness. Bindi surprised me by announcing that he was joining Carla and Kurt in New York in December for a few days, and going along to see the opening of the smash London hit that everyone was talking about – *The Bliss of All* with, to quote "that cute Amanda Adamson."

"Amanda's a great friend," I stated. He was enthralled. I gave him a brief résumé of our long-standing friendship and added that she and a mutual designer friend had been with me for Christmas. An idea was rapidly forming in my mind. Of course, the way to introduce Reggie to them all. He would join me in New York to view the new offices, we'd go to Amanda's first night, doubtless there would be a party afterwards to await the reviews, and then I would give a party for Amanda during our few days' stay. I was sure that Carla and Kurt would be soon planning something similar. In fact, better still, Christmas in New York.

I went on to air these thoughts, bringing up Designs Unlimited, Amanda's apartment and the fact I would be in NY planning the new offices with Reggie joining me. "My God!" I looked at Bindi. "It's gone four." We laughed. "We have been talking for some time."

He offered a brandy. "You may as well. I would then suggest a shower and breakfast – we can doze on the flight down. This isn't usual for a Texan backwoodsman," he added.

I smiled. This man was a charmer and I could feel his appeal. He was so natural with it all that I was beginning to regret my initial thoughts. He looked at me over his refreshed glass and spoke.

"This young man, Reggie, you have been talking about!" I looked at him startled. He said gently, "Yes, RA, for the past fifteen minutes, whilst talking about Amanda, Designers Unlimited, and Reggie, especially Reggie, you have become totally alive." He paused. "I take it he's your guy?" I stared dumbly at Bindi. "Oh sure, I know the scene," he continued. "Take our darling Monica and Angela. Those girls were lovers in Hollywood. Hank Du Barry was a great guy, a great friend and he always would say to me that should anything happen to him, and then Angela, would I still make sure I took care of Monica. Hank was gay, but he and Monica loved each other so dearly. Hank and my Daddy were close friends and he advised Hank on a lot of his oil deals. I sometimes feel their friendship went deeper than I will ever know," he nodded. "Oh sure, I'm sure there was more to the two of them than simple friendship. Hank used to be so marvellous about me. He used to say quite openly to my Daddy, in front of me – I don't know how you can have that young man in front of you all the time, Jake Wainwright, and not have one teensy thought of incest! You look surprised. Hank meant no harm, and I was as saddened the day he died as was Monica. Monica was like my mama but then again, she and Angela are a wicked pair. I'm not gay, by the way," he added, "in case you have been wondering. The fact that I am in my thirties (Christ, he must find me in the realms of Monica) and still a bachelor makes them determined I am gay. Monica and Angela do not matchmake with Texan ladies of quality for me – like that sweet girl there tonight. Tonight was no exception; Monica wasn't sure about you but Carla had told her she thought you were gay." (So much for my tell-all lunch with Carla!)

I was riveted and helped myself to the decanter. "May I?"

"Of course, top me up as well, please." Bindi leaned forward holding out his glass. He settled back comfortably and smiled, before continuing. "You seem surprised? I'm not shocking you, am I?"

"Good heavens, no," I said, as if incest and society lesbians were part of my everyday scene in London – and I thought the English were meant to be the decadent race.

"Usually," Bindi went on, "those dinners comprise of Monica, Angela, myself, an enlightened couple Monica knows and always three or four young suitable men. You laugh? Monica sees herself giving me away at some fancy barbecue and wedding I shouldn't doubt."

We both laughed.

"Seriously, the nights I have had to give some young man a lift back into Houston are beyond count. A drink or a disco is suggested, but I always have the excuse that there is something wrong. I must have had more imaginary doses than the whole of the US Army has had genuine goes. Monica is always on the telephone at sunrise to see how I am. We never discuss the matter too seriously, she would hate to be disillusioned and her game to end. One day I shall stun her and say, "Wait a second, speak to the young man yourself."

"Then there's the other side to it. She imagines that love to a big bruiser like myself will be with some delicate young person, never a physical equal. No, don't get worried," he grinned, "I won't put you on to the telephone to her this morning!"

More laughter but I had had a momentary thought.

"Bindi!" I had to say it. "You are one hell of a nice guy."

There was a knock on the door. "I was going up to call you both sir," – it was a smiling Max – "breakfast in half an hour. Would you care for your coffee here or in your rooms?"

"In our rooms, thank you Max." Bindi stood up. "Wear a shirt and a pair of slacks, RA. There are some reefer jackets in one of the cupboards in your dressing room. I'd bring one of those as it will be a bit cool when we set off."

The flight to Key West was perfect. Bindi's jet, a Lear, specially decorated with an interior comprising of bar, small micro kitchen, reclining armchairs for six, a sleeping area and a shower, was manned by a pilot, co-pilot and a camp steward, called Pete. 'Pete the Treat' Monica called him. There had been a nasty moment when Monica imagined Pete was Bindi's treat and was, to quote, "mightily worried, Bindi, mightily worried."

"That's another thing," said Bindi, strapping himself in and taking a large bullshot from the chocolate-box cover Pete, "this plane. When I mentioned to Monica I was getting one, she was against the idea and said I was being extravagant. Extravagant! That, from Monica is quite something." He took a long draw from his tankard and smiled at Pete. "Perfection – the drink," he added, with a wink. Pete grinned and disappeared into the cockpit with two mugs of coffee. "Now I have to ask Monica if she isn't using the plane. She thinks nothing of a day trip to New Orleans or a spin to Dallas. I said to Angela that there must be a flighty piece in the French Quarter Monica fancied. I have not made that sort of joke again!"

We chatted for a while. I had a further bullshot and, like Bindi, reclined my chair and was soon asleep. Pete fussed with a pair of warm cashmere rugs for us. He woke us a few minutes before beginning our descent and handed us cups of steaming coffee. I sat, leaning against the window taking in the aquamarine-coloured sea and the series of islands joined with the fine tracery of the causeway bridges.

The jet taxied towards the airport building. I could make out only a scattering of palm trees and a rather collapsed fence. A few taxis stood by the small building – more of a shack and in need of some repair – and the whole area, apart from a lone figure guiding us in, looked deserted.

The light breeze and the smell of the sea, after the humidity of Houston, was very welcomed. I was surprised to find I was not feeling at all tired. The brandy from the late night gossip, plus the bullshots on the flight and the short doze, seemed to have buoyed me up to a state of pleasant euphoria. We all descended from the aircraft. Bindi was having a few words with the pilot about times for our morning return. Pete was standing next to me, pulling on a cigarette. "Do you know Key West?" I asked.

"Sure." He threw the cigarette on to the ground and stubbed it out with his highly glossed Gucci boot. (Texas, where the stewards wear Gucci, I made a mental note to tell Reggie when I spoke to him that night.) "Great place," he drawled. "Every scene is available." I looked at him and he grinned. He jerked his head towards the giant figure of Bindi. "Bindi will show you around. I'll probably see you later. The two of you will make quite a show." He smiled wickedly. Bindi came over to us.

"Has Pete been trying to corrupt you into the ways of the island already?" he asked. "There's Keith." He waved at a tall, rangy young man who came loping over to us. Keith Whatsisname was a dish.

Tanned, with long brown hair held back off his face by a brightly coloured headband, he was clad in a pair of cut-off jeans and was barefoot. His drooping moustache and narrow beard gave him a Christ-like look. He was blessed with a pair of deep green eyes and was – to use the typical KW expression, very laid back.

"Hi Bindi," he said, in a husky, slow tone.

"I didn't realise we were being met," I turned to Bindi. "You've planned everything. Hi," I added.

"Hi." husked Keith, in response to my comments. "Monica telephoned and told me when you would be here. I checked with the airport and they gave me the time of your arrival." He grabbed our bags and loped off towards a station wagon. "I'm sorry you have to be at The Pier House," he said over his shoulder, "and not with me, but Conrad (the writer friend) is due in later on the Miami flight and he has two house guests so there simply won't be room."

He organised the bags in the back of the car. I got in alongside him and Bindi squeezed himself onto the back seat. Pete was cadging a ride with us into the town. Keith opened a case on the seat alongside him. In it were four mugs and a thermos. "A welcome Key West special by courtesy of Sloppy Joe's," he drawled.

The drink was an iced rum punch. I spluttered with the first swallow. At this rate, what with Texas hospitality and now Key West, I'd be taken immediately in The Priory on my return to London.

"I've got a couple of houses for you to look at," Keith continued. I was impressed. He had not been all that laid back. He changed gear – "I'll get you to your hotel, let you check in while I wait. We can then go and look at two before lunch. There is another one we cannot see until later. That is the one you'll go for. It needs a lot done to it but it is one of the original conch houses, just by Hemmingway's house, and they are becoming very rare to get as the islanders are now realising what these properties will eventually be worth. We're here!"

We stopped outside a single storey dwelling with a set of plate glass doors and a few clumps of oleanders on either side. Keith sat sipping his rum and looking as if he was about to slip into a trance.

Pete got out with us, said he'd see us in the morning if not at Delmonico's later and sauntered off in the direction of the main street.

"Where's he staying?"

"Oh, some friend with a guest house," said Bindi.

We moved into the cool reception area. A blonde young man with long fair hair and the inevitable moustache, was sitting behind the desk. "Hi, welcome to the Pier House. You must be Mr Wainwright and Mr Anderson?"

We were soon to learn that Key West was a very small town and everybody knew everybody and everybody's movements. I wasn't quite sure what Keith had said when making our reservations, but the welcome was certainly a warm one. A lot to do with Bindi's influence on Keith, no doubt.

Bindi and I were put in adjoining rooms in the annexe at the hotel. My balcony, like his, was right overlooking the sea. I splashed my face with some tepid water from the tap, ran a comb through my hair and went out to join him and Keith.

We viewed the first two houses, and although they held considerable charm they were not quite what I was looking for. I was enchanted with the island, however, and knew, should I find a suitable property, whether on this brief visit or on my return, I would certainly consider spending a certain amount of time here. We stopped at the famous Sloppy Joe's Bar for drinks. The bar, on Duval Street, the main artery street of Key West, was filled with young hippies. There was a jazz quartet playing and everybody seemed to be in a quiet and convivial mood. We lunched at a beachfront restaurant slightly out of the town, and then returned to view the final house.

It was the lucky three all over again.

The house was perfect. The garden was heavily shaded with camellia bushes, oaks and banyan trees. The house, built in the eighteen twenties was finished in clapboard and the windows, with their tall louvred shutters, were well proportioned and elegant. A sagging veranda, partly screened, ran around three sides of the house.

"I'll take it," I said.

Bindi was brilliant at organising the preliminaries. It was arranged that the purchase would be organised via Houston and through his and my lawyers.

Bindi and I were discussing it enthusiastically as we walked over to Mallory Dock to see the late buskers and watch the sunset, a Key

West tradition. Keith had left us with the owner, an elderly gnarled local who thought Bindi was Burt Reynolds and kept muttering about actors and foreigners – my accent causing the latter hostility. Keith was making his second trip to the airport for the day. We were expected at the house for dinner at ten.

"You've made a very good buy there," Bindi said to me, as we made our way between the various side-shows and over to the wall by the water's edge. He stood staring for a few minutes at the setting sun. "Quite a sight, isn't it?" I nodded my head in silent agreement as I stood alongside watching the vast orange globe giving the appearance of gaining speed as it fell onto the horizon. Within a few minutes it had totally disappeared behind the darkening sea.

We turned and began to pick our way towards the hotel which stood nearby. Bindi and I began discussing the purchase again and methods of payment, plus the proposed occupancy date.

"There is really no hurry," I said, "but doubtless the sooner one can get started it does mean that the house can be ready for suitable leasing when not in use by me or friends."

Bindi smiled. "I like your mention of leasing out the property. Knowing Monica she will be first in the line of 'friends' for a lovely long stay. No doubt she and Angela will be down here to settle it all for you." I glanced at him. "And," he went on, "from what I can gather, they will be working hand in hand with Reggie. I have a very strong feeling that you have found yourself a great working force there!"

We continued talking for a while at the hotel bar, and then I went off to my room to have a short rest and also to ring London. The latencss of the night before and general excitement of the day were beginning to take their toll. I looked at myself in the fluorescent lighted mirror in the bathroom. I was not too impressed with what I saw staring back at me. Reggie would not have anything to worry about from a competition point of view. As he would no doubt say 'there is no need to advertise that vast age, is there?'

I suddenly felt a tremendous surge of loneliness. The melancholy blue black of the sea and the now darkened sky, plus the solo cry of a few sea birds as they settled in for the night, added to my rapidly spreading depression. I checked the time. It would be the early hours of Sunday morning and I would wake him up with a call, but I could not wait. I wrapped my bathrobe around myself and lay down on the bed, my head and shoulders propped up with an army of pillows. I took a sip of my Scotch and then called the hotel operator to place the call through to London.

The telephone gave two rings and was promptly picked up.

"Reggie?"

"Oh, RA. I'm so glad you called. I've been lying here feeling so low and even Petrina seems to have caught the mood."

"Darling! But why? Is there something wrong?"

"No, not really. It's just that everything seems to be so rushed and exciting and then there's the weekend and instead of organising anything I stayed in, and the more I sat listening to music or staring at that ridiculous box, the more low I became."

"Well, put it down to tiredness. You have been at it non-stop you know. Why didn't you call Manda?"

"I thought of that, but she does two shows on a Saturday and I feel sure the last thing she needed was a lovelorn queen grizzling into a drink over dinner."

"I like the lovelorn bit. But she wouldn't have minded. In fact, the two of you always cheer each other up."

"I know, but RA, I cannot run to Amanda when I get into a state. It's you I am missing and our feelings are so very private. I mean, the way I feel, only you can understand."

"I was feeling depressed, too, darling. That's why I've called now as opposed to telephoning at a more suitable time for you."

"Is Key West fun?" His voice sounded so small.

"It's a lovely island. I've seen a marvellous house which I have decided we should buy."

"Oh?" He chirped up a bit.

"MmMm. It's a typical Conch house, very similar to the sort you and I have discussed. You'll be delighted to hear it needs a great deal doing to it."

"Oh, RA. Have you really bought it?"

"Well, yes. Unless something unforeseen occurs.

"I arranged the deposit this afternoon and shall organise the various financings when I return to Houston. Once completion is arranged I suggest you pay a visit, perhaps we can tie it in with your trip to New York? I did have plans for that, too, but with the house it will certainly be more practical to be here earlier." I went on to explain my thoughts over the proposed Christmas visit and the combination of viewing the offices, Amanda's opening and perhaps a few days in Vermont.

"I would very much like you to see the Woodstock Inn," I went on, "and I know you haven't done much skiing before but there are some excellent slopes for beginners and, of course, there is always those known runs like Suicide Six once you are expert."

"Had you said that a few minutes ago," said Reggie, "I would have suggested Suicide Six on an immediate one-way ticket."

"Well, it would have been a bit awkward with no snow as yet," I retorted with a laugh.

"RA?"

"Yes!"

"I do love you so much."

"I love you, Reggie."

"I miss you."

"I miss you too, darling."

"When you get back, can we go straight from the airport to the Cottage, please?"

"Of course, Reggie."

"And straight to bed?"

"I'm not too sure about the word 'straight', but definitely to bed."

"I feel much more perky, now."

"How perky?"

"Not that perky... have you ever done it talking to someone over the phone?"

"Reginald. No."

"Nor have I." Silence for a second.

"Would you like to?"

"Like to what?"

"Play schoolboys?"

"What, now?"

"Yes. I would... please?"

Reggie's phraseology at times fascinated me. For one who could be so basic and wanton in bed, he became quite embarrassed when talking about actual sex.

"Yes, I'd like to."

"Well, darling, of course. I may take some time as I haven't got you next to me."

"I'm starting."

I opened my bathrobe and began rubbing myself with my right hand. Reggie began whispering endearments over the receiver. I began whispering in return. His voice got harsher and I could hear his breathing quickening. "Oh Reggie, Reggie," I started to moan.

"Oh, RA," he gasped. "RA!"

"Reggie!" I lay back, my heart thudding loudly against my ribcage. I was drenched with sweat.

"Did you come?" A plaintive whisper into the telephone.

"Oh yes, darling." I looked at the mess on my stomach. "Oh yes."

"I feel so much happier," murmured Reggie, sleepily. "It's a lovely sleeping tablet."

"I am happy too, darling... Reggie?"

"Mmmm?"

"Sleep well, darling, I'll call again when I get back from dinner."

"Mmmmm, g'night dear RA, I love you." And a click.

"I love you too, Reggie," I whispered, staring at the receiver. I put the telephone back on the cradle and heaved myself off the bed. I grinned. "Schoolboys indeed." I headed towards the shower. The telephone rang.

"Hello?"

"Mr Anderson. Switchboard here. I was simply checking that your call to London was satisfactory?"

I stammered into the phone. "M... m... most, thank you."

"Thank you, sir!"

I had the decency to blush.

*

Conrad was charming and his house guests, a dentist from New York with his boyfriend who was an ear, nose and throat specialist, nicknamed Linda, because of the latter, were in an exuberant mood when Bindi and I arrived.

Babe, a local character, who had a clothing boutique shop on the island, was also there looking as if she had had the fear of a possible burglary and so was wearing all the items of clothing from the shop. She was a mountain of colourful fabrics and looked like a combination of a Gingold and the Michelin Man.

The laid-back Keith, now in white cotton trousers with obviously no underwear, was busy plucking a guitar in the corner, in between smoking a joint and taking long draughts from a can of beer. Several other locals had been invited. There was the local gay lawyer and his friend, an amusing vivacious woman from Los Angeles and her scowling Cuban lover, and Pete the Treat with a hairy Spaniard who was fascinated by Keith's obvious talent. Bindi and I were given a warm welcome and in a few minutes we were deeply engrossed in conversation with the other guests.

Conrad was delighted about the house I had seen. "Keith told me you were serious about it, and I'm delighted to welcome you to the island. It's an idyllic place, but it is becoming very commercially orientated, even though Babe claims her profits deny this!" He waved at Babe who was peering up at Bindi and who looked round when she heard her name mentioned. She gave a vast wriggle, rolled her eyes heavenwards and went on looking up at Bindi with complete adoration. Conrad called over Richard, the lawyer, and we continued talking about the purchase and any problems that may arise. Richard was more than helpful with his advice, and I asked him if he would be good enough to act as my legal advisor on Key West and liaise with Bindi's man in Houston. Richard was more than happy to oblige. He then called over his friend who was a local handyman and decorator. Casey listened to my enthusiastic plans for the house and kept nodding with my basic suggestions, but then coming up with several good ideas of his own. The house was known to most of those present and they were audibly relieved that it had been bought by a gay.

"Key West is creating a marvellous private gay community," went on Richard, "and there are a number of very good gay guest houses opening. We have our local gay elite, and trendy names such as Williams and Co., and now it is up to us to introduce a more permanent and stable tone. A lot of the locals are happy to sell and it would be preferable if we basically retained the gay syndrome."

"What about me?" This was Bindi, who came over to us.

"There's always me," quivered Babe, joining him.

"Well, that answers that," grinned Conrad. "Bindi will no doubt come over to our way of thinking." We all laughed. "Babe's boutique is a front," continued Conrad. "She's actually employed by the Gay Mafia on KW to convince any hunky straight that the grass is greener on the other side of the fence." He pronounced grass 'grr-arse' and there were more guffaws from us.

"Don't fence me in," beamed Bindi, his hands held up in supplication. More laughter.

Keith joined us, flopping as well as lopping, to check if anyone's glasses needed refilling. He also handed around a box of neatly rolled joints. "If anyone needs a line," he added, "it's all set up over there."

He had neatly laid out a mirror with two small bowls of white powder and two spoons.

Several neatly stacked clean dollar bills lay alongside. It obviously was going to be some party. And it was.

My mood, taken to cloud nine by my recent call to Reggie, was enlivened by the general company, the excellent wine and several puffs on a joint. I avoided the coke, but Pete and José, his Spanish friend, were well into it. Keith was keeping up with them in the snorting stakes and I could see José's brain beginning to buzz with the plans to get hold of Keith later. It looked as if Pete was to miss out his Spanish treat that evening after all.

Dinner was a delicious serving of barbecued ribs and chicken pieces with side salads and dressings. There was an enormous fruit salad that had been marinating in a gallon of rum for at least several hours. Keith had arranged large jugs of a potent Sangria and it was well after midnight when we all staggered off towards Delmonico's, the main gay disco on Duval.

Delmonico's was jumping. The bar area was crowded with a sea of young men, mostly in shorts or simply jeans and T-shirts. Couples were strolling arm-in-arm through the gardens at the back, and I could make out a moving mass on the large dance floor. The surprise at Delmonico's were the busy pool tables where more god-like young creatures were energetically playing. Richard beckoned to me and I followed him through to the bar. Conversation was not easy due to the pulsating music tearing out of the speakers. The harassed barman took out drinks and we stood around eyeing the morass around us.

Bindi had caused his usual sensation. One frail young man clutched his chest, gave a piercing shriek and cried, "I have just seen heaven and I am now prepared to die!" Bindi gave him a wink.

"Oh, my Gawd!" shrieked the queen, "he reacted! Ms Myrtle!" he slapped a dazed, swaying lookalike next to him, "why didn't you tell me I was dead? He winked at me!"

Bindi threw back his head with a roar of laughter. The young queen, turned to study our group again. She looked me up and down with a rapid movement. "Ms Myrtle," she shrieked again, "she's brought her twin sister. Don't tell me Heaven is double vision!"

And so the night continued. José and Keith had disappeared to the dance floor and I later saw them strolling out to the back, oblivious to us all. Pete had also disappeared. I looked at Bindi. "A nightcap at the hotel?" He nodded, looking somewhat relieved.

He had been subjected to another attack by the 'death wish' queen and Ms Myrtle, who had been dismayed to be told by Bindi that I was his lover, and although flattered he would not do anything as I would be furious. The first I got to hear of this was when Ms Myrtle and friend flounced by, paused, glared up at me and hissed in 'Supreme'-like unison 'Butch Bitch!' tossed their heads and glided on.

We said goodnight to Conrad, Babe and the rest of our group and made our way to the entrance.

"Oh no, trouble," groaned Bindi. Standing in the doorway, looking like The Unhappy Hooker, was Ms Myrtle and her friend.

"Goodnight," I muttered, and with Bindi tried to push our way past.

"Here, one minute handsome!" This was Myrtle, grasping Bindi. "My friend and me suggest perhaps the four of us, huh? You come back to our place, we've some good coke an' rum...?"

Bindi stopped and looked at them. "That is very sweet of ya," he drawled, "but my friend and I have this problem between us."

Myrtle and friend looked up at him and then at me. I was fascinated.

"What sort of problem?" This from Ms Death Wish.

"Well," said Bindi, standing with his legs apart and flexing his massive thighs. Ms Myrtle crossed herself. "It's like this. My friend and I are just SO big..." He held his hands in front of him at about twenty inches apart, "and SO thick," he circled his thumbs and forefingers, "that we can barely manage each other and so we have this pact that we NEVER, EVER, attempt with anyone else. But thank you and goodnight." He smiled and led me off into the night.

Shrieks rent the air. I glanced back quickly. Ms Myrtle and Death Wish were clutching each other with screams of girlish giggles. They waved and blew a kiss. "I knew I was in heaven but I didn't realise I could have died so happily as well!" screamed Death Wish. They had to hold each other up.

"Well done, Bindi," I laughed, as we walked back to the hotel.

"If only it were true," he bellowed, tears of laughter in his eyes. We both stood in the street, holding each other and howling with mirth, looking no less like bigger versions of Ms Myrtle and her friend.

Our flight back was uneventful. Peter was nursing a massive hangover, as were Bindi and myself. I had managed a few words with Reggie when I got in. He was on his way to lunch at Elvira's – no time for 'schoolboys' on this occasion.

We arrived back at the ranch with half an hour to spare before Monica and the other guests arrived for the magnificent barbecue magically created by Max. Guests arrived either by helicopter, or else in a series of amazing limousines. Monica had been fascinated by the anticipated purchase of the house. She had roared with laughter when Bindi had described the incident with Ms Myrtle and her friend.

I returned to the hotel and after a quiet supper in my room, I collapsed. Monday was spent at supervising the final details to the auction but, as Monica had said, the planning had all been so skilfully taken care of that I almost felt as if I were in the way. I had so much free time on my hands that I was able to take Bindi up on his invitation to lunch at his Club. He was a tremendous person, and his warmth and total ease was very contagious.

Monica's dance was the hit of the whole week. The First Lady was there and led off the dancing with Bindi. She was in great form, and her enjoyment was conveyed with the opening speech she gave at the Fair the next day. She complimented Monica on the dance of the night before, adding that her feet were so tired after all that dancing that whilst privately touring the Fair before the inaugural start, she had simply had to sit in the prettiest of chairs for a moment. That sitting, she added, in the prettiest of chairs that she couldn't refuse, had cost her five thousand dollars. As everyone at the Fair had been to the Ball, if not necessarily the dinner, no doubt they would be cajoled into unplanned buying too! She had received a tremendous ovation and the Fair had got off to a fine start.

Bindi took a good selection of paintings and I was commissioned to supply any others or relevant pieces of furniture I may feel would enhance the house. I returned to New York very pleased with the whole venture. I had made a great deal of money, a new friend in Bindi, and I was delighted with the house on Key West which I saw as a tremendous catalyst in bringing all these wonderful people together, particularly with my Reggie.

I had a very cheerful lunch with Carla and we laughed a great deal over my fears about her reaction and Kurt's over my relationship with Reggie. I had one more conversation with him before I set off for my flight back. It was the Friday night flight and he would be meeting me at the airport in the morning and we would drive straight on to the house.

"I've reserved a double room at The Old House," he concluded, before hanging up. The Old House was a stopping over point for us on occasions when we left latish on a Friday. We were always assured of a warm welcome and a very good dinner.

"What on earth for?"

"Well, it's a bit more comfortable than a lay-by. I don't think I could last until the cottage!"

"Randy sod," I laughed. "I'll see you in the morning and see to you at the cottage."

Chapter Ten

First night fever was already running high when I called by Pimlico Road on the Monday to have a brief viewing prior to the official 'opening' planned for the Thursday. The frontage to the premises was complete and there in the display cases were six magical jewel-like stage settings. Elvira's yellow and blue drawing room, her lapis dining room and her bedroom in the palest of rose tones had been sketched, painted, cut out and beautifully mounted by Ray. Competing with these were the models for Amanda's new apartment. Her magnificent space age in emeralds and whites, with its unique floating sofas – A Designs Unlimited special – her emerald and amber dining room and her white and saffron bedroom, brought gasps of admiration from passers-by. Business was not merely brisk, it was phenomenal. The main showroom and reception were complete, but the offices behind the calm façade were still unfinished and the atmosphere was electric. Joe and Chris, recovered from their St Tropez sojourn, were continually dashing in and out. They were busy working in Wilton Crescent for the ever-watchful Elvira and, apart from this, Reggie had already undertaken two other projects – "more cosmetic as opposed to design" he told me blithely, "but good basic bread and butter stuff." His way with all his staff and the additional outside contractors he was dealing with never failed to amaze me. He threw some spectacular bouts of temperament, but when it came to knuckling down and dealing with a problem, no matter the intensity of it and no matter in which field, Reggie was always capable of seeing a way around it. "Make your mistakes your deliberate mistakes," he used to say. "As long as it looks intended it will be accepted as intended. If your blue is not your blue but it works, employ it!" When I questioned the morals behind such an attitude he used to turn on me and cry "but RA, I'm a commercial designer, I'm going to be the most commercial designer of them all. When I say rich, I mean RRrrrrrrrrrich!"

I had returned with the various plans for the new offices in New York. I gave these to him and said, "Calculate your fee and once we agree we'll go on from there." It was determined from the very start that I was to be treated as a client, deliberate mistakes or not, and our whole working arrangement had to be professional or not at all. He had treated Elvira in exactly the same way and it was like witnessing a Jekyll and Hyde transformation to watch Reggie as Reginald Forbes, Designer, as opposed to Reggie Forbes, friend or friend and lover. I had broached the time factor fairly cautiously, but Reggie had taken this up without further ado.

"Obviously, if Key West is to be redone, it would seem ridiculous not to be supervising the New York project as well. I appreciate the Christmas plans, RA, but seriously, once we have got the promotion over with I really would like to get cracking with the States – if you are serious."

I protested that I was certainly serious, but felt that his other clients should take priority.

"You're a client when it comes to these two projects," he replied. "We have to schedule you in with our works programme exactly as we would anyone else." He went on, "The sooner we start, the better. I can begin with the preliminaries as from the details you have let me have on the Madison offices. I really feel that Steven and myself may have to go over there within the next few weeks. Tourist, of course," he added sweetly, "Key West included."

And so I was to be regulated into the channels of the new Designs Unlimited. Whilst I did not care for the idea of being a mere client, yet having insisted on being treated like one I had to admire Reggie for it.

Before leaving for America I had presented Reggie with a large leather-bound book filled with heavy blank pages in pale grey. The cover had been inscribed in pewter letters with 'Designs Unlimited Vol. 1'. "You'll soon require the second scrapbook to follow, at the rate Pete and you are going," I had joked.

On my visit to the showroom on the Monday, I sat having a cup of coffee with Reggie in the reception area and idly flicked through the scrapbook which had been placed prominently on the chrome and glass coffee table. There were at least seventeen pages of cuttings since the initial mentions prior to our break in the South of France! Photocopies of choice press pieces from the scrapbook had been neatly pinned together to make up a handout for that evening's opening. The front of the handout was again in the grey colouring and I was flattered to note that the type of lettering I had originally used for the first scrapbook had been adapted for the handouts. I had to admit that I had, in turn, been inspired by the original notepaper that Martin and Reggie had designed. This too was grey, with the pewter printing and an inset perimeter line of saffron and blue. The Reginald Forbes colour bands were soon to become his trademark. Included with the press copies was a photograph of Reggie, in laconic pose taken in the same Wassily chair alongside the William Kent commode at Ennismore Gardens. I looked up at him when I saw the photograph. He smiled and shrugged.

"Well, what do you expect. After all, we are together and I want you to know how very dearly I care that you and I belong."

*

Party promotion time. The guests had been asked for seven o'clock. It had turned out to be one of those perfect September evenings, still warm but with a freshness to the light breeze which was enough to set the grey and saffron banners on the posts outside the shop front, waving theatrically. The television crew had arrived in the late afternoon and had set up their required arc lamps and reflectors and a small crowd had already gathered to watch the arrival of the guests. There had been an hysterical moment when the arc lamps had caused a massive explosion and the shop, plus part of the Pimlico Road, seemed to be doomed to eternal darkness, but the ever vigilant team of contractors headed by Joe and Chris, had the lights back to normal within a breathless few minutes.

Reggie had arranged for a carpet of yellow, edged on either side in grey, to run from the edge of the pavement up to the main door. A doorman, resplendent in a grey uniform (Reggie had hired him from one of the gay nightclubs) stood at the ready to help the arrivals from their cars or taxis.

The invitations had stated the dress as 'Casual Chic' and the watching crowd were certainly getting the full benefit of what the evening had to offer.

Reggie had arrived direct from the flat in Fulham. I had managed a few words with him before I set off from the office back to

Ennismore Gardens to change into dinner jacket. I had arranged a dinner in the private downstairs dining room at Burkes and we were scheduled there for ten o'clock. Reggie had only wanted a few people to dinner, the members of his staff from the office, Sarah and Angus, Peter and a girlfriend and Amanda, and some of the cast he had become friendly with were coming in after the show.

I parked the car in Holbein Place and made my way round to the Pimlico Road on foot. It was seven fifteen and I had decided to arrive fairly early and then leave with Elvira, have a drink with a business colleague and his wife at the Dorchester and proceed to Burkes. This would leave Reggie with a free, unfettered run. After all, the night was his and his alone.

I walked towards the crowd around the brightly illuminated shop front. A large Phantom Rolls had drawn up alongside the pavement. A figure was helped out and there was an appreciative buzz followed by a loud cheering from the watching throng. Puzzled, I quickened my pace and stopped on the edge of the onlookers and smiled. Posing by the door to the limousine was Amanda, in full theatrical makeup, ready for the curtain which would be rising at eight o'clock. The crowd were delighted to see one of their most glamorous and successful stars. The mere fact that she was so totally unexpected by us all added to the excitement of her arrival. She was joined by her leading man who again drew more cheers and some shrieks from the female members of the audience.

Reggie appeared in the doorway. If Amanda had made an entrance, Reginald Forbes was not to be outdone. He stood there, in the arc lights, savouring every moment. The TV cameras were swung from the smiling Amanda to an amazed but oh so controlled Reggie. Even I took a sharp intake of breath. He was sheer show time. He slowly extended his arms, leaned his head to one side, and began to smile with 'the smile' becoming broader and broader. "Amanda," he said simply. "How special!" Amanda blew a kiss at the crowd and advanced towards Reggie, her arms outstretched to meet his.

"Reggie," she cried. "Congratulations! Only your show-stopper could have stopped my show." A roar of approval greeted this. Reggie smiled even more and freeing one of his arms, waved to a waiter who had been hovering in the doorway. The waiter appeared with a tray holding three glasses of champagne and apricot juice. Amanda took a glass, Reggie handed one to the leading man and took the third for himself. "To Designs Unlimited," said Amanda, raising her glass. She took a sip, kissed Reggie and with a wave made her way back to the car. At the door she paused and the noise of the crowd was silenced. "How sad I cannot stay," she cried, "but at least we got here. Good luck." More cheers and she was swept away whilst a beaming Reggie waved back at the people watching.

A newscaster came forward and questioned him eagerly. No, Reggie had not realised that Amanda would be making such a gesture and wasn't it wonderful of her to race from the theatre just to wish him good luck. Yes, he was doing her apartment for her and he would also be working on the apartment she would be taking in Los Angeles when she began work on the film of *The Bliss of All*.

I was dumbfounded. Other celebrities were now arriving. A rather disgruntled Elvira emerged from her car, but smiled charmingly when she saw the battery of cameras and the television crew in particular. She told me on the way to the Dorchester that she thought it intolerable that a queue of cars had to be kept waiting whilst "that actress frolicked." I gave her a warning look when she said this and she kept quiet for the rest of the journey.

Elvira had dressed in soft blues and yellows and did look sensational. Topazes and sapphires were brilliantly on show and she caused almost as much excitement as Amanda. Fortunately she did not hear one rather piercing comment from a large woman with her hair in bright yellow net, who had obviously stopped on her way to do some late night shopping and was standing there in her slippers, an old coat, and puffing a cigarette. "Not bad for someone her age. But then it's all that plastic and those injekshins in Switzerland, ain't it? And those young men!" she added darkly.

The crowd grew and Reggie never seemed to be still for one second. At no stage did he look frantic or agitated. He remained calm, solicitous, smiling and always the charmer.

Sarah came up to me. "Almost frightening, the confidence, isn't it?" This was not said maliciously, but with a smile. I knew exactly what she meant. The whole evening was so brilliantly contrived. Amanda had suggested the arrival and that had necessitated some former arranging with the traffic around the shop and also making sure Amanda got back to the theatre on time. Peter had handled all this for her and Reggie. Reggie's staff, impeccable in beautifully cut casual clothes, the girls in outfits from the likes of Sandra Rhodes or

Ossie Clarke, the boys in outfits from Blades or Mr Fish, seemed to combine the same ethereal aura and professionalism. Steven and Ray looked so dishy and Sam, in a sequinned dinner jacket, white slacks and a cream shirt and bow tie, looked devastatingly Dietrich. I was so proud of them all. But the outfit of the evening had to go to Reggie.

His suit was in saffron yellow silk with a silver thread through it. His shirt, in shot grey silk with a matching stock, was artfully pinned with a brooch of topaz and diamonds (loaned by Elvira). His boots were in suede, half yellow and half grey. "...'e looks bloody marvellous, don't 'e," said Joe, moving next to me for a moment.

"You're right, Joe," I agreed, "bloody marvellous."

Peter was very much in the public eye. Although in a plain dinner jacket he cut a striking figure in his dark gypsy-like way. For a moment he looked almost like Bindi! His companion, who was joining us for dinner, was a vivacious blonde who had just started her own TV series. She was a popular singer and Peter was promoting her into the big time. She, too, had received her fair share of crowd adulation on arrival.

Dorella Devene, with her young, muscle-bound escort, was floating around shrilly claiming how wonderful it all was and that Reggie had met her when a mere boy (two months before!) and how he was going to stun London and New York with her new salons.

In the middle of all this I caught Reggie looking over at me. He mouthed, "I love you" – and smiled.

"I raised my glass. "I love you too, Reggie," I whispered.

The cacophony reached a crescendo. A smiling Elvira advanced towards me. "Darling, isn't this fun and what a triumph? I am so happy for Reggie. So happy for you." She blinked at me in her mysterious way. "How clever all this is," she gestured in a swirl of chiffon. "I am so glad he is so understanding. My house is not at all vulgar, but then, here he has to sell it all, doesn't he?" She smiled again and made to move off. "Let me know when you want me to leave. The Dorchester will be quite dull – and silent – after all this." With a tinkling laugh she moved off to where Peter and his protégé were standing. I hoped she had heard one of the poor girl's songs, though I imagined that Elvira would never had heard anyone more modern than Doris Day and her 'Moonlight Bay'.

Steven and Ray came over to me. "Hello, RA," they chorused, rather like Tweedle Dum and Tweedle Dee. Ray was beginning to look rather cosy and portly for one so young, but they were obviously so devoted to each other and so happy that there was no criticism to be made. "What do you think?" Steven ventured this question solo.

"A great success," I said, "and I wish you all the best of luck. Long may it continue."

"Isn't Reggie marvellous!" breathed Ray.

"That seems to be the general opinion this evening. Yes, I have to agree again. He is."

More people kept coming up to me congratulating on Reggie's success. I was starting to feel like an aged parent – or uncle. I smiled, young Reggie had probably explained me off in this role to anyone who should enquire. "No, I tell them you're an extremely close friend and in some cases I tell them straight out that you are my lover," he answered me when I asked him about it later. He noted my incredulous expression. "Well, you are both," he claimed, "and the majority of our friends are totally aware of this. One is only cautious with the clients. I mean, I am after all in the role of the mistress... even if I am not drenched in diamonds and furs!"

"Oooh, there you are, charmer." I broke out of my reverie. A giggling Viv and Pearl were standing alongside me, clutching full glasses of a lurid champagne based drink.

"Viv and Pearl – as lovely a pair you'll never find."

"Hark at him, Pearl," and the screams of mirth began.

I glanced at their cleavages – even Dolly Parton would be on trial with their lot. "I see it's no holds barred and all holds bared tonight," I continued. God, was I really being this corny?

"We're just trying to compete with Joe and Chris's handiwork on the shop front," shrieked Viv.

"What's that, wet paint then?" It was Joe, heading into one of his usual evening states. "Hands off the paintwork. Do not touch!" More yells. I smiled rather weakly and moved off to find Elvira. The Dorchester was exactly what I needed – dull and extremely silent.

The dinner went better than I expected. Reggie, like myself, had been concerned that the rest of the staff may find it a bit inhibiting with clients being there and particularly as they were not too sure as to how aware someone like Elvira was of their particular scene. Elvira was being magical and Angus and Sarah could not have been more charming. Reggie and the rest of his office staff had arrived a few minutes before ten o'clock. When I mentioned to Reggie that perhaps it would be awkward for him to leave his reception, and did he perhaps wish to postpone a celebration dinner until a few nights later, he had been adamant that he would be there on time.

"Look, RA. I'm going to be there from seven o'clock. People have been asked for a drink and not to a dinner – hence only a few snacks or niblets being served. I won't stop the serving of drinks at nine thirty, but I am leaving at nine thirty. Always leave when a party is at its peak – assuming this one reaches that exalted height," he added as an afterthought.

Amanda and a few friends arrived as we were halfway through dinner. Elvira looked slightly put out at having to move her chair to accommodate a friend of Amanda's who squeezed in next to her, but in a few minutes he had got her into a heavy discussion on civil rights or some such deep topic and Elvira, who had strong personal views on every subject, almost forgot her crème brûlée.

Dinner finished soon after midnight and Reggie and myself dropped Elvira off at Wilton Crescent. She thanked Reggie for the evening, kissed me on the cheek and trilled to Reggie from the door, "now don't forget me, will you!"

"God, does she never let go?" breathed Reggie, settling back in the passenger seat and leaning his head against the headrest.

"Tired?" I asked.

"Not really," he yawned, belying his comment.

"Oh dear! Well, what do you think?"

"Tremendous Reggie. You were all superb. I thought that touch of Amanda's lightning arrival was nigh on genius."

"That was good, wasn't it?" He yawned again. "Thank you for the dinner party too, RA. That was a very super touch and it was rather a relief to be able to sit and simply talk as opposed to buzz!" We slowed past the Carlton Tower to turn right into Sloane Street.

"RA?"

"Yes, darling?"

"Do you mind if..."

"Of course not. I quite understand."

I reversed the indicator and turned left down towards Sloane Square. We proceeded along Lower Sloane Street and turned into the top end of the Pimlico Road. The lights were still on in the display windows to the shop front and several late nighters were looking in at these. We drove past slowly.

"It looks good, doesn't it?"

"Stunning," I said. "Rather like its owner. I've been meaning to tell you, the get up was fairly amazing."

"Yes," he giggled. "Would you believe it but Elvira actually asked me if the yellow was a fabric from one of the coverings I had selected for a series of scatter cushions in her drawing room. I mean, I appreciate that there is a very extravagant yellow silk with a gold thread being used but..."

"Is it?"

"Of course." I laughed and so did he. "But I must say there is someone else I would prefer to be stuffed by as opposed to Elvira's upholsterer!"

"What a coincidence. I'm happy to say that it so happens I am in the upholstery field and certainly would not mind doing some overtime work on a particular cushion."

"We won't bill the Duchess this time!"

"How envious she would be if she ever realised that her cushions can be pumped up as well as plumped up."

"Or the ideal mixture of feathers and going down!"

The papers were full of enthusiasm with their covering in a late night news coverage, of the promotion party for Designs Unlimited. Photographs of Amanda and Reggie were in practically every daily and they had appeared on endless TV screens. There were also glowing reports as to his well-connected clients. Elvira was mentioned endlessly as was Dorella Devene. Comments on work in the States and work virtually everywhere one would wish to consider, were made. Reginald Forbes had arrived with the big time and all in a matter of months.

Again, I kept having a nagging fear as to how he would cope with the sudden success and the tremendous workload that was being pressed upon the company. The enquiries, from hotel groups, private individuals, building developers and all facets, kept coming in. Sam was operating full time at the switchboard. Reggie was threatening to take on extra staff, 'ICK!' ICK was the office motto – meaning the words 'I can't cope'.

Reggie had postponed his immediate trip to New York but had finalised a date for the end of October. I flew over with him and Steven. We checked in at The Pierre and spent a hectic few days viewing the offices and fabrics and papers. Reggie's plan of operation was to return to London and commit the relevant designs to paper, utilising the available goods he had earmarked in New York. A contractual team arranged by Carla, had seen Reggie and Steven at several meetings and the basic works to the offices were put into hand without delay. Reggie and Steven worked diligently on the preliminary architectural details, utilising as much of the original interiors that they could without spoiling the effects they were striving for. Electrics, adjustments to the air-conditioning, plumbing, conduits for telex and telephone cables, plus required partitions for the new office and gallery areas, were sketched out physically in coloured chalks on the premises. I had barely any spare time with Reggie and he would be exhausted when he returned to the hotel in the evening. He and Steven would invariably have a late drink together or with friends of Steven's when they had finished their work for the day. Steven, with his unfailing energy would then go on to dinner or a few bars, but was always at the hotel room at eight o'clock to go through the day's briefing with Reggie, and then the two of them would set off to meet the contractors or else view additional items for selection as required by the project. Steven seemed to have an endless list of introductions to soulmates in the city.

Reggie met Carla and Kurt and whilst they got on together I did not feel that the rapport that I had been hoping for was there. Carla was studiously quiet at their first meeting, although charming, and I brushed this aside as part of the atmosphere in general being rushed and fairly strained. Their second meeting, which was to have included dinner, ended up merely as a drink at The Sherry Netherland. Reggie was rushing off to meet Steven and go off to a warehouse over the river. He and Steven were leaving for Key West the following morning and returning to London direct from Miami. I explained to Kurt and Carla that this was the only time that Reggie could get to view this particular assortment of proposed furniture and she had seemed pacified.

Reggie, for once, did not seem to totally relax with her. I again was surprised as I appreciated at how good a friend she was of Amanda's. They had talked about Amanda and her apartment. When Carla asked for details as to how Reggie was planning Amanda's 'new look' he said, rather irritably. "Oh God, can't it wait until it's in a glossy! That is by far the best way to have it described to you." I had looked at Reggie, slightly askance and on noticing my expression he had turned on his most brilliant smile and said to Carla. "I'm sorry if that sounded a bit snappish, but I seem to have done nothing else except talk about design for the past three days and the subject is slightly overpowering at the moment."

Carla understood, but I could see that she had taken offence. After all, she had been more than helpful in introducing a first-rate team of contractors for Reggie to work with, and it had meant cutting into her own highly valued business time. Reggie eventually left us and we went on to dinner. The dinner was not as relaxed as usual. We discussed Amanda's show and plans for the first night.

"Will Reggie be with you or will he be too involved?" questioned Carla. I looked at her curiously, but the remark did not seem viciously intended. Perhaps I was becoming too sensitive, too preoccupied and too possessive about Reggie and his effect on others – particularly friends of mine. I was sure Reggie would be at the opening night – "He'll be attending to final bits and pieces for the office so he will be in New York, anyway," I stressed, and then wondered as to why I was sounding almost apologetic. I decided to ignore it. I spent a few more moments with Carla and Kurt and they kindly dropped me off at my hotel.

I undressed, got into my bed and attempted to read. I checked my watch. It was only eleven thirty, and I expected that Reggie had gone off with Steven to have a late night supper at Uncle Charlie's or some other comfortable and relaxing restaurant/bar. I got up, poured myself a late night Scotch and got back into bed. I checked my watch again. Midnight! How slow time seems to go when you are anxiously waiting for someone, particularly a lover.

I got up again, went through my briefcase and collected my address book. I dialled Houston. In a few minutes Bindi's voice came over the wire. "Good evening, is that big Bindi? It's your twin."

"RA!" he laughed. "Good evening."

"I didn't wake you, did I?"

"No, I've just got in. Everything okay?"

Bindi and myself had taken to calling each other fairly regularly. He was becoming a staunch friend and he was so easy to discuss one's doubts or problems with. There were matters I felt I could talk to Bindi about far more easily than to Amanda. Even though he was not gay, Bindi was one of those incredibly humane and civilised heterosexuals who was capable of understanding and discussing personal problems without adapting a holier than thou attitude as to whatever the relationship was based upon. I brought up the conversation of the evening in general and also vented my feelings over the attitude of Carla to Reggie.

"Oh, I think you are reading too much into this, RA," he said. "Carla was no doubt doing her heavy 'I am a woman of the world' bit and I can see more into a person's soul than the average woman. She's doing this with me the whole time."

"Anyway, there we are," I surmised. "It cannot always work."

We carried on discussing the house, the deal over which was now concluded.

"I'll see the boys tomorrow," concluded Bindi, "and no doubt Reggie will ring you from Key West."

"Whatever. I'll call on my return to London."

Reggie and Steven were flying to Houston where they were being met by Bindi. They were then flying straight on to Key West, staying with Keith and after two days returning to London. I had suggested to Reggie he take a break on Key West for a few days but he would not hear of it.

"I simply have to get back," he argued, or rather, stated. "There is too much at stake. Elvira is out of the way, thank God, but Dorella did spring Bond Street on me rather earlier than envisaged and besides, it's simply not fair on the rest of the staff and – surprise, surprise – the clients, if I am away with Steven."

After a few more reassuring words Bindi rang off. I made myself another drink and got back into bed with my book. I must have fallen asleep because I woke up with the bedside light still on. I glanced over to the bed next to mine. This was neatly turned down and Reggie's outrageous multi-striped dressing gown from Turnbull and Asser was still lying across the foot of the bed. Imagining I must have simply dozed off I looked at my watch again and did a double take. Six o'clock!

I leaped from the bed and went to check the bathroom to see if Reggie had come in by chance and possibly fallen or gone to sleep in the bathroom. He had seemed to be drinking a good deal recently and I was bracing myself to bring up the matter with him. He simply could not hope to keep those elfin features forever if the intake of vodka – nowadays mixed with a glass of champagne – was to continue at its present rate, never mind an increase in consumption. There was no sign of him in the bathroom. I raced over to the main door to the room to check as to whether, by some error, I had accidentally put the chain on. This was hanging unattached. I opened the door cautiously and peered into the quiet corridor, inwardly praying that I would find Reggie in a blissfully, crumpled heap against the door. The doorway, like the corridor, was deserted.

I hurried over to the telephone and punched the number for the message desk. One of those over-bright early morning American voices answered me after the first ring. "Good morning, message desk."

"Good morning, this is Mr Anderson, Room 3017. Has there been an emergency message for me that I may not have picked up?"

"Good morning. Hold on please."

There was a silence. "No, no messages, sir."

"Thank you," I muttered, totally distraught by this piece of information.

"Thank you, sir," smiled the voice. "Have a nice day."

I dropped the telephone. "Have a nice day." My mind was racing. Of course. Steven! If there was no reply from his room it would mean that at least the two were together. And although this would alleviate my wildest panics for the moment, I still could not believe that they would not have come back to the hotel. I had imagined that they would have taken a cab to their rendezvous the night before, but perhaps there had been an accident and the two could be in hospital. I was beside myself. I kept on hearing terrifying stories about New York at night, but that wonderful attitude – it could never happen to me – seemingly dismissed such thoughts. But first, Steve. As I lifted the telephone once again I planned a panic campaign. If Steve was not there, I would get hold of Kurt and obviously we would have to contact the police. But what if Steve was there! I couldn't believe that Reggie, my Reggie would have gone off on his own. Extraordinary as it may seem, Carla's face sprang to mind and her strange eyeing of Reggie.

"Hello."

Christ, it was Steve. "Steve, it's RA. Have you got Reggie there?"

"Uh... hold on a moment." I could hear the murmur of voices and my heart bounded with relief.

"Sorry RA. No. I was just speaking to someone here who is just leaving. (So much for the devotion to Ray).

"But Steven, it's after six and he's not come back. Where for fuck's sake did you leave him?"

"I can't talk," he gasped.

"Hold it, I'm coming down to your room." I tore into a pair of trousers and sweater, pulled on a pair of slippers and raced out of the bedroom, along the corridor and to Steven's door. As I got to the door it swung open and a heavy set young man, in denims and a peaked leather cap, was leaving.

I pushed past him, ignoring his 'watch it, mister' and confronted a sheepish Steven who was standing in his dressing gown, looking very tousled and very hung-over. The curtains were tightly closed and the room reeked of amyl nitrate, sweat and sex. The bed was in total disarray and the bedside lamp was on its side. A large bruise on the side of Steven's face told me all I needed to know.

"Saved by the bell – literally," I said grimly. "It looks as if your friend could have been a bit rough. Steven, for Christ's sake, what the hell have the two of you been up to?" I exploded.

Steven gestured helplessly and sat down. He was beginning to tremble. I pulled open the curtains, opened the window and picked up the telephone. I called room service and ordered coffee and a large brandy. Steven suddenly burst into tears.

"Oh RA," he sobbed, "I am sorry. I cannot tell you what I would have done had you not telephoned. That guy – he seemed so nice at the time, absolutely fine until this morning. He then demanded money – all I had on me was about thirty dollars which he took. He was then starting to get nasty and he hit me a second before you telephoned. As soon as I started speaking to you he was heading for the door and then seemed to change his mind and made a rush at me, and oh..." He began sobbing hysterically.

I put my arm around him. My heart had totally sunk. I was feeling sickened and wretched. "There," I said in a choked voice. "Come on, it's all right now. He's gone. I'm here. Oh God, Steven, what about Reggie? Please, you've got to pull yourself together. He's probably desperately in need of help as well. Only you can help me help him."

There was a noise at the door. I looked up expecting to see room service.

"What a pretty sight." A swaying, dishevelled Reggie was standing in the doorway. The words 'pretty' and 'sight' were spat out at me as I knelt cradling Steve.

"Reggie," I cried.

"Reggie," he mimicked.

I was stunned. "Reggie," I repeated, softly.

"Oh SHIT," he screamed and spun round crashing into the aged bellhop with the tray of coffee and brandy.

"You idiot," he shrieked at the startled man, "can't you look where you're bloody well going?"

He disappeared from view. I had jumped up leaving a huddled Steven on the chair. Apologising briefly to the bellhop and asking him to hold on, I raced along the corridor after Reggie, whom I saw disappearing into our room. The door crashed shut as I reached it.

"Reggie," I said, knocking on the door. "Please open up?"

"Reggie." No reply. I knocked again, aware of the early hour and also horribly aware of the rest of the occupants nearby. "Reggie," I commanded, "will you please open this door?"

Exasperated, I turned away and went back to the bellhop who had begun to pick up the pieces of china and glass from the carpet. "Have you a master key?" I asked.

"Yes sir."

"Well, would you please let me into my room. My friend isn't very well and has closed the door." I glanced beyond him to Steve, who was still sitting curled up on the chair, holding the side of his face. "I'll be back in a minute, Steve."

Again to the bellhop. "When you've let me in would you be kind enough to get him some more coffee and give it to him with the brandy. These young men!" I laughed hollowly, making an empty gesture with my hands. He nodded in agreement and shuffled with me to the room.

The door to the bathroom was closed but I could hear the sound of the shower. I knocked lightly on the door. The water continued running but there was no reply. I knocked again, not quite sure as to what reaction I expected. Again, no reply.

"Reggie? Are you all right?"

"Oh, for Christ's sake!" The voice was angry and distorted. I stared blankly at the door for a moment, contemplated trying the handle and then decided against this. I looked around the room wildly. He had thrown his shirt and jacket onto the bed and his trousers were in a heap by the bathroom door. His shoes lay where he had obviously kicked them off, one looking rather soulful on its side. I picked up his coat to hand over the back of the chair. In doing so, his wallet fell out on to the floor. Glancing back at the door, I knelt down and quickly picked up the snakeskin wallet. I flicked it open and checked inside. It was still filled with bills and it did not look as if his credit cards were missing. Unlike poor Steven, he obviously had not been rolled. Steven! Reggie still seemed to be showering and so I walked back to the room I had recently left.

The elderly bellhop was fussing round a much happier looking Steven. Some colour had come back to his face and he had moved from the main armchair to one of the smaller chairs at the serving table by the window. He had also combed his hair and so was more like his usual self. I thanked the bellhop, gave him a bill and waited until he had quietly closed the door behind him.

I moved over to the window and sat down on the chair facing Steven. He had been staring at me since I came back into the room and now licked his lips nervously. I gestured towards the coffee and the spare cup. "May I?"

"Oh, RA, of course. Forgive me but I wasn't really thinking..."

"I understand," I said, and poured the steaming coffee into the cup. I added some sugar and sat looking at him as I stirred the coffee slowly. "Do you want to tell me about it?"

He looked at me. "Is Reggie all right?"

I nodded. "He sounds all right. He doesn't seem to be in the mood for speaking, somehow!"

Steven nodded glumly. "What a cock up," he said grimly.

"I suppose one could agree with you over that twofold," I said, starting to smile. He looked so miserable for himself and I thought it really would not help to start lecturing him on the dos and don'ts of life. He was after all, like Reggie, an adult and I was not his lover, keeper or whatever.

"You silly buggers," I continued. "I think I've got the picture. Just consider yourself lucky and be a bit more cautious next time."

"There won't be a next time," said Steven determinedly.

"Well, let's say should a similar happening come along."

"Ray would kill me if he knew about this."

"Well, he certainly won't know about it if you don't say anything, so let's consider the matter forgotten. I don't suppose you have any idea who that young man is or his whereabouts? I mean, do you want me to do anything about getting that money back?"

"No, RA, please. It was only a few dollars and I simply want to forget about it."

"Well I should have tried to get him stopped on the way out, but I was too occupied with seeing if Reggie was all right. Were you two together?"

Steve filled me in briefly with the events of the evening. He and Reggie had gone off to look at some furnishings as planned. They had come back into Manhattan and moved over to Regent's East, a discreet drinking bar off Third Avenue, for a few drinks before going on to dinner in The Village. Dinner had been followed by more drinks in a bar on Christopher Street. Steven had been approached and chatted up by the leather number he had eventually returned with to the hotel. He admitted to getting fairly drunk and together they had ordered more drinks before getting into bed. The night had been fairly wild and the pickup had produced several joints as well as the amyl nitrate. Steven had even gone so far as to ask what his companion would like for breakfast as he, Steven, would have to start getting ready and also had to pack as he was due to leave for the airport at nine o'clock. It was then that the scene had changed and the paramour had become paranoid.

"A typical tale of wanderlust woe," I said to him, getting to my feet. "It's happened to us all, young Steven. Now, you get yourself organised and I'll go and deal with Reggie. You have half an hour to pack and check out. I'll deal with the bills as arranged." I reached the door.

"Thanks RA," said Steve, still sitting by the window.

"Don't mention it."

I returned to the room. The door to the bathroom was open. Reggie's case, already packed, was still lying on the bed unzipped. Reggie was standing, dressed, staring out of the window down at the Park below.

"Good morning," I said. "Shall we try a fresh start to the day!"

He spun round and stood glaring at me. I was prepared for tears, recriminations, anything, but not this continued anger.

"Don't you ever stop being so bloody parsimonious?" he snarled.

I moved back, as if stung. "Reggie," I said, shocked. "It's been a bad time. Leave it!"

"Don't you want to know what happened?" he went on. "Don't you want to know what your darling, whiter than white Reggie, has been up to?"

"Not particularly," I replied, staring at him curiously. "You're either still stoned or smashed or both – and behaving rather childishly."

He kept glaring at me, unblinkingly. "If you must know," I added, "a scene like this is inevitable. I have told you before to have some time to yourself – it's only human nature – but if you do decide to go on a bender or get your rocks off elsewhere, do it discreetly next time and don't come back, covered with guilt and therefore take it out on me in a pathetic outburst of queeny temper. It's not that good for the image you've created," I added.

He went purple. "You bastard," he shrieked.

"Oh, come on Reggie," I said, totally exasperated. "Now you are making a total fool of yourself. Get yourself together as you have a plane to catch. This whole incident is better forgotten."

"Fuck the plane, fuck your New York offices, fuck Key West and fuck you," he screamed.

I slapped him hard across the face. He looked at me, his mouth moving, and then fell sobbing on to the bed.

"No dear Reggie," I said, looking down at him. "You fuck you!"

I was furious and angry with myself for reacting in such a way. Moreover, I was so totally disappointed in Reggie. I put on a pair of loafers, collected a jacket and picked up my wallet. "I'll be downstairs," I said to his now silent figure. "I suggest you get your luggage, collect Steven and I'll see you in reception. I'll get a cab for you." I walked out.

In the lobby I was shaking. I could not work out what had happened to cause this reaction. Guilt I could understand, but the attitude towards myself by Reggie was fringing almost on hate. I remembered Carla again from the night before. But Amanda had always been so pro Reggie. Even the enigmatic Elvira seemed to be a loyal devotee. No, I was now reacting.

But how was I reacting? I did feel immense anger, confusion and also embarrassment. I was only sorry that I had seen Reggie descend to such a state. I felt sure that his own feelings at his outburst must be the same and I was determined not to mention the matter unless he brought up the subject. I could not believe that in a few hours the whole concept towards our relationship could have changed so seemingly drastically. The same time yesterday there had been a feeling of mutual pride and respect. Now it seemed as if these two emotions, so vital in the foundation of any relationship, whether heterosexual or gay, had been viciously abused and subsequently shattered. My mind was whirring with a stream of jumbled thoughts. Peter's first words at The Raging Bull – was it not even a year ago when he had hinted at Reggie's behaviour and subsequent hurt involving a friend of his, came rushing back. Was this now going to happen to me? Was I the next? I could not believe this. Whilst I could appreciate Reggie's ambition and his determination to succeed and the fact that I was a considerable help in his achievement of these aims, I still felt that there was more to our relationship than this. I appreciated the difference in our ages, hence my remarks on occasions that he should be by himself, and hurtful as it may be, I would turn a blind eye to any dalliances as long as they did not destroy what I felt we were creating and had already created. I did not for a moment believe that there was anyone else. Reggie was too involved with me, his work and our general way of life simply did not seem to give any notion that this could be happening. A fairly wry thought was as to when he would get the time! No, I put it down to pressure and to tiredness. He had been working extremely hard and, as he had quite rightly pointed out the evening before, he was always on show and responding to questions about his work and business plans and it always had to be the charming Reginald Forbes. But even the bouts of his temperament that I had heard about regarding the office and business surely did not dissolve as what I had witnessed upstairs. I decided to leave it until I possibly spoke to him later that day, in Key West. For a wild moment I thought of travelling down there myself instead of flying back to London that night, but that was too obvious and too Barbara Cartland.

Further thoughts were dispelled by Reggie's arrival with Steven. Reggie ignored me completely and Steven, who had been smiling and talking with him as they stepped out of the lift, looked merely confused. The doorman was holding a cab for them. Reggie walked straight out through the front, down the carpeted steps and got into the waiting cab. He slid across to the far side and sat staring at the wire mesh in front of him. Steve, again with his sheepish expression – for the second time within an hour – supervised the cabdriver putting the two cases in the boot. He looked at me and smiled nervously and then glanced in at the window to the cab.

"Enjoy Key West, Steven." He turned round. I held out my hand. "My best to Bindi and I'll see you and Ray down at the cottage over the weekend." Reggie had arranged for Ray and Steven to stay. Ray was to travel down with me on the Saturday morning and we would collect Steven and Reggie from the airport. It did not look as if it was going to be as enjoyable an arrival as the original those few months before.

The cab swept off. I stared at it for a moment and then walked back into the hotel. I made my way to the dining room on the first floor. I ordered myself eggs, toast and a Bloody Mary. "So much for love," I said, to the flowers in the cornucopia on the table.

I suddenly missed London, Amanda and Peter. I was looking forward to getting back. Reggie would no doubt sort himself out and the whole incident would hopefully be laughed at in time to come. Or would it?

I returned to London that evening as arranged. The rest of the morning had been busy and productive. I was delighted with the initial effect to the new offices. Reggie had been brilliant. The preliminary sketches and colour tonings, to be finalised in London, were sufficient to give a fair idea as to what the final effect would be. He had managed to epitomise his phrase 'updated trad' and the other phrase 'contraceptive decor' seemed stylishly safe without being sorry!

Dorella was in New York and had snared me for one of her luncheons. This meant the end of the afternoon and I had arranged for a limousine to collect me from her apartment on Park and take me straight on to Kennedy Airport. My baggage would be collected from the hotel by the chauffeur and from then on it would be a vague and pleasant flight to London. It also meant that I would be unable to telephone Key West even if I had wanted to.

I presented myself at the apartment at one o'clock. Dorella lived in magnificent splendour on Park in a duplex of some twenty rooms, all of which appeared to vie with the other for magnificence. She had tried every decorator in New York with the same ferocity she tried all her own cosmetics, and the result was a patchwork quilt of highly extravagant ideas. Her luncheon guests were all gathered in the Parrish Hadley drawing room for pre-lunch drinks before going into the tented splendour of the Valerian Rybar dining room. Coffee and liqueurs, after lunch, were noisily shared with Billy Baldwin in the library.

Among the familiar faces I spotted the waif-like Warhol and some frenzied blonde who was appearing in one of his avant-garde movies. Barbara Walters was there, looking more soignée than she did in her breakfast show, which means to say she was super soignée and I was looking forward to meeting her. Amanda was to appear on her television show which was a sure-fire way for an introduction to millions of Americans. The publicity for Amanda was already taking on monumental proportions as only the American media seems capable of doing it. Everybody knew of Amanda's show and was making sure that they had made the relevant reservations even before the show had opened and the sacred critics had cast their pearls.

Reggie had been asked to the luncheon but had declined, due to having to fly down to the Keys 'on business'. "When I go to a lunch at Dorella's," he had said to me, "it will be given for me."

"You're beginning to sound exactly like Elvira," I had laughed. I was now beginning to see how controlling of his destiny Mr Forbes was being. Even his absence seemed to have had an advantage for him. Dorella kept apologising for the fact that this wonderful new designer who was the toast of London – "I mean, darling, he even has Elvira eating out of his hand. And you know how Elvira only nibbles" – was not able to be with us today. She explained that he was on his way to Key West to look at a house "a Streetcar stop away from Tennessee's" and she could not wait to see what he would be doing to her new garden room.

Even this bit of information took me by surprise. I had known that the Bond Street premises had been extended to the New York premises, scheduled for the following year, but I did not realise that Reggie would be adding his own unique patch to Dorella's quilt. It did, for a split second, cross my mind that Reggie was outgrowing me. Though rich and of fair social standing myself, I was not a movie star, international name nor a title. I glanced round the luncheon table at the various animated faces. One particularly dashing young man, now the owner of a successful gallery, was there with his wife, a woman at least thirty years older than himself and even considered by the New York rich as 'super rich'. Her young husband, in name only, was one of those charming young men who, at an early stage, become 'walkers' to the many lonely widowed or single women who always need an escort for those seemingly endless parties and functions they never tire of attending. He had been notorious in the gay world, but had disappeared from the scene the higher up the social ladder he had climbed. There was a rumour – strongly supported by Dorella – that his latest boyfriend was the live-in chauffeur and that the elderly wife, a latent voyeur, spent many a happy hour watching husband and chauffeur making out. "So much better than an old movie on a late night channel," remarked Dorella dryly.

Perhaps Reggie had his eye on a cosmetic empire! I smiled. Or, God help us, the everlasting Elvira. He knew no princes so his aspirations at being a princess or principessa were not too good. I must be getting drunk, I thought, as I had another mouthful of wine (the breakfast Bloody Mary had been followed by several stiff martinis at The Oak Bar en route). Anyway, my smile was broader, at least he was acting like a queen in his own right. Reggie Regina! Of course! I laughed out loud causing several of the luncheon guests to look at me curiously. The name had been born.

"You seem to be enjoying yourself," Dorella remarked afterwards.

"Oh, I always do in New York, Dorella," I answered. "In fact, I have been having a right royal time."

*

Reggie rang once from Key West. He was enthusiastic about the house and made some original design suggestions, but his general attitude was cool. Bindi had not spoken to me and it was not possible to call him as I remembered he was going on to the West Coast for a business conference and would not be returning to the ranch for several days.

Reggie's attitude had again stunned me. He had been brilliantly professional and correct with his call, but it had been of a 'call to the client' nature. Adding insult to injury was a call from Ray to say that Reggie had spoken to him at the office and suggested he check with me that the plans for the weekend were still in order. Ray had gone on to say that Reggie had said for Ray to call him back if the weekend had been cancelled.

Reggie was planning to spend some time during the weekend with Ray and Steve going over the details they had worked upon in New York and the Keys. He had set up a small studio for himself at the cottage, in one of the outside sheds, and they would either be there or else he would return direct to London with Steven and they could meet in the office.

Not being the type of person who sulked nor bore grudges, I could not condemn Reggie for his attitude. After all, I was his lover and to change from hot to so cold after one flare-up in New York, seemed so very strangely wrong. Amanda realised something was upsetting me, but regrettably I had not had a real chance to speak to her. She was making her last appearance in *The Bliss of All* that Saturday and had to organise final pointers before she, and part of the original cast, left for New York on the following Monday. She had three weeks rehearsal with the New York crew before the grand opening.

Peter was equally as frantic with business and I did not have a chance to see him. I confirmed with Ray that he was expected with Steven, as previously arranged. I also suggested he came to dinner on the Friday evening, spent the night at Ennismore to save him journeying up at dawn from Bromley. We would leave at six in the morning to meet the early overnight flight from Miami. "You can lock yourself in the spare room with Petrina," I laughed.

Ray came along to the flat after the office had closed on Friday. He had a small overnight case for himself and one for Steven. I showed him to his room and then returned upstairs to wait for him to join me. I had already poured myself a Scotch and fetched him a gin and tonic when he eventually arrived. He and Steven are really quite odd, I thought to myself, as I sat listening to him chatter on from the chair in front of me. Whilst Steven was the more delicate of the two, Ray seemed more motherly. I found myself wondering what on earth they got up to in bed. But then, one never could tell in gay relationships as to which partner was which. Most couples I knew were definitely either active or passive, and though some were both through mutual affection or demand, these particular two remained an enigma. However, judging from Steven's preference for a bit of rough trade in New York a few days before, I gathered that Ray was the boss man of the couple.

He went on rapturising about Steven. They had been together for several years and lived in total domestic bliss in remote Kent. 'A proper pair of Dora Domestics' Reggie had once sniffed when Ray had cancelled an evening out due to Steven having a slight cold and therefore requiring looking after. Their small detached house was very stylish though a bit flamboyant for my tastes. One always felt that even Emily Merryweather Post would have to be on her best behaviour there. They were almost caricatures of a gay couple, 'a real Mr and Mrs' to quote the sardonic Peter.

Ray became fairly mellow and then became girlishly confidential. "I wouldn't tell anyone else, RA, but I feel I can trust you," Ray giggled. "But, do you know, whilst Steven was away, I almost had a naughty!" My dear Ray, I felt like adding, when Steven was away he had it away.

I took him to La Popote for dinner. As it was a fairly mild evening we nipped down through the mews and crossed the Brompton Road over towards Walton Street. Addy raised a studied eyebrow when I walked in. "And how is Reginald?" he charmed.

"Fine, Addy," I said.

Christopher came dancing over. "Ah, Mr A." he chimed. "And who is this?" I introduced Ray who was staring at Christopher with open admiration. "London's most devastating restaurateur," I said to Ray.

"He even says that about Bill Staughton!" hissed Christopher and swirled away to greet a mink-coated party who engulfed him with cries and kisses.

Dinner was fun and made more so by the cheerful crowd Christopher always seemed to attract. When he moved on to create Hunter's and then the hysterical 'Country Cousin', it was the case of the Pied Piper with all of London's fun café society following him with blind devotion from Chelsea to Fulham and then the nether regions of World's End.

The waiters had the restaurant in hysterics. The outrageous, camp Welsh Hugh, flew from table to table dishing out insults with the vegetables. The diners adored it. We staggered out at one thirty in the morning. To exit was rather like running a gauntlet of camp, ribald remarks. "How sad you're taking away that Ray of Sunshine," arched Christopher from the door.

"No doubt Mr A's planning to see the sunrise," hooted Hugh.

Chapter Eleven

A decidedly hung-over Ray and a not too chirpy RA were at the barrier to greet Reggie and Steven as they came off their transatlantic flight. The two of them looked exhausted as they came through from Customs and Immigration. Terminal 3 was crowded and throbbing with noise, even at this early hour of the morning. Ray and myself had just made the airport on time. Knowing that the two passengers would not have to wait for luggage I left the car on a yellow line and grinned rather pathetically at a hostile-looking warden. He looked the typical sort who had at last achieved 'his rights' with the aid of an ill-fitting uniform and I expected to find the car fluttering with tickets on our return. Or worse still, smile or no smile it would probably be towed away.

Reggie greeted me with a warm smile and a cheerful wave as he came through the doorway. I was so relieved – I had had no idea as to what his mood would be. How sad I had said to myself earlier, that instead of looking forward to Reggie I was more apprehensive as to how Reggie would be.

Steven and Ray were delighted to see each other and Ray flung his arms about Steven with no hesitation. Reggie smiled rather foolishly at the two of them hugging each other and then came over to me.

"Hi," he beamed, "how marvellous of you to meet us."

I took his hand baggage from him, as did Ray with Steven's. Chatting vigorously about the horrors of Miami airport, the airline and the Customs at Heathrow, we made our way through the crowds and to the main doors. My smile must have worked as there were no tickets on the windscreen and no sign of the warden. I mentally retracted all I had been thinking about him!

The drive to the cottage went unimpeded by any slight hints of temperament and I simply shrugged off the whole American incident as a phase. I merely hoped that these were not going to begin surfacing too often.

We spent a quiet weekend. Steven and Ray disappeared upstairs as soon as we arrived and did not reappear until a half hour before lunch. Reggie remained charming and announced that he would be going upstairs to have a bath and then would come down and join me for breakfast. We breakfasted in a slightly strained silence, me busy with the paper and Reggie going through an *Architectural Digest* he had bought at Miami airport. Both he and Steven had got on famously with Bindi. We discussed the house, Keith, Mallory Dock and referred to the offices in New York. I repeated how impressed and delighted I was with them. Meanwhile, I kept looking at Reggie. If only he would be the old Reggie I knew and fling his arms around me, I would have felt we were back to our normal, well-established selves. I decided to break whatever ice there was remaining.

"Dear Reggie," I said, putting the paper down. "It is so wonderful to have you back."

He pursed his lips slightly – was this a show of annoyance or perhaps irritation?

"Thank you," he replied. "It's nice to be back."

Silence.

Petrina, who had been lying at his feet looked up at the sound of his voice and then flopped with her head back on the floor. I was becoming sensitive. I was even assuming that the dog was aware of a slight friction or tension.

"Do you think we can disturb Ray and Steven?" I ventured. "I thought we may go over to Lulu's and perhaps have lunch there or else the Old Bell." The Old Bell at Hurley was a favourite of Reggie's and we had enjoyed many a happy light-hearted, loving meal there.

"Of course we can disturb them," said Reggie, rising to his feet. "I mean, if I wanted to do some work on those jobs they would have to jump to it. I did say that one of the reasons they were coming down here was to do some work on the projects."

"Hardly," I rebuked him gently. "Come on, they haven't seen each other for a week and you have the whole of tomorrow to work on my jobs." Christ, if I had done or said something that demanded punishment, I certainly was getting my full dose of it.

"You wouldn't have thought their separation so telling had you seen the way Steven was cavorting about in that bar in New York," said Reggie, still standing by the table. "He must have blown everybody in sight."

"For Christ's sake, Reggie, don't start again. Simply belt up, please." I added the 'please' slightly desperately. He glared at me.

"Look, I'm sorry about New York," I went on, "but if you are upset that I slapped you, I can only apologise and swear that I will never, ever do that again. I give you my solemn word."

"I doubt if the situation will arise again."

"Reggie, I was distraught with worry! You know my feelings for you and you must appreciate a fact. You are so vital to me and so much a part of me and I hope you feel the same way about me as I do about you. Come here, darling." I held out a hand.

"I'll call the boys," he said, and walked out of the room.

Steven and Ray came into the sitting room where I was going through a catalogue. They were flushed and very cosy with each other. I felt alone and an alien in their midst. Reggie came into the room. "Are we ready?"

"Ready?"

"Yes RA, aren't we off to Lulu's and then lunch? I rang the Old Bell and booked a table. You haven't forgotten you asked us?" he added.

Steven and Ray looked from me to Reggie and then back at me.

"No, of course not. How very good of you to call them, Reggie. Hold on, I'll get my coat and the keys. Would you like a drink before we leave?" I asked Steven and Ray.

"No thank you, RA. Reggie has already offered us one but we'll wait until we get to the pub."

Brilliant, I said to myself. Now I am being shown up as not only being a forgetful host, but not too good a one either!

Reggie was charm personified in the car. The conversation was light-hearted and brisk and he had us in fits of laughter with some wild tale about a scene in Papillon on Key West. This involved a young man in a stetson and someone who sounded very like Myrtle.

Lulu was delighted to see us and charmed Steven and Ray who had not met her before. Hector was as gloomy as ever. "He really does look as if he has taken an overdose of his own nutrients," laughed Reggie in the car afterwards.

"More likely an overdose of Lulu," I retorted. More laughs. Thank God we seemed to be reaching a normal keel once again.

We returned to the cottage around five o'clock. We had stopped in Henley to buy some additional provisions for dinner that evening.

Steven and Ray had insisted on cooking and the main course was to be a surprise. Ray had arrived the evening before with a large plastic carrier bag which had been smartly dumped in the refrigerator at Ennismore. Petrina had been very curious over the container. The bag had almost been forgotten in the early morning panic to get to the airport, but Ray had remembered this as we were going out of the front door.

We were all sitting in the television room having a cup of much needed tea. Reggie had checked the fires and turned towards the boys who were sitting together on the floor, their backs supported by the edge of the sofa.

"Well," he said, "now it's our turn."

I looked up at him.

"Come on RA," he said, smiling and holding out his hand. "If they can spend part of the morning in bed I see no reason why we shouldn't do the same. Shall we say dinner at nine?"

I was somewhat taken aback, but got to my feet, still holding his hand. "See you later, then," I said.

I followed Reggie up the stairs and into our bedroom. He closed the door behind him and gave me a shy look. "Forgive me?"

"Darling." He rushed over to my arms and buried his head in my shoulder.

"Oh RA," he squeaked, his voice muffled against my shirt. "I've been such a bitch. Please, please forgive me. I'm so sorry."

"There, there," I said, shushing him gently. I moved over to the bed and sat down pulling him down alongside me. "It's all right, darling, you're here with me and we're all right again. That is what matters more than anything else."

He sniffed and sat up looking at me. He looked so incredibly beautiful and vulnerable. "You're too good to me," he said, looking so woebegone that it was almost laughable.

"Nonsense, darling. I just know when I am on to a good thing." So does he, said the cynical side of my nature to my mind.

"I've been acting like a stupid, spoiled queen," he continued. "Oh God!"

"Oh, Reggie," I almost admonished him for the scene – it was getting a bit too much.

"Sorry." This was better.

"Come here," I said.

He tentatively leaned his shoulder against my chest. "Have I been awful?"

"Pretty bloody."

"Am I forgiven?"

"Could be."

"I'm sorry about New York. I... I didn't do anything..."

"Shhh... it's all forgotten. That was all yesterday..."

"RA?"

"Hmmm?"

"I really do love you."

"I love you too, Reggie."

"That's nice..." He nestled more closely against me.

"RA?"

"Yes darling..." I kissed him gently and began to undo his shirt. Our kissing became more passionate. I quickly pulled his shirt off him, then his trousers. I kissed him on his eyes, his nose, his mouth, his chest. I kissed his stomach. I buried my face in his crotch. He moaned. "Oh Reggie," I gasped. "Oh darling."

*

I did not have a chance to see Amanda before she left, but we spoke twice on the telephone. I had spoken to Carla and it was arranged that we would be there in New York for the opening night of the show. I had confirmed that Reggie would be with me and Carla had replied, rather slowly, that she looked forward to seeing him again.

The Houston Fair was having better results than I had anticipated. My company had received several commissions regarding the advising on and purchase of antiques and paintings. One enquiry covered a major aeronautics company's headquarters in Houston and we were also becoming involved with a hotel chain who were expanding worldwide. They wanted a basic English quality as their 'look'. How strange I often said to myself that it took an American company and American money to finance the 'Englishman Abroad' look. However, the contract, a seven-year term, was solid and extremely profitable. I then began making enquiries as to the possibility of opening a branch office and sales room in Houston. Sotheby's had been brilliant at doing this on a large scale in New York and I saw no reason as to why I could not repeat the formula even if on a lesser scale. I found the

Texans stimulating and enthusiastic and I looked forward to this additional challenge to my rapidly growing minor empire. I had toyed with the idea of involving Reggie with the design side, but he was so busy with his own particular venue that I decided to leave it for a while. The offices in New York were going to be a great success, but I had got a slight warning light when a client had seen this in it's initial stages and had commented. "It's very dashing, Mr Anderson, but it's not really like those wonderful cosy 'English' London offices of yours. This is more New York, isn't it?"

Reggie, of course, was a very theatrical designer and his interiors were more international as opposed to typical. The success of Elvira's house had been due to the introduction of colour more than any structural work. The word to describe Elvira's schemes was Cecil B. DeMille 'cosmetic'. Reggie had been brilliant in emphasising mouldings and plaster work, plus his use of totally alien fabric patterns and colour. It was Elvira's own particular brand of the theatrical that enhanced these new backdrops and the result was an overwhelming blending of two catalysts – Elvira the fairy tale Duchess and her fairy tale castle as created by Reggie.

Amanda would also be an ideal client. She had requested an apartment of the Seventies. Her demands were for the use of clean lines, clear colours and the techniques of the time in respect to lighting, textures and furnishings. Dorella had been of a similar vein and so Reggie's approach had already taken on its distinctive and bold feel. I had therefore deliberately toned down some of the effects stipulated for New York. When Reggie had reacted to these changes I did remind him that in the very beginning I had warned that I may be having to do just this. "I did say," I repeated, "that they are offices for a particular look and not a new look such as you have created so successfully for Elvira. Elvira wanted a change and though you have been brilliant in working around her an aura that still imbues the old – and I mean that kindly – my customers are coming to me for something tried and true." This seemed to calm him down and I compensated for my criticism by allowing him to turn Key West into a technique of ocean colours and effects which made even the most blasé of visitors comment most agreeably, and in an awed tone, over the final decorative results. I did say to myself on more than one occasion, that the house on Key West looked like some amazing Hollywood set for an underwater scene in a gay porno version of *The*

Waterbabies played, no doubt, by a frolic of Adonis-like nude young men. But Reggie was very pleased with the effect. Monica loved it and floated through the house like some magnificent mermaid with Angela tagging behind like some demented shrimp.

The hiccough of New York had seemed to be forgotten and I put this down as part of the 'growing together or growing up pains', a relationship had to endure to survive.

Reggie was looking forward to our return to New York. The reports from the contractors were favourable and he and myself would be attending to the final finishing touches when we were over for Amanda's Broadway debut. Dorella had already booked him up for several hours' work to her proposed designs on the garden room and I sensed he was more than keen to concentrate on this as opposed to help me with the end details to the offices. Like most designers, if he could not get his own way his interest waned and he was secretly relieved when I had said that I would be happier bringing as much of the London look to the new premises myself. The whole concept was still essentially Reginald Forbes, but a watered down version. As he said, and quite rightly, it looks as if someone had bleached the original coloured perspective. The designs and proportions were little short of magnificent and this again was a fine tribute to his excellent eye for form and a basic architectural inner instinct. "Perhaps I should decorate in chiaroscuro alone," he said, contradicting his reasons given to me over a year ago, for going against architecture in the first place.

"Why not?" I replied.

This then is exactly the look he eventually gave Dorella in her New York salon. The greys, blacks and tones of white looked sensational and to these Reggie introduced a flame red which looked like an outrage and became the most talked-about design point in Manhattan.

Bindi became a regular voice on the telephone. He was travelling up to New York the week before we were due to arrive, and was looking forward to a Sunday luncheon being given by Carla and Kurt. Amanda was to be there. He was wildly enthusiastic when he called me after the luncheon. It was in fact the day after. He and Amanda had taken in a film in the village after the lunch and then they had enjoyed a leisurely supper in some bistro down there. He was clearly smitten and kept referring to her as 'L'l doll'. Reggie took this up as quick as a flash and in our private conversations Amanda was referred to as Dildol! Elvira had become la grande Douche and Monica was eventually to become Ms Macho and Angela Ms Angst! Our relationship had become more strong and what I found to my delight was that I was having so much fun with his company and his introduction to his own way of life. Reggie introduced me to a loving, enthusiastic and impressively talented young group of people. Their attitudes towards politics, life and in particular sex, were of a tremendous variety. On politics it was usually a case of definite black or white; life was as you made it, and sex was regarded as extension of a basic affection and whether it was of your own sex or the opposite sex, nobody seemed to really care. I became used to straight couples staying with us, gay couples, and on one occasion, we had a ravishing transvestite who totally captivated the humdrum Hector. It would easily have been a case of St Tropez all over again, but Zoe, our house guest, was pining for her lover who had left her for a trial separation and so she was disenchanted by any advances or flattery. "She sees herself as Wyman in *Magnificent Obsession*," whispered Reggie evilly. "Her sadness is that her lover may not be Rock Hudson but Rock Hardon somewhere else."

Reggie was spending more time at the flat in Fulham. He felt it unfair that I should be wakened at all hours with his late homecomings and so we tried to keep our weekends at the cottage as selfish as possible. Friends coming to stay were now invited down in time for lunch on Sunday and we would all set off for London on the Monday morning. Reggie would leave at some unearthly hour such as six o'clock to miss the traffic. I would spend the earlier part of the morning dictating letters and notes for Clare to deal with when I reached the office early afternoon. I would usually lunch at The Old House on my way up to town or else go straight up to London for some luncheon appointment. Elsie would see that the house guests were taken care of breakfast-wise and they too would eventually set off around mid-morning. Mostly, they would leave with Reggie if they had to be in town for an early start. We both found that this weekend arrangement suited us both admirably.

Reggie's skill at manipulating his finances fascinated me. For someone who gave the appearance of being rather vague about money in general, he would have been a wizard on the Stock Exchange. Although he could not be deemed mean, he was shrewdly cautious and any spare money was carefully reinvested. His brother, Richard, had supplied him with a great amount of work in Yorkshire requiring only design fees and sure enough the design work from the north was also growing. Our visit to New York was a success. I remained in the city for a week, but Reggie spent two days only and most of this time was devoted to Dorella's apartment.

Dorella had been in constant touch with Elvira and knew as much about the Wilton Crescent house and details as Reggie's glamorous client did. The slightest toning, the arrival of the new swags – "My dear Dorella, the pelmet boxes to the drawing room are divine! Reggie took up the original shapes designed by dear Syrie and outdid her – he redid them in one of her most famous trademarks in mirror! He has then festooned the mirror with swags of the sheerest silk and you still have the idea of the tails, but the fringings and tasselling is all on the mirror. It's magnificent."

The more Elvira oohed and aahed the more the fashionable magazines clamoured to see, photograph, study, and naturally – meet Reginald Forbes. Reggie took all in that unruffled stride. However, he certainly enjoyed playing up to his newly discovered audience. He was subtle enough to calm down for more of his sober clients, but when it came to what he claimed as his PR persecuted, all stops were pulled out. Reggie was elevating Elvira within himself. He was a great admirer of her taste which, though verging on the flamboyant, was too intelligent ever to offend. Whilst comments were made, there was little criticism and admiration of his innovative techniques and disbelief at some of his more outrageous combinations and design complications kept his reputation generating itself with almost a pop star frenzy. "Regina" became the nickname in the office, between his gay friends and even Amanda was referring to him by this name. Elvira retained the very definite "Reginald" or "Mr Forbes" when introducing him, and did not seem too pleased when meeting Peter at a reception and being told "I hear Regina has come up with something larger than life for you this time, Elvira dear!"

Dorella and Reggie in New York created a minor whirlwind of excitement. Dorella's publicity team made sure that *Home Furnishings Daily* interviewed Reggie, *Women's Wear Daily* talked to him, and one of the leading male fashion magazines cornered him for a feature. A very frantic few days. Reggie revelled in his image as the effete English designer abroad. His colour combinations and the flamboyance of his style and mannerisms began a minor cult following. He taped a television chat show and starred - there was no other word for it - at a sumptuous cocktail party Dorella gave for him. The press referred to him as a "reincarnation in style and looks of Wilde's 'Bosie'" and immediately counteracted any sueable claims by following this up with a hint that he had a lady in his life who preferred to keep out of the limelight.

She was hinted at as being a writer of some repute. Where Reggie had thought this one up I had no idea but I was thankful to read that she was not an antique dealer - fingers pointing at me - or of Austrian origin - Petrina! Reggie kept the New Yorkers happy with his long curly hair (Paul at the Berkeley had recently entered his life with hair and tongs), fastidiously cut suits from Tommy Nutter or Dougie Hayward, brocaded waistcoats and cravats or stocks with bejewelled pins. I cast it off as connoisseur camp, as opposed to camp camp, and again even the cab drivers flattered him with their admiration even though basic Bronx was nothing as bright as the comments passed in London. After a photograph had appeared on the front of one of the dailies, showing Reggie and Elvira arriving at a large charity event in Berkeley Square, one cabbie was said to have shouted to Reggie who was standing waiting to cross by the Ritz - "'Ere Reg. You got one of 'em tarara things like the old Duch wears?" Hoots of laughter and much waving and tooting accompanied this comment as the cab swirled off. Reggie waved graciously.

America also began the "Reggie says" quotes, and although these were extended to "Regina Rules" remarks in London, he was certainly working his way to whatever it was he so eagerly and ruthlessly pursued. I found myself becoming more of the "rock behind the scenes" or "rock of ages" as Reggie put it.

I chastised Reggie for his drinking - he always had a glass of champagne in his hand - and also for some of his behaviour. Mostly the scenes would end in tears and nobody understood him but, as I patiently explained, I understood too well, and far better it be me as opposed to someone else who would see this hysterical side. Petrina had reached a stage of not flinching when a sudden shriek and flounce of bad temper occurred with growing regularity in our domestic life. Whilst he remained calm in the country, a quiet evening in London, usually at his suggestion, resulted in a pouting and claiming of "come to the Cabaret. Why am I wasting time when I should be out being seen by doing my thing and benefiting the work scene?"

On more than one occasion I would claim a business dinner when Reggie announced he would be free. There would be a minor sulk, but he would then be out and spend a happy few minutes on the telephone the next morning telling me what I had missed.

At times I confessed to Peter that it was like having the most impossible, talented glamorous star as a mistress. Peter's sardonic reply was, "Well?"

The office continued to flourish. Reggie employed more staff and came up with the announcement that he was eventually going to open a salon in Mayfair and the Pimlico Road operation, under Steven and Ray, would handle the contractual side. At no time, though, did he shirk even the most minuscule of decisions or site visits. These visits alone were worth witnessing, but nobody could hoodwink Reggie nor excuse an error. He was always lethally professional. Joe and Chris remained brilliantly supportive and they, too, were going from strength to strength as a result of the never-ending contracts that Reggie was pulling in and putting their way. His social flair and influence among the Elviras and Dorellas saw him meeting women whose husbands were the demons of the hard business and commercial world. Through the influence of their wives Reggie was getting contracts that he would never have dreamed of even as short a time back as two years before. A contract to design the boardroom and several executive offices for a financial company in The City saw Reggie's break into the Arab market, which had been on a rapid increase in London. Flats with extravagant budgets for the design and furnishing became a specialised sector of Designs Unlimited. Reggie had even fitted in two rapid-fire trips to the Middle East on Concorde who had just carried out her inaugural flight.

Chapter Twelve

Amanda's show was a tremendous hit and the official opening exceedingly glittering and very glamorous. There was an enormous party afterwards given by Carla and Kurt for her. She and Bindi never seemed away from each other for a moment and I must admit that they made a splendid couple. Amanda had become Broadway's darling and wherever she went she was greeted by enthusiastic and adoring fans. After the reticence of the English public she found this new fan magic overwhelming at first. In London she could walk through Harrods and there would be a few nudges and whispers, whereas in New York she would find herself mobbed. On one occasion in Bloomingdales they had to sneak her out of the staff entrance, but not before she had signed endless autographs and shaken hands with numerous avid admirers behind the scenes of the great Lexington Avenue store.

I took off to Texas again. Bindi was to join me, but stayed on in New York. I gave the Warwick a miss this time and stayed at the ranch. Although this was some way out of Houston, it was ideal for me and Max was marvellous at being a 'nanny' figure. Monica was on great form and determined that Bindi had at last 'come out' in New York. I explained that the coming out was more a fascination for Amanda Adamson than A Man and although I felt the pun pretty terrible she had shrieked in her wonderful, bawdy way.

I also travelled down to Key West. Work had not started on the house, but the workmen were scheduled to move in immediately after Christmas and I planned to be using the house in early summer. Reggie had said he would prefer to be in the Key's for Christmas as opposed to go to New York or Vermont, and so I agreed to making the relevant reservations at the Pier House. This also meant that the initial work to the house would be supervised by Reggie- "after all, I have to earn that fee," he had said, smiling.

It was at this stage that I began calling Reggie, Regina. The term was used as one of teasing endearment and strictly in private. Peter had been staying with us one weekend and had heard me call Reggie by the nickname on several occasions. It was only a few weeks before the name became a fact and Regina out of Reggie was born yet again.

I had always loved New York, but it fascinated me to note when we were there for the second visit that Reggie did not seem to be over fond of the City. We were discussing this one evening when we were back in London – and long after the Christmas and New Year break on Key West – when he had confirmed the point to me. "I loathe it," he said, suddenly quite violent. "I find it crude, brash, filthy, noisy... actually, I find it pathetic. Rather like a tacky cripple who is making a last attempt to stand up straight!" I found this a strange comparison and simply could not see his reasons for such vehemence. "Everyone goes on to say how New York influences this and that," he continued, "but they are desperate for US. They are the city of the en masse. Their designer labels are en masse. There is nothing exclusive. Even an intimate restaurant is en masse, their helpings are en masse. If they have a choice they go for something European – they need us. We don't need them." Whether it be a film director, a writer or whatever, he always brought in a European influence. It was a thrust and parry argument. I could parry away all his digs against America as simply as he could with all my pro-American enthusiasm. I ended by asking why his enthusiasm for Key West? His answer had been simple. "Key West is not America – Key West is lotus land, it is the land of the never never. It's sea and sun and sex, if you want it. It is an island of no time."

It was not long after this particular discussion that we were both down at the cottage for a solitary weekend. Reggie had gone off with Petrina to Wallingford and would no doubt drop by to see the ever jolly Lulu. I had been checking out some figures for the planned Houston project when the telephone rang. I answered it, expecting it to be Peter who had telephoned the office the day before and had left a message saying he would be calling over the weekend.

"RA?" There were some cracklings and a few atmospherics, but I recognised the voice.

"Darling, where are you? You don't sound as if you're in New York. You sound as if you are in the middle of the jungle."

"We are – well, almost."

"Who's we?"

"My husband and I." There were a few giggles.

"Oh yes." I realised Amanda sounded slightly tipsy.

"Yes darling."

"You haven't," I yelled. "That's fabulous news!"

Of course she had. Carla and I had discussed it and it was inevitable. Bindi and Amanda.

"But seriously, darling, where are you?"

"Hold on, here's my beautiful, wonderful, magnificent husband to talk to you."

"RA?"

"You old dog! Congratulations to the two of you."

"Thank you. We wanted you to be with us today. I wanted you as best man, but the lil lady had no time to spare so we made do with Kurt and Carla."

"Where are you?"

"Cuzco."

"Where!"

"Cuzco – Peru!"

"Why Cuzco? For God's sake."

"Manda wanted to see Machu Pichu."

"Oh yes." I started to laugh. "Put her on Bindi."

"RA."

"Dirty cow."

"You guessed!"

It was a standing joke. Amanda and myself some years back, had been going through some travel brochures in a light-hearted way. We were planning a few days' break and one of the brochures showed a colourful picture of the two massive, upright volcanic peaks, known as The Pitons, on the island of St Lucia in the Caribbean. "Goodness," Amanda had laughed, "do you think that it is a hint as to what those large black men can offer!"

We had roared with laughter. Mount Fuji we had decided, looked very Japanese.

"I always imagine them to be short and rather fat," Amanda had giggled. I had poured us more champagne.

We had whooped over Kilimanjaro. "You killa man with dat," I had suggested. More giggles and shrieks.

Mount Everest. "Forget the rest," whooped Amanda, but we had both agreed that the shot of the peak at Machu Pichu was the ultimate.
"Machu Pichu."
"Your verdict," I laughed.
"Bindi is best," she exploded. Bindi grabbed the phone back.
"What are you terrible wenches on about?" he drawled.
"Ask Amanda," I spluttered. "If you are half the man she's claiming, you will have the decency to blush."

They eventually rang off. I was delirious with excitement and happiness for the two of them. I considered them so very close and dear and I was delighted at their news. There was so much to discuss with them but I would leave that until Amanda was back in New York. What a story it was. Rich Texan, good-looking and charming, marries international star. It was the thing movies are made of. I immediately dialled Carla in New York. She was delighted to hear me. No, she had not telephoned me as Amanda had insisted that she would be breaking the news. We spoke about the show and Carla assured me that Amanda would complete her contract on Broadway, but she had her doubts as to the film. "They want to start a family as soon as possible," Carla continued. "They really are so happy and Manda is simply prepared to forget Amanda Adamson and totally involve herself in her new career as Mrs Bindi Wainwright, wife and mother."

Reggie was as delighted as I had been when I told him the news. After the initial bout of enthusiasm he did come out with one rather cryptic comment which caused a slight embarrassed silence – "so much for my entrée to Hollywood – for the moment."

I missed Amanda enormously. Although we spoke to each other virtually every second day, it was not the same as having her in London. I did see a great deal of Elvira, but there was really no comparison between the two friendships. Elvira's coverage in the fashion magazine could not have pleased her or Reggie more. There were stunning photographs of Elvira 'at Home' and full page colour shots of the house. There was a dashing portrait of Reggie with the article. He had matured so much over the past two years and it was very noticeable. The elfin charm was still there, but the prettiness had given way to a devastating handsomeness. There was also an amazing poise and charm. He looked like a graduate with distinction from the most glamorous academy of glamour.

He was becoming very in demand. He and Richard, whom I had now met on several occasions, were negotiating on the purchase of the shop next to the original in Pimlico Road. Amanda still remained on the board, but her role was now totally negligible. Reggie had created a space age fantasy with her flat, as planned and here again more publicity followed. Amanda had come over to London with Bindi for a few days – she had left the show on Broadway a few months after the wedding and had officially announced her retirement from show business – and was photographed for several magazines in the apartment. One of the highlights of her visit was a dinner party she gave with Reggie to introduce the new apartment and, she added as a wicked afterthought, Bindi!

Originally Amanda planned a discreet dinner for ten or twelve. I could tell from our several conversations that she must have guessed Reggie's reactions about the proposed Hollywood contract and its cancellation. Reggie had not mentioned this again to me, but he must have said something in passing when seeing Amanda on her return. Amanda, being the ever-loving and diplomatic Amanda, did exactly what one would have expected – she did have her intimate dinner party for a few close friends but, with Reggie, she gave a large buffet-style supper to which several influential journalists and magazine correspondents were asked, as well as what Bindi claimed as London's "café oh lay and gay society." In contrast to Elvira's 'look' Reggie had created a science fiction setting for Amanda. The main drawing room caused gasps of admiration and stunned, incredulous looks from the arrivals. Although the interior had been well publicised it was a case of 'seeing is believing'. The main room, which opened onto a large terrace, had been divided into two areas with an enormous log-burning fireplace at either end. The total walls were mirrored with the fire recesses suspended into these. Reggie had raised the floor, thus creating seating scoops in the areas in front of the fireplaces. His famous floating sofas, wondrous snake-like units, softly upholstered and lying on curved acrylic mirror plinths, gave the effect of large, fluffy clouds. The vertical louvres to the long windows were in mirror and a cornice effect of mirror strips and lacquered plaster added a further undulating dimension to the room. The whole area, in tones of white and the silver effects of the mirror, housed a centred display splitting the two conversation areas containing a mirror-based fountain with clear acrylic shields and shelves hosting a collection of jade in tones of green and opaque whites. Silvered pillars held tumbles of greenery and the ceiling, in mirror, had been painted with swirling clouds to take on the theme of the cloud-like sofas.

"It's how I imagine heaven, darling," crooned Elvira, in a wraith of Jade green chiffon and sparkling with the Lewes emeralds (she had checked her colours with Reggie earlier).

"She's old enough to have been there and back," muttered Reggie on hearing this remark.

Amanda was radiantly happy and looked almost celestial – again Elvira's phrase – in silver. Elvira had not quite got round to describing me in simple black tie, but no doubt I would be 'funereal' to keep in with her heavenly aspirations of the evening. Bindi was 'god-like' and Reggie looked an angel.

"A somewhat fallen one," hissed Reggie to me. He was in a white jacket, piped in silver, and green trousers. I did a double take and had it confirmed by Steven. "Yes, there are total silver streaks in his hair. Be thankful it isn't emerald."

"Amanda," Peter boomed his welcome from the silvered doorway.

"Peter darling." Amanda swirled over to him dragging Bindi. Peter shook hands heartily with Bindi and raised his eyebrow at Amanda.

"My dear, lovely to have seen you but I can't stay."

"Oh? Tell me."

"There's a night flight to New York which means I may make Texas by the afternoon," said Peter, widening his eyes.

"The greatest compliment," laughed Amanda. "Dear Peter." She kissed him fondly and then moved off with Bindi to greet some other guests.

The buffet had been arranged and sparkled with Reggie's inventiveness. He had insisted on all food being green and white. There was fresh asparagus to start, or avocado soup. This was followed by sole veronique, cold lobster or sturgeon on a bed of lettuce and cucumber. The main courses were turkey breasts in a white wine sauce or slices of delicate veal. Salads and vegetable were all in tones of green and the sweet course was a green fruit salad of apple, Kiwi fruit, figs and grapes, or green sherbets and pear sorbet. Green veined cheeses with celery and apple rings added to the decorative interest of the separate tables.

Reggie, with the inevitable glass of champagne, flitted with professional and somewhat venomous ease through the thronging guests. Peter joined me at one stage and we stood surveying the room.

"It's a long way from temperament and The Raging Bull. Isn't it?" he commented.

"Let's say from The Raging Bull," I replied.

The majority of the guests had left by one o'clock. Reggie had left with Peter, Steven and Ray to go on to some disco and I ended up sitting in the small green study – with Bindi and Amanda.

"A fairly substantial success," I said, swirling my brandy slowly in my glass.

"Thank God we've done 'our bit'," said Amanda from the sofa where she sat, her feet tucked up underneath her, her head on Bindi's vast shoulder. "As much as I adore Regina, he doesn't seem to stop. The energy is frightening."

"No more than yours, darling," I said. "When you were doing a show and filming you were never not 'on the go'."

"Yes darling, but Reggie has to be so original the whole time. That must be exhausting. I simply had to repeat written lines to leap about to a routine. He's like the Liberace of the palaces as opposed to the pianos."

I laughed. "Palaces being the operative word. He's now got some crazy idea of getting a house in Cheyne Row or a studio in Glebe Place. No wonder he's Regina and Regina rules, okay?"

Bindi rumbled from his side of the sofa, "He looks like a Regina, more so than a Reggie." He leaned forward, "I must tell you, on Key West, that first time we went there, he was quite something. His energy came to the fore in every possible way."

Amanda gave Bindi a quick, warning glance which did not escape me.

"Oh," I said, "do tell me more."

"Nothing more to tell, really," Bindi said, rather lamely. "He just seemed to enjoy himself and was never out of those discos until dawn..."

"Sounds like Reggie in London," I laughed.

"When are you next in Texas?" said Amanda, changing the topic and holding out her glass to Bindi. "RA?"

"Thank you, a small one please, Bindi, I know your Texan ideas of a nightcap!"

"So do I," smiled Amanda, wickedly. Bindi leaned over and kissed her.

"Well, if Houston takes off, I can see myself there for several weeks if not a month or two out of the year." I looked at Amanda. "Darling, I hope you were thinking I may suggest this, but I would be so happy if you would like to help me with the business over there. I mean, you in Houston and with some spare time!"

Amanda looked at Bindi. "What did I tell you?" she said. "Darling, I would have been desolate if you hadn't suggested me getting involved. I mean, I am still a director of Designs Unlimited so why don't you keep using lil Amanda in any family offshoot?"

We sat talking happily about the Houston venture, Bindi and Amanda's plans for a family, life in Houston, Reggie again – not in too great a detail this time, except that Amanda conferred that he should calm down slightly. Even Elvira had commented that he was becoming a bit 'excitable'.

Amanda and myself planned to speak in the morning and arrange a quiet lunch. She and Bindi were off to Paris and then to Venice for a few days. They were planning to return direct to America from Rome.

I got back to the flat, let Petrina out into the garden and sat for a few moments savouring another brandy and the quietness that comes with the lateness of the hour. I smiled when I thought of Amanda and Bindi together. They were so happy and seemed such a complete unit. I thought of my own situation. Whilst I loved Reggie very dearly I did feel that the relationship of now two years and a bit, had been taking on a dangerous swing. Reggie's success and notoriety – I preferred to use that word as opposed to popularity as Reggie was not really all that popular – could easily account for this. The majority who knew him, apart from his office staff, the workmen and myself, never saw the temperament and the hysteria he could evoke. At first I had thought this was due to pressures he had been unused to, but it was actually simply in his makeup. "I'm the bitch – goddess of the design world," he had camped on one or more occasion, "when I say drag it, honey I mean the paintwork and not your butt!" Yet he was such a complex of contrasts. One moment he would be sweet and faun-like – 'strychnine sweet' he would purr – or else an impossible monster. I was beginning to find it very exhausting. I had to confess that I was still infatuated by this feline creature. Our sex life had not diminished, in fact it had seemed to be strengthening and Reggie had always been one for new ideas and innovations in bed. I smiled as I thought of a weekend not too far back when we had been alone at the cottage. Reggie had been sitting on the floor, his head resting against my knee as we sat watching the late night Saturday film, *Singing in the Rain*. He was absently stroking my foot.

"RA?" he said suddenly.

"Mmmmm?" I smiled down at him and stroked his hair. Moments like this were so special and so treasured, and it was on these occasions that I felt I could forgive him for even his most outrageous bouts of selfishness and egotism.

"Are you ever kinky – I mean, kinky kink?"

I looked down at him. "How kinky?" I was slightly taken aback. Our sex life was basically wholesome and fairly straightforward. "You're not going to tell me you have suddenly been inspired by the title of the movie, to take up membership of the golden shower syndrome or...?"

Reggie laughed. "No thank you, though... it could be..."

"Not tonight, young man," I laughed. "Don't forget we had asparagus soup!"

"Correct!" Reggie laughed. He looked back at the screen. "Steven and Ray were telling me about something they tried the other night and it sounded rather odd – but fun."

"Come on. What?"

"I'm not suggesting we do it."

"Well, if you are suggesting you'd do it with anyone else..." We both laughed, but I had a faint glimmer of doubt. If Reggie was now going to experiment into kinky sex and I wasn't too keen to partake, then what?

"What do you want to try?" I said. "Come on, we'll do it."

"RA, I'm embarrassed."

"Don't be ridiculous," I snorted. "Tell me anyway." I was curious.

"Well... no let's forget it."

I laughed and teased him for a few more moments. I sat holding his hand and went back to watching the antics of the dancers on the screen. The little devil had got me quite turned on. A silence followed, but I could sense Reggie glancing at me and then looking back at the television.

"RA?"

"Yes, again?"
"Have we any alka seltzer?"
"I think so... why, have you a headache or something?"
"No."
"Come on, Reggie, out with it."
"Or in with it!"
"In with it?" I started to laugh. "You don't mean..."
"Well, it's something Steven told me about. An alka seltzer and an ice cube."
"A bit cold, don't you think?"
"I don't know... would you like to try?"
"Why not?" I roared with laughter and pulled him to his feet. I gave him a hug and moved over to a side table. I picked up the ice bucket. "Reggie's Ice Cram Parlour?" I questioned.

Reggie giggled.

"Your order sir," I continued, holding up the bucket. "One cool milkshake coming up."

We both roared with laughter and, arm in arm, made our way to the stairs.

"Though," I added, smiling down at him, "knowing my Reggie, perhaps Bucks Fizz is more appropriate!"

Chapter Thirteen

Reggie was determined to go ahead with the purchase of the property in Upper Cheyne Row. Although I thought this a tremendous extravagance and potentially a serious drain on the finances of the company – even though these seemed to be accumulating very healthily – he and Richard planned it as a company house and I was given all the sound arguments such as a tax loss and so forth. As the deal would not be influenced by me in any way, I left the two of them to sort this out. Although it meant that Reggie would concentrate his time at the house and I could see the nights spent at Ennismore Gardens lessening, I was secretly rather relieved. The weekends at the cottage were our main stabiliser and Reggie did really require a showplace of his own. More and more clients wanted to see Reginald Forbes in his own environment, and although the flat in Fulham had been ideal at the start, as he was now onto the big time it was only right that the necessary background was duly created to emphasise his widely accepted style.

Reginald Forbes had, quite simply, become the style of the Seventies. With the recession and general gloom and despondency abounding, his colourful personality and flamboyant attack on the work in general, created an aura which was admired and on occasions, envied. Reggie was a phenomena in his own right. A star success.

I spent a few minutes looking at the house when he first exchanged contracts, and then promptly left for Houston. I was spending more and more time in the city and of course Amanda and Bindi were a tremendous lure. Amanda had joined in her side of assisting me with a vigour that made even her days on the London stage seem lethargic. Her marriage to Bindi was a tremendous success and this was added to when Amanda announced she was pregnant. Bindi was hysterical with delight and caused much mirth and merriment. He fussed around Amanda to such an extent that Monica was heard to observe, "I think he's the one who's pregnant!"

I had seen a house in River Acres which I decided to buy. The property, styled on a Texas idea of an old coaching inn, was ideal for me. Basically it comprised of one enormous high beamed room with a study and two bedrooms leading off these. An enormous kitchen and dining area completed the house. There were also staff quarters and a rather splendid garden with a pool. I checked out the property with Amanda and left her to organise it for me. I requested bland tweeds and plaids and supplied the remainder of the furniture myself. I sent over a fair amount of good quality oak from England and several faded Kashmiri rugs. The house was simple and comfortable and ideal for me. Monica was swanning around Key West – she now claimed herself as the matriarch of her newly created family – and so with Bindi and Amanda, Monica, Angela and Reggie, plus the toing and froing between London, New York, Houston and the occasional quick flits down to the Keys, I was constantly on the move.

Reggie retained his own lifestyle in London. He spent a tremendous amount of time with Elvira and the name James Young, kept cropping up. Elvira had spent several weekends with James at his house in Gloucestershire and I was faintly surprised when Reggie told me that he had been down there on two occasions by himself.

"You had better watch him," I said to Reggie. "He's probably doing a latent switch after all."

The house in Upper Cheyne Walk became pure Reggie. The property, though registered and therefore subject to endless bylaws regarding existing structures and inner finishes, proved no problem to his ever inventive mind. The garden went so far as to boast a Jacuzzi whirlpool and the house, mirrored in a brilliant effect of applied panels and in banded ceramic tiles to the floors, gave one the impression of walking inside a brilliant child's kaleidoscope. Furniture, designed by Reggie, was integrated with modern classics, such as the designs of Mies van de Roe, and he also introduced an enormous amount of African art. His collection was completely that of the eye. If Reggie saw something he liked, he bought it and somehow it always managed to look as if the area he eventually sited it against had been especially created for the piece and the piece alone.

I had arranged to lunch with Peter on my return to London after a particularly gruelling time in Houston. I had a few days planned in town before flying off again. This time, to Italy.

We met at Morton's in Berkeley Square. I found Peter leaning against the long bar, heavily conversing with a young man whom I took to be the latest friend. Peter had been alone since his final bust up with Tim, and although he always seemed to have some young companion in tow, he had never actually brought up the subject of the current companion nor bothered to really introduce him into our circle.

"Peter."

"RA. Welcome back again. God, you look fit. I take it that tan is partly Key West as well as Houston?"

"Almost. Basically it's partly convertible. You get a very good tan sitting in the sun in those traffic jams on those so-called freeways!"

"RA, meet Lawrence."

"How do you do," I said, glancing at the young man. Lawrence was extremely camp and I was surprised at Peter's choice. I had always been used to a fairly heavy number being alongside Peter, but Lawrence was the other extreme. He was tall, very thin and best described as gangly. He had pale hair, large grey eyes and a highly prominent Adam's apple. I took it that he was either brilliantly endowed or brilliant in bed, or both.

I mentioned this quickly to Peter when Lawrence excused himself to go off to the toilet for a few minutes.

"The latter," smirked Peter. "He's got a built-in magimix. I've never known anything like it!"

Lawrence returned, but not before Peter had said casually, "I hope you don't mind if he joins us for lunch." I was slightly put out as I had hoped to have a soul talk with Peter and catch up in general on news and events, but this was typically Peter.

A rather large, well-upholstered woman sidled past me and perched on a stool next to where I was standing. She joined two other women and there were shrieks as they greeted each other and admired whatever the other was wearing. I heard Reggie's name mentioned and my ears pricked up.

"My dear, we've got Reginald Forbes to do the house. Harry wasn't too keen - he's very pricey you know - but I simply insisted."

"I loathe what he did to Martha, dear."

"Oh, do you? I thought he was quite brilliant really. He captured her so well, don't you think? I mean, she is exactly like the flat – dark!"

Peter smiled at me. We went on talking amongst ourselves.

"My dear," said the woman next to me. "There he is!" I glanced around to the main door. Sure enough, there was Reggie. I was faintly surprised that he hadn't mentioned that he, too, would be at Morton's, but then neither had I, and we had certainly reached the stage where every minute of our working lives was not being accounted for. I had to admit he looked outstanding.

Peter nodded. "Your friend looks well. Don't tell me he's joining us!"

I shook my head. At that moment, James Young walked in. Reggie turned and smiled at him. James Young looked more elegant than I remembered him. He was wearing an immaculate black and white checked jacket, light grey trousers, a white shirt and a black and grey striped tie. Reggie was literally identically dressed.

"The Bobsey twins," smirked Peter. "Don't tell me they have taken up shopping together!"

"What do you mean 'shopping' together?"

"Oh, it's common talk that James Young and Reggie are seen almost everywhere together. Poor Elvira is feeling slightly left out. Her two major escorts seem to be only interested in escorting each other."

Peter glanced back at me again.

"Don't tell me this is news to you?"

"Reggie and I are still together," I said, rather stiffly.

"I realise that," said Peter, "but you have been away a great deal and whilst you're away methinks young Reggie's turned James Young gay!"

I stared at Peter, the blood rushing to my face. I could quite understand Reggie seeing someone, but I did think it extraordinary he had not mentioned James to me, but then, of course, he had. "I know that Reggie spends a good deal of time with him in the country when I'm abroad," I continued, "but I hardly think James and he are bedfellows."

"Bedfellows," guffawed Peter. "At times your expressions are amazing. I hear," he added conspiratorially, "James Young has one of the biggest in London too – I won't ask you if you've noticed a slackness up there lately."

"Shut up, for Christ's sake, Peter!" I snapped. I looked over at Reggie again. He and James Young had moved to the bar, quite oblivious to anyone else there. James ordered two glasses of champagne, handed one to Reggie and they silently toasted each other. I simply could not believe it. Surely Reggie could not be acting so indiscreetly, particularly in a place like Morton's where everyone knew everyone and also he must have known that I would be sure to hear of his luncheon out. Perhaps that was exactly what he wanted.

"RA, darling." I spun round. Tracy Reed had made an entrance. Spectacular in scarlet and black and looking like some devastating Velasquez, she stalked over towards me. "And Peter," she smiled.

"Trace darling!" I kissed her and introduced her to Lawrence. Lawrence was looking at her with open-mouthed admiration. I had to admit, Tracy was looking the epitome of glamour, but then she always did. Lawrence was to say later at lunch, "She looks exactly like a movie star."

"She is," commented Peter.

"And how is Houston?" continued Tracy, accepting a large glass of champagne from Peter (Tracy had protested 'no' at first as she was meeting a girl friend, but we were happily able to persuade her to change her mind).

"Marvellous," I replied. "I must arrange for you to come out there and then go onto the Keys."

"Promises, promises," pouted Tracy. "Oh, there's Regina!"

"Yes, with the latest rung," said Peter.

"Peter," I cautioned.

"Now, now, don't be silly wenches," brillianced Trace. She dazzled Lawrence with another smile that would make any dental advert look inferior. "Have you known these two old quags for long?"

Lawrence muttered that he had known Peter for a few days and had met me only a few minutes ago.

"On occasions the best way," replied Tracy sweetly. "Oh, there's Liz," she cried. "I must go. Be in touch darling," she cooed to me, "and I'd love to meet for a drink in Florida."

She sailed off, towering above the rest of the bar, stopping to pat Reggie on the shoulder. She smiled down at him, said something and pointed at where the three of us were standing. She threw us another dazzling smile and went over to join an equally glamorous companion.

"The league of the BBs never fails to amaze me," said a bemused Peter.

"BBs?" asked Lawrence.

"Beautiful Birds, ball-breaker bloody bitches... whatever. Trace is a stunner though. You can understand why they all fall to her charms."

Reggie had glanced back at us when Tracy had spoken to him. He muttered something to James Young and edged his way towards us.

"Ooh, Mr Forbes," carolled the woman on the stool next to me. I had forgotten about her.

"Mrs Larkin," Reggie waved, "how nice to see you. I'll ignore the calorific cherry in that drink."

"Oh, Mr Forbes!" Mrs Larkin trilled with excitement at having spoken to Reggie. She pantomimed another wave with her plump, beringed hand and returned to her companions excitedly.

"Good afternoon," pursed Reggie.

"How's Lady Forbes today?" said Peter. "The two of you look like a fucking Burberry advert in matching checks."

"I'm very well, thank you Peter," Reggie said, in a clipped tone. He looked at Lawrence and I saw his eye flicker as he noticed the poor man's Adam's apple. Peter did not.

"Reggie," I said, "what a surprise and how nice to see you."

"Aren't you two still living together?" smirked Peter.

"RA," said Reggie, ignoring the last remark. "Had I known you weren't doing anything important at lunch I would have suggested you joined James and myself. However, your time is usually valuable when you are back here for a few days and I know we are meeting this evening, so I assumed..." He shrugged delicately.

"Assumed he wouldn't catch you out with your paedophile. Why can't you accept the fact that one should grow old gracefully, Reggie?"

"Now you two," I interrupted. I turned to Lawrence, "They love each other, really. They simply go on like this the whole time."

James Young was now looking over at us, with a slight scowl.

"Your GP is missing you," went on Peter.

"GP?" This from Reggie.

"Your Gloucester Park," said Peter. "We hear you're into big estates and bigger things."

"Well, you cannot boast to that claim," whipped back Reggie. He looked cruelly at Lawrence's Adam's apple again and then back at Peter. "One can see the limited length with which you left your morning load." He spun on his heel and moved back to his baleful baronet.

"Little bastard," growled Peter. "One day…"

"You two always ask for it," I said. "Come on Lawrence, Peter, let's go upstairs and have some lunch."

"What did he mean?" Lawrence was asking Peter, plaintively, as we walked out past Reggie, who totally ignored us.

"I wouldn't go into that answer too deeply," I smiled at Peter. He threw back his head and roared and put his arm affectionately around Lawrence's shoulder. We made our way up the mirrored staircase.

*

Reggie and myself planned to dine at Hunter's. Reggie had wanted to go somewhere more formal, but I felt I needed something light-hearted and noisy. I was tired as a result of my recent trip. I had not been too happy about Peter's innuendoes at lunch and I was rather bad-tempered with Reggie. He had not returned to the office that afternoon which I found almost sacrilegious. At no time would I expect him not to turn up at the office. I understood that a Mayfair property had been seen and negotiations were going on, but I felt it high time to give young Reggie a talk about the business falling too much upon the shoulders of a Steven and a Ray. A new designer had been lured away from one of the large design companies and although there was no cause for alarm I simply felt it time that Reggie should be gently reminded that stars do burn themselves out.

He had telephoned me at the flat to check as to where we would be meeting as it would be more convenient for him to come direct to the restaurant as opposed to come over to the flat.

"Where are you?" I demanded.

"Albany," he replied. "With James."

"Oh, I see. Well, I've booked a table at Hunter's."

"Hunter's. That heap! I thought we were Savoying. That's at least convenient for here."

"Well, not for here. Would you prefer to cancel then and I'll call you in the morning?" I was furious and made this a statement as opposed to a question.

"No, no. Of course not." He paused, "I'll see you at Hunter's."

I arrived at Christopher's ivy-bedecked new restaurant and Christopher joined me for a drink.

"How's Regina?" he asked, with his usual charm and solicitude. I looked at Christopher. God, he probably knows something I don't know. I said to myself, Christopher would be too kind to say something if he knew it would genuinely hurt. I looked at him. "Difficult!" I conceded.

"My dear, all these girls when they become grand, are!"

A large party of dark-suited men appeared at the top of the stairs, just as I was about to ask Christopher when he had last seen Reggie. "Excuse me, Robin." He jumped to his feet.

"Mrs Peyton," he cried at some towering, florid-faced gent, "you've never looked prettier." More shrieks and greetings ensued. I sat nursing my drink and nodding to several people who greeted me as they arrived. I could not believe it. He was over an hour late. I decided a further ten minutes and then I would go. Rather than sit alone even though Christopher would be constantly there in his never-ending role as soothsayer, father confessor, what have you, I planned a quick snack at Le Poisonnerie in Sloane Avenue and then back to the flat and the ever loyal Petrina. I found myself getting rather maudlin and drunk. I asked for one final Scotch and sat there eyeing the menu for the umpteenth time.

"Regina!" This was from Christopher. I looked up. A very drunk Reggie was standing at the door with an even more drunk James Young behind him. For a moment I had a flashback to the doorway at The Pierre and Reggie appearing there only with the bellhop, the substitute figure for James.

Christopher saw James Young and beamed evilly. "Or should I have said Lady Forbes!" He danced across to where I was sitting. "Mr Anderson's over here at a table for two which I shall now change to three!"

I glowered at Reggie. He had obviously been back to Cheyne Row to change. He was wearing an apricot velvet jacket, open neck pale yellow shirt and deep brown velvet trousers. An array of chains and bracelets had appeared since lunch and to my added reaction to this amazing glitter was the fact that he was very obviously wearing violet eyeshadow and an outrageous velvet patch on his cheek. James Young, in a velvet smoking jacket, looked devastatingly elegant and exactly like the wicked baron.

"Darling Christopher," breathed Reggie, his strident, but elocuted voice, hushing the conversation in the restaurant. "Don't you think I look madly Margaret Lockwood in *The Wicked Lady*? Note the beauty spot!" He spun round for the benefit of a bemused Christopher. I would have happily fallen through the floor.

"You are the beauty spot," smiled Christopher.

"And everyone's visited her," I heard a voice say. Titters of laughter greeted this remark.

Reggie spun round. "My dear," he hissed, "if it isn't Rachael Rimmer!" A total silence awaited his next follow through. "Darling." He turned back to James. "That one's husband is legendarily mean. She has never been known to have even bought a paper in her life - even a newsworthy one - but we all know of Rachael's busy little tongue. Apparently they enjoy a sticky time together."

Chaos ensued. The person, billed as Rachael Rimmer, uttered a shriek of pure fury and crashed through the table to attack Reggie. Reggie, not to be outdone, grabbed the ice bucket from a nearby table and hurled the contents straight at his would-be assassin. Christopher, as quick as a flash, grabbed Reggie and flung him across to me, instantly grabbing the sopping, staggering Rachael in a ballet-like movement. James Young moved forward, grabbed Reggie's arm and whooped with fiendish glee... "Let's leave these shits."

I stood up protesting as Reggie and he disappeared through the door. What amazed me was that both James Young and Reggie were shrieking with mirth as they exited.

I collapsed back in my chair. The whole restaurant was in an uproar of excitement.

"Cabaret's on Sunday," commented Christopher, and received added yells and whistles.

I waited until the general excitement had died down.

I nodded goodnight to Christopher and made my way downstairs. I was appalled and humiliated at what I had witnessed. Drugs? Drink? Sadly, on analysis as I drove towards the flat, I had to admit to myself it was Reggie. I deliberated for a second on my first plan of stopping at Le Poisonnerie, but felt too sickened and enraged to do this. I let myself thankfully into the flat. Petrina was there to greet me and I gave her a warm hug and pulled her on to my lap. I dialled Peter.

Peter, as he always did, stopped his sarcasm and teasing when he realised how genuinely upset I was. "RA," he sighed, "I warned you about this. He did the same to someone years ago. He was still at school and got a master sacked. There was quite a scandal about it. I am not too sure of what actually happened, but he apparently denounced the master at a speech day. He – Reggie – was up on stage giving some recitation when he changed the whole context of what he was saying, and came out with this shattering denouncement." Peter laughed, "You have to give it to him, he did things with style even then."

"What happened to the schoolteacher?"

"He killed himself."

I was silent. "Christ, is that really genuine?"

"I'm afraid so."

"I don't know what to do," I groaned. "Christ, I cannot believe this and what I saw happening tonight."

"It's time to cut loose, RA."

"But Reggie!"

"Forget Reggie. This thing with James Young. The two of them are impossible and seem to lead each other on with no thought for anyone else or any consequences. Young seems to have given up his parliamentary interest; he's loaded and he and Reggie seem to find each other's company riveting and obviously satisfying."

"Do you think that they are having an affair?"

"RA, don't be so bloody blind. You are the laughing stock of London. Elvira, the whole gang know about this. At least your friends are concerned."

"So concerned, that someone – for example yourself – hasn't even bothered or considered telling me?"

"Dear RA. You try telling yourself something one day. You're impossible. You make a mule look malleable."

I sat for a long time after we had concluded our conversation. I felt physically sick. I did not attempt to ring Reggie – mainly because I was afraid that he would not be there to answer. He and James Young. I gave a sob. I would not accept it. I could not and yet I knew it to be so. My Reggie.

I got up and poured a drink and went back to my chair. My mind wandered back to our first meeting, our first weekend and the subsequent wonderful times we had spent together. I remembered Saint Tropez, times in Italy, the magical Christmas period on Key West. The triumph of Designs Unlimited. What had happened to it all? Was I too stuffy, too old-fashioned, too boring? I sat analysing myself, our relationship again and again, and it was only when dawn was breaking that I fell drunkenly into a doze, still fully dressed, and with tears still glistening on my face.

I wakened to the ringing of the telephone. It was Clare to see what time I would be in at the office. I looked hurriedly at my watch. Ten o'clock. I sat upright and gave a groan. My head! I told her I would be there within the hour.

I undressed and put on a dressing gown. Slipping my feet into a pair of espadrilles, I shuffled through to the stairs and up to the kitchen. I put on the kettle, tottered over to the letterbox and took out the post and the papers. There was the usual pile of bills and circulars and nothing of note. Petrina was already in the garden. I had left the doors open when I had finally tottered to bed. I felt dreadful.

After two cups of coffee I began to feel a bit more human. I poured out a further cup, glanced guiltily over my shoulder and then added a strong splash of brandy to the cup. I carried this downstairs with me and proceeded to shower, shave and dress.

Clare had quickly gone through my diary for the day. I had a business lunch with a city company and, apart from one late afternoon appointment, there was nothing for that evening except a drinks party at Elvira's. I groaned again, this time at the thought of Elvira's drinks party. She had recently become involved in some charity to save some weird form of bird life on some islands off South America, and the party was for a leading ornithologist on the particular type of bird.

I anticipated Sarah and Angus being there and decided that I would see how things went and possibly suggest supper to them afterwards if they had nothing planned. I was, of course, secretly hoping that Reggie would have telephoned by this stage. There would have been the usual apologies and recriminations, and no doubt it would be the Savoy Grill after all. Reggie did not call at all. There were no messages for me and when I eventually gave in and rang Sam I was told that he would not be in until the morning.

"Oh," I said, "was that planned?"

"Oh yes, RA," said Sam. "He went to Paris for the day. He's looking at some premises there for a tobacco company we have done some work for recently here in London."

"Thank you, Sam," I said. "Oh, you don't know when he will be back do you? I mean, is he booked on a definite flight or was he on the usual open return?"

"No, open return. When I say morning RA, it will be mid-morning. I made a reservation for them at the Ritz."

"Them?"

"Oh yes, he's travelling with James Young."

I spent a tiresome afternoon checking previously checked export papers for goods going to America. I had been looking into purchasing items from the Far East and decided to go and see a dealer in St James's before going on to Elvira's. I collected my topcoat and left the office. I advised Clare I would be back to sign any remaining letters and collect the car. "Any messages please leave on my desk," I said. Clare looked surprised at this instruction to something she had been doing automatically for many years, but made no comment.

The afternoon was fairly mild but there was a hint of a change in the air. Autumn was on its way. We had not gone off to the South of France that year. I had been too busy in the States, but Reggie had managed a few days on Hydra and Mykonos – with James Young as I was to learn later.

Anthony Edwards, the dealer, was pleased to see me and we went through to his office where he produced a bottle of champagne. Anthony had been a boyfriend of Peter's – who hadn't? – many years before and he and Peter were still very close. I was now envious at the easy relationship they had slipped into. I could never see my relationship with Reggie ever being like this should it end – if it had not already done so.

"How's Regina?" he asked.

"Not a good topic at present," I said.

"I hear that there has been something rotten in the state of Designs Unlimited," smiled Anthony. "Anyway, cheer up, old thing. We still love you."

We sat talking about Peter and Lawrence. "If that is how he pictured me," said Anthony, "please leave me at Westminster Bridge, Cabbie!" Anthony and I also discussed a combined business plan for the future involving purchases in the Far East. I was more than willing for Anthony to use some of the space in the Houston showroom as the floor space still smacked to me of gross extravagance after the tight-fisted way we had to utilise floor space in London's West End.

Anthony had recently returned from the Far East and suggested I made a trip there as soon as possible. He mentioned dealers in Hong Kong and Bangkok I should see in particular.

"Why not arrange to go within the next few weeks?" he encouraged. "Quite honestly, Peter and myself were discussing it the other night and we are concerned. You look sodding awful, if you don't mind me saying so. It's a perfect time weatherwise as well. Take a few extra days and go and collapse on Bali. Let Regina get on with it here. We don't know how serious this James Young thing is, but it has been going on for a bit but nobody really thought there was much to it. Basically, nobody considered Young gay. We knew he was perverted, but perverted perverted." He put out his hand for the bottle. "He seems to have gone over the top though with Reggie. The two of them are becoming quite notorious with their carryings on. Apparently they are the talk of Gloucestershire. Peter was saying something to me the other day about them giving a gay dinner party at which all the guests were in drag!"

"Oh Christ," I said, "it gets worse, doesn't it?"

"But this James thing is typical," Anthony continued. "He's obviously had this bottled up inside him for years and now he literally has thrown the bonnet over the windmill. You can understand Reggie's fascination – with due respect, RA, – but all that money, that amazing house, and of course Reggie's own success and notoriety are simply too stimulating."

"But he was never like that," I added, not too convincingly.

"Like what?"

"Well, like that. He really is a genuine, sweet caring person. I have spent moments with him that you simply wouldn't believe."

"Unfortunately, that is what James Young is saying."

"It's that well known, then?"

"No, not really. But for someone who has been as discreet as Young before – and that publicity about his so-called dabblings with young girls a few years ago saw him having to really tow the line. It did considerable damage to his political career, hence his devotion over the past few years to developing his racing stable and concentrating on the house which he now opens to the public on occasions. I should think that if he continues at the rate he is going, and with Reggie to help him, the public will be queuing for a look at them as opposed to the property. Reggie should love that."

"Oh shit, Tony. What the hell am I to do?"

"RA, that is the question that friends have asked friends since time immemorial. The sad thing is, should a friend give any advice and it proved to be the wrong advice, the friend would be in the proverbial shit. If, on the other hand, Peter – like myself – told you to cool it for a while and perhaps hopefully Reggie would come to his senses, that is if you ever think he will or else do that desperate thing and make a complete break."

"I couldn't do that. Not now."

"Oh, come on RA. You had the same problem with Michael. Only he did it to you and we didn't seem to notice any remorse from his side on the final severance."

"But it must be a phase. Perhaps I've been ignoring him. There's the pressure of work. There are so many things that could be the cause."

"Crap! And you know it. He thrives on his work – Reggie can put more into a day and a night than most people would even consider tackling in a month. Take that latest Arab deal on the hotel in Riyad. He went out there, with one of his henchmen and a visual artist, and in five days they had the basic designs off the ground. He has that extraordinary back-up team who handle the costings for him and he cleverly introduced a major contractor to cope with all the financial headaches for the privilege of having a major intro into that virtually untapped resource. Reginald Forbes is laughing all the way to the bank, staggering under a huge percentage introductory fee. Do you know he offers deals to the suppliers direct so that the financial handling involving Designs Unlimited is now being taken out of his hands and totally managed by Yorkshire and beady brother? The Queen of Commissions is what he is now known as in the trade. How long it can last nobody can say in this game. He is like an actor. One day you're box office and the next day you're opening your wrists alongside your scrapbook. If he is shrewd enough, he will continue building his team and mini empire – Empress as well as Regina, is another title involuntarily bestowed upon him and which he covets – and by the end of the decade will not only be an international figure in his field, but a very rich one. James Young is an ideal foil for him. You, my dear RA, are too nice and sober for what Reggie wants. He and James are bizarre enough to generate whatever scene they decide to fill the day with and people will flock to the charade."

I sat stunned. "That was quite a speech."

"Yes, and we all rehearsed it. Peter, me, even Elvira who, for all her nonsense, is devoted to you and blames herself for introducing Reggie to James at Wiltons those months ago. He shrugged. "But that is Elvira. She had to be a major factor for the success of the drama."

Anthony looked back at me. "He's done an amazing amount for himself in a very short time. You were intrinsically responsible for a great deal. Your introductions to Amanda and Elvira were the fan to those oh so eager embers. He deserves an Oscar – not of the Wilde variety, he's got plenty of those! – for his performance of the sweet young thing. We are only sorry that you are now being hurt."

The talk continued in this vein for a bit longer. I was saddened and sickened with what I had been told and even more so that my friends had been so aware as to what had been happening. Whilst I understood their actions I felt betrayed by them as much as I did by Reggie. I was not prepared to change course without taking the matter further. I simply had to talk to Reggie if I could see him privately for a sober talk and – hopefully – during a sober moment.

I walked back to the office. There were various messages left for me, but no message from Reggie. I dialled the flat and listened to the recorded messages. Nothing there either. I busied myself with a few papers and then sat down on the sofa armed with a large Scotch. I looked at the glass ruefully, at this rate I would be drinking as much as Reggie. I looked at the empty cushion next to me. Was it only so short a time ago that we had sat here and toasted the instigation of Designs Unlimited? I remembered the moment so clearly. I felt myself becoming choked up again. He could not have changed so completely so quickly. There was still the basic Reggie there – the one I had exposed and the one I had begun to love. I gave a weary sigh and collected my jacket from the chair alongside the sofa. I stood up, put on the jacket and made my way slowly to the door. At least Elvira's drinks party would help fill in some time before I tried Reggie's number. I had decided that I would call him and arrange a meeting. If there was going to be a reconciliation, it had to be now. If there was to be a break, then the time was as good as any.

Elvira's party was more amusing than I had anticipated. Elvira was particularly solicitous and seemed to do a great deal of arm-clinging. She whirled me round to several different people and gave me a pointed look when she left me standing next to some solitary young man she had no doubt weaned from someone a few parties before. "Now, are you sure you are going to be all right?" She said. I assured her I would be. Elvira the evangelist was something I felt could become a fair strain. I spoke to the young man for a few minutes and then made my way over to Sarah. She was full of news about Amanda and Bindi. Her quick-fire delivery of various anecdotes and her total charm soon shook me out of my numb and depressing state, and I found myself laughing along with her as she continued with her latest snippets of gossip and digs at Elvira. "My dear, have you heard that she, too, is off to Machu Pichu in a few weeks' time? Amanda has no doubt inspired her with tales of wild, dark-eyed young men glowering over their pisco sours in the likes of The Piano Bar in downtown Cuzco. Yes darling, would you believe it. Trust Bindi and Amanda to find The Piano Bar. Elvira talks continuously about the delights of late night suppers in the main square by the famous cathedral and its larger than life Black Christ. No doubt she sees herself being ravished by some dark soul clean from confessional as he spots her eating her aphrodisiacal roast guinea pig."

"Perhaps she'll have to sublimate all on the switchback motion of the train up the mountain instead."

"Darling!" Sarah chortled wickedly. "That is too divine. Elvira satisfied by a train of the track version as opposed to one of events!"

So the evening continued. The ornithologist became very drunk and locked himself in the downstairs cloakroom which Reggie had decorated as an elaborate birdcage. "He no doubt finds it a home from home," sniffed a not too amused Elvira. Sarah, Angus and myself slipped away and went on to a quiet supper at Le Perroquet at the Berkeley round the corner.

"I really loathe all those limp cocks hanging from the ceiling," Sarah had said as we sat down. "Such a waste." Angus had guffawed in a rather embarrassed way and muttered something about 'theatre talk'. I laughed uproariously and found that I was enjoying myself immensely. We all got very happy and rather tight by the end of the meal. Angus lifted his glass in toast to Elvira "a damn fine woman" and Sarah toasted Amanda, Bindi and me. We walked slowly back to Wilton Crescent where we fell into our respective cars. With much hooting and tooting we drove off. The lights were still on at Elvira's. "Her bird in the gilded cage is probably still there," snorted Sarah.

I let myself into the flat half hoping that Reggie would be there. I had imagined our making up, the tears, the promises and his swearing to me that the business with James Young was merely a phase. The flat was totally deserted. Petrina was asleep on her favourite chair and greeted me with a few snuffly barks and a wiggle before settling back to sleep again. At least she is loyal I said to myself, rather forlornly, the high spirits of the evening evaporating rapidly.

By the next morning I had made a major decision. I would call Reggie at his office and demand a meeting. I would offer him two alternatives, either he squared with me, or else we would simply have to stop seeing each other – not that we were, really anyway. If we agreed to the former I would insist he took a break from the business and came away with me. The more I mulled it over in my mind the more I thought of Anthony's suggestion that now was the time to visit the Far East. I saw ourselves together for a few blissful days on Bali and then on to Hong Kong for some fun, and finally Bangkok before flying home to London. I did some rapid mental calculations and worked it out that we would not be away for longer than two weeks and if Reggie did have any sincere concern for our relationship, he would agree to the trip without any avail.

To my amazement, he did.

My telephone call saw us meeting for a quick lunch. Reggie had a meeting at Pimlico Road so I suggested we met at Waltons. "Yes how ideal," he replied. "The yellow and grey decor will match my bruises."

I was intrigued. Were he and James now heavily into sadomasochism, or what?

Reggie's bruising turned out to be minimal and for a moment I was traitorously disappointed. There was a slight swelling to the side of his face and neck which was partly hidden by a softly tied cravat.

"What happened?" I said, after the preliminary hellos.

"If I told you, you wouldn't believe me," he said. "The truth of the matter is James hit me."

"That I could believe."

"But not deliberately. We were dancing!"

"Dancing?"

"Yes, dancing. He's put a disco into the house in Cadogan Gardens and we christened it last night."

"Oh, a big party?"

"No, simply the two of us."

"I see."

"Do you? It was great fun actually. I wore this amazing shimmy dress..."

"You what?"

"Dress... with tassels... very Twenties. Well, we were doing a tape of rock charleston and got rather carried away I suppose. Anyway, James did this amazing hand gesture and twirl and caught me on the side of the face. End of simple story."

"You've gone quite mad, haven't you?" I smiled up at Rolf, the maître d' who was standing looking fairly bemused. "Champagne Reggie?"

"Please."

"A bottle of the house champagne, thank you, Rolf. We'll order later. How much time have you...?"

"I have to be back at the office by four."

"Right." I looked at him. Apart from the marking on the face he looked fairly marvellous. The hair was now a champagne and pink with touches of silver, but sensibly trimmed. His suit was of pale crushed strawberry with a grey shirt to which the strawberry and grey cravat added the final sense of colour and style. Several people had looked at him as he had walked into the restaurant and I had seen several heads move together. Reggie was certainly talked about.

"How's James?" No doubt it was best to take the bull by the horns. A raunchy image of me grabbing James by the crotch caused a slight smile to play around my mouth.

"Divine. But he always is." He looked at me from beneath his long lashes – delicately dyed, no doubt. "I'm very fond of him, RA, but you must realise that I am still very fond of you."

I noticed the inclusion of the word 'still'.

"I realise that our relationship seems to have been on the wane, but that is not so."

"Oh, and what is 'so'?"

"You must appreciate how I and circumstances have changed, RA."

"My dear Reggie, I, of all people, am totally and utterly aware of the changes."

"Seriously, I have grown up a great deal since we first met."

"Reggie, Reggie," I shook my head. "You are talking to me, not a child. Of course you have changed, grown up as you say. We all grow up and we all grow older. You have changed incredibly. Whilst I admire your business success – everybody admires that – and your very obvious talent, some of the changes are hurtful. I find the change in our relationship the most difficult and as for your public image..."

"I don't need to have my public image discussed. I have created an image and I am happy with that image. With regard to us... when I try to tell you we are still friends – don't interrupt – of course we are friends, we are still lovers, but there is a change in that. I cannot be the sweet, innocent young boy you basically want – a plaything..."

"I do not want or require a plaything," I responded. "Had I wanted a mere toyboy I could have found one"– I snapped my fingers – "like that. What I wanted was someone of intelligence, of fun, a companion, a friend, a lover... I wanted what I felt I had found in you and now I don't know."

"Typical. I, I, I, I, did you ever stop to consider how often you use that simple little word. What about 'me'? I want what you want, but I also want me."

I looked at him as if I had been slapped.

"Yes," he cried, "I want an identity too. I am not a mirrored image of you. I want to be an individual. I want to be different. If you cannot accept what I want, don't accept it. You may criticise James, but he understands. He was an image until he accepted what he wanted most and hence he, too, has become what he wanted. I adore him, he's an amazing friend. I know what people say. I do go to bed with him, but we have fun. FUN." His voice had risen to a shriek and I realised that all the tables were riveted. "You have no idea how heavy you can be, RA, what a BORE. There, I've said it. You are a nice, cosy, loveable, kind generous person, but at times you can be such a bore. Mr Right, Mr Saying the Right Thing, Mr Diplomacy."

Rolf, who had already replenished our glasses twice, scuttled up and poured another glass each. He looked questioningly at the nearly empty bottle. I nodded in affirmation.

"Go on," I said, playing the injured party to the hilt. Oh God, I thought, if I show I'm reacting I will be deemed a bore on that score as well.

"Please RA," he said quietly. "There is still something between us. I know there is, but it has all changed. It can never be as it was in the beginning... too much has happened. I cannot give up my friendship with James, I value it too much. I cannot give up my friendship with you for the same reasons. You are so stable and I know that whatever happens you are always there... perhaps that is part of the reason why I do take such liberties with you."

He looked so appealing and so adorable and my heart went out to him, even though it did seem that the whole blame for any reactions was now being swung over to me.

"What we should really do," he said, looking at me seriously with those enormous eyes, "is get away together for a few days." He had fallen right into my hands.

"That's telepathy," I began, as Rolf brought over the other bottle of champagne.

The rest of lunch had passed in a pleasant, champagne-induced whirl as well as an almost pre-holiday atmosphere. I explained to Reggie that the possibility of a trip to the Far East was imminent and how I felt that it would serve as a good foundation for the two of us to get away for a few days together. I specified the importance of time, both in Hong Kong and Bangkok, but I felt sure that a break on Bali would give us the therapeutic start we both needed to get over the unfortunate atmosphere that had recently evolved.

"I don't know much about Bali," I said, "but there is that amazing new Hyatt Hotel which I feel you should see. They are brilliant with their interpretations of local culture and gaining the local atmosphere. Apparently the one on Bali excels."

"Isn't that the one on Sanur Beach where you can sail to the nearby Turtle Island?" questioned Reggie excitedly. "Some friends of James's were there not too long ago and they found it enchanting. The hotel has these amazing compounds set in the most heavenly tropical gardens and you can have a double-decker suite there with your own dining room and so forth. They made it sound very civilised. I would suggest a house perhaps in a village, but as we are only there for a few days..."

He went on planning Bali and talking about trips to view the volcanic lake, to see the Barong dance and the famous monkey dance. I was fascinated at the knowledge he had about the island. "Oh, not just a painted face," he laughed, when I commented on this.

"When do you think you could manage to leave for two weeks?" I asked again, as we were on our coffees and brandies.

"Really RA, I do think it's more a case of when you plan to go," said Reggie, being charmingly affable. "After all, I simply tell the serfs as to when I plan to take off and then I am yours." The last comment was made with a flamboyant flinging out of his arms which unfortunately connected with the waiter who was arriving to serve more coffee.

"Oh dear," said Reggie, when the mopping up and excitement had died down. "I do seem not to have lost that habit I picked up in New York, of knocking into coffee trays!" His wicked grin became theatrically sickly. "There, I'm being wicked, aren't I? But seriously RA, I think it is a marvellous idea and I shall invest in reams of exotica out there... and no doubt a few jewels. Isn't Bangkok noted for its sapphires? I shall be the Star of Sapphires, naturally – or unnaturally – I cannot wait."

So it continued. For all his apparent sophistication Reggie could be so childlike when treated to the equivalent of a new toy. I settled on a week to ten days' departure as from then – I did not want to go through the traumas of a changing of mind – depending on availability of hotels and aircraft bookings. We decided on the Hyatt on Bali, the Peninsula in Hong Kong and the Imperial in Bangkok. Reggie was enthusiastic as he had heard about the hotels in question. I had simply suggested these as Anthony had mentioned them when the Far East was mentioned as places where he usually stayed.

I returned to the office in high spirits and immediately set Clare to work on the various reservations. I rang Anthony to give him the suggested dates and he was delighted.

"I shall write to various dealers tonight, and send over copies of my letters to you," he said. "I do think it is a very good thing that you are going off, RA."

"Reggie will be with me."

There was a stunned silence.

"Anthony, are you there?"

"Yes," wearily, "did you say Regina was going with you?"

"I did."

"RA, you're mad. The whole point of the exercise is to get away from London, him and the general atmosphere."

"Maybe. But we have had this talk and he feels that we should have some time to ourselves—"

"*He* feels? How does he feel about the various cavortings that are now being reported back to you and your general upset over the whole matter?"

"Whatever may have happened, he still feels the same about me and the relationship has only been going through some growing up pains."

"Nonsense! He's the only one who should be suffering some growing up pains – not the relationship. Okay. We'll all be here to receive the first telephone call."

"Thank you for your concern," I said sarcastically.

I spoke to Sarah too and she was delighted about the trip. She, in turn, was preparing to go over to Houston and join Amanda for a few weeks. The baby was, as Sarah succinctly put it 'about to hatch' and she felt that Amanda would appreciate some more stable female company as opposed to the crushing camaraderie of Monica when the great event occurred.

"Keep in constant touch," I said, "or else get Clare to contact me when you have any news. Clare virtually knows even the colour of my daily selected socks when I am abroad!"

Chapter Fourteen

We set off from Gatwick for the long flight to Bali, via Jakarta. The flight was comfortable, but monotonous and Reggie spent most of the time asleep. I read a paperback rather listlessly and seemed to drink and doze a great deal.

We arrived on Bali the following evening and were both instantly enchanted by this magical island.

"It's total Hollywood," crowed Reggie. "One expects Mitzi Gaynor to come lurching out from between the palms armed with her bottle of anti-dandruff and warbling."

"Highly romantic," I answered.

The hotel was spectacular in its decoration. The staff were angelic and our suite could not have been more perfect. We had a long, slow walk along the beach before returning to the pool terrace for drinks. Reggie was looking elegant in white and had raised a few eyebrows when he appeared in the dining room with the addition of several orchids laced into his hair and a bracelet of the flowers on his wrist. He had stopped to talk to an enchanting Balinese girl who was arranging flowers in one of the lower ground floor boutiques to the immense, thatched open-air lobby, and she, in turn, had offered Reggie the flowers as a token of welcome and friendship.

"Sweet child – probably thought I was her angelic, bleached sister," said Reggie, merrily, as he buried his nose into the foliage decorating an immense fruit cocktail. He leaned back in his chair and studied the exotic surroundings. "Oh, I approve. I do approve, RA. This is wonderful."

The time on Bali passed too quickly. Reggie was a delight. He quickly made friends with various people at the hotel and became a Pied Piper in his own way, in that his decision to go to the volcanic lake, or to Turtle Island, or any such place, was immediately agreed to. 'Reggie says' or 'Reggie suggests' became the saying of the day.

I sat back rather like an elderly uncle and approved of it all. There were several flirtatious looks from some devastating Balinese boys and young men, but Reggie ignored these and seemed only interested in being with me and making a tremendous fuss of me. Within a few hours of being in that heady atmosphere I found all my resentments and doubts, which had travelled with me on the flight out, were disappearing.

From Bali we flew on to Hong Kong. I had not been to the Colony before and again was taken up with the total enchantment and magic of the island and its unique harbour.

Reggie spent his time visiting the endless small bazaars and shops near to the Kowloon Ferry and I, in turn, was seeing various dealers. The Peninsular Hotel with its Piano Bar (no pisco sours and certainly not gay I wrote on a postcard to Amanda) and Gaddy's famous restaurant where we stuffed ourselves with delicious carpetbagger steaks, proved to be a stunning stopover. There were several dinner parties to attend, one at the famous Repulse Bay Hotel, and another with a gay dealer who lived with his oriental friend on the Peak. In a second card to Amanda I claimed to have climbed the peak and met a gay Chinaman but simply 'no peek'. Armand, the dealer, and Ming (called Min by Reggie) took us to a gay disco which was rather like being in a demented cage of parakeets. As I said to Reggie afterwards, when you get an oriental queen you get 'A' queen. Appalling, amorous, ambidextrous, but not 'A'ppealing! He had to agree. "My God, even I looked butch," he sighed, collapsing into giggles alongside me. "Me plitty?" he asked. "Me Chong and I play wit dong?"

We were sad to leave Armand and Min who came to the airport to see us off. Min kept rolling his eyes at Reggie - a remarkable feat for a Chinaman - and insisting "Leggie, you leturn, plis?" Leggie, amidst more giggles - he was getting as bad as Min - 'agleed'. More girlish shrieks as the two of them kissed each other irrespective of a few curious tourists. As I said to Reggie once we were strapped into our seats, "God, the two of you looked like Sindy dolls in local dress."

"Plis?" questioned Reggie.

The light-hearted mood showed no signs of abatement. I sent off a happy letter to Amanda and had been very jovial with Anthony when I spoke to him. Peter happened to be at his flat, having a drink, when my call came through and I could tell that Peter, though relieved, was not too convinced. "You still have four more days together, he said in his rough way. "Perhaps little Reggie is already getting the itch to bang other cock in old BK."

"Ridiculous," I said.

"Don't tell me he's been secretly putting crushed pearls in your ribena," guffawed Peter, "so as to make you chop chop more with that old chopstick!" We finished our talk laughing loudly. Reggie, who was perched in a scarlet kimono, cigarette in a jade holder and a glass of champagne alongside him, looked at me.

"Everyone sounds very happy," he said.

"Aren't we?"

"Of course." He struck a pose. "Don't I look madly Rita Hayworth without the rain?" I laughed. Reggie moved over to the long window and looked down at the Chao Phya River below. "It's fabulous RA," he said. "I'm loving every magical minute of it. Are you?"

"Of course. With you every moment everywhere is magic."

He gave me a rather old-fashioned glance and flicked his ash into an ashtray on the coffee table. "That isn't, I trust, from something by dear Uncle Willie." We laughed again.

I had arranged with a friend of some years standing to join us for dinner at the Normandie Grill. Douglas had been living in Bangkok for many years and he and I had always kept in contact. I saw him on his rare visits to London. He was a great admirer of Elvira's, but she and I had never been able to assess his sexual preferences. Elvira was slightly more down to earth than I was. I suggested a beautiful, lotus-like maiden secreted away in the mahogany depths of Thompson's compound. "He's more than likely doing it with one of those bald monks," sniffed Elvira.

Douglas was looking very smart and tanned in his white silk safari jacket with matching trousers and a dark cravat. It was almost as if Reggie had planned to match him and they were identical in their getups. "My, we do go well together," said Reggie, fluttering slightly blued eyelids.

I looked at him and then at Douglas. Douglas was obviously intrigued. One up to Elvira for getting the basic gist, if not the exact type. I felt a slight quiver of jealousy and then put this aside. Nonsense, not Douglas. I appreciated that Reggie was probably feeling slightly starved of a new audience for his wiles and aberrations, so I let it pass.

We enjoyed a splendid meal and afterwards went on to a bar Douglas knew, for coffee and drinks. By this stage we were all getting along famously and Douglas's friend had joined us at the bar. He, in turn, was a very attractive Thai who worked in one of the jewellery shops and seemed to be highly possessive of Douglas. Reggie and Wang got on brilliantly and no doubt were discussing jewellery too.

"Are you going to see a show?" Wang asked suddenly, looking at me brightly.

"A show?"

"Yes, sex show. Velly good in Bangkok."

"I'm sure."

"Oh yes, RA, we must see a show," said Reggie, "and I don't mean a cobra and a mongoose either." We had witnessed one of these unnerving shows at the floating market earlier that afternoon.

"No, sex show," said Wang.

"Oh get on with it Wang," said Douglas. Wang started to explain in pidgin English. Reggie and I began to laugh. "Wait a moment," I cried, "please Wang, more slowly."

"Let me explain," said Douglas. "There's this place run by a friend of Wang's in downtown BK. It's in an alleyway right opposite Chedok, the Russian tourist office, would you believe! Kinks in the Kremlin no doubt." We laughed. "Anyway, I've been there once or twice before. It's fairly primitive, but it is amusing and certainly not touristy. It caters for your locals as if it were."

"Oh, RA, let's go," said Reggie, clapping his hands with glee and looking, to quote him, rather like Dorothy Lamour in *The Road to Ruin*.

It was thus decided. Douglas would not join us but we planned to lunch the next day at his house. He offered us the use of his car and driver, and Wang sadly had to refuse to join us. "I must go wiz Doug," he explained.

"I'm sure you do," said Reggie.

We sailed off in great style in Douglas's rather resplendent Rover and within moments were lost in a maze of twisting, dimly lit streets. The driver suddenly drew to a screeching halt by the darkest of alleyways.

"Plis," he lisped, gesturing to us to get out.

We did, and he moved the car on a few yards before locking this and joining us. "God, I thought he was leaving us here stranded, for a moment," hissed Reggie.

"Plis."

"Let's follow 'Plis'," I said, and walked after our guide into the darkness.

The alleyway was about forty yards long. 'Plis' stopped outside a small door to a dimly lit building which sagged drunkenly up to about four floors. He knocked discreetly on the wooden frame.

"Shades of St Tropez," whispered Reggie.

A shutter quickly opened and an eye blinked out at our driver guide. 'Plis' spoke rapidly in Chinese. The shutter smacked shut and in a few seconds the door was pulled open.

The smallest Chinaman, and the oldest, stood there beaming at us. He was completely yellow. Yellow skin, yellow eyes, yellow teeth and yellow robe. "Ah!" he squeaked, raising a gnarled finger above his right ear. "Welcome Inglis gentmen. Flend of mista Dig's. Glate honah!"

I raised an eyebrow at a snorting Reggie.

"Kum in, plis." He gestured with the flat of his hand to the downstairs room which we took to be the main bar. It was pure Somerset Maugham. A lethargic fan clicked away on the drab ceiling. In the gloom I could make out a few dismal chairs and cane tables, plus a long, scarred bar. Leaning at the one end of the bar, in a sweat-stained creased dirty white linen suit was your archetypal Englishman abroad, clutching a drink and staring into space with red-rimmed eyes.

"Us in a few days' time," hissed Reggie, who was clearly enjoying himself. "I can see why Douglas says this is off the tourist beat," he added. "Anyone trying to get here would die of thirst trying to find the place. I cannot imagine what sort of show we can expect to see."

Just then, our host came shuffling over to us. "Plis? Dlink onka house?" I looked a bit bewildered, but Reggie already saw himself in his role as the beautiful planter's wife ("I felt very Claudette Colbert dear with you as an older Jack," he said, in the confines of the hotel room later) was devastatingly glamorous and poised.

"Thank you," he said, and smiled over at the Englishman who had been somewhat shaken out of his reverie by our arrival. "I'll have a gin and lime please." I swear that if he had been wearing a large picture hat – with trailing scarf – he would have taken it off and tossed his curls in a madly, madcap way.

"Yes, a large gin for me too, thank you," I said.

"Two velly larg ginin lime, kumin up," beamed our host. The hand with pointed finger rose to the side of his head again. "Afta dlink, you see show."

"Plis," said Reggie.

Suitably armed with our drinks, we started to follow our grinning, gesticulating host up a flight of narrow stairs. Our driver – to be known as 'Plis One' was busy talking to our derelict compatriot at the bar. Reggie went ahead of me and gave a loud shriek as I lightly goosed him.

Our yellow friend turned round, still grinning.

"You happy? You lookee, lookee?"

I did not follow him for a moment. Nor did Reggie. I took it that he meant we both looked happy – doubtless a good omen – but then Reggie and I realised that 'lookee, lookee' meant what he said. He was pointing to a small eyehole in the door on the half landing. Reggie peered in, and then so did I.

The view was on to a bed in a dimly lit room. Lying on his back, with an energetic Thai lady jumping up and down on the most enormous erection, was the most enormous Chinaman. He gave a large grunt with every one of her shrill leaps – quadrophonic copulation I later said to Amanda – and the two of them were oblivious to anything else except each other.

"There goes my theory and Amanda's," I chuckled to a riveted Reggie.

"My God, she must be hollow," he gasped.

"Or a blow up doll," I added.

"With that pump and pumping she'll explode," Reggie chortled.

"Goodee goodee," chuckled our Chinaman. He gave another of his strange gestures and pointed vaguely past his ear to the ceiling. "Show upastair," he hissed.

We lookeed, looked through three other doors and viewed two frail gentlemen wriggling over a large black man, a lady with another lady and then a solo young man "Solitary con't find it," quipped Reggie eyeing the neatest of mini erections.

"No, show!" puffed our host.

We had arrived at the main room at the top of the house. A large bed, with what I could only describe as a marbleised mattress – such were the markings and stainings – sat in the middle of the floor. At the far end were two upright chairs to which Reggie and I were led. "The seats of honour," I hissed.

"Nonsense – a throne from throne," sniggered Reggie. "We're in for a thrill, Phil," he added.

"Gee whiz! Really Liz," I gasped. We exploded with merriment, our gins shaking in our hands. We were beginning to find ourselves – like the situation – hilarious.

"Show to stlart sloon," guffawed our host along with us, his head bobbing more and more quickly and his hand going up past his cheek again.

"Do you suppose we are the lookee, lookee?" I said, tears rolling down my cheeks.

"Oh yes, nookie nookie makes lookee lookee," shrieked Reggie.

At that moment a few more spectators filed into the room. Apart from our two chairs there were also three wooden benches, two alongside the bed and one at the foot end. For one mad moment it reminded me of Sunday School! Becoming more and more agitated our midget host greeted another gnarled being of indiscriminate sex, who came in. This person was in charge, we discovered, of the musical effects. A large wind-up gramophone was rapidly attended to and the head placed on the bobbing disc. At that moment the centre light, a naked, fly-blown light bulb, was put out and two wavering beams directed from the corners of the room on to the bed. Reggie squeezed my hand in excitement and naughtiness.

The music, wailing and typically oriental, began. Sadly there was a severe crack in the record so each wail was distorted by a resounding 'click'. Our little host scuttled over to my chair and squatted down alongside it. "Show now stlart," he whispered, his yellow teeth glowing in the light. Two Thai boys skipped through the door and jumped on to the bed. They were naked and began to frolic about, crawling over each other without any particular purpose. The music got faster and another figure appeared. This was a large man who appeared to be carrying a chicken. I gripped Reggie. It *was* a chicken. He then proceeded to plant the poor chicken on his rather impressive length. The poor bird gave a rather hysterical squawk and the two boys jumped up and down with more enthusiasm.

"Now I understand the appeal of chickens," hissed Reggie.

I dug him in the ribs.

Now a girl appeared and she seemed to jump about with the boys. The man withdrew himself from the chicken and jumped on the one boy who promptly fell on the girl. The chicken squawked with renewed enthusiasm, but was immediately attacked by the solo young man. More figures joined in. Audience reaction was rising to fever pitch. The big black man we had lookeed at earlier appeared and jumped on the young boy and his chicken and all seemed to be having a very energetic time. The music, squawkings, gruntings and shouts were reaching a crescendo. Hopping up and down with excitement as he watched the goings on, our little man saw Reggie beckon to him. He leaned over, looked at Reggie incredulously and jumped up and down with added enthusiasm, flinging both hands up and down into the air. I was flabbergasted.

"Stlop show! Stlop show," he screeched with instantaneous effect.

The participants halted in their antics, the audience gaped at him, the disc jockey raised the head off the record.

"Englishman want to join in," he proclaimed with a proud shriek.

"No! No!" gasped a wide-eyed Reggie. "I simply said I'd like another gin!"

We left.

Reggie and I were still laughing as we made our way into the suite. "Darling," I said, doubling up once more, "a gin?"

More shrieks. I fell over towards the bar table to help myself to a drink whilst Reggie collapsed, still shrieking, into the bathroom. With shaking hands and my whole body suffused with giggles, I unsteadily poured ourselves a brandy each. What an evening and what fun we had had. How right I had been about us all along.

The telephone rang.

I made my way towards it and picked up the instrument.

"Mr Anderson?"

"Yes."

"Hold on please. America is calling, and has been trying to reach you all evening. Did you not have a message?"

"Er, no. I didn't check." I noticed then that the message light was still flashing, "is the party on the line?"

"Yes, hold on plis."

"Robin?" It was Sarah.

"Darling," I laughed, "how are you?"

"Darling, it's too terrible," said Sarah's cool voice. My blood ran cold.

"What's happened. Is it Amanda...?"

"No, Bindi. He's had a flying accident. He's dead."

"Oh my God," I grasped blindly at Reggie who had come up to join me. I took his hand. "How, when?"

"Today. Amanda had a son this afternoon and he was piloting the plane back from Galveston. We aren't quite sure as to what happened – RA?"

"I'll be with you as soon as I can possibly get there," I said. "I'll let you know my flight time."

We had a few more words and I put down the phone. Reggie was sitting looking stunned. He put his arms around me and started to croon like a mother to a child as my tears began to fall.

The following hours to Sarah's call were agonising. Due to the lateness of the hour it was impossible at that stage to make any sense with air bookings, but I did contact the main desk at the hotel to explain that there had been an immediate change in plans and we were leaving within the next few hours. I had tried to persuade Reggie to stay on the few extra days as I planned to return to Hong Kong and fly through to the West Coast and on to Texas. He was adamant that however complicated the connections and required flights to return to England, this is what he was going to do.

A very tense and strained Reggie saw me off from the hotel to the airport. I had already sent acreages of telex instructions to Clare and had by this stage reached that total non plus stage. All I wanted to do was to be with Amanda as soon as possible. A major contribution to the atmosphere had been Reggie's cruel remark over a distressing cup of coffee whilst waiting for my taxi to take me to the airport. We had gone down to the main coffee shop as we felt the slightest human activity would be advantageous to the depressive pall that had fallen upon us. I was still stunned and deeply upset, but Reggie was seeming to cope more realistically and philosophically with the situation than I was.

"It could have been both of them," he had said gently. "You know that if it had not been for the imminent arrival of the kiddiwink Amanda would have been with Bindi."

"Perhaps that would have been for the best," I had replied dully. "I don't know how she will survive without him. He was her life."

"He was. But there was a lot of life before Bindi and Amanda is a survivor. She at least has his son, a tremendous gift and that in itself should give her a tremendous will to continue. She also has you," he added quietly. "In this she is very fortunate."

I looked at him seriously.

"I wonder," he continued, looking at me seriously, "if there was a similar situation regarding me, if you would react in this way." It was said as a statement not a question.

"React? What do you mean?" I looked at him incredulously. "Reggie, it's Amanda, my friend, our friend. She needs me and I am going to her. Surely you cannot resent that?" I was stunned, outraged, hurt. This surely was not a time where he would be so selfish as to adopt one of his 'B' grade Hollywood roles and begin to revel in a self-pity which would only sicken and disgust me.

"The situation between us would never be of a similar nature. If you were hurt, obviously I would come to you. In these circumstances, the situation is not even comparable. Amanda has lost Bindi, whom she adored. She gave up everything happily for him and they were a unison. If something happened to you – God forbid – I know Amanda would react as I have. She would down everything to be with me. And you, if it happened that something occurred involving me."

"I doubt it," said Reggie. I jerked my head at him. "Darling," I said, "I know you are as shocked as I am. Please let us stop this conversation." I saw to my relief the man from the front desk making his way over to the table. "Look, the taxi's here." I stood up and picked up my coat from the chair alongside me. "Look, get back to London safely and ring me as soon as you are there. I shall either be at the ranch or with Monica. I will try and ring you as well as soon as I arrive. Whatever happens, one of us will be in touch. Right?" I smiled at him, but he continued to stare ahead, still blowing on his now cool cup of coffee. "Reggie."

"Oh? Yes." He stood up and put out a rather limp hand. "Isn't life curious." He paused and then looked at me with a terrifying directness. "First of all I lose Amanda to Bindi and lose Hollywood and now it looks as if I lose you to her. She certainly now does have her cake and her favourite long-standing companion to eat it with."

"You bitch!" A couple of bland Orientals sitting near to us jumped at my scream of fury. "Take that back," I pleaded, "please don't let me leave you like this. Take it back!" I hissed between clenched teeth, balling my hand into a fist.

"No," said Reggie, putting down his coffee and reaching for his cigarette case. He sat down again, eyeing my fist. "You promised never to hit me again. Don't tell me that in one night you break your promise and I lose a lover."

"You know, you are sick. Really sick, Reggie." I felt I was suffocating. I took a deep breath and pointed a finger at him. "I don't believe this conversation. I put it down to shock and reaction. You cannot mean this. Apologise or I walk out of here and you will never see me again." Silence. The two Orientals' gaze switched from Reggie to me and back to Reggie. Like fucking Wimbledon, I remember saying to Peter later. "Please," my last word.

"I think something has happened to my vision," said Reggie, lighting his cigarette. "I can't see you. Goodness, I must have gone blind."

*

I was in Houston for two weeks. My flight had passed in a drunken, tearful fury, much to the concern of the sweet air hostesses who gathered some of the facts for the reason of my journey. I was sick with fury and a sense of betrayal. The evil switch in Reggie had proved a point I had been so unwilling to accept. I had gone through these doubling back in affections before, but this was the penultimate, this was for real and it hurt. A tearful Peter had met me at the airport and drove me straight out to the ranch. Amanda, looking pale and drawn, but still my stylish amazing Amanda, had been on the steps to greet me when I arrived.

"Bless you, dearest RA," she had said, coming down the steps with her hands outstretched. "How kind and how sad we have to meet again in such a way." I held her close to me. She felt so tiny and frail. Her tenseness relaxed and she fell against me. "Oh RA, why?" she said, simply and brokenly. Still with my arm around her we walked slowly up back into the house. Sarah was there, and Monica, both looking old and tired eyed, but neither would have shown any more emotion than this nor break down in front of Amanda. I kissed both, overwhelmed by their simplicity and warmth and gentle smiles. Amanda, in her turn, apart from the moment when she greeted me, was calm and serene and filled with such a simple dignity out of her love for Bindi and with the tragedy of that love, that my pride and love for her increased more and more by the moment. As she said after the funeral, "Grief is so personal. Bindi knows how I am sharing it with him and my dear, dear three precious friends."

We had met, a few days later in the office of the salesroom back in the city. Amanda, in a simple grey suit and still pale, had insisted that we met to talk matters over. I had already been to one meeting with her and Bindi's lawyers. He had, as expected, been meticulous with his papers and his will. Amanda was his sole heir. Naturally he had left simple instructions for endowments to a few of his loyal staff should anything unforeseen happen to him, but Amanda, in that simple wording, became the fourth richest woman in Texas.

Their son, to be called Bernard Robin Howard Carter II, was a joy. A tough little baby, with dark chestnut hair and a voice that Monica swore could be heard by every cow poke or poking cowboy throughout the state of Texas, he seemed to grow even within the two weeks I was there. Amanda had created a temporary nursery with a unisex theme and work was being carried out on the main nursery which, on completion, made the boy's section to the annual Toy Fair over Christmas at Harrods, look sparse.

"I had hoped Reggie would do the nursery up for me," Amanda had said to me after dinner one evening. "I had spoken to him about this you know. He did send a sweet letter from London about Bindi but never mentioned anything about Bindi Jnr." She looked at me. "I take it everything is still all right between the two of you? I mean, the Far East was the soothing balm it was meant to be... or wasn't it?"

I had not wanted to bring up the matter concerning Reggie. Amanda's own tragedy and grief was too consuming and of concern. I had skipped over the subject but here, in the office, the subject had been raised again.

"Quite honestly, Manda, things aren't good. I had hoped that our getting away would have brought some sense to the situation, but he simply has developed these rather unpleasant traits which Peter says were always there, but seriously darling I must have been blind to."

"Well, he was always difficult but I did think that you, if nobody else, would have been the answer for him. You and only you would have the strength and the patience – yes darling, patience, he is very demanding and difficult as I have said and he would be mad to throw all this away. He knows you have turned a blind eye to some fairly ropey behaviour and I am only disappointed that he does not seem intelligent enough – when he should be – to see what he is doing or—" she looked at me – "if I am not mistaken, what he may have done."

I had not mentioned the scene at the hotel to Amanda. I knew Peter would bring this up with Sarah, but apart from the two of them our bond of loyalty to Amanda would see that she never heard about this.

"There was a play, years ago in New York," continued Amanda, "*Will Success spoil Rockwell Hunter* – sadly, and surprisingly enough Bindi saw it immediately, we both felt that it was a case of 'Success is spoiling Reggie Forbes'."

Amanda, in a few days, had taken to mentioning Bindi quite calmly and in a way that seemed so natural that nobody felt embarrassed or uncomfortable. She was not prone to histrionics as some people in a similar situation would be. "At a moment like this I don't need an audience," she had said. I disloyally thought of Reggie. He would be Regina to the hilt and though I am sure there would be no tears unless of the Versailles variety, that is, a single diamond stuck on the cheek. "In any situation, diamonds are a girl's best friend," he would have explained why the precious stone and been a dramatic Lana lookalike in a heavy spotted veil.

"Is he still seeing a great deal of James Young?" she asked.

"Yes."

"That explains a great deal," she finalised. "The two together could be lethal for each other. The Pit and the Pendulum. Oh dear!"

We had our first guffaw for a few days. "You're right," I exploded. "From what I hear James is certainly the pendulum and let's face it, dear Reggie the willing pit."

"Behaving like the pits," shrieked Amanda.

I hugged her. "I do love you so much my darling," I said.

"I know, it's mutual," she answered. "Thank God I have you. Bindi always said that too. He used to sit in that giant chair of his and say, 'L'l doll'," Amanda did a brilliant mimic of Bindi's drawl. "If anything happens to me, you have RA to look after you. I know he likes the boys, but you two are sane enough to sort all that out."

*

I returned to London via Washington, on Concorde. The 'In Flight' magazine had an article by Compton Miller on 'Style' and Reggie featured heavily. *Town and Country* carried a major feature on Dorella and her designer. I put the magazines down in disgust.

I had not heard a word from Reggie. His answering service had taken my messages with monotonous regularity and a new receptionist – Sam had been promoted to PA – with the exotic name of Sharoo, had blocked any demands to speak to him with alarming expertise.

Several plans were being formulated in my mind. The American venture was doing so well that I decided to spend more time in the States. The business in London was stable and with Clare and my general staff there were no problems. I decided to concentrate on New York, leaving Amanda to occupy herself with Texas. The work was ideally suited for her. It gave her an opportunity to promote her own business authority with that incredible personality. It also gave her unlimited time with young Bindi. She was delighted at the whole prospect. I had decided to sell the cottage although I would offer Reggie the opportunity of buying this before I put it on the general market. I smiled ruefully to myself. Six weeks ago I doubtless would have signed it over to him and simply had the legal document sent over to his lawyers. How circumstances can change in a moment! I also toyed with the idea of selling Ennismore Gardens and staying at either The Berkeley or The Connaught when I was in London. Amanda had decided that her flat would go on the market and I was to instruct Stewart Wilson & Co. to handle the sales. Stewart was an Australian whizz-kid who could sell eucalyptus trees to the Abbos – Reggie's favourite saying – and he was always involving Stewart in deals. "I don't know how he manages so much time at the office," Reggie once exclaimed. "Whenever I speak to him, his wife has always just dropped another."

There was no note from Reggie at the flat. I spoke to Elsie to find that Petrina was still with her. I expressed surprise. "Oh, Reggie hasn't even telephoned me, Mr Anderson. I thought he was with you and poor Miss Amanda in America... what a shocking business. How terrible." I spent a few moments murmuring suitable platitudes to Mrs Law. How typical I thought, that the likes of Elsie demanded more consoling than the nearest and dearest. I spoke to Sharoo again and said in an exasperated tone that I was tired of leaving messages for Reggie, either long distance ones or local. "I don't want to sound rude, Mr Anderson," said the silky voice, "but that, in fact, is the message I was told to give you by Mr Forbes, but have refrained from doing so as I did think you may be offended."

"What message exactly, please?"

"That Mr Forbes is tired of receiving your messages and it must be obvious and he stressed, I quote this – even to a blind man – that the messages are being ignored."

"I see, thank you."

I had expected to feel crushed, defeated, humiliated, destroyed, finished, but surprisingly enough I felt delightedly elated. It was beginning to dawn on me how great a strain Reggie's relationship with me had become. In four years I had become an obsessive boor. The time to change all this had arrived.

I checked further messages with Clare. Elvira had been on the telephone and Clare had said that I was due back that day. Elvira had something important to discuss. I rang her.

"Elvira."

"Darling, you must be back. You wouldn't call me long distance." Her voice was full of reproach.

"How are you?"

"Darling, more important, how are you?" She did not give me a chance to answer, but went on, "I mean, I know I never cared for her, but I was so sorry to hear about your friend. That lovely man." Trust Elvira to get her knife in. She disliked Amanda, certainly knew her name, but kept the identity anonymous and had to come out with the comment on Bindi.

"I hear she's now worth millions too," added Elvira with utter dismissal. "Darling," she cooed.

"Yes, your important news."

"Are you free this evening? I realise it's short notice – you must be exhausted but then you will have flown Concorde, won't you darling, so if I ask you to escort me to the Opera House you will say yes."

"What's on?"

"Oh, it's a ballet." Elvira's knowledge of the Arts was purely social. "Mauna and Algernon Jamieson have a box and have invited us – (I liked the 'us')– and we are dining at the Savoy afterwards. Such fun, wouldn't you think? You know I'd never ask you at the last moment in normal circumstances, but you are a dear friend and I knew you wouldn't mind." Elvira, in that sentence, had accepted that I was going to be with her, irrespective as to whether I was dining at The Palace or whatever.

"It sounds a lovely welcome home," I said. "What time? Right, I'll collect you at seven and we can have a large glass before we meet the Jamiesons. We'll need it," I added under my breath.

I called Clare and got her to ring the car hire firm the company used on such occasions. The thought of Elvira walking from a car or being 'dropped off' at the door would be too much for Elvira.

I changed into my dinner jacket and was at Wilton Crescent a few minutes before seven. I was shown into the drawing room and offered a glass of champagne. Elvira appeared on the minute of seven.

"Darling," she twinkled from the large doors.

"Elvira." I strode over to her and kissed her chastely on her cheek. "How ravishing you look." And she did. Her dress, in simple black tulle, showed off her pale colouring to perfection. A pearl choker, brooch and bracelet with matching ring, completed the outfit.

"I do think one has to contrast with all that gaudy red, don't you think?" She blinked. "I am sure Mauna will be the ultimate in clashes. She's prone to crushed wine velvet." Mauna happened to be wearing exactly this and Elvira gave me a knowing blink. Algernon was bluff and hearty and we chatted in the Crush Bar prior to going to our box.

Elvira had been full of gossip in the car on the way to Covent Garden, but had avoided the name of Reginald Forbes.

"Oh really," muttered Elvira. We had taken our seats in the box. The orchestra was already tuning up and there was the high tension buzz of conversation from the well-dressed stalls below and the rather more raucous noise from the tiers above us. I saw Elvira looking across the auditorium to the box facing us. Whereas we were only four, the box over from us contained eight chairs. Eight gentlemen were entering the box and stood hesitantly waiting for their host to seat them. Their host was James Young and his obvious hostess was Reggie, looking every inch a Regina. James was in a resplendent blue and gold brocade jacket with gold waistcoat and blue velvet trousers. He looked intensely elegant. I could see from even this distance that he was heavily made up. His hair was now immaculately white and waved out in a spectacular array of curls about his fine head. Jewelled rings flashed on his fingers as he gestured to the remaining six gentlemen to be seated. A hush had descended on most of the audience who had noticed various others in the crowd looking up at the box.

Reggie – and I could not believe it for a moment – was in pure gold with a pink waistcoat. His hair can only be described as pre punk. It had a solid pink streak to the left hand side. He, too, was fairly bedecked in rings and a heavy gold bracelet. The remainder of the box were more soberly attired, but there were three elderly men and three younger ones, one who looked like a more anaemic Reggie and two who looked like two guardsmen out for an evening and definitely in something from Moss Bros.

As quickly as it had died down, the buzz of conversation began again. I suddenly realised that the occupants of the box were the cause of it. I should have known. James, with the promotion on his house, a gay lib rally in the grounds, and endless television interviews, had become almost a household name and so had Reginald Forbes. Reggie had been asked to design the sets for a new play opening later in the season and this, too, had gained him tremendous publicity.

"Good heavens," blustered Algernon, "isn't that James Young? Queer kettle of fish as I always thought. Who are his friends?" He went on talking to a pained Elvira.

I looked at Reggie. Although talking animatedly to James and over the shoulder to one of the young toughs – he obviously fancies him I said to myself, feeling an old twinge of jealousy, but then shrugging it off and how easy that was becoming – whilst his eyes darted about the vast amphitheatre. He caught my glance from our box and froze. He leaned over and said something with a smirk to James. James looked up and glanced at me and at my companions. He in turn said something to Reggie, who laughed. Reggie looked back at me just as Elvira glanced in his direction. Reggie gave a regal wave from his elbow.

"Really, Reginald," hissed Elvira.

It was inevitable that we should all converge upon each other in the Crush Bar during the interval.

"Elvira! Mauna," cooed Reggie – very graciously I thought to myself. He's even making Elvira look gauche – "RA!" he exclaimed. "How nice – and Algernon." I was surprised as I had not realised that Reggie knew the Jamiesons, but then by this stage, whom didn't he know! "You know James, of course," he continued, and then proceeded to introduce the others.

Algernon did not seem at all phased by the peacock parade and stood having a long talk with James about problems with a horse he had recently invested in. James, for all his coming out, was still a brilliant business man in between the pirouettes and eccentric "let's stun them" attitude. As I had said to Peter after I heard about his planned gay rally, "I'm all for it, but why oh why does James – aided and abetted by Regina at his side, no doubt – have to turn it into a painted circus."

"What James doesn't realise – and sadly –" replied Peter, "is that clowns always hide behind paint and that is exactly how he is showing himself – as a clown. Instead of acting like a demented old painted queen he should actually present his arguments soberly and objectively. He sees it as an excuse for another champagne party and that is all very well for publicity, but publicity of the wrong sort. He's causing a hostile, as opposed to a hoped for, reaction."

I turned back to Reggie who had said something to me. "Sorry. What?"

"How is Amanda and the deposit?" This was said with a syrupy smile.

"If you mean the baby, both are fine," I said rather uncomfortably. I glanced at Elvira who was chatting to one of the bedazzled young men. "She would love to hear from you."

"Oh, I'm sure. But no doubt she is very busy investing. I'll call her when I have a moment. Mauna, you are going to come to the first night of the new play I'm doing the sets for, aren't you..." I wandered over to Elvira.

"Darling," said Elvira, "this young man is a weightlifter!" She stood back and looked at him in amazement as if expecting him to produce a bar bell from one of his stretched pockets.

"How fascinating," I said. "Robin Anderson, good evening." I put out my hand.

"Hi, Bert," he said.

"And where do you practise, er Bert?" continued Elvira. I smiled and moved back to Mauna and Reggie. Just then the first warning bell went. I raised my eyebrows at Reggie. "Lunch next week?"

"Oh, could Clare speak to Sharoo," he replied, tossing his hair and running his beringed hand through it.

I could not help noticing the watch. A Corum spectacular for evening wear only, in gold and diamonds.

"I beg your pardon!"

"Sharoo. Clare can check with her to see if I'm free."

"Oh, piss off Reggie," I muttered, as Mauna turned to collect Algernon and Elvira.

"What?" He turned on me, his face going red, "if anyone should piss off, I suggest it be you. Go on, piss off back to your little operation 'cover up' group. You should be a bit more discreet in what you say to the Peter Browns of this world. He obviously isn't employed by you to give you good PR coverage."

I gaped. I was totally taken aback. I came out with a last snipe at him. "You should consider your PR, young man. You and your James are an embarrassment. You would make any queen cringe."

"Dear RA," purred Reggie, looking at me, "as *you* are making me now. Don't you ever give up? You're like some fucking family nanny who, after she's changed your pants, never realises that her use is over. She stays on and on hoping that she is still indispensable. Well she isn't. Go back to your nursery Robin, and find someone this time who will be happy with his little lot. And in parting – your little lot. God, were you boring!" Needless to say, not only was I stunned, I was too stunned to even retort or strike back. I simply decided never to have anything to do with Regina – he was no longer Reggie – again. He ignored me during the rest of the performance. As we stood to leave I gave one last glance at their departing party from the box. James Young gave me a mock salute and followed Reggie out. "Queen Deadly Nightshade and her consort," I said later to an amused Amanda – dear Manda, she always got everything into perspective. "Long may she pain," she replied.

Chapter Fifteen

I glare at Peter and look at Regina. Of course he looks divine.

"Regina," I say stiffly, standing up and offering my hand. He looks at it as if am holding something repellent.

"RA. A surprise." To Peter, "You should have told me and I could have dreamed up some wonderful excuse as opposed to a scheme." To me, "You look tanned and Texan light. Obviously all that money agrees with you. I expect it's the new soap opera sensation, 'Aids and the Older Man'. Financial aids, I stress."

I began to splutter. Peter laughs. "Now you two. Truce," he says.

"No, you do look well," says Reggie sitting down. "Champagne," he says to nobody in particular.

"On its way," says Peter.

"I understand I must congratulate you," I say, attempting to regain my composure. I cannot believe that I am still reacting to him after a time lapse of seven years. Whatever happens I am not asking him to join us for lunch, not at any price.

"And I, you. Rather rash, RA, wasn't it? But I suppose a ready-made kiddiwink prevented the ultimate intimacy or have you gone back to your bi-bi days?"

"Regina, I don't have to put up with you now and I have not had to put up with you, thank God, for the past few years. Peter asking you for a drink is entirely news to me. I can assure you that the hostility is mutual with the exception that I am barely holding myself in check."

"Goodness, we are verbose. But still, not every emigrant to Texas can be expected to be strong and silent. Very well, I apologise for whatever sensitive point I seem to have touched. (Everything was said with the most horrific innuendo.) How is Mrs Anderson and B. R. H. Carter-Anderson?"

"Amanda is fine, thank you, and so is Bindi."

"Good. Now that wasn't too painful, was it!" Regina crossed his legs and lit up a cigarette. "Has Peter told you?"

"He's mentioned something of a sickly nature."

"Now who's breaking the truce."

"All right, Reggie," I say in an exasperated and totally defeatist manner, "I hear you're getting married. Congratulations. Who is the victim?"

He sits back in his chair, takes another draw from the holder and a slow sip from his glass.

"Victim?"

"The lucky woman."

"Oh, no dear, the lucky man!"

"I beg your pardon."

"James."

"James?" I look at him incredulously. Peter is huddled up with mirth.

"James Young."

"Regina, don't be ridiculous. What do you mean, you and James Young?"

"It's in all the papers. Some say we've taken gay lib too far, but we are officially marrying – to set a new trend. You must come."

I am speechless.

"Two weeks on Saturday. In Gloucestershire. I've done the most marvellous decor for the chapel. Glamorous Gay Gothic in Gold is in."

"Tell me this is a joke," this to Peter.

Peter shakes his head. "The lead in several dailies is not a joke. It's for the movement. More harm than good though, but Regina does not accept that."

"You can't."

"Oh but I can and I am." Regina stands up. "Well, you cannot say you haven't been asked. What a pity you won't come. Had I thought about it you would have been such a perfect matron of honour." He blows a kiss and turns to Peter. "I'll talk to you later." A last look at me. "Yes, it is a miracle after all. Thank heavens I am still blind."

In no way am I allowing Regina the last word. "Yes, blind you certainly are and how lucky for you, Lady Young-to-be, that you remain so. Should you have the courage to open your eyes, your favourite story chant would appear somewhat changed..."

"Favourite fairy story chant?" He pauses and raises a well-groomed eyebrow.

"Uh huh, favourite chant. Mirror, mirror, on the wall, who is the most odious, poisonous little queen of all?" Peter joins me in the answer, "REGINA!"

I hate to say this but he still manages a regal exit.